I, CHE
GUEVARA

ALSO BY JOHN BLACKTHORN

Sins of the Fathers

I, CHE GUEVARA

A NOVEL

■

JOHN BLACKTHORN

WILLIAM MORROW AND COMPANY, INC.
NEW YORK

Library of Congress Cataloging-in-Publication Data

Blackthorn, John.
I, Che Guevara : a novel / John Blackthorn.
p.   cm.
ISBN 0-688-16760-8
1. Guevara, Ernesto, 1928–1967 Fiction.   2. Cuba—History—
Revolution, 1959 Fiction.   I. Title.
PS3552.L34286I3   2000
813'.54—dc21   99-39243
                                                                            CIP

Printed in the United States of America

First Edition

1 2 3 4 5 6 7 8 9 10

BOOK DESIGN BY BERNARD KLEIN

www.williammorrow.com

For *la niña de la muñeca de palo*
(the girl of the wooden doll)

Ernesto "Che" Guevara, born in Buenos Aires in 1928, was reportedly killed while leading a revolution in Bolivia in 1967. An asthmatic licensed physician, Che joined the Castro brothers and seventy-nine other revolutionaries on the Granma, *the boat that landed on Cuban shores in 1956, and, as a* comandante, *played a key role in overthrowing the Batista government on New Year's Day, 1959.*

"Che" is an Argentinian colloquialism for "pal."

I, CHE GUEVARA

PROLOGUE—OCTOBER 1967

∎

He lay on his side, his hands and feet bound, the bullet wound in his left calf untended and bleeding. On his mud-caked feet makeshift leather wrappings had replaced the long-lost boots. His muddy, tangled hair had not been cut in weeks; his clothing was that of a tattered beggar—not a warrior. He had not bathed in six months. Nearby on the dirt floor of the primitive, mud-walled schoolhouse in the village of La Higuera lay the bodies of two of his fallen comrades, Orlando Pantoja (code-named "Antonio") and René Martinez Tamayo (code-named "Arturo"). The only sound from the wretched survivor was that of raspy breathing.

"He looked like a piece of trash," Rodriguez wrote later—after Che was disposed of.

Felix Rodriguez was a veteran of the Brigade—the 2506, which landed at Playa Girón, at the Bay of Pigs, just over six years before. But when his helicopter landed in a field outside La Higuera at 6:15 A.M. on the ninth of October, 1967, he wore a Bolivian Army uniform and introduced himself as "Captain Ramos." He was the CIA's man in Bolivia, sent to oversee the capture (he said) or the death (others said) of the most famous revolutionary in the world, the notorious Ernesto "Che" Guevara.

The previous day a small band of seventeen guerrillas had made their way down from an overnight camp at an elevation of 6,500 feet in south-central Bolivia into a narrow ravine three hundred yards long and less than twenty yards wide, only to find themselves surrounded by Bolivian Army rangers. Sighting rebel movement, at just after 1 P.M. on the eighth, the ranger patrol on a ridge above the guerrillas opened up on the ravine with mortars and machine guns. The ragged creature now trussed up on the schoolhouse floor had his M-2 rifle disabled by a machine gun round and, reaching for his pistol, found its magazine gone. He was disarmed. Then he took the bullet in his leg.

By three-fifteen in the afternoon on the eighth, the revolutionary war in Bolivia was over.

Lieutenant Colonel Andres Selich of the Bolivian Army interrogated the leader that night in the heavily guarded La Higuera schoolhouse, calling him *"Comandante."*

"Comandante," he said, "you've invaded my country. Most of your men are foreigners."

Looking at the bodies of "Antonio" and "Arturo," the ragged leader said, "Colonel, look at those boys. They had everything they wanted in Cuba. Yet they came here to die like dogs."

Selich said, *"Comandante,* what made you decide to operate in our country?"

"Can't you see the state in which the peasants live?" the captive asked. "They are almost like savages, living in a state of poverty that depresses the heart, having only one room in which to sleep and cook, and no clothing to wear, abandoned like animals." Briefly he paused, his gaze distant and absorbed. "The Bolivian lives without hope. Just as he is born, he dies, without ever seeing improvements in his human condition."

The following day, the ninth, around midday the Bolivian high command radioed its officers in La Higuera to execute the *Comandante* and the other two prisoners. Selich and his superior, Colonel Zento Anaya, left by helicopter for their command post in Vallegrande. Lieutenant Colonel Miguel Ayoroa, commander of the forces that captured Che, was given responsibility for carrying out the executions.

Felix Rodriguez, "Captain Ramos," had radioed a coded message to CIA headquarters for instructions for the disposition of *el jefe guerrillero*—instruction that never came—when he heard a shot. Running into Che's room in the schoolhouse, he saw the ragged warrior looking up at him from his place on the floor. Che's bodyguard, Simon Cuba, whom he called "Willy," lay slumped across a table in the adjoining room gasping out his last breath.

Perhaps stalling for time—waiting for a radio message authorizing him to spirit the captive guerrilla away—or perhaps for ego and history, Rodriguez took the *Comandante* outside for a last picture. The guerrilla leader looked like a wild man, his hair long and matted, his eyes and cheeks sunken, rags hanging from his skeletal frame. This picture would be his last. Some who knew him best would later find it virtually impossible to find their *compañero* in this picture.

Then Rodriguez took him back into the schoolhouse to await his destiny, only to hear another shot. This time the execution was for Juan Pablo "Chino" Chang, another member of the tiny revolutionary band wounded and captured that morning. *El jefe guerrillero* became silent and dropped his head, his face now pale. His life, he knew, was now measured in minutes, and only a few of these.

As Rodriguez started to leave, the guerrilla said, "Captain, I know you work for some intelligence service, probably the Yanquis. But I want to ask a last favor. Please let me see the teacher of this school—alone."

Rodriguez said nothing as he left. Outside, waiting nearby, he saw the woman, the village schoolteacher. She was called Julia Cortez and she was twenty-two years old. Rodriguez gestured to her, searched her for weapons, then motioned her inside.

She stood against the mud wall, tears streaming from her terrified eyes, as she looked at the half-beast, half-man.

He smiled and nodded his head toward a sentence on the chalkboard. "The punctuation in that sentence is wrong. You must correct it." She sobbed loudly. Then he said, "You must never tell. Never!"

She sobbed more softly.

"Let them think what they think. It is important—for many people. Let them think it. They must think it."

She shook her head no.

"I have loved you since you were a girl. I love only one thing more than you. I love these people—our people. I have done my best. The other one . . . he can do more than me. You must help give him a chance—by remaining silent. As long as he stays free, our revolution of dignity will survive." He waited.

Finally, hand to her mouth, she looked up and nodded yes.

After the young woman left, Rodriguez returned. In a fit of passion that, even years later, he could not explain, he suddenly embraced the captive and said, "I am sorry."

The guerrilla's face became pale and he said, "It is better like this. I never should have been captured alive."

As Rodriguez left the schoolhouse, he passed a short, rugged Bolivian Army sergeant, Mario Teran, who carried a semiautomatic rifle, stank of drink, and grinned.

Rodriguez said, "No head shots. And his wounds have to look like they came in battle." Rodriguez walked up a nearby hill and looked at his watch. It was 1:10 P.M.

As Teran came through the door, rifle leveled, *el jefe guerrillero* looked directly at him and said, "Shoot, you coward. You are only killing a man." Then he fired one burst and, seeing the victim writhing on the ground, fired a second.

Within an hour the army helicopter arrived and took the body of the thirty-nine-year-old man to Vallegrande, where it was cleaned up by nuns and nurses and put on display for senior military officers and their photographers outside the laundry house at the Nuestro Señor de Malta hospital. Nurses who prepared him kept cuttings of his hair.

Within hours word had sped around the globe that Bolivian Army units had killed in combat the world's most famous guerrilla revolutionary—feared by dictatorial governments and revered by millions of the poor—Ernesto "Che" Guevara.

Three days later the guerrilla's body was dumped in a trench dug by a bulldozer, the grave unmarked. His body had no hands. They had been severed, placed in formaldehyde jars, and sent to government crime laboratories in Argentina for fingerprint identification.

About the time the severed hands were being shuttled from office to office in Buenos Aires, a lone, clean-shaven figure with a battered straw hat covering his close-cropped hair, wearing simple, worn peasant work clothes, jumped off a smoking, clanking farm truck on a narrow Andean mountain road near the Peruvian border.

He was just beginning an odyssey that would last more than thirty years.

PART I

■

SUMMER 1999

There is that story del norte—*what is it, Rip, something?—about a man who goes to sleep, wakes up years later, and is surprised to find out the world has changed. The story is interesting not because the world had changed, but because he was surprised that it had changed. Why should he be surprised? Why should anyone be surprised? That Greek told us twenty-seven hundred years ago, the only constant thing is change.*

The only issue is whether we change or don't change. For me, it got down to whether I could find a way to be a revolutionary in a different world than the one during the last revolution. And the key to that was . . . timing. I had to pick the right time. I've always believed that ideas have power. Look at all the people who have had any real influence on events—Plato, Jesus, Muhammad, Marx—any of them. They didn't have money or armies or any of those things. They had ideas. The money and the armies came later, created by schemers who figured out how to use the ideas to get power.

You have to come along at the right time. And the ideas have to fit that time. That was the case with Fidel in '58. Right idea. Right time. His idea was to get rid of the oligarchy, Batista, the Mafia. Cuba for the people. Some kind of socialism. We convinced him there was only one kind of socialism that mattered. He got into the test of wills with the Yanquis and from then on it was easy. So, as I said, right idea—but also right time.

The big difference between Fidel and me was that he liked the power and the position, the big meetings with politicians and dignitaries, receptions at the airport, long dinners, talk, talk, talk, into the night. How many times have I seen old Fidel put the whole table to sleep. It's two or three in the morning. He's been flying to some distant country for eighteen hours. They're all rested and he just talks them head-down onto the table. I always found the diplomatic stuff boring as hell. First of all, no politician wants to talk about ideas. It's always about territory and relations and who gets what. I liked to go to some little peasant restaurant wherever I was with some of those hot-eyed, firebrand revolutionaries and have an intellectual brawl. Most of them had never gotten past a hundred pages of Das Kapital. *What they called "objective logic" was usually just opinion, and you could tie them in knots with their own "logic." After the revolution, they tried me out at the Ministry of Finance—what a joke—then other places. No use. I didn't like administration. You have to be some kind of clerk or behavioral engineer to want to administer something. The whole idea makes me creepy.*

*Medicine and revolution have one thing in common—immediacy. Here's the patient. Here's the country. It's sick. Deal with it. Make it well. No administration. It's right here, right now. That's what most people don't understand about my business—revolution—they think it's about politics. Wrong! It's about fixing something that's broken or sick—right here, right now. I can't stand a job where you organize other people to do things—fill out forms, keep records, count beans. Revolution is grabbing something by the throat and shaking the devil out of it. I'll always be a revolutionary. It's what I was meant to be. I actually love that word—*revolución.

I am still a revolutionary. In that respect, nothing has changed. Otherwise, everything has changed. Here I am, back in Cuba, starting yet another revolution. And, as I believed before, if it works here, it can work anywhere. The big difference this time is that I've had a lot more time to think about it. Thirty-two years to be exact. And this time my ideas are even more radical. Because they are not Marx's ideas. They are my ideas.

■ ■ ■

1

The old man sitting at the small table outside the narrow door of the cantina was so still he might have been dead. Even as the lazy whirlwinds of dust stirred around his feet and deposited their tiny particles of brown earth on his white hair and beard, his white long-sleeved shirt and white pants, he did not move. A young boy leaning against the corner of a shaded wall across the square of the dirt-poor village studied the old man. It was early on a Sunday morning in the summer. The planting had been done and few people in the village would be up so soon. Yet, the old man sat, impassive, implacable as the barren earth whipping and drifting around his thin, bare ankles, and the young man watched. This was a stranger and few strangers made their way into this village high up at the end of the narrow mountainous path, barely wide enough to get a cart down to the market, on the rugged southern slopes of the Sierra Maestra mountains in the Granma province of eastern Cuba. The watching boy thought he saw the old man briefly smile beneath his wispy white mustache and imagined that the old man was dreaming of a dark-haired beauty whom he had loved from afar or with whom he had spent a never-ending night of bliss in an age long before the boy himself was even born. The boy could not know that there had, indeed, been a dark-haired beauty in those days, more than one in fact, and some fair-haired ones as well, more than enough to keep an old man dreaming for the rest of his life. But the old man was not thinking of them now. He was thinking of revolution.

Presently the large woman they called Conchita pressed her broad face against the narrow front window of the cantina and then threw open the door, pulling the shifting miniature dust storm indoors. She uttered a curse as warm as the morning sun and went for the broom.

When she returned, she pushed small wisps of dust outward through the hanging beaded curtain now blocking the sun's rays from the shop. Then, almost on top of him, she saw the old man sitting as still as death at the lone outdoor table. He looked as if he had been quickly molded from white plaster and left on her doorstep overnight as a prank to addle her mind, already confused from the heavy dose of Saturday night rum. She started backward and gave the same soft curse. Across the square, the boy, almost twelve now and learning the ways of the world, suppressed a chuckle. The old man, his back to the door, seemed not to notice, so lost in thought was he.

The heavyset woman propped the makeshift bristle broom against the outside wall and carefully eased around the immobile figure, afraid he might have died during the night. If a lost old man had to die somewhere, she muttered, why did it have to be on her doorstep? It would be months or years even before her regular customers came back, afraid that she and her place had been cursed. She sidled around him until she could see his face straight on. His eyes were open. Then, to her horror, his left eye twinkled like a demon's and he winked at her. *"Café, por favor?"* the old man asked politely.

For a long time afterward, when she came to know him well, or at least as well as anyone would know him, she would remember the sound of his voice. It was not deep, but it was . . . firm. Firm was the only word she could think of. A voice that had given some orders in its day, orders that were used to being obeyed. Yet, it was a soft voice, like an aged rum, a soft voice full of amusement. This old man was amused about something. Maybe life itself.

It took a few minutes for her to grind the beans in the antique grinder old even in the days of her grandmother. Then she boiled the water. As she did so, she could not help but wonder who he was and where he came from. Old men didn't just show up on every Sunday morning in this forsaken place. Bandits perhaps, but only ones that could climb like goats. Maybe this old fellow had one of those slippery minds that came and went and he had just wandered off from his children or even grandchildren. Well, at least it would give them something to talk about for a while. No real stranger had shown up here for quite a long time.

The water passed through the badly ground beans and makeshift filter and poured out thick as syrup into the small cracked cup. She filled her own larger cup and carried them outside. The fumes of rum thumped against the inside of her head. She wanted to get this old man's story before anyone else.

In the other of the two chairs at the single table now sat the young boy. Her nephew Eusebio. Where did he come from? Always sneaking around, peaking into the window of every woman in town, some kind of sex fiend already. The boy never slept. He was leaning forward to hear what the soft, firm voice was saying as she banged the cups down and threw herself down on the creaking third chair she had dragged outside. At first she could not hear. Then it sounded like someone giving a school lecture.

"It's going to be your country, you know, and you're going to be responsible for it."

She thought she must be dreaming. First a dead old man or at least dead-looking old man. Now he's giving lessons to the children. She would warn the others fast. He's probably one of those queer ones.

"You don't understand now, and neither will your parents or the people in this town. But for the first time since the *conquistadores* slaughtered the Indians, you people are going to have a chance to save yourselves."

"*Señor, por favor*, how can we save ourselves? From whom? For what?" The boy's earnest forehead wrinkled in confusion.

"Save yourselves from ignorance, from the politicians, from the bosses." The dusty white-haired old man sipped the thick, steamy coffee and bowed his head in thanks to his hostess. As he made this declaration, she had made a spluttering motorboat noise in her coffee.

She peered into his dark, brown eyes, deep-set and, like his voice, amused. "Are you crazy, *abuelo*?" she shouted. "We can't save a cat from drowning. Save ourselves? Where do you come from, *señor*, maybe the moon?" This last was given with a bit more deference, given his advanced years.

He smiled. Unlike most old people in that region, he had a lot of teeth that looked like they were his own. Suddenly, when he smiled, he looked about thirty-nine years old. She sat back, stunned at the transformation. "If you will remember what I say, then you will understand my meaning in the coming days. There are going to be some big changes on this lizard of a country and you better get ready or you're going to be slaves again to some new bosses. You're going to have to learn how to take over your own lives or you'll get your pockets picked just like every other time things changed in the last ten thousand years."

The boy was transfixed. Usually the old men talked about the weather or the baseball or going down to the sea to fish, or sometimes, he heard them talk about getting into the underwear of *la Señora Gonzalez*, the tall widow who lived above the village. Because his pal Juan always laughed at this, he understood he should know what it meant. He would find out sooner or later why these old men wanted to get into her underwear. Always when he thought of them walking around in her underwear, the idea made him laugh, too. But this old man was talking a different kind of language. Almost like a priest. By now the boy had discovered that sometimes, rarely, it was best to listen. You could learn things, things you needed to know to become a man. He instinctively understood this to be one of those times. And it was particularly to him, with an occasional nod to his aunt, that the old man spoke.

The woman put a thick hand covered with cheap jewelry to her protruding chest. She looked around. This was some kind of seditious talk that would get the whole town locked up. The boy's eyes were wide with the shock of recognition revolution produced at all times everywhere in the world.

"This place"—the old man pointed with an animation made more startling by his previous stillness—"this place should have its own government run by its own people. You people here ought to elect your own officials. Fix your own roads. Build your own schools. Hire your own teachers. Set up your own clinic. It may not be much. But it will be"—he stuck his finger at the boy's eager face—"yours."

The old man sipped the hot coffee. The boy and the woman both sat back at once and stared at him as they would at a lunatic. He showed those teeth again, more white than the hair or the beard or the shirt or the trousers. Again, for a startling second, he became a young man. If he can do a trick like making himself young like that, the woman thought, then he can do any kind of magic. She wondered if she should throw his cup away afterward or just boil it a long time. There was always the possibility of having the Santeria priest, the *babalao*, take a look at it. But that would cost a chicken.

The man was thinking again, absorbed, as still as marble. The boy wondered if he should leave. Presently, the large woman muttered something about breakfast and rose from the chair that uttered a cry of relief. She had plenty of tortillas from last night, maybe a cold tamale and some cold frijoles she could heat. There were also those *dos huevos* she had bartered for on Friday. But they were valuable and she didn't think the old man looked like someone with pesos for eggs. She stood, torn between the opposing forces of commerce and hospitality. Much to her own surprise, and somewhat against character, hospitality prevailed. She burst sideways through the beaded curtain to offer the old man a proper breakfast with *huevos*.

She saw her nephew now standing in the middle of the square looking toward the road leading back down the mountain. The old man was gone.

■ ■ ■

All those years, traveling through the countryside, delivering babies, teaching school, I learned so much. Everywhere they gave me room and board, all the frijoles I could eat. Campesino *food. Best in the world. Rice and beans. Maybe when the crops came in, there was a little money, then some pork, or a chicken, or fish. Thirty years I did that! In some ways, the best years of my life. For a year or two I had to look over my shoulder all the time. You never know when the* federales *might show up. I hated those guys—imperialist lackeys, capitalist lickspittles. Then, when things cooled off and I got more philosophical, I thought about it. They're just doing their jobs—most of them. Now, you have your sadists and murderers and torturers and so on among the cops, drawn to a job with a license to beat up on people who can't beat you back. But most of them are just plain working guys, like truck or taxi drivers,* campesinos, construction workers. Guys like that.*

Pretty soon the people in the villages just took me for who I was. When I was still young, in the early years after I was "killed," I didn't do much medicine, because I didn't want to get any rumors started. "Hey, this guy looks like Che and, hey, look, he's a doctor or medicine man or something, like Che." I didn't need that. So, I just taught the kids—to pay people back for the food and the bed. At first it was kind of pesky. Sometimes you had these bad kids. Not too many, but some. Mostly, they were just ignorant, poor kids. They couldn't read or write even. Maybe the priest would have taught them a little. But mostly they didn't even know what a school was. These were, of course, the tiny villages—way up in the mountains or at the end of the road or totally off the road. I had to stick to those places for a long time, many years. It was a long time before TV got there and in most places they didn't even have a radio.

So, after a while I finally figured it out. I got brave. What do you think about the revolución *in Cuba? I said. What* revolución *is that,* señor?

they said. What revolución is that? That's the revolución to save your skinny little ass! I said. Oh, señor, they said, there is no revolución in the world can save my skinny little ass. So, I gave up on that. What about Che? I said. You know, the most feared revolutionary in the Western Hemisphere. Oh, señor, they said, Che? He must be somewhere in the next province— here we have seen no revolutionary for many years. Our padre, he tells us that Jesus, he was the only true revolutionary. Madre de Dios!

When I had enough of these conversations, then I realized I didn't have to worry about the soldiers. Anyone who finds the courage to travel from the capital to these godforsaken villages is not going to be looking for Che. He is going to be looking for . . . El Dorado! So, then I began the medicine. Babies and more babies. Sometimes if somebody was going down to the town, and I had saved a few pesos—or lifted them from a passing peddler—I gave them a list, some medicines, and instruction to go to the place with the sign FARMACIA. *I used those elementary medicines—antibiotics, aspirin, pain-killers—for infections, birthings, toothaches, and so on. They thought I was God. Then it came to me. These people didn't want a revolutionary. They wanted a doctor. And, they wanted a teacher. So, I had two careers. After starting to be a doctor, I became a revolutionary. After I was a revolutionary, then I became a doctor . . . and a teacher.*

Maybe it is, finally, the same. Maybe to be a doctor and a teacher, you must be a revolutionary. Maybe to be a revolutionary, you must be a doctor or a teacher. In this way, I can summarize all that I learned in my life. How many people can do that?

Anyway, I was writing about priests, my only competition in the vil-lages. I hated these people, you know, when I was a revolutionary. I con-sidered them bloodsuckers, reactionary witch doctors, the worst. But there they were. Before me, in the villages. In every goddamn village. They may not have anything else—water, toilets, decent health, food. But they had a priest! The only thing more common in these villages than the lice were these priests. My God! For a while they looked on me as the enemy. Very smart, these priests. Of course I was their enemy. They wanted these poor damn campesinos to remain poor and stupid . . . so they could con-tinue to scare the shit out of them. You preach death and hell and dam-nation to anybody, you're going to scare the shit out of them. Then, once you scare them to death . . . then, you save them. Body of Christ. Blood of Christ. Etc., etc. I was about thirteen years old when I figured out that business.

But, after a while, they understood I was just a traveler, some guy on the run—from the law, or his wife, or his creditors, or all of them—so, they left me alone. I didn't preach—at least in the early days—my revolutionary stuff. Too dangerous. You preach revolution, two things happen. You attract the army. And, you attract the church. Between the two, I take the army any day. Those poor dumb soldiers, they're just looking at one thing. Shoot whoever threatens the economic system, meaning shoot whoever threatens the rich people. Now, the priests, that's a totally different thing. Those Jesuits, they're like really clever commissars. Now that I think about it, when they take themselves seriously, they are Communists. Thank God they don't take themselves seriously that often.

■ ■ ■

2

■

Two *campesinos* of middle age, both of average height and both wearing the worn, light-colored work clothes that were the near universal uniform of their trade, stood smoking long, thin cigars near the ubiquitous statue of José Martí in the village square. Unlike its mounted counterpart in many other villages, this Martí stood with left leg thrust defiantly forward and left arm raised to challenge his followers toward the Valhalla of Cuban revolutionaries. This Martí, alas, was doomed for eternity to seek Valhalla on foot. This village could not afford the marble for a horse.

"It's him," said the *campesino* called Jorge.

The other one, called Pedro, laughed. "Rum is still your very good friend."

Jorge said, "This man is the right age. He is the same size. Look at that mustache." Jorge puffed. "Look at those eyes. My father knew him well—here in the Sierra—he saw him often. 'The eyes,' he said. 'When you have seen those eyes, you will remember. There are no other eyes like his.' "

"Eyes?" said Pedro. "Eyes every man has. His are old and wrinkled around the edges, like my own father's. In old eyes one sees only old age. One sees no difference in the eyes of an old *campesino* from those of an old revolutionary."

"Here you are as wrong as a dumb *campesino* can possibly be, Pedro. There are no eyes like the eyes of a revolutionary. They never change—never get old. They have a fire that does not die. It smolders beyond death." Jorge puffed. "When the soul is burning, the fire shows behind the eyes."

Pedro snorted, smoke pouring from his nostrils. "Such a great poetic figure like you would know nothing of dumb *campesinos*—or revolutionaries. 'When the soul is burning . . .' *Dios mío!*"

Together the two men walked slowly back to the corner of the square, where four facing weathered wooden benches formed the same square in miniature. Two men sat on each of the benches, their faces matching the cracked, weathered wood. Except for the stranger, all had long since exhausted the younger generation with their half-mythical tales of the magnificent revolution that had swept down from those volcanic slopes now four decades ago to drive the bastard Batista from Havana and into the exile from which he would never return. Several of the men had battered cups, some containing coffee, some containing rum. The two somewhat younger men stood respectfully behind them, the setting spring sun warming their backs.

"Fidel will never leave," one of the old men said.

"Unless he has found *la Fuente de la Juventud*," said another, "he will have little choice."

Another said, "If he finds it, I hope he is truly a *comunista*—so he will share it with all of us."

They laughed.

"If he shares it with me," one man muttered, "I will find a young wife. It is too late for my old one."

They laughed again.

"He will leave," the stranger said.

They all looked at him. There was silence. Then he said, "He will leave because he knows it is time to leave."

"*Con respeto, señor,*" Jorge said. "Who can know what is in Fidel's mind?"

The old stranger smiled, as if to himself, beneath his drooping white mustache.

One of the older men said, "If *el Jefe* had been like other men, he would have died long ago from one of those diseases he was always supposed to have or the Yanquis would finally have got him. I swear," he said, glancing heavenward, "if he is not some kind of spectacular ghost, then he should be called *el Gato* for the superior number of lives that he has."

Another said, "As we all know, there is more than just one of him."

That brought a general chuckle—the *campesino* fable that Castro had a double or even a triple.

"If that is true, Jesus," said one, "how do we know the real one is still alive and has not instead died and been replaced by the double—or the triple?"

"If he can give the long speeches and stomp on the toes of *Tío Sam*," Jorge said, "then it doesn't matter who is Fidel."

"What matters," said the stranger, "is not who is Fidel, but what happens *after* Fidel. All three Fidels cannot live forever."

Pedro leaned sideways and whispered in Jorge's ear, "He is from the State Security Department . . . for sure."

None of the men said anything.

The stranger said, "There are some choices." The men remained silent. They were waiting for the strange old man to explain himself. "Things can go on, with the same bosses in Habana. There can be free heart surgery for all," he said, tapping his chest, "but we have no aspirin." He leaned forward with his elbows on his knees and his thin hands clasped. "Or the Miami crowd can return, put in power the sons of their age"—gesturing at Jorge and Pedro—"take back their land, and we can resume as things were forty years ago."

Only the rim of the sun now could be seen over the top of the buildings framing the square's western perimeter. At this altitude it would be cooling down soon, the humble houses off the square habitable for sleeping. No one stirred except for one man who persisted in looking over his shoulder, watching for Fidel—or Fidel's security agents.

"Before Fidel," one man said, "we didn't even have the first choice. So it does not seem like much of a choice to me."

"The choices are not finished," the stranger said. Now two men looked quickly behind them. "You have the choice to run your own lives, to govern your own village, to make your own decisions." One man stood as if to leave, saw the others remaining, then changed his mind and reluctantly sat down again.

The old stranger spoke quietly yet forcefully. "Nobody has the right to tell you how to live your life. Who knows what's best for this village, you or somebody in Habana? I think here in this village are men and women who can make decisions for themselves. They can farm this land and get education for their kids and find doctors for their old folks. You don't need big shots in Habana or Miami to tell you how and when and where to do these things."

Jorge said, "*Señor*, you speak about politics. Yet you speak too simply to be a politician. We are merely poor *campesinos* here. So if you have been sent to discover if we are loyal to the power, please say to the power that we are not making a welcoming fiesta for our cousins in Miami. We are accustomed to leave the politics to those who have read the books and know the big ideas."

Several of the older men nodded in agreement.

"Bullshit! Don't try that 'poor dumb *campesino*' salsa with me, *che*," the old stranger wheezed out with a barking laugh.

That was the moment, Jorge later said, he was absolutely sure of the stranger's identity. His father had told him often how the famous nickname came to be. The great revolutionary called everybody by the Argentinean colloquialism for "pal." Jorge studied the faces for a hint of recognition. They had all missed it.

"I am the last thing from a politician," the old stranger said. "I used to be a teacher—a little kid teacher, not a *profesor*—so I guess I still am. I'm my own man. Always have been. I don't work for anyone—in Habana or elsewhere. It's a little late for me to learn how to be afraid. So I say what I think."

Dim light began to come on in the rooms above the shops as dusk settled on the village square. One of the men emptied a final swallow of rum into each of the empty cups.

One of the men said, "I don't know what you call this politics of yours. What we now have—*socialismo*, I guess—I think I know. *Capitalismo*, or whatever we had before, I also think I know. What you are now explaining—the village for the village—I do not know it."

"It doesn't matter what you call it," the old stranger said. "It's the idea that matters. A very long time ago—the longest time, to the very beginning of Greece in the ancient times—the people in the village chose who would make the decisions for their village. But they all took part in making the decisions work. They all believed in protecting the village and making it a good place for everybody. Some people had more wealth than others. But they all played an equal role in picking leaders and carrying out his decisions."

His muscles and joints now beginning to stiffen in the evening cool, the old man put a hand to the small of his back and winced as he stood. Slowly, all the men stood with him, stretching muscles permanently creased through many years of labor.

"They called it *la república*," the stranger said. "It was their word for free men running their own lives in a fair and just way for all."

One of the men said, *"La república."*

"It's only for people who decide to be free. It's only for people who believe in themselves and each other." He stooped to pick up a tattered hemp bag. "Do you know any Cubans like that?"

"Señor," the oldest man said, "you will honor my wife and me by staying the night in the room of our daughter who is now in Santiago."

It was hard to make out the expressions in the eyes of the men. The deepening shadows were sharpened by the rising half-moon.

"Muchas gracias, señor," the stranger said. He smiled and shook the hand of each man. He followed his host out of the square of benches, then stopped and turned back. "Remember," he said, still smiling. "All men are created equal."

No one spoke as the two men passed out of the square toward the cluster of small houses at the end of the main street.

"It's him," Jorge said almost to himself. "They didn't kill him after all."

■ ■ ■

Anyway, the priests. After a while they understood that I wasn't out to take their pitiful poor parishioners away from them. After that, they pretty much left me alone. They taught the little kids their catechisms and I taught them how to read and write. It was really wonderful. I had been so busy saving the world and making revolutions that I forgot the world I was saving. It was the world of children. We don't live that long when you think about it. We show up, we struggle, we fail, we die. What's it all about? Children. That's the only other thing I've learned in all these years. Jesus said something about letting little children in to see him, because they're the kingdom of heaven. Someday somebody really smart will rule the world, and when he—or she—really has the power, they will make every decision based on one thing—what's best for the children. You can't go wrong looking at things through those glasses.

That's what got me started on this idea of mine. Capitalism doesn't protect children. Communism doesn't protect children. Monarchies, and oligarchies, and anarchies, and all the rest of the "archies" don't protect children. Those of us who were revolutionaries in our time claimed to want to create "justice" and "freedom" and things like that. But we never asked ourselves, "For whom?" There is only one answer to that, when you think about it very much—and I had the time to think about it a lot!—and it's children. That's what the whole thing is about. That's the only reason to make a revolution. For children.

When I thought about things in this way, then the teaching was easy. I figured every little kid in every one of those thousands of goddamn little villages all over Latin America was a "Che," a revolutionary. If I taught enough of them to read and write, I would create more revolutionaries that way than I ever had fighting in the Sierra Maestras, or Angola, or Bolivia. It's a laugh, even right now. Wait till the oligarchies have to deal with those thousands of kids up there in the hills of Bolivia, and Colombia, and Peru, and Ecuador, and Venezuela, even up in Chiapas. Right now I'm imagining looking at a watch on my arm, which I don't have, but if I had one. And I'm thinking in about eight hours—which, when you think about it, isn't much shorter than eight years (at least when you're my age)—and all those kids are pouring out of all those little pissant villages down into Bogotá, and Santiago, and Mexico City, and they're going to start teaching reading and writing in those goddamn barrios and favelas and tin-roof shantytowns in every capital in Latin America. It makes me laugh to think about it. It's the ultimate form of subversion.

One thing happens when you can read and write. You begin to think for yourself. And thinking is the last thing in the world the aristos want the poor goddamn campesinos to do. The very last thing. Because when you begin to think, then you begin to be free. Thinking equals freedom. And a

free man is a dangerous man. "Freedom's just another word for noth
to lose."

I spent all those hard years in the Sierra Maestras, and in the Cong
and in Bolivia, trying to convince those slaves to throw off their chains. But
I had to get "killed" to get the point: The way to get people to throw off
their chains is to teach them to read and write. They'll figure out the way
to throw off the chains themselves.

■ ■ ■

3

■

Compañeros y compañeras, buenas noches," began the voice made familiar through years—decades—of public address. "After forty years of
our glorious revolution—the revolution of the Cuban people themselves—we now come to a crossroads, a point of new departure."

There was a crowd in El Papagayo, a popular cantina in the center of
Manzanillo, the seaside city in western Granma province—so named
after the famous leaky tub that had transported the eighty-two revolutionaries on their desperate seasick voyage from the coast of Mexico to
the southeast coast of Cuba in 1956 to launch their laughably quixotic
assault on the corrupt government of Fulgencio Batista. Around the perimeter of the congregation watching the small television screen, some
backchat about baseball or muttering about politics created a dull rum-
ble. But most people, drawn by rumors of sensation, watched carefully.
Indeed, they had been watching carefully as el Comandante had spent
the last hour and a half, almost two hours, rehearsing the achievements
of the glorious revolution, even in spite of, and in the teeth of, and
against the strangling backdrop of, the efforts of the perfidious neigh-

el norte, their antihumanitarian embargoes and their wretched ...ions and their pathetic pressures. None of it, of course, they were ...nded by *el Comandante*, none of it had brought down the proud Cuban people or their revolution or their success at achieving justice for the people.

"Justice I have had for dinner these last four nights," one regular murmured to another, "and my stomach thinks my throat has been cut."

El Comandante paused, sipped a glass of water, then looked directly into the camera. His notorious beard was now more white than gray. Though noticeably receded from the widow's peak of his glamorous youth, the gray-white hair on top and sides framed his universally recognized long, rectangular face. Sorrow more than vengeance now characterized his observant brown eyes; his gaze was now more distant than penetrating. He studied the camera lens as if searching for his destiny.

The effect of this uncharacteristic silence was to draw the crowd perceptibly closer to the screen. Some in the audience moved forward in their seats; some leaned elbows on knees to get a closer look. If something important was going to happen, it would be now. The canny old thespian had his audience and he was center stage.

"In a few months a new century will come over the horizon like a sunrise. Also, by the way, a new millennium. A new era for mankind. What will we do with it? Will we stay in the past? Will we permit history itself to leave us behind? For five hundred years we have been the crossroads of the Western Hemisphere. We have linked north with south, the Western Hemisphere with Europe. That is, and always has been, our destiny. But, if we stay where we are, we will be left behind."

Suddenly, he stood up and the camera was focused on his belt buckle. Quickly, the stunned cameraman, accustomed to the unexpected, adjusted the lens jerkily upward until it looked at Fidel from below. It made the already tall man seem like a stupendous giant. Then the camera itself rose upward on its hydraulic stem until it was once again at eye level with *el Jefe*, who then began, totally without script, to pace back and forth behind the prop desk in the outdated television studio. The camera continued to struggle to maintain focus and perspective. Sometimes it sought to keep up by swiveling back and forth as he paced. Sometimes it maneuvered spastically on its rollers back and forth with its subject. Overall, the effect was cinema verité and dramatic.

Fidel stroked his beard, a familiar gesture. He was thinking. Then, he suddenly turned to the camera, his idea clear, and the words poured forth like a torrent.

"I did not spend my life being a revolutionary to see the world now pass me by. Once a revolutionary—a true revolutionary—always a revolutionary. Look at what's going on." Now he left the confines of the desk and began to perambulate the whole studio. The outmatched camera did its best. "The whole world is trading. And we are left out. The whole world is getting computers. And we have only a few. The whole world is opening up. And we are closed." He was stumbling over television cables and pausing in front of stunned technicians and wide-eyed staff members holding cups of coffee. With wildly gyrating results, the cameraman had lifted the camera from its mount and was now producing combatlike footage as he followed the restless warrior around the studio.

"No more," shouted the scarred old veteran, his combat fatigues clashing dramatically with the technological cage that, for the moment, contained him. "No more." He suddenly reached in the breast pocket of his green jacket. He produced a signature Cohiba Esplendido, the kind his doctors made him give up a decade before. "No more," he shouted once again. With a flourish and a wink at the camera, he struck a long wooden kitchen match and, with the style of a seasoned professional, slowly rotated the tip of the cigar in the blue flame until it glowed.

Pursued by the sweating, beleaguered cameraman, he resumed his pacing, puffing as he went. "We have to make some changes here. Changes *muy grande*. Despite the Yanquis, we will open this country up. Everybody can come and damn *Tío Sam*. We're going to give every Cuban kid a computer."

The crowd in El Papagayo cantina in Manzanillo was mesmerized. Where in the hell was all this going? Had the old man finally gone over the edge from the lifelong battle with *el Norte*? Until the time that Castro got up from the desk, those in the back had been silent. But when he lit the Cohiba, a cheer went up from them and people began flocking in from the street to find out what was up. Outside, the street traffic was thinning. All across Cuba people were scrambling for the nearest television set.

"The revolution brought health care to the Cuban people . . . better than anybody in Latin America. We have fewer babies dying than in Washington, District of Columbia, capital of the U.S.A." He poked the cigar at the camera, which jumped back as if from a heat-seeking missile. "We have schools for our people. The best in the southern part of this hemisphere." He paused; then, his eyes widened dramatically, he shoved the cigar at the camera: "Now, it's not enough. Now we have to have computers if we want to be civilized and give our kids a chance. The next revolution is . . . computers." This last was delivered more softly and thoughtfully. His voice was sad and wistful, as if he were contemplating a mystery which he could not fathom.

In the back of the cantina sat a solitary elderly man dressed in the simple clothes of the mountain villages. Though crowded about by intense auditors of the performance, his dress, age, and demeanor marked him as singular. As he listened, he gazed more often out of the window into the night sky than at the fuzzy electronic screen. Seeing his occasional enigmatic smile, those around him assumed him to be slightly drunk or at least, like the leader to whom they now listened, of an age unable even to contemplate the wonders of the silicon chip and the microprocessor.

"That is why I am going to let others take over this new revolution." An impressive figure even at five inches on the television screen, *el Comandante* now stood behind the desk. He puffed on the cigar thoughtfully. "Nobody should stay in one place forever. I'm going to start traveling to countries that don't even have what we have, countries in Latin America and in Africa and in Asia. They need to know what we've done here and how we did it." He started to sit down, then changed his mind. "If I travel the world speaking about revolution, then I don't have time to run this country anymore. We have to pick some new leaders."

The cantina crowd, like thousands of cantina crowds all across Cuba, watched in stunned silence as an inch of ash fell, unnoticed by *el Jefe*, onto the desktop. He reached into an inner pocket of his green combat jacket, his eyes twinkling and a slight, provocative smile on his lips. He pulled out a folded sheet of paper and opened it up. He put on reading glasses. "Here the U.S. president says, just two days ago, 'Our policy toward Cuba will change when the Cuban people can pick their own leaders.' " Through the thick beard, large white teeth gleamed as Castro held his large hands palms up and shrugged dramatically. "I thought that's what we've been doing all these years. But, I guess *Tío Sam* still doesn't understand our system.

"Okay, Mr. President. Okay." The old revolutionary consulted a pocket calendar. "Now it is the twenty-sixth of July, the anniversary of the triumphant uprising against the Moncado barracks. Okay, Mr. President. On the first of next May—why not pick the day of the anniversary of communism?—on the first day of May in the year of the new century, *el primero de mayo*, 2000, there will be national elections here in Cuba—on one condition—elections in which any political party can participate. They can put forward their candidate for leader and everyone on this island can vote. Open elections. But, on one condition."

Castro puffed three quick times on the Cohiba. As if signals to a native tribe on a distant hill, the small clouds of smoke drifted upward in the airless television studio. "Here's the condition," he said, once more peering directly into the camera lens. "No embargoes. No sanctions. Full, official, and complete diplomatic recognition. An embassy and an ambassador. Nothing more and nothing less than you gave the Soviet Union and that you still give China, the largest Communist country in the world. We don't want to be treated better than anyone else. But we certainly don't expect to be treated worse."

The cantina crowd in Manzanillo applauded enthusiastically.

As if magically hearing the applause, Castro held up a hand. "One other thing. You send Bill Gates and his computers down here. When we get enough money from the Yanqui tourists, we'll pay him back. The Cuban people do not accept or need your charity. We wouldn't accept it if you offered it, anyway. You take off your stupid embargoes and your sanctions, and let your people come down here to see this beautiful country, and we'll earn enough to teach our children about these computers. They're smart so they'll learn fast."

Castro puffed more signals. "So there it is. Recognition in exchange for your kind of elections. I just hope ours aren't as corrupt as yours have become. All that money. Every interest with a wallet in one hand and the other one out for something. You're going to find out, you *del nortes*, that a lot of our people will choose to keep the system they've got, especially if the choice is your kind of dog-eat-dog capitalism." Again the cigar became a pointer. "Don't even think about packing up that lot in Miami, with their Mafia friends, and sending them back down here in the name of 'democracy.' We can't keep those that still have our citizenship from voting in this election. But for those that are now Yanquis, tell them to stay where they are. We don't need them back here trying to take over things again."

The tall man stood up, wandered restlessly to the corner of the studio, puffed some more, and stroked the beard. He strode back to the middle of the studio, looked at the camera, and gave a big grin. "Now you won't have Castro to kick around anymore." Still smiling, he waved at the camera, said *"Buenas noches, amigos,"* then strode, trailing a stream of smoke like a locomotive with a head of steam, out of the studio doors. The cameraman followed him, as if he were the Pied Piper, until he ran out of cable.

Several of the people in the cantina spontaneously stood and applauded. Then seeing their dumbstruck neighbors still silently seated, they sat down. The room was silent for a long moment; then murmuring began; then it swelled in volume until it seemed everyone in Manzanillo was shouting at everyone else.

"Did he really say what he seemed to say?" someone shouted.

"Is he truly leaving?" someone laughed. "It's Fidel's joke. You watch," she said pointing at the television set playing the Cuban anthem, "he's coming right back and he will laugh and give us the true speech."

The cantina manager, also the local party boss, said, "It's not a joke. He's just testing the mood of the people. He will not abandon the revolution. The party won't let him. There is no one else . . . I mean like Fidel. He is making us think about the new future. It's his way of leading . . . making people think about things." He pointed at the screen and laughed delightedly as if to reassure himself. "He sure gave it to those bastards in Miami."

Debates and shouting matches had broken out around the room. The furor spilled out into the cooler night air. People had come out of their flats and small crowded houses and were drifting like sleepwalkers up and down the streets, thinking they must be dreaming. Everywhere the mood was the same. What's he talking about? Elections? Diplomacy with the Yanquis? Computers? What in God's name does this mean for Cuba . . . what does it mean for me?

As the crowd disbursed, a lone waitress restored order to the chaotic room. Starting at the front, beneath the television set that had mesmerized them all evening, she put chairs under tables and loaded her tray with empty *cerveza* cans and glasses. As a slight breeze from the open windows now cleared the smoky room, she emptied ashtrays and shards of corn chips used to perpetuate the drinkers' thirst. In ten or fifteen minutes she had worked her way to the darkened back of the room and looked at her watch wondering if her boyfriend would still be awake by the time she got to their tiny room.

Suddenly, she started. Someone was still there. She looked into the gloom and made out an old man in village work clothes. She was terrified that Fidel had given him a heart attack. The boss had gone. The cook had gone. Most of the people had drifted away. She started to scream for help. Then she saw his eyes open and he smiled.

"Madre de Dios!" she gasped. "You scared me to death." She came closer and looked more closely at him. He looked like her old grandfather with all the white hair and the white mustache and beard. He had to be as old as Fidel almost. She couldn't imagine anyone older. Poor old guy had just drifted in from the village, didn't know where else to go, and ended up here with the crowd. Probably slept through the speech. People had been mostly quiet when Castro started all that stuff about the computers. He could easily have just drifted off. Poor guy wouldn't have a clue about all this. Maybe somebody could explain it all to him. Just not her. And just not tonight.

He said something, something so quiet she couldn't understand.

She stepped closer and started to help him to his feet, as she did with her grandfather. His thin arm was surprisingly taut for such an old man, she thought. Must be one of the *campesinos* who never knows when to quit. Scared if he quits working he will die.

She heard him say something again and this time she leaned closer and said, *"Por favor?"*

"I knew it," he said with a chuckle. "I just knew that's what he was going to do."

4

■

Overnight the lights had stayed on at the offices of the Cuban desk, the assistant secretary of state for Latin American affairs, and the secretary of state herself. The national security advisor had been called back to the White House at 1 A.M. Memos were hastily prepared at the CIA and the Department of Defense. The president's regular quarterly press conference had been scheduled for ten that morning. No doubt Cuba would be Topic A. The U.S. government had been taken totally off-guard. The old fox had struck again. *Tío Sam* was once again reacting.

"Let me say this about that," the president began, having preempted the topic at the top of his comments. "Obviously, we welcome any suggestion that any long-standing dictatorship is going to hold free and open elections. But the proof of the pudding is in the eating. Having made this grand gesture, Mr. Castro now has to perform. We will watch how this proposal unfolds. If legitimate political parties are allowed to form and achieve legal recognition, if they can be guaranteed freedom of speech in their campaigns—including freedom to criticize those in power—if everyone can vote without retribution, then perhaps this initiative is genuine."

Out of the forest of hands and babble of dozens of "Mr. President!" he acknowledged Victoria Savidge of The Political Network. TPN, as it was called, now was a force to be reckoned with. "Mr. President, will you grant Cuba recognition? President Castro seemed to indicate that— now that he has made this proposal—it was your turn—sorry, our turn—to reciprocate or there would be no deal."

The president smiled. He liked—maybe even more than liked—Victoria. She was, or at least had been, easy to like. "Ms. Savidge, we in the administration will consult on that in the coming days and announce a decision—sooner, rather than later. If it's a question of a kind of horse-

and-cart, chicken-and-egg thing," he said, maintaining his reputation for mangled syntax, "we don't want to be the last out of the barn. But we won't be made a fool of . . . if you understand what I'm saying . . . either."

Someone else asked a follow-up about timing. When would this happen?

"Can't really say, right now," the president said looking at his political advisers on the far wall to see if any fingers were being held up for days or weeks. "Soon. Very soon."

For an otherwise cautious administration, sooner turned out to be much sooner. Within seventy-two hours the secretary of state announced that she was sending a personal representative, the former head of the U.S. Interests Section in Havana, to begin negotiations with Olivero Ramirez, the Cuban foreign minister, to establish full-scale diplomatic recognition and the establishment of official embassies. The president had decided that he had little to lose by the exercise. If Castro reneged, he would merely pull out his ambassador—he already had in mind a very good friend, a Cuban American who had given a lot of money to his campaign, whom he could appoint in repayment—and they would return to the status quo ante. Nothing ventured, nothing gained. If elections were rigged, or were not held, Castro would be the loser. This was the kind of no-lose political deal the president loved, but rarely saw.

"The U.S. Department of State today announced," the press release read, "that it intends to test the good faith of the Cuban government by beginning the process of diplomatic recognition in exchange for the first free elections in Cuba in more than forty years. If the Castro government keeps its commitment, the Cuban people will have an historic opportunity to shape their own democratic destiny."

5

T here was very little of life that Victoria Savidge had not seen. Revolutions, earthquakes, famine, slaughter, terrorism, elections. And virtually all of that she had seen through the lens of a television camera. In her early years as a new and rising network reporter, her throaty voice and distinctive thick red hair quickly earned her something of a following. "Victoria Savidge, here on Capitol Hill." "Victoria Savidge, reporting from the campaign trail." Then she had covered the UN, the fall of the Berlin Wall, the freeing of Nelson Mandela, the Persian Gulf War, tribal slaughter in Rwanda, King Hussein in his last days, and had gotten exclusive interviews with Boris Yeltsin. On the way up, she was a bidding item among the networks. As a celebrity journalist she earned a great deal of money and lived very well. There was scarcely a dinner table on Park Avenue, in Georgetown, or in Beverly Hills that did not have a place for her.

And, of course, with fame and fortune had come the men. At first, the fellow journalistic stars, then the politicians, some single and some not so single, then the wealthy bachelors and business executives. Off camera, Victoria could wear the clothes whose cut and fit revealed and accentuated a body that was nothing less than flamboyant. Early in her career she had become accustomed to the reaction to her entrance at social events small and large. Three steps into a room and other women's eyes began to take her apart bit by bit, while the men's eyes started to devour the famous face and then proceeded slowly downward, very slowly. She loved the sudden silence that accompanied both reactions.

Victoria was not without cleverness. Raised in rural Kansas in a bankrupt farm family, she had learned the harsh lessons associated with slender means. Her ambition was for financial security as much as for fame. Very early she selected an astute financial planner and had, under her advice, sacrificed luxury for security. Early on she had hoped eventually—later in a successful career—to marry, someone who could watch over her of course. But some of the likely Prince Charmings had turned out to be intimidated by her fame, some by her ebullient sexuality, and some by her independence. By the time she decided to adjust her standards somewhat downward, time itself had begun to intervene.

The first shock of recognition came when female—and some male—friends mysteriously lost the tiny wrinkles around the corners of their eyes. Hers had appeared so gradually and so naturally that she refused even to acknowledge them. Then one or two friends and a network program director hinted less than subtly that they knew of really good doctors who could take care of such things—and those lumps along the jawline while they were at it—and she would be back in public, younger than ever, in six or eight weeks. But there was always an assignment, and a competitive one at that. And, though she couldn't admit or even explain it, there was some instinctive resistance to tampering with the natural order of things. By the time she rationalized her way around these scruples, it seemed almost too late. The nips and tucks would have to become cuts and patches that, once healed, would make her look almost a different person, one of those modern people wearing the cosmetologist's mask. In her business, the last thing she could afford was to look desperate.

But industry gossip treated her move to The Political Network exactly as that. Poor Vic, the last desperate stop on a downward slide out the door. She had maybe two years left—tops. Then she'd have a year or two at KOLD-TV in East Tin Cup, and possibly a term at some second-rate journalism school. Then, like Dorothy, back to Kansas. Well, said one of her more virulent critics, she wouldn't even have TPN to halt the slide if it weren't for—you know—shtupping that toad Marshall Stuart. They deserved each other, was the common response.

Long acquainted with the vitriol of jealousy, Victoria's skin had become thick enough to repel most assaults. But time had worn the skin of the psyche thin as well. Now, the hypocrisy of the Georgetown dinner circuit, the meanness of the Park Avenue cocktail party, the transience of Beverly Hills loyalty, were taking a heavy toll. Caught in a process that spiraled downward with a speed that still mystified her, she was suddenly without an assignment for the first time in her career.

When Sam Rapport had told her the previous day that he knew she would be given something important in the 2000 elections, she had at first been grateful, then excited, then suspicious, and finally realistically depressed. It had taken the whole cycle to put her position in perspective. Whatever she would be given would be a kiss-off on the way out the door. She was in the final months of her contract at TPN, the Mediterranean idyll with Marshall had been a disaster, and he would no longer return her insistent phone calls. Indeed, her office and home phones were both becoming more and more dormant. What next? Where would she go? What could she do with the rest of her life? Was there, she laughed ironically as she strolled along Madison Avenue in the high seventies late one afternoon, life after television?

She could not bear another session with her psychiatrist and, on the way to her office, had abruptly canceled her regular appointment. What to do now? She looked behind her at the small old church and heard a voice say, "Pretty warm, isn't it?" On the steps was a middle-aged man with a paunch and a thick black curly beard enjoying the sunlight. She suddenly realized he had been watching her. She nodded agreement absently and looked down the street, trying to decide what to do now, where to go. She was having a hard time remembering why she was here and what she was supposed to be doing.

"Care to have a seat?" the man said, patting the worn stone step. "Nice place to watch the world go by."

She briefly sought a reason not to and, finding none, slowly walked over and sat a few feet away from the smiling man. He looked relatively harmless and the smooth stone step felt surprisingly comfortable. "It is a nice day," she agreed. "Is this your neighborhood?" she asked by way of conversation.

"Yeah, most of my life," the man said. He stuck out his hand. "Warren," he said.

She shook his hand, surprisingly calloused and rough, and said, "Vicky."

"I know," he laughed. "You're pretty famous. I knew it was you about a block away. I expect just about everybody knows who you are." He paused, then said, "You live around here?"

"Yes," she said. Then, "Not exactly. A bit farther down." She gestured vaguely down the street. She had had enough experience with people on the street—men—following her to her apartment building.

"I used to watch you all the time," Warren said. "But since you went to TPN, I don't see you much."

"Let's just say I'm being a little more selective about my assignments." The irony made her smile.

"Must be tough, that business of yours," Warren said. "You have to follow people around, ask them . . . you know . . . personal questions. Get into their lives—expose their secrets." He shook his head. "Don't think I could do it."

"You could do it if that was your job," she said with surprising bitterness. "That's what they—we—do in my business now."

He looked at her and smiled. She was momentarily taken aback by the warmth and kindliness of his eyes. They were the kind of eyes you didn't see very much in the city these days. "You don't like it, do you." He wasn't asking. He was telling.

Victoria suddenly felt uncomfortable. "No," she blurted. "But . . . how . . . I mean, that's kind of a . . . personal observation, if I may say so."

"Sorry," he said. "Didn't mean to get personal. It's just that it comes across. On television. You can tell—I hope you don't mind—you can tell you don't enjoy what you're doing."

She was stunned at his directness and sought to change the course of the conversation. "And how about you?" She wanted to say, What makes you a television critic? but couldn't bring herself to do it. "What kind of work do you do?"

"I'm one of the ministers here," he laughed as he gestured over his shoulder. "Actually, I hope to be. I'm studying . . . in the seminary." He rubbed his rough hands together. "I guess I really don't look like a minister. I'm coming to this a little late in life. Most of my life I've been a stone carver."

Victoria stared at him as if at an endangered species. "Stone carver. I never heard of such a thing. I thought they disappeared in the Middle Ages."

Warren laughed. "Somebody has to do it." He gestured at a worn gargoyle above her left shoulder. "You don't think that was just dug out of the ground like that, do you? Stones have to get carved. Actually there's a connection. The only work in my craft now is cathedral restoration. I went around city to city, mostly in the old cities in the East, helping restore old cathedrals. So, the more I carved cornices and capitals and gargoyles . . . gargoyles are my specialty"—he laughed—"the more I got to thinking about what a cathedral—or for that matter a synagogue or mosque—was for. You see, a place of worship is meant to symbolize the human soul. We build places of worship as a kind of external manifestation of what we are meant to do with our lives and our souls. It sounds kind of old-fashioned, I guess, but as I carved these gargoyles I realized life was supposed to be about creating cathedrals and mosques and synagogues—in our souls."

"So that made you go to the seminary?" Victoria asked.

"Pretty much," he said. "It seemed like the next step—if you know what I mean." His direct gaze studied her. "In your case, for example, you report on events—political events. In a way you carve gargoyles." They both laughed out loud. "No, I mean, you adorn the event. But, what if you put yourself inside the event? What if you could shape not just its appearance but also its meaning? Its . . . soul. Now that would be something. That would be truly participating in the life and soul of the society."

She shook her head. "That's not what our business is about. We can't participate. We just report."

Warren put a rough hand to his mouth and smothered a snort. "Please, Ms. Savidge. We both know better. You build the structure around the event—the politics. You shape and carve it. You show people what it looks like. You tell people what it means. That's participating." He paused. "What if you put the microphone down—the same as I did my chisel—and helped make the event, helped make it a better and more meaningful event. Wouldn't that be more challenging? Wouldn't that be more fulfilling? Wouldn't that be more . . . fun?"

Victoria laughed in spite of herself. "You're right. I've carved some gargoyles in my days. In fact, I've even dated some." Then they both laughed. "But being a politician never appealed to me. Maybe because I know too many of them."

Warren said, "I've dealt with a lot of people, too—some not so nice— but I haven't met one yet who wouldn't like to find a way to make his life into a cathedral—even just a little one."

Victoria started to laugh again and was surprised to feel a tear starting down her cheek. She turned away and got up to leave. She swallowed, afraid to trust her voice. Then she said, "Thanks . . . ah . . . Warren. It's been very good to talk with you." She dabbed her eye, pretending to extract a bit of urban grit.

The bearded man stood up and took her arm. "When I watched you on television, all these years, I thought to myself, This woman is not doing what she wants to do—what she was meant to do. It showed—at least to me."

She took a step or two away and turned back. "I didn't think it showed. But thanks anyway. And . . . good luck with your cathedral."

He smiled and waved. "And good luck with yours."

6

■

Even as the celebration continued into the night following Castro's announcement, a dozen or so successful businessmen and -women, leaders of the Cuban-American community in Miami, made their way to a small restaurant called La Casa de Pedroso. Some ordered drinks and the others coffee. They settled into a large banquette off the main dining room and exhibited a curious mixture of exhilaration and apprehension.

"We got a lot of work to do," Olivero Sanchez said.

"Where do we start?" Angela Valdés said.

"We start by forming a political party," her husband Virgilio said.

Angela said, "How in the hell do you do *that*?"

Virgilio said, "Do you think those Commies created any rules for organizing political parties? We make it up. We just go down there and file some papers with somebody. And we're in business."

"Money," someone muttered.

Olivero pulled an expensive handmade leather wallet from the right breast pocket of his elegant Armani suit, extracted a crisp thousand-dollar bill, and launched it toward the center of the table. "I want the record to show that I made the first contribution." The bill made two gliding circles and settled in the middle of the table. "Anybody else in?"

Others reached into purses and wallets. A small collection of thousand-dollar bills accumulated. Angela said, "I'll be the party treasurer—at least until we elect one," and she pulled the drifting pile of bills toward her.

Ramón Heredia drank coffee, then grumbled dourly, "It'll take a hell of a lot more than that. A lot of money."

"There are a lot of friends of a free Cuba, some 'businesspeople,' who will be interested in contributing . . . once we get organized and start rolling," Eduardo Pons said.

Lucia Martinez said, "Careful. Careful with those 'businesspeople.' I think I know—think we all know—who you're talking about."

"Why careful?" Eduardo asked. "I haven't checked recently. But I'm willing to bet that pile there—our 'party treasury'—that Cuba doesn't have and *will not have* any kind of campaign reporting laws like we have up here." He laughed wryly. "Those guys don't even know what a campaign is. We'll kick their butts." There was giddy laughter around the table.

Ramón Heredia said, "Diego, your company does a lot of political media, doesn't it? You were all over the last mayor's race here, if I recall."

At the end of the table, already on his second Glenmorangie, Diego Falla smiled smugly as he put both hands behind his head. "I think it's safe to say that no major campaign has carried south Florida in the last ten years without our help." His broad face was dominated by thick horn-rimmed glasses, whose lenses reflected the table's guttering candlelight, and a thick salt-and-pepper beard. "We usually link up with Wager-Down—they're the best consultants and pollsters in the state— maybe the country—and—"

"Wager-Down?" Angela said. "Are you kidding?" They all laughed.

"—and we can turn out spots overnight to reflect their tracking polls. If ten old codgers out on the Beach have angina watching Clinton one night, Wager-Down picks it up, and we'll have anti-Clinton spots on the old-folks channel by six the next night. Hell, we can probably design a spot and put it on videocassette for just those ten old-timers." Falla smiled like a fiend. "That's what's known as targeting."

"How are you at targeting Raúl and his pals?" Lucia asked sarcastically.

Falla said, "I've been thinking about that all evening. I've already designed about three spots for Cuban TV right here." He poked a pudgy finger at his left temple. "Let's send the comrades back to Moscow," he sang to the tune of "Get Me to the Church on Time." He was now on his stubby legs, swaying to the rhythm. "Let's send them back to their old paaaaals. You play the tuba"—pointing at Lucia—"We're back in Cuba. Get me to the polls on tiiiiime." There were loud hoots and hollers and pounding on the table. Late drinkers in the main bar peered into the dark side-room. Falla beamed like a maniac.

"Okay, Diego, you're the media guy," Lucia said. "But 'Wager-Down' . . . ?"

"The best," Falla said. "Don't even think about it."

Angela said, "I don't think they're even Cuban."

"Yeah, they are," Heredia said. "Both moms married Yanquis. Integrated. Assimilated. They speak the Cuban Spanish, *señorita*." Angela used to be married to Ramón, and she loathed him.

■ ■ ■

Which, in a way, is how this strange odyssey started. Here I am in one of those villages. Once the local priest figured out I wasn't going to kill him, or bugger him, he let me sleep in the stable out back, with the parish mule and the goat. God, the smell! He even gave me some pollo con frijoles *and, God bless him, some wine that he had stored up for God knows what. Maybe the next visit of the pope, no doubt. Maybe it was the communion wine. Anyway, we finished off this bottle of partly vinegar—didn't they give Jesus some vinegar on the cross?—and he looks around like some goddamn revolutionary conspirator. Can I trust you? he says. If you can't trust me, padre, you're in deep shit, I said. He thought about it; then he nodded his head up and down. He goes to a shabby bookcase—just some wood boxes stacked on top of each other—and from behind some moth-eaten old biblical commentaries he brought with him from the seminary years ago, he pulls out an even more moth-eaten old book. It was really a mess. Covers falling off, pages curled up, mildewed. All that stuff. He carried it like it was old sticks of dynamite. You won't believe what it was.*

Selected Writings of T. Jefferson, it said. In Spanish. Where in God's name—sorry—did you get this? I said. He said, When I came down here from Mexico as a young man, my grandfather gave me this to bring with me. You'll need some serious revolutionary ideas to get you through down there, my grandfather said, and this is about the most revolutionary thing I've ever seen. It was the most honest thing the old man ever told me, the priest said. So, a little drunk, this priest gave it to me to read.

Well, I hadn't read a book in about three years at that time—let's see, maybe the early '70s—but the last thing I wanted to read was a book by some long-dead Yanqui who thought that setting up the American colonies as a homegrown oligarchy to get the English monarchy off the backs of a bunch of rich plantation owners was serious revolution. But, as I've said, it wasn't like I had the Biblioteca Nacional Argentina ready at hand. So, over the next few weeks while I was hanging around that village, teaching the kids and birthing babies, I read it. Actually, I read it several times. Then, some rumor got around the province that I was a troublemaker of some kind from over the hill, and so, as usual, I had to move on.

Well, to make a long story short, I patted the kids on the head, as usual, kissed all the pretty señoritas, *as usual, shook hands with the major, as usual, and started down the road. All of a sudden, I hear these hooves pounding up behind me and I was sure it was the* federales. *I was starting to head up into the hills when who should pull up on this old mule but this padre, Padre Gustavo, or Carlos, or Pedro, one of those priest names. He has big tears in his eyes (he must have found some more wine). Here, he says, take this. And he pushes a little package at me, wrapped in an old ragged cloth. I said,* Muchas gracias, padre, *and moved on. That night, I camped out by the side of this stream and started a little campfire. I opened the little package and, presto, it was T. Jefferson.*

■ ■ ■

7

■

It was late at night in the Palacio de la Revolución. Although the building itself had become well accustomed to late-night governance during the four decades of the *revolución*, this was something extraordinary. Most of the offices were lit, almost every conference room was occupied by cadres arriving from all over the country, and even more consequential conferences were taking place in the hallways and anterooms throughout the sprawling palace. Within hours, even minutes, after the shocking speech by *el Jefe*, political chaos had erupted and now, twenty-four hours later, it showed no sign of succumbing to any kind of order.

There was considerable anger at *el Jefe*, most of it unexpressed, for his decision to step down, but even more for the fact that he had not prepared the party. Here they were, the backbone of the *revolución*, the vanguard of the party, indeed, the party itself, the *jefes* and the toilers, the faithful, the bearers of the standard of socialism through all the bad days. He had not told them. He had not prepared them. He was abandoning them to their fate. What was their fate? To slip farther down the slope into collapse like the Russians? To split up like the Czechs? To turn into money-grubbing capitalists like the Hungarians? There was bitterness that *el Comandante* had traded a guarantee of free elections . . . for what? For diplomatic recognition? For ending the embargo? For a welcome back into the suffocating embrace of *Tío Sam*? And that, after years of promises of *Venceremos*, of go-it-alone, of up-yours, of the triumph of the *revolución*.

"How do we do it?" Antonio Oliverez asked. "How do we prepare for this stupid democratic election campaign?" Occasional shouts of anger, furious controversy, chairs banging against walls, could be heard echoing down distant corridors. But this was the command post where the most senior party officials had been meeting virtually nonstop since last night's speech. The dozen or so officials in the official state conference room on the top floor of the Palacio were no less angry or confused than the others; they were just more controlled and serious.

Victor Pais, Raúl's right-hand man, had been drawing boxes with connections on a yellow pad, a kind of primitive organizational chart. In the silence following Oliverez's question, he said, "Like this. At the top is the new party. Down here, under the new party committee, we have the campaign committee. Pretty much the same people as in the party committee, or it may be their representatives. Then down below that"—here those in the room began to gather to Pais's sides and back to see the diagram—"you have these groups. This one is the field organization of the campaign—"

"We got that already," someone said. "It's our party organization—the provincial committees, the town committees, the village committees, the cadre."

Pais said, "Right. But now they have to be given new assignments. They have to get everybody out to vote for us."

Vilma Espinosa laughed. "That's easy. We been doing that every election for the last forty years."

"This is different, Vilma," Oliverez said. "They're going to have some kind of choice. And they get to vote in secret."

"The hell with that," Vilma said. "One of these little pissants votes for somebody else, we'll figure out who it was. They won't have any coffee or pork for about a year."

"What kind of choice?" Felipe Morales asked. "You telling me somebody else is going to start another party here? Not a chance."

Pais shook his head. "Look. Here's what's going to happen. The Yanquis and the UN are going to be all over us. Secret ballots. International inspectors. Serious counting. And . . . and other parties if somebody wants to start them. No choice about that."

Vilma flipped her cigarette the length of the table. "You know what that means. That means our 'cousins' *del norte*. Those bastards. I bet they're loading up their fancy boats right now. They'll be all over us down here. Those bastards'll steal this election."

"Not if we steal it first," Oliverez said. They laughed. "What are they going to tell the *campesinos*? Happy days are here again? Welcome back,

Mafia. Welcome back, casinos. Welcome back, prostitutes. I don't think so. We'll kick their butts."

Pais said, "That's the whole point. Those guys will come back. They will start a party here. They'll promise the goddamn moon. And we"— he thumped another box on the yellow pad—"are going to remind everybody about the bad old days." The group gathered around the pad again. "This group here does the advertising. We control the TV. We control the radio. We've got the billboards. So when the Capitalista Party of Miami shows up here, we put up big pictures of Batista and his thugs all over the place just so everyone understands who these guys are."

"Victor," someone said, "I got a little surprise for you. My kids are now in their thirties. They will vote. And I'll make sure they vote for us. But a lot of their friends don't have an old man like me around talking about the bad old days. Except for the schoolbooks, they don't remember anything about Batista or the time before the *revolución*."

"They will. They will," Pais said. "We'll make sure they get the message. Now," he said, pointing at the pad again, "now we got organization, we got advertising. . . . This group, they have to raise the money. We're going to need money . . . to pay for the campaign workers and to pay for the advertising."

Vilma snorted with laughter. "Pay? For what, Victor? I know we'll probably have to pay a lot of the *campesinos* to vote, but you just said we own the TV and the radio and the papers. What do we have to pay for?"

"All these international observers are going to demand that there is equal chance for the political advertising. So, we'll have to have some kind of system to charge for the media stuff. We can cut some corners for ourselves, but we'll have to pay for some of it. So, you got to have a finance committee."

"*We're* the finance committee," Oliverez shouted. He gestured down the hall. "Last time I checked, that little locked room down there outside *el Jefe*'s office still was pretty full." They all knew he was talking about the special party treasury that had been kept stocked with hundreds of millions of pesos for "contingencies" over the years.

Pais held up a hand as cautious warning. "Let's just keep that down, Antonio. Now is not the time to have that discussion or to be talking about things that should not be outside this room. Of course, that's the treasury of the new party. But we may need that for other things later, also." More than one person in the room understood that to mean the getaway account in case things went bad or the other side took over. "Anyway, we have organization, we have advertising, and we have finance."

"What's that?" Ricardo Gomez asked, pointing at a separate box on the right of the hand-drawn organizational chart. "That one that says"— he frowned and squinted—" 'special activities'?"

Pais said, "You never know. We need a unit that sort of keeps up on things. You know, that keeps its eye on the other side. Maybe checks up on what they're doing. Maybe puts a skunk in their garden party once in a while."

"Special activities." Vilma smiled malevolently. "Let me have that one. I'll take over 'special activities.' "

Pais looked around the room. No one seemed interested in challenging her. "Okay. At least for now. We'll see how things go later on."

José Puerta said, "Who's the candidate?"

There was silence. The question had been on everyone's mind since Castro's speech last night. Indeed, one way or the other it had been on everyone's mind for a long time. Who would succeed Fidel? That was the real question. But, up until now, no one wanted to raise it. Sooner or later, though, it had to be faced.

Pais shrugged. "Maybe you, José. You announcing your intentions?" There was laughter, but it was nervous. "The party has to decide. Raúl, I am sure, is it. But we at least have to go through the process."

"We don't have a party," someone muttered.

"That's the next step," Pais said. "Here in this room we have the authority to call a meeting of the party central committee. Let's do that in about sixty days, no more. We'll have to check with Fidel. He must speak. We'll get everything ready. All the laws. All the paperwork. At the party conference we go through all the proper procedures, take all the votes, all that stuff, and we simply replace the Communist Party of the Socialist Republic of Cuba with the . . ."

"The . . . what?" Oliverez asked.

"Any ideas?" Pais said. "What do we call ourselves?"

Felipe Morales said, "The Socialist-Workers-Laborers Party of Cuba."

"Too long. Besides, it's almost the next century. We don't want to be the last 'Socialist-Workers-Laborers' party in the world. Hell, even the Chinese don't call themselves that."

"How about the Democratic Socialist Party of Cuba?"

Pais sighed. "Nobody's going to like this, but we can't be 'socialists' anymore. It's old-fashioned and nobody cares. Nobody's a socialist anymore."

"Okay. You tell us."

"The Social Democratic Party of the Republic of Cuba. The Social Democrats."

"Why that?"

Pais shrugged like a man too weary with the world. "Because that's what every other Communist party in the world has done. That's why. It's just the thing you have to do. It's acceptable. It doesn't scare anyone."

"Why be in politics if you can't scare people?" Vilma asked. "You know, the people that ought to be scared."

Pais sighed. "Maybe in the old days. Now, you have to make people feel good. You can't scare them or sound like . . . well . . . Communists. That scares people now."

"Can we scare them again after we get elected?" Vilma laughed and others joined her.

Pais smiled. "Maybe. But first we have to get elected."

So, the plan was made, subject to Castro's approval, to call a plenum of the Central Committee of the Communist Party of Cuba, transform the party to a new "Social Democratic Party," and launch a campaign to win the open election and maintain power in the country. Pais, who was Leader of the Parliament, delegated the staff of the Parliament to draft legislation designating the first of May, 2000, as the day for the next national election, establishing the formal procedure for creation of political parties and filing of official papers for registering parties, registering of eligible voters, and regulating the conduct of the election. The group intentionally decided not to pass a law regulating political advertising or requiring disclosure of campaign financing. They assumed they had the advantage and didn't want to limit themselves.

Those in the room were, in effect, the Politburo of the Cuban Communist Party. They controlled the day-to-day affairs of the party and determined its course. They held the power. If they stuck together and established what seemed at least to be a new political base, a new party, they would have a lot to say about how the more-or-less democratic election of 2000 would be held and, possibly even, who might win. They had no doubt that they would win. There was no way the Cuban people were going back to some kind of revisionist oligarchy from the old days. But they were going to have to play by the rules, more or less. There would be international observers to deal with, Jimmy Carter and his nosy friends looking over their shoulders, making sure they didn't try to steal the election.

A few days later, after they had a chance to make some refinements and get their story straight, they presented their plan to Fidel Castro. He listened silently, brooding. Except for those restless, startled eyes, his face was expressionless. He seemed like a big, bored cat trying to decide if one more pounce was worthwhile. He nodded as they talked but seemed distracted and distant. It suddenly occurred to Victor Pais that, for the first time in half a century, the future of Cuba was being discussed in a way that did not include him. What a horrible shock that must be, Pais thought. It must be like attending your own memorial service. This doesn't involve him at all. Here was a man who had dominated the life of his country longer than any other leader in the world. And they were talking about life after Fidel . . . to Fidel!

Castro suddenly stood up and repeated an old Spanish proverb. *"En boca cerrada, no entran moscas."* Then he left. In a closed mouth, flies do not enter.

Pais and the other members of the executive committee looked at each other. That was it. They were on their own. *El Comandante* had handed his mistress, his Cuba, over to them. He had surrendered to a new age, to the world of consumption, of markets, of videocassettes not ideals, of capitalism triumphant. He had lived too long. He had outlived his quarrel. It wasn't so much that he had lost. It was more that he had become redundant. Irrelevant. One of the supreme children of the age of ideology, he had been replaced by . . . a computer, a satellite, a Walkman.

After a stunned moment, a moment in which each person in the room understood in his or her own way that they had seen an extraordinary thing—they had seen the last dinosaur walk back into the veldt never to be seen again—they silently stood and one by one walked down the hall to their traditional conference room. Once there, they sat down. The room was silent.

"He doesn't care," Morales said.

Vilma said, "Oh, yes, he does, you stupid ass. Of course he cares.

What do you expect him to do? Blow something up? Of course he cares. But, what can he do?"

Oliverez said, "My God! We've all lived too long. It's a curse."

"Tell that to the Santería priest," José Puerta said. "I look around this room. I see people I met in the Sierra forty-three years ago. I'm"—he paused, thinking—"sixty-one years old. I joined the revolution, I was . . . I was eighteen years old."

"Me too," Pais said. "It's been my whole life. And now look what's happened. The whole world has changed. The kids don't care about politics anymore. They think it's boring. They think it's stupid. What do they care about revolution. They have no idea what the whole thing was about."

Morales said, "You old farts can sit around here feeling sorry for yourselves. But I'm a politician. I don't know anything else but politics. You take away politics, I'll shoot myself. So, you old-timers go on to the retirement home. I'm staying. I'm going to win this goddamn, stupid 'election' and I'm going to stay in power. And I'm going to do that for one reason only! I'm going to keep those bastards in Miami from coming back—if it's the last thing I do in my life!"

Spontaneously, his comrades cheered. People in the hallway looked in the door of the conference room, seeking consolation. Someone brought out a bottle of rum and they set up glasses all around. The choice had been crystallized. They could head into retirement, turn in their badges, check in their weapons. Or . . . they could fight. In varying degrees, they were all committed to fight.

But this time they had to fight with somebody else's weapons. This time instead of a Kalashnikov rifle, they had to use a television camera.

8

■

I want to sign up. I been hearing what some of the people around here are saying. About pure democracy. About running things ourselves. They're saying you taught them this. They're saying you put this idea in their heads."

The old man continued to walk briskly down the road almost as if he were ignoring the tall, thin, equally old man who had, with considerable exertion, fallen in beside him as he continued away from the village. Finally, without breaking stride, he looked sideways at his new companion and said, "Sign up? Sign up with what? There's nothing to 'sign up' with, *che*."

"I want to sign up with the idea," the taller man said. Then they walked a hundred yards in silence as the shorter man thought it over.

"How do you do that—sign up with an idea?"

"I don't know exactly," said the taller of the two, "but I thought you might help me figure that out." He paused. "I call myself Alejo." Then, to his own amazement, he said, "And what do you call yourself?"

The shorter man tugged at the point of his white mustache and laughed. "That's a good question, *che*. I'm from Argentina—a long way back—and down there we called a pal *Che*. So you could just call me Che." He laughed again as he strode steadily, kicking up little puffs of dust along a road that badly needed a shower of rain.

The tall man's eyes were wide. "Don't call yourself that. I know who you are. But I don't think you want every *campesino* up here in the Sierra calling you that. You'll get some crazy stories started that way."

The shorter man shrugged indifferently, suggesting perhaps that whatever name he used, stories would get started.

"I tell you what, *che*, why don't you just call me Blanco. Ernesto Blanco." He pointed at his hair and tugged the mustache again. "It fits, don't you think. You have any objection to 'Ernesto,' *che*?"

"*No . . . señor*. Ernesto Blanco it is." They walked another hundred yards. Then the taller man said, "I was with you up here, you know. Back in the original days. You wouldn't remember. But I dropped my hoe . . . back over there a few miles"—he gestured back and to his left— "when I heard what you guys were up to. The big man's foreman chased me with a gun. He was on a mule and I just took off running." He chuckled to himself, recalling the chase. "Almost got me. Shot right over my head a few times . . . the stupid bastard. But I was pretty fast then. The crops were high, so I went right through the cane fields. I could hear the donkey snorting right behind me a couple of times. But I got away." His companion said nothing, so he continued. "Then I walked around for about three days. I had heard some rumors about where you guys were hiding out. I went everyplace the rumors said and, of course, you weren't in any of those places." Both men laughed, recalling the excitement of the times. The same thought silenced them both at once. Those were the old days. They would never come back.

"I don't want to quarrel with you about who was where forty years ago, *che*," the mustachioed one said, "but you're right about one thing. I don't remember you."

The taller man padded along a half step behind like a patient old dog. "No reason. I was just one of those foot soldiers. Ran some errands. Stole some weapons. Liberated some food. But, I'll tell you one thing. I was at Moncado barracks. And I fought at Santa Clara." He thrust his right fist toward the sky, and his voice choked with emotion. "And I went into Habana on New Year's Day." He rubbed a fist in his eye. "It was the happiest day of my life. My God, what a party!"

The lead man seemed lost in thought. He didn't respond. Presently he said, "Why are you following me?"

"I'm not, *señor*. I just heard you were up here. So I been trying to find you. Like I told you, I want to sign up."

"Sign up to what? I told you, there's nothing to sign up to."

"What you're doing. This thing you're up to."

"I'm not 'up to' anything, *che* . . . Alejo. I'm just trying to get these *campesinos* to think a little bit. They don't have to work for the man for the next six generations. They can work for themselves . . . for a change. That's all."

Alejo said, "That's a revolution, Che . . . sorry, Señor Blanco. That's a big revolution. Maybe as big as the last one."

"Bigger," Ernesto said.

"Bigger," Alejo agreed quickly. "Bigger. So, I been waiting for something big . . . for a long time. Here it is. I got a little pension. The old woman is gone. The kids are in Habana, becoming big shots of some kind. So, what have I got? I got one more revolution. You said once . . . I mean Che said, 'Once a revolutionary, always a revolutionary.' I never forgot that. It stuck in my mind ever since."

Hearing these words come back to him, Ernesto laughed. "Look at you." The two old men stopped in the middle of the road. Blanco gestured at his companion, half a head taller, stooped, arms at his sides like a skinny scarecrow, weak, nearsighted eyes blinking in the dust. "A revolutionary."

"*Sí, señor.* I am still a revolutionary," the skinny man said meekly. "Once a revolutionary, always a revolutionary. I cannot help it, Señor Blanco."

Blanco threw his arms in the air, as if in despair, thinking what can I do with this old codger. "I don't exactly need full-time help, *che*. I just do what I do. There is nothing for somebody like you"—he gestured again at the thin, vulnerable figure—"to do. I just talk."

"There's plenty to do . . . as before. I can get food. I can find us— you—places to stay for the night as we travel. I can help bring people to you. I can go ahead and, maybe . . . prepare the way." Then he looked off into the hills. "Before, in the old times, I was a lookout. I was on the point. I stayed down the road from the camp at night. I was a guard." As he talked, his old spine began involuntarily to straighten. The memories seemed to wipe years from his face and an age of burdens from his thin shoulders. He was becoming, once again, a young man, a warrior. Even Blanco was moved by his transformation. "I can do that again, *señor*. I can be a watchman against troubles."

Blanco snorted and started back along the road. "No one's going to cause an old man like me any trouble, *che*. I'm harmless, don't you know. All I do is talk. And I only do that when someone asks me a question or says something stupid like . . . we got to stick with the guys in Habana to keep out the guys from Miami. Dumb-ass *campesinos*."

"No, Señor Blanco," said the taller man, bent forward as he loped to keep up. "You're going to stir up big trouble. Big trouble for the guys in Miami and big trouble for the guys in Habana. Both of them want to control things. Both of them want the power. You're saying to the people, You keep the power for yourselves. Don't give it away to those other guys. That's a very dangerous message for the old power. Maybe even more dangerous than the last revolution. Very dangerous, *señor*. You're going to scare a lot of people. They're going to want to stop you from doing this revolution."

"Let 'em try, Alejo. What have I got to lose?" He gestured at his ever-present hemp satchel. "This is it, *che*. The whole thing. Everything I own. Some old books, a clean shirt, and some socks. You think anybody wants this stuff?" He snorted again.

Alejo pointed at his head and drew a bony finger across his throat. "No, Señor Blanco, they will want your head. They will want to silence your tongue. And your idea. That's what they're afraid of."

Blanco shrugged, as if to say, What will be, will be.

"Try it a little bit, *señor*," Alejo said. "Let me try to be your helper. Just a little while. If you don't like it, I'll go away." He pointed the bony finger, as if at a dangerous apparition, down the road. "You're going to need me." They walked farther in silence, Blanco considering the offer. Then Alejo said, "And . . . I need something to do. My life is not over. I have one more battle," he said thumping his thin chest, "in these bones."

Blanco looked sideways at him, then picked up the pace. He raised his right hand to shoulder level and waved his companion forward.

■ ■ ■

How did I know when it was time to come back? I just knew. I had this feeling. But, as usual, there was some calculation. Fidel is getting up there— hell, aren't we all? This forty-year experiment down here wasn't going to last forever. Once Gorbachev began to shut down the enterprise, and quit giving us cheap oil for our sugar, then it was just a question of time. If anything, I'm amazed Fidel has held out as long as he has. It's just this thing he's got about Tío Sam. He's spent his whole life trying to frustrate the Yanquis as much as they've frustrated him—and he's pretty well succeeded.

In any case, I knew the time had come. It just came to me one day. Now is the time to go back, and start all over again. I was along that river in Ecuador, over in the jungle in the east—I guess it's the one that begins the Amazon—been there maybe six months or so—and I just packed this old

*hemp bag and set off for the Sierra. It's funny how you know these things.
I hadn't thought about it a lot for thirty years or so. I knew I'd come back
some day. When it came time to come back, I'd know it. And I did. It's my
destiny.*

*But it was that old T. Jefferson book that got me started. After I had
practically memorized that old book, I knew I had a lot of reading and
thinking to do. And that's about the time when it came to me that I was
not coming back here anytime soon. That must have been about '71. I just
settled in and began to organize my education in political theory. About then,
too, my need to get my hands on books overcame my fear of being caught,
and about once a month I found a way to get close to a town big enough to
have some kind of library. In most parts of Latin America, that means pretty
much the national capital or a city that size. I carried out my teaching and
medicine closer to the city and got good at finding the libraries. There is
actually quite a good collection of books on political philosophy at the library
at the University of Caracas. I spent almost five years working in the favelas
all around Caracas and spending one or two days a week reading in the
library.*

*I understood that to teach myself how to really think about political ideas
I would have to start at the beginning. I read* The Republic. *Over and
over and over. I must have read that book a dozen times. A lot of it seemed
pretty obscure and abstract. It had little if anything to do with the poor
people of the world. Then Plato wrote something that stuck in my mind.
"The only system that protects the interest of poor people," he wrote, "is the
republic." That was the beginning. Suddenly, it came to me that a lot of
thought had gone into class issues before Marx. Plato doesn't have much to
say about capitalism, but he does know something about republics versus other
forms of government—monarchies, theocracies, oligarchies, and so on. Even
in medical school I was a political theoretician, always trying to find out why
societies were unjust, why they divided between the few (rich) and the many
(poor). The more I saw, the more radical I got. The more radical I got, the
more I gravitated toward the most dramatic opposition to a system that
tolerated vast inequities in the distribution of wealth. That happened to be
Marx. I wasn't very patient in those days. If you hated poverty the way I
did—still do—and the system that tolerated it, you didn't take thirty years
to read and think about it. You did something—you made a revolution.*

*Then when I turned up not to be dead, I was forced to learn patience.
While learning patience, I decided to try also to see if there was any alter-*

native to capitalism on the one hand or collectivism on the other. My pun-
ishment for impatience was this crazy form of autodidacticism. A "dead"
revolutionary taking several decades to learn about a lot of other dead rev-
olutionaries. Except some of them are a lot less dead than others. Anyway,
I found out that I'm a better student than I am a teacher.

■ ■ ■

9

■

The first thing is the money. I've got some campaign people—media people mostly—doing some calculations. And it looks like we'll need
twenty-five, maybe fifty million." The speaker was Miguel "Micky"
Mendoza, Florida's leading political consultant.

"By our standards, Micky, that's nothing," Emilia Sanchez said. "But
for Cuba, that's huge. Twenty-five to fifty million? That's a lot of money
for down there."

Micky said, "We don't know yet. It's a guess. But look, they got
maybe three million voters? That's just sixteen–seventeen bucks a voter,
tops. We've spent more here for a key statewide race, let alone the
presidential."

"That's not that much money for what we're talking about," a man
they called Pat said. "We're talking about bringing democracy to Cuba.
You don't think we can raise twenty-five to fifty million bucks in this
community for that?" He snorted derisively. "There are guys in this
state that would put up that much money in a heartbeat just to get rid
of Castro. The money's nothing."

Emilia said, "What kind of a campaign do you get for that money?"

Micky said, "The whole load. Full media buy. TV. Radio. Billboards
all over the country. A blitz. Slick stuff. But not too slick. Don't want

to shock the *campesinos*. Got to break them into our kind of politics slowly. But good stuff. High concept. Power to the people. Freedom. Free at last, free at last. You know, that kind of thing. Get some Cuban actresses, singers, whatever. Endorsements. Shake and bake. Happy times are here again."

Pat said, "Does that budget get you headquarters and staff? You got to have storefronts in every little burg all over the country. Sign up the voters. Hand out leaflets. Maybe even door-to-door. How about a nationwide canvas? Knock on every door in the goddamn island."

"The fifty covers that, for sure," a rosy-cheeked young man they called Pinky said. He scratched some figures on a pad. "Fifty covers it. The problem is finding the space. We've talked with some of the recent boat people. Space is crowded down there. To get a storefront, you need to move out some shopkeeper and his family. Where do they go? It's a problem."

There were about fifteen people jammed into a conference room at Wager-Down, the highly successful political consultancy and polling firm that had dominated Florida politics for a decade. The firm had started out twenty years before helping establish the Cuban-American political ascendancy in Florida. In the last decade, however, it had been sought out by Anglo, black, Haitian, and every other kind of campaign. The firm was hot. Most of the people in the room were full-time employees. But others, like Pat, were themselves freelance consultants who signed on with Wager-Down on a campaign-by-campaign basis. One way or another everyone here would be focused on the first-ever national political campaign in Cuba. They were mostly Cuban Americans, at least on one side of their families. All considered themselves Americans first, hyphenated Cubans second. Cuba was the old country, talked about by the parents and grandparents endlessly. One or two had gone down there when the pope visited in 1998. But most didn't have a clue what it was like. Cuba was a kind of curiosity—an anachronism—to them. Maybe a place to visit or vacation in eventually, when things settled down and some kind of democracy was restored. But for now it was a unique political challenge. Reputations would be made on this campaign. Those responsible for bringing early-twenty-first-century politics to Cuba would be famous. They would be sought out for campaigns all over the country, maybe all over the world. They would be the pioneers in how to do it, how to take countries from the old politics to the new politics. This was going to be a big one, a big notch in the political gunslinger's belt.

And they had a sense they would be well paid. Wager-Down had been told by the Committee for a Democratic Cuba to clear the decks, write off all other campaigns, focus like a laser on Cuba. This was all or nothing. This one they could not afford to lose. They were betting the firm. But it wasn't an especially high-stakes bet. Word was that the CDC had a bundle. Word was that the committee was planning, as soon as Cuban law permitted it, to form a new political party in Cuba, the Free Cuba Party, and go for the presidency and control of the new congress in the 2000 election. The CDC had deep pockets. Every rich Cuban American, and even some Cuban Spanish, were being tapped, hard. Hundreds of thousands, millions, would be raised. If ever a campaign was oversubscribed, it would be this one. Ninety percent of the budget would go to media, just as it did in the States, but there would still be enough left over for a victory party that would last about a month. The campaign for Cuba would be exciting, a hell of a lot more exciting than the American presidential campaign in 2000, and a hell of a lot more fun.

"I've been in a lot of campaigns where there were a lot of promises of big money," Pat said, smoking his seventh cigarette, "and I've lost money in all of them." There were snickers around the table. They knew he was telling the truth, but they also knew he had made big bucks on the ones that came in. Pat charged top dollar for his polling analyses. "When do we see the color of the money?"

Someone muttered, "Show me the money." They all laughed.

Pat ignored them. "I'll need"—he looked at some notes—"quite a bit to get started. Look, these people are going to be tough. I polled in Hungary in '92. You know what that was like? You can't use the phones. First, they don't work most of the time. Second, nobody's going to talk to you on the phone. So, you got to go door-to-door. Same response. They think you're secret police. '*No sé, señor.*' So, you got to give them something." He rubbed thumb and forefinger together. "You know, a little present to talk. Just to show good faith. Maybe a chicken. A bottle of rum. Whatever. Even then, they're going to tell you what they think you want to hear. '*Oh, sí, señor,* I vote for the people who have been so good to me all these years, *señor.* I love Fidel.' Sorry, *señora,* Fidel he is not running. 'No? Well, then I vote for Raúl. He is so good to me.'

Yatta, yatta, yatta. It's going to be tough." He rolled his bulging eyes heavenward and massaged a presumably aching forehead. They all believed he was padding his fees already.

Micky waved a hand dismissively. He had heard it all before. Every campaign the song was the same. It's going to be so tough, I have to charge extra. "Get your team together, Pat. The committee has promised the money. They're good for it. Just get started. And get real Cubans. These people"—he gestured at his own staff in the room—"can barely speak Spanish. These suntanned Anglos." There were some smirked laughs. They knew it to be true. "Get some people down there as soon as you can. Recruit some bright young Cubans and begin to teach them the trade. We'll want some preliminary results in"—he consulted a pocket calendar—"no more than ninety days."

Pat barked out a harsh laugh. "You got to be kidding!" His jaw dropped dramatically and the large eyes rolled up again. "You can't be serious. Ninety days? You got to be kidding!"

"Not kidding, Pat. Get it done. Even if it's a little . . . dirty. You know. The money guys will need some numbers. And"—he looked pointedly at Pat—"they must be 'good' numbers. Winnable numbers. You hear where I'm coming from?"

Pat nodded. This wasn't the first time he had been asked to cook the books. In fact, usually with first-time, rich, wannabe senators, it was becoming standard practice. Sure, Mr. Fat Cat, you can win this race. Look, they all love you (even though they don't have a clue who you really are). You're exactly the kind of candidate the people are looking for (because the poll questions have made you out to be Jesus-JFK-Reagan). In fact, we think you're the next John Kennedy. The magic button. Out came the checkbook. The first of many millions poured into Pat's damp palm as automatically as a slot-machine payoff. The system had taught Pat, originally a young idealist, that the road to riches, along which he had already traveled quite a ways, was paved with the surplus dollars of dreamy young telegenic millionaires who wanted the title senator as a trophy, like the latest young wife, and who were willing to pay equally large amounts of money for both.

Emilia said, "Can we begin to do the same thing with the media, explore the market?"

"You bet," Micky said. "Get going. Get down there as fast as you can. Find some young hotshot in Cuban television. Hire him . . . or, you know . . . her. Right out of there. Find out how the system works, how the Commies intend to allocate time. They'll try to cheat us, of course. No surprise there. But we have to be smarter. Get our government to raise hell. Get some do-gooders in Washington to demand equal time. That kind of thing. Don't worry about that. Pinky knows how to stir that up. You just get down there. Take a good Cuban-speaking translator. And hire the best person, smartest person, you can out of the system. Let's crack the code. Find out how we get the time. How much we can have. How much it will cost. That's the least of our worries. Then put a budget together. Show it to me as soon as you get back. We'll get the money. Just get it done by"—here he checked the calendar again—"by, let's say, November one. That gives you about ninety days also." This time it was Emilia's turn to roll her eyes at what was meant to be an impossible assignment. But she knew from experience, she would have it done sooner.

Micky said, "Pinky, set up a Fair Play for Cuba Committee in Washington. Make it a pressure group for free elections. Get Jimmy Carter and George Bush to chair it. Get Kissinger on it. You know, that crowd. They'll jump at the chance to be in the action. Draft a list of demands. Open access to the media. International election observers. Poll watchers. Independent vote counters if necessary. A real democratic process, like we got here."

Pinky said in his quiet voice, "You want campaign finance disclosure, too? Open and honest. Limits on contributions?"

Micky looked pained. "Pinky. Please. Why should we burden these poor oppressed Cubans with a system that doesn't even work up here? Are you kidding me?"

There was laughter and table thumping around the room. These were people who hated campaign reporting and spending limit laws.

"Let's break them into democracy slowly," Micky said, clearing his throat. "Let's not give them an overdose. Besides, we're going to need some, shall we say, 'flexibility' to maneuver down there. We can't exactly tie our hands behind our backs."

Pinky said, "I got an idea. Let's have the Fair Play committee call for disclosure of spending *after* the election. We get the 'good-government' credit. But by then it's old news and no one cares."

"Great idea, Pinky. Do it. Just get that committee formed before the guys down there stack the deck against us."

"How're they going to raise their money—the Commies?" a woman named Angie asked.

Eddie Alonzo said, "Don't worry about it. They got a bundle stashed down there—mostly getaway money." A specialist in political "research," otherwise known as intelligence, Eddie was believed to have close ties to U.S. intelligence sources. People laughed at this insight. "These guys'll spend as much as they have to to stay in power. Most of them have a place over in Nicaragua or somewhere. But they don't have to worry about being invaded or arrested or anything now. So, even if they lose, they can hang around. Besides, they're going to try to steal this thing. Control access to TV and radio. Run the papers. They already got a political network—all those commissars in the villages. They don't have to pay for that. They just turn over the treasury of the Cuban Communist Party—hell, the treasury of the goddamn country—to this campaign. Don't worry about money. They're going to have a bundle."

Angie said, "But they won't know anything about our kind of political campaigns. Those dummies are dinosaurs politically. We'll kick their butts."

Micky hummed a distracted, off-key tune to himself. "I wonder," he said. "Let's not underestimate these guys. Big mistake to take this for granted. They have to have watched events in Central Europe. Remember how all the big-time political consultants showed up over there after the Iron Curtain. All made a bundle on it—somehow. Probably the Agency paid them. Who knows? Point is, the wall comes down, every hack political type and his brother shows up telling them how to do it."

Pat said, "Wait a minute. I was over there—Poland, Czech Republic, even a little job in Hungary. I'm no hack."

Somebody strangled a laugh, until it came out like a nervous cough.

"That's the point," Angie said. "We're not the only political professionals in the world. Think of the outfits like ours in California and in New York ... D.C. especially. If we're thinking like this, they must be—"

Pinky interrupted, "—doing just what we're doing. You're right. Some consulting outfit will show up down there to show the Commies how to put together a respectable campaign. They'll make them look like regular democrats. There have to be about a dozen groups like ours having meetings just like this in Washington alone."

"They're just not as good," Micky said.

"Or as expensive," Pat chimed in.

Emilia smilingly said, "Yeah, and most of all they're not Cuban."

"They will be," Pat added. There was general laughter.

"Just means we gotta get going," Micky said, standing up to end the session. "You all have your assignments." He made a note in his calendar. "Let's have this meeting once a week from now on. Those of you with assignments in Cuba, get going. Keep your head down while you're there. Don't talk to anybody—bars, restaurants, anywhere—that you don't have to to get your jobs done. We only want to show up on the radar screen after this thing's over. After we've won. For that matter, keep it down up here. Word will get out that we're involved. But we don't want to talk about it. So, button it up."

"We're just trying to support democracy," Pat said.

"That's our motto," Angie added. "Democracy supports us, we support democracy."

As they started to file out, Pinky murmured to Micky, "Shouldn't we probably have a code name?"

"Right," Micky said, stopping everyone. "From now on this is Project . . . Project—"

"—Cigar," Emilia added. "Project Cigar?"

Angie said, "Isn't that kind of . . . should I say, phallic?"

"For you, Angie, everything is a little phallic," Pat said. Everyone laughed.

"Project Cigar, it is," Micky said. "Let's go get Fidel's cigar."

"Hmmmm!" Angie said. They really laughed at that.

■ ■ ■

It will be interesting to see how the so-called democratic governments react to our little experiment down here. If they truly believe in democracy, then they'll support us. But if what they've got is a kind of hybrid government with centralized power and instruments of state designed primarily to protect the big corporate interests, not the people's interests, then we'll scare them to death. Here is another lesson it took me a long time to learn. The best way to challenge a system sometimes is not to attack it head on but to confront it with a purer version of itself, one that takes its principles literally. After years of study, I've come to conclude that pure democracy is the most radical form of government yet imagined. The problem is that it has never been tried before.

We are going to try real democracy for the first time here in Cuba.

But first we have to explain this idea to the people. These poor folks have been enslaved, beaten up, beaten down, robbed, lied to, cheated, manipulated, impoverished, and generally reduced to dirt. Now they are going to hear from the old Communists calling themselves some kind of social democrats— whatever that means. We may have not run things very well in the past, they're going to say, but now we know the right way. Stick with us. Then the old oligarchy del norte *are going to come down here sounding like Ronald Reagan and Margaret Thatcher shouting, "Free markets, free markets." Free markets, like free press, all right, so long as they own them.*

Somehow we have to find a way to convince these people to trust themselves, to have the confidence to believe they can govern their own lives. All they've heard for centuries is how dumb and stupid they are, how they can't figure out how to walk across the road without some boss—rich landowner or commissar—telling them how to do it and breaking a stick across their backs when they don't do it fast enough. But these are smart people. They are a lot smarter than they have ever been given credit for. They know what is best for their villages and their families. They know how to farm their own land. They know how to sell their stuff in the markets. They can improve their houses if they have the materials and the tools. They don't have to be told what to do and how to do it by some Havana bureaucrat or some corporate bureaucrat, either.

That is the key to real democracy. You either believe in people or you don't. If you do, then you have to give them control and support. Help them do what they decide, acting together, is best for themselves. One of the old political theories is that people need bosses, that they need to be told what is best for them, that they really are not smart enough to figure things out for themselves. Del norte, *they can't even get people to vote. Some people say that means the people simply don't want to have anything to do with their government. Well, I guess there is only one way to find out, isn't there? Let's give them the power. Use it or lose it.*

■ ■ ■

1 0

■

Alejo nudged his shorter companion, thinking he might be asleep. The man who called himself Blanco nudged him back and winked sideways at him. He was listening to it all. The monthly town meeting in Media Luna had been rancorous and it would end in either a brawl or some unnecessary and long-lasting enemies. The two strangers just happened to have bumped into the *alcalde* at the cantina before the meeting—or had they just happened to? Alejo wondered—and he had invited the visitors to the small village to join the citizens. No secrets here, he had said. And indeed there had not been any. Everybody in the room was upset. There had been a great uproar. Media Luna had the distinction of being near the coastal site where Fidel Castro and the rebels had stormed—well, not exactly stormed—had struggled ashore when the good ship *Granma* had run aground on a sand bar a couple of hundred yards offshore back in '56. It had not been an auspicious start for the revolution. But when success came more than three hard, trying years later, then Media Luna had come to be considered and certainly considered itself a site that generations of Cubans, history itself, would consider virtually holy. Thus, the rancor of this particular town meeting. The topic had been life after Fidel.

Led by the local party boss, a full third of the hundred or so people had demanded that a delegation be sent to Havana to insist that Fidel reconsider. This faction was convinced without question that *el Jefe* wanted exactly that. He wanted an affirmation by the people that they could not, they would not, do without him. He must stay. He must continue to lead them. Otherwise, there would be chaos. They would be at the mercy of *Tío Sam*, who would let the old Mafia crowd come back. Then they would eventually have to go through the whole thing all over again. Fidel, or another Fidel, would have to rise up and throw the bastards out again. How many times must a small country like Cuba relive its destiny? In response, another third shouted that the smart people in Havana would come up with the right person to follow on, to keep the revolution alive, and keep the old Miami crowd out. Fidel wanted to go, they said. He must spread the revolution to all the new emerging countries. There were people all over the world who must hear his message. *Libertad! Igualdad! Socialismo!* He had work to do. They were strong enough now to move forward. He would be around. He wasn't totally going away. He would be there when they needed him.

The last third were fed up with the whole thing. They wouldn't admit it in so many words; but they, the realists, knew the whole thing was a disaster. Socialism hadn't solved their problems. They didn't work for the rich landlord anymore. They worked for the big landlord in Havana, something called the State. They had better medicine, at least part of the time when they could get it, and their food was better, when they could get it. And their houses were mostly better, but they were jammed full of generations of families. No, something else had to be tried. They didn't know what it should be called. They assumed it was some kind of democracy like most other countries had. But they didn't know how to get it. They didn't want *Tío Sam* to run it. And, every time they talked about it, fistfights broke out with the other two factions.

In the back row with Ernesto Blanco and Alejo, there was a young man, or maybe just an older boy. He was maybe fourteen, maybe fifteen or so. There were fair wispy hairs on his upper lip. But his arms and legs were long and thin, lacking the muscles maturity usually produced. He moved awkwardly, all angles and confusion like a badly managed puppet. He listened intently, Blanco noticed, to all the arguments of all the factions, seemingly fascinated by the give-and-take but with frowns when violence threatened to break out. He seemed disappointed at the lack of resolution that characterized the closing arguments.

Searching for a way to wind things down, the mayor used a momentary lull in the mayhem to thrust a hand toward the back of the room where the two old men and the boy sat. He acknowledged the boy, Rafael, and commended him for his civic concern, his maturity, his faithfulness over the past months at attending—as no other teenager in Media Luna did—the town meetings. He was an example to his generation, the mayor said, a future leader of the community, and who knew, maybe even a future leader of Cuba. As the citizens applauded enthusiastically, the boy reddened and studied his scuffed sandals. Then the mayor acknowledged the strangers who were passing through, and made them know that, in the finest historic traditions of the ancient town of Media Luna, all strangers, especially the grandfathers of someone, were welcome, always welcome, to the full hospitality of their community. What they had witnessed there that night, he assured them, was proof against the silly prejudice *del norte* that Cuba did not have democracy. If the back-and-forth in this room in this village wasn't democracy, he shouted, then he didn't know how to interpret the word.

Then, seeing two faction leaders still glaring at each other across the center aisle dividing the meeting hall, he had an inspiration. Democracy applied even to strangers in Media Luna, he said. Pointing his hand, palm up, to the two men, he said, "Why not say a few words on the subject of the evening, *compañeros*? You have the venerability of the years, the wisdom of a lifetime. Tell us your thoughts of the future of our great country."

There was silence as, row by row, heads began to turn, necks craning to make out the strangers. Alejo hunched his bony shoulders and slid down in his seat. He would have a heart attack before he would speak. He would have a heart attack if he spoke. He squeezed his wrinkled eyelids shut, hoping the mayor would forget him, hoping that he would be invisible to the rows of curious eyes.

"What makes you think you don't have any more choices?" Blanco said, still sitting down. "Why does it have to be Fidel or some young Fidel or some Batista hack?" His voice, though quiet, had carried across the small, crowded room like the solitary cry of the hawk across an open field.

A hundred people, turned at the waist, seemed frozen in time. What? Another choice? What was he talking about? And, besides everything else, who was this character?

"There are some other choices," the old man said, putting both hands in the air. "I can think of several." He slowly got to his feet and started down the side aisle toward the front as he continued talking. He seemed totally at ease, as if he had spent a lifetime of town meetings in Media Luna. His tone was reasonable, his manner diffident. In deference to the mayor, the old man held his arms out, palms up, as if to say, is it okay? The mayor nodded dumbly.

"Do you understand what happened here tonight?" Blanco asked as the heads gradually swiveled forward to follow his slow progress. "What happened here tonight, as the mayor rightly says, and what happens in this town every month, it's a form of government. It is democracy. The only difference is, you have no power. What have you been shouting at each other about? It's been about what to ask Habana for. Please stay, Fidel. Or, give us another Fidel. Or, maybe, some of you have been thinking, let's get a McDonald's hamburger, some Coca-Cola, a new movie house. How do we get these things? Or maybe, like Fidel said the other night, let's get computers for the kids. How do we get those? Well, since everything comes from Habana, let's ask Habana."

In the back Alejo was wringing his hands. This was it. His pal, his *che*, was going to get himself strung up by these hotheads. Next to him, the boy Rafael was mesmerized. He had moved forward in his seat, eyes glued on the old man. He had nodded agreement at the last statement, as if anticipating where old Blanco was headed.

"What if this town," Blanco said, waving his wiry arm across the crowd, "what if you people made your own decisions? What if you didn't have to ask for everything from Habana or wait for Habana to tell you what to do? What if you could build your own movie theater, or school, or hospital?" As the mayor backed away toward the side of the room, distancing himself from the stranger and his words, Blanco propped himself against the edge of the mayor's table in the front of the austere meeting room. Outside, the night was settling in and doves could be heard calling for reassurance and companionship across the lengthening shadows. "Do you hear what I'm saying? There is no rule of nature that says somebody else always has to have the power. They have no secret knowledge in Habana. They have some secrets . . . but it doesn't mean they're smart."

Someone in the back snorted, then coughed.

The party boss stood up. "Ah, look, *señor*, we're happy to have you here. You and"—he gestured at Alejo—"and your friend are welcome here. But"—he shook his head—"we're going to figure this new thing out, ah, you know, pretty much by ourselves. You stick around as long as you like, but, ah, we'll work this out, you know, with the help of our leaders in the government. They've thought about all this and they'll let us know presently what we ought to do."

His rival across the room said, "Yeah, like they always have. Pedro, my neighbor, is losing his few chickens one at a time. Hungry people are stealing them, he thinks. My family, we haven't had good pork in weeks . . . maybe a couple of months."

Somebody in the back said, "The teacher's not coming back. She got a better job in Santiago. She couldn't earn enough to live here. Who's going to teach our kids? The guys in Habana?" In the back, Rafael nodded vigorously. The mayor started to say something, but Blanco cut him off.

"Look, *compañeros y compañeras*, this isn't really about the guys in Habana. They're only the evidence of the problem, not the problem itself. The problem itself is power. Who has it, who doesn't. They got it, but they don't know what to do with it. It's like a mule. The mule doesn't do you any good unless you can get him to carry things and to move. Right now they got the mule—but they can't make him move."

A lot of the people laughed, understanding the point.

"I say, you ought to have the mule and you ought to be able to figure out how to make him move," Blanco said and there was general applause.

Rafael stood up, eyes wide, startled at his own sudden determination to be heard. "*Señor*, what do you call this idea . . . this . . . politics of the mule?" Around him, the elderly women chuckled, amused at his stammering awkwardness.

"I call it '*la república auténtica*,' pure democracy," Blanco said.

"Why, *señor*?"

"Democracy is about people running their own lives, Rafael," Blanco said. "Democracy is the most radical idea anybody ever invented. It's more revolutionary than communism. It's so radical it scares most people. That's why it's never been tried before. Pure democracy—real power to the people—has never been tried before."

The room was silent. Still standing, the party boss started to speak, but his wife pulled him down. People looked at the mayor. For the first time anyone could remember, he didn't have anything to say. There were murmurs in the room, quiet side conversations. Blanco stood up from the table and started toward the back of the room. "Think it over," he said as he started down the side aisle.

Rafael was still standing, uncertain what to do. "*Señor*, I am ready."

Blanco hesitated. "Ready for what, *muchacho*?"

"I am ready to take over the mule. I believe I . . . I believe we can . . .

make him, you know, we can make him . . . work . . . work for us." Rafael started to sit down. Then he said, "Show us how, *señor*. Show us how to make the mule work."

Blanco put his head back and laughed. It was a kind of delighted cackle. Alejo spontaneously laughed with him, then self-consciously put his hand over his mouth. Blanco started back toward the door and Alejo stood to follow him. "If I knew that, Rafael, I would be . . . I would be some kind of king. No, there is no kingdom in the pure democracy. That's the point. It is not a king-dom. I would be some kind of . . . T. Jefferson." He stopped at the end of the last row of seats where Rafael still stood and put out his hand.

Confused, Rafael stuck out his hand and they shook.

"You'll figure it out. That's the point. We all have the ability to figure it out." Blanco turned back toward the room where the crowd now had fully swiveled back around again. "You people can figure it out. Make the mule work. Make him carry what you want him to and make him work for you. Go find that teacher and bring her back. Go down to Santiago and get a doctor up here. But, I'll tell you something," he said, pointing at Rafael, "you need this fellow's help. If anybody can make the mule go, he can. And pretty soon this is going to be his country."

Blanco gestured to Alejo and they started out the back door. The mayor charged after them and caught them out in the street. "I don't particularly appreciate you taking over my town meeting," he said. "But"—he looked the two old men up and down—"you can't go down the road this late. Come on, I got a place for you to stay." Behind them they could hear a new uproar, but with a slightly different tone, erupting.

They followed him down the street, Alejo loping along behind the quicker, shorter man. They went two blocks, then made a turn past the cantina where the evening had begun, and were led around behind it. There the mayor showed them a battered shed that belonged with the cantina and that was used to house itinerant visitors to the town. Inside he lit an antique oil lamp, warned them to keep it free from the dry hay and blankets spread out in each corner. He promised them coffee in the morning and bid them good night.

The two weary men stretched out. Just as Blanco was passing into sleep, he heard Alejo say, "T. Jefferson. Pure democratic mule. Someday, you'll get us strung up with that stuff." Then he laughed softly and passed into sleep himself.

After their morning coffee and good-byes, the men started up the canyon road into the hills and back eventually to the Sierra Maestra mountains. Once or twice Blanco stopped and looked around. He sniffed as if to test the air. Then he walked on. After repeating this procedure several times, he said, "We're being followed."

Alejo turned totally around, convinced a marauding band of brigands would instantly spring upon them from the thick shrubs set close to the narrow road. He pointed a long, bony arm at the movement visible in the underbrush, his eyes wide with terror. "*Señor,*" he said, then made a grab at Blanco who brushed past him to leap into the thick lowland shrubs. There was a gasp and a whine and Blanco emerged from the leafy jungle with Rafael's ear in his hand and Rafael firmly attached to the ear.

"*Por favor, por favor, por favor, señor.*" A small boy's voice wrenched itself from Rafael's angular adolescent frame. "*Por favor, señor!* Let me go. I am coming with you. I am coming with you to find the mule and to give him to the people."

"Okay, *che.*" Blanco's laughter echoed through the mountain greenery as the three figures moved on up the road.

■ ■ ■

Now, what am I trying to do here? I've already said this crazy country is my destiny. Why not? Here you have the Caribbean, you have España, you have Africa, and you have some pirates and some castaways and some smugglers and some desperadoes of all kinds. All of this potpourri dropped right on the doorstep of Tío Sam. You mix all this up and you get some interesting things (like señoritas muy espectacular, for example). But, at least equally important, you get política muy espectacular. I know that firsthand.

I also know this country and I love this country. I know these campesinos. I know the Sierra and the Escambres. I know the villages and the roads and the mountains and the rivers. I know how to move around here, and that's critical to what I'm trying to do.

What am I trying to do, after all? It's a little complicado to explain, even by me to me. Create something. Start fresh. Take a new approach. Invent a new revolution. Imagine a new kind of politics. Something like all of this. In a small country like this, with the old oligarchy gone and with communism disappearing over the horizon, it's a vacuum. Several things can happen in a political vacuum, and most of those things are treacherous. These people deserve a chance, at least one more chance. If I can help these people build a kind of society that they own, that belongs to them, then maybe the same thing can be done in Russia, or Ecuador, or Mozambique, or who knows where.

Here is my idea. I call it the true republic. It's a republic because everyone has certain rights, but they also have duties. They have to participate in selecting their leaders and seeing that they do their jobs. The people have to participate in the civic life and take responsibility for the common-wealth. It's easier to do, though, because every neighborhood has its own government. T. Jefferson called it a "ward republic." A ward was a neighborhood or a township, as they called it in New England. Anyway, the people in the ward elected their own government to deal with all the local issues—the schools, the hospitals, the roads, taking care of the old folks and the children. Things like that. If they were poor and couldn't get much money from taxes, then the national government helped them out so they could afford these public things they need in common. But these local governments have to decide what's best for everyone, not just now but in the future. The local govern-ment decisions have to be based on creating the best public inheritance for all the children.

That's it in a nutshell. True republicanism. It sounds pretty theoretical and even impractical in this day and age—until you think about it. Then it makes sense and you realize how radical it really is. It's radical because it's never been tried before. And it's radical because it threatens the old political systems and structures of power. So, if I can convince these people that it really can work and they ought to give it a try, who knows what can happen. We could really start something here.

I have an idea that if we let this republican genie out of its twenty-five-hundred-year-old bottle, it will require some truly desperate dictator to put her back in again.

■ ■ ■

The waiters dipped and swirled, gliding around the spacious dinner table with an elegance normally reserved for Olympic ice-skaters. Here and there a heavy silver knife or fork could be heard to strike high-quality china or strike a bell-clear tone as it brushed against a cut-glass crystal goblet. The chimelike tones varied only according to the level of the wine in the glass, with most of them being in the lower range. This special cabernet, raised from a stock kept separately in the cellar at "21," was going fast. Seven bottles so far among the twelve of them and they still had salad and desert to go.

From fifty-five floors up in the penthouse corporate dining room of The Political Network, the skyline of Manhattan twinkled with magic delight as if arranged for just these twelve, the corporate hierarchy of TPN. Marshall Stuart, the founder and chairman of TPN, had only five years before been a line producer for CNN International. Now, as he rapped on his wineglass, he was finding it a considerable challenge not to be totally delighted with himself.

"Now listen, folks," he began, his voice unconsciously dropping an octave in the manner of the newscasters he had so long been required to turn into celebrities. "This is going to be a little hard for you people to take, I know, given the volume of the stock options your goddamn greedy business agents demand every time your employment contracts come up. But the quarterlies are in and"—here he put on his familiar half-moon reading glasses and consulted a sheet of figures from a manila file on his right—"and it looks"—there was a sudden silence—"it looks . . . awful." From a couple of executives who had just laid out a bundle for houses in the Hamptons, there seemed to be a slight release of carbon dioxide. "Just kidding! They're . . . *great*!"

The room erupted in cheers. The pirouetting waiters brought on more cabernet, and a toast, to themselves and another brilliant quarter of profits, was sounded. "Now look," Marshall Stuart said, "we gotta quit making so much money. It really is . . . obscene, isn't it? I mean, remember all those critics when we started TPN? Nobody's going to watch politics. Nobody cares. Blah. Blah. Blah. Well, we've showed them. You guys have taken the American people behind the scenes. You've undressed these pols. You've really given the American people warts-and-all leadership. The real nitty-gritty. Elected officials who are real human beings, with bunions and piles and girlfriends and boyfriends and who knows what all. And they've loved it and the advertisers have loved it and ratings are up and . . . and we're a little 'richer' for the experience." He held up his glass to more cheers.

"This quarter is this quarter, Marshall," a vice president named Walter Myer groused. "In this business every quarter is a new century. We have to create this business every quarter." The executives at the table had heard this cranky speech too many times. Besides, they were here to celebrate additional heft to their already large bank accounts.

One of them said, "Walt, it's okay. Tomorrow we'll begin the new century."

"No. Let's engage for a minute on Walter's point," Marshall said with a thoughtful swirl of the wineglass. "What are we going to do about this election? In less than a year from now, we're going to have a national election. The year 2000 is a real milestone for our country. Every candidate and his . . . er, her . . . cousin are going to want to buy time on our network and we're going to have to give the whole campaign—all the candidates—wall-to-wall coverage."

"Oh, God!" a woman named Cynthia, the director of marketing, said to much merriment. "Marshall, do we really *have* to? I mean, *really*, it's too much! Can't we add some soap operas or exposés or *something* to break the monotony?"

Hal Stern said, "Way ahead of you, Cyn. We're working on a pilot that breaks a scandal every week. My guys have recruited this cracker-jack investigative outfit. Starting this fall they're going to turn up some dirt, some really juicy stuff, on a different politician every week. 'Now it can be told,' *Hard Copy*, 'You, the voters, ought to know' kind of stuff."

"Got plenty of politicians to go around," Walter said. He was an old-timer, a traditionalist, who hated the new journalism, and loathed himself for occupying this lucrative, career-capping job. "Let's see, there are four hundred thirty-five congressmen, one hundred senators, a vice president, and a president. That's five hundred thirty-seven weeks. Every one of them has something to hide. So, that gives TPN about ten years' worth of programs. This is a no-brainer."

"You forgot the governors, Walter," Hal said. "There are—"

"Fifty, Hal," Cynthia said. "Same as the number of states." The laughter was raucous.

"Do you have the libel lawyers ready, Hal?" Marshall worriedly asked.

"Not to worry, Marshall," Hal said. "Our lawyers reminded me of something they call the Sullivan case. Some guy named Sullivan sued *The New York Times* for libel and don't you know the Supremes said he loses unless he can prove 'actual malice.' Anybody sues us they have to prove that we broadcast a false story that we *knew* was false and did so *intending* to injure our subject. We're clear." He turned to Cynthia. "Hey, Cyn, do you want to hurt a senator?"

"You betcha. There are a couple of them that I'd really like to clobber," she shouted. They all pounded on the table. "One of them jumped me in an elevator when I was covering the Senate. I'd like to clobber that old bastard," she hissed.

"He wouldn't remember, Cyn. That had to be quite a while back," Sam Rapport said from the end of the table. Cynthia had once been a real looker, but not recently. She threw the dregs in her wineglass at him. "Besides, Cyn," Sam said from under the table, "you cover the Senate; why shouldn't the Senate cover you?" This time she threw the glass.

"Okay. Okay." Marshall's voice was raised to restore order. "Okay. So, we do the weekly exposé. That will also serve the purpose of the soap opera. We get two for one." An idea brought its own smile to his face. "What if we let the congressman respond, like, the following week? He comes on, wife crying, kids crying, How could you do this to us. We're honest, decent people, just trying to serve our country. You are ruining our lives. It's *real-soap*. Authentic like. People will love it. Dramatic, don't you think? Charge, defense. Countercharge. If he lies when he responds, if he denies cheating or stealing or whatever. We catch him. Gotcha. Then we have a third week. 'Last week Congressman Shlump denied our investigative report'—show footage of the wife crying—'but we now have proof that he was keeping not one but *three* mistresses with funds siphoned off from an unreported campaign fund illegally created with money from gangsters in Taiwan.' " Marshall's eyes were shining and distant. "It's great," he said with delight. "It's . . . it's . . . endless."

"Let's see," Walter said, his voice heavy with irony, as he consulted some jotted figures. "Five hundred thirty-seven politicians, three pro-grams each. That's . . . one thousand six hundred and eleven programs which will span . . . thirty years. Hell, Marshall, no wonder you're a ge-nius. We just solved our content problem."

The swirling, dipping waiters silently materialized with more precious wine. Outside, the New York City skyline glistened with despair like an uneven line of dejected Rockettes. The cynicism in the air of TPN's luxurious corporate dining room was approaching toxic level. Marshall checked his biscuit-sized Rolex. "Well, tomorrow is another day and, yes, Walter, a new quarter, a new century in America's troubled political life. We must continue to do what we do best, to enlighten the voters concerning the issues affecting our increasingly complex democracy. But, as I have said, we must find some way to bring life to what promises to be a very, shall we say, unpromising and unrewarding national elec-tion at the turn of the century."

The sober Walter, worn with the weight of a lifetime of viewing human folly from both in front of and behind the stage curtains, said, "One thing we must think about is the international aspect, the glob-alization of everything. So far your creation, Marshall, this unique net-work, has had a predominantly domestic focus. But we all know that everything is interconnected now. The economy. Politics. Wars. Pretty much everything has some international aspect to it. One thing we could do in 1999 and 2000 is to show how, increasingly, everything that we do in this country affects a lot of people outside this country. And, where there is something unique or interesting, we could actually cover some other elections in other countries. We could contrast them with our own, show how ours are better, show how much the others have to learn about democracy."

Marshall shook his head in thoughtful agreement. "Like where, Walt?"

"Like in Russia," Walter said. "Like in . . . ah, let's see . . . who in Europe has an election next year? Like in Italy."

"The Italians don't have elections, Walt," Cynthia said. "They have operas and call them elections."

"Watch it, Cyn," Hal said. "That's not PC."

"It's okay, Hal, *mamma mia* was a Sciolino."

"Where else?" Marshall asked.

"Somewhere in Latin America," Hal said. "Somebody down there has to have an election in 2000. It's a cultural pastime."

Sam added, "Besides, we have an increasing audience in the Hispanic middle class. That's a great idea. Cover a Latin election."

"Anybody know where there's any action?" Marshall asked.

There was silence. "We can have it researched in the morning," Marshall finally said. "Walter, can you have somebody look into it?"

Walter nodded, then said, "Wait a minute." He smacked a palm against his forehead. "What's wrong with us? It's right on our doorstep. It's a great story." They all looked at him, waiting. "Cuba!"

"Cuba," they chorused. There was excited chatter around the table. Then Sam said, "It's a joke, Walt. Castro's never going to let democratic elections to be held."

"I think he is," Walter said. "I think he has no choice now. We called his bluff. This week negotiations started on full diplomatic recognition." He turned to Marshall. "We even reported yesterday that a group of Cuban Americans in Miami are planning to form a political party and present candidates in the election."

"If we reported it, then it must be true," Sam said gleefully.

Cynthia said, "Yeah, I heard those guys hired a consulting firm, a polling firm, the whole works."

Marshall signaled for one last glass of wine. "There it is then. Cuba."

Hal said, "I'll get some researchers on it tomorrow. We'll get up a memo on the background, the parties that are forming, what the Commies are going to do, all that stuff. It's a great idea. The last bastion of communism adopts democracy: a case study. Great stuff."

Sam said, "Work in a profile of Castro. The tired old lion of the Caribbean." Cynthia was making notes. "Time passed him by. All that stuff. Maybe even do a reprise on the missile crisis. Lot of young people don't have a clue about that. Very dramatic. Very scary."

"Not a bad idea, Marshall," Walter said. "Responsible journalism." For a change, he thought to himself. "Might even get some kind of award."

"That's thinking too far ahead, Walter," Marshall said. "Right now we have to assign someone to it. Cuba. And, at our last staff meeting my recollection is that all our senior reporters had assignments for our own elections. Do we have anyone who could take this on?" He looked at Sam, who had assignments.

Sam shrugged. He and everyone else in the room knew they had one deadweight. But no one was going to touch it. This was Marshall's problem. Marshall had to solve it. Suddenly, the contents of the wineglasses or the melancholy skyline contained new mysteries to be studied.

Marshall cleared his throat. "Ahm, well, we haven't quite decided what . . . you know . . . Vicky will do. Victoria." They waited. "She's still . . . I mean . . . she has well-established credentials."

Cynthia smirked into her wineglass. On her back, she thought maliciously. She looked up and nodded in sober agreement. Others nodded in vague and silent agreement.

"She is still . . . I mean . . . she still has great credibility. An audience, you know. She . . . even has some foreign experience," Marshall floundered on.

That would have been the "research" trip to the Mediterranean this spring, Cynthia thought. Marshall and Victoria, "researching" the Med. Sicily, Corsica, Sardinia. The jet set ports on board Marshall's new 120-footer. Poor Mrs. Stuart unfortunately couldn't go along.

"I say that we give Cuba to Ms. Savidge," Marshall said, raising his glass.

They all smiled and raised their glasses. The boss had just solved a sticky little personal problem. Why not celebrate.

"How do you know she will go, Marshall?" Sam asked. "I mean, it's not quite the garden spot of the world like it was."

"Frankly speaking, Marshall," the unknowing Walter waded in, "I have to say that I think Vicky's a little . . . ah, well . . . perhaps we should say her best days are behind her."

Cynthia turned a snicker into a little sneeze. It didn't quite work. Marshall glared at her, then at Walter. "Walt, Ms. Savidge needs reassignment. We owe it to her to give her a last . . . another chance to . . . ah, salvage . . . ah, recuperate her career. This is the chance. There aren't a lot of opportunities in television now for ladies . . . ah, women . . . at her stage in life. I mean, she has put in many good years in television and she deserves one last . . . I mean another . . . assignment."

Cynthia maneuvered a fork to the edge, then off, the table. She buried her face, now red with unreleased laughter, at knee level until she regained composure. Marshall the old fool had used up this has-been and now had a guilty conscience. His way of dealing with a bad bargain was to ship it off to Cuba and out of his hair. Out of sight, out of mind.

Finally, the ever-blunt Sam said, "Marshall, I know you have a good deal of . . . ah, personal regard for Vicky. But I have to tell you. She's considered by many people in our business as kind of a . . . well, a . . . joke. She's been through two of the major networks. She's been back and forth between two or three affiliates. She's blown . . . ah, you know, messed up . . . a couple of big stories. The Chinese fund-raising connection in '96, remember, she totally missed. Had it handed to her, and she decided it wasn't important. So, I would send her to Cuba, speaking frankly, only to ease her out the door. A place to hang her hat for a few months and then"—here he drew a forefinger across his throat—"gone."

Marshall Stuart compressed his lips. He didn't like a woman who had, however briefly, attracted him demeaned like this. Yet, she had become a pest. Calling all the time. Faking business to call his house. Asking him over for dinner all the time. Showing him off to her friends. Then there was the hair and the jewelry. . . .

"It's her hair, Marshall," Cynthia blurted out. Her eyes were glassy and her face overly red. The cat fight between her and Victoria was hardly a company secret. "Cuba is the *only* place you can send someone who insists on wearing that . . . that . . . trailer-park hairdo. *Really!*" That stung Marshall badly. He knew there was something not quite right about Vicky. He thought it was perhaps just the new wrinkles around the eyes and mouth. Now he knew. People had been laughing at that hair. Oh, God! he thought. They were laughing at him, too. How could he not have seen it. While he had been transfixed by the still-lush body, everyone else was laughing at her hair. "And," Cynthia said, now sailing straight down the dining room table all guns blazing, "that god-awful jewelry! So *much* of it. And so *cheap!*"

Marshall cut her off. "Now having the benefit of your personnel review of Ms. Savidge, Cynthia, I think we can give her a trial in Cuba. If she performs well, she stays on. If not, we will review her contract which, I believe," he said, looking at Walter, "runs out in any case next—"

"April," Walter said, "the first."

"That's appropriate," Cynthia said as she drank the last of Sam's wine.

Marshall stood up and headed for the door. The quarterly meeting was over.

1 2

■

Who is Señor Blanco?" Rafael queried, his youthful face a troubled maze. He and Alejo had trudged down the mountain donkey trail almost two hours before he summoned the courage to confront his lanky old companion.

Alejo looked worried and studied the path, as if for clues, a dozen steps ahead. "Who wants to know?" he grumbled. He had been repeating the shopping list—flour, black beans, rice, coffee, a little sugar—so he would not forget when they got to town.

"Whenever we go to the towns and villages," Rafael said, "I see the older people pointing and whispering." He took a dozen steps. "They say he is not really Ernesto Blanco." He hesitated again. "They say he is . . . Ernesto Guevara."

Alejo stopped and scowled at the wide-eyed youth. "Never repeat that, *joven*. It is too dangerous a thing to even think—let alone to speak. Do not even *think* it!"

Chastened, Rafael resumed, then quickened, the pace. Presently he said, "It's just that—"

"Just that what?" Alejo almost shouted. "It's just that nothing. *El jefe* tells me to call him 'Ernesto Blanco.' I say, '*Sí*, Señor Blanco.' That's it. No more." Alejo muttered, "Blanco. He says 'Blanco,' he is Blanco."

Ten minutes down the silent trail, Rafael said, "If he is Ernesto Guevara, then he must be some kind of ghost."

Alejo's thin, scarecrow frame was shaken by a shudder.

"And Señor . . . Blanco does not seem to me a ghost," Rafael continued, as if to himself. This clearly was a puzzle, even to a more than usually thoughtful fifteen-year-old. He put his palms up, shrugged, and shook his head sideways.

Ten minutes farther down the trail, Rafael said, "Whatever the old people say, he cannot be Ernesto Guevara. From my earliest school days, I have learned that Ernesto Guevara—the great and world-famous Che—was made a martyr of the revolution by the reactionary Bolivian forces and the capitalist CIA." He considered the matter further. "So Señor Blanco cannot be Che."

Alejo nodded his long, narrow head, an old pony glad he was headed to the right stall.

"But if he is not Che," Rafael mused moments later, "why do the old people keep whispering that he is?"

Brought to the very precipice of distraction by the boy's persistence, Alejo's voice rose and cracked as he stamped his long, worn sandal. "Goddammit, *joven*, they are longing for a hero. They pray for someone to save them . . . from this mess. We"—he paused, startled by his own slip—"they are led by pygmies—*el Comandante* now departing, of course—little men who have no spirit, no . . . vision, no . . . no soul!" His eyes were startled. He could never have brought himself to deliver such a statement in Ernesto's presence.

The boy nodded in affirmation. This was an explanation he could understand. "So . . . so, they *dream* that he is Che. *Verdad?*"

"*Verdad, joven.*" Alejo sighed deeply, pleased at the clarity of the boy's insight. "He is their dream that their great hero has returned to deliver them."

"Señor Alejo," Rafael said presently. "What was he like—the Che of the revolutionary times? What do you remember of those times?"

As Alejo permitted his mind to return more than forty years ago, his stride lengthened, his stooped, thin shoulders seemed to straighten, and his eyes took on a distant, almost youthful shine. Remembering, he shook his head in wonder. "It was a hard time. But there was a . . . a magic in that time. We lived so near the edge of death that I saw its face every night before I slept. If I woke up at night, or if I had to stand watch, death was there beside me. I was then only a few years older than you. But I was also more alive then than I have ever been since—that is until a few weeks ago, when he—Ernesto—found me."

"He 'found' you?" Rafael asked.

"No," Alejo said hurriedly, "I mean when I found . . . you know, when I . . . crossed his path."

Rafael looked sideways at the older man. "You crossed his path? Is that truly how it happened?"

Alejo coughed, as embarrassed as a child. "More or less." They walked on. "No, it was different," he continued. "But if I tell you"—he stopped and thrust a bony finger under the boy's nose—"you will never retell it. Never!" It was a command that sounded more like a plea.

Rafael held a hand up, swearing a silent oath.

Alejo studied the young man from the corner of his eyes, searching for mischief and finding none. "I . . . I knew he was coming." He paused, thinking how to explain a complex phenomenon even he did not understand. "It was a feeling, a thing in my bones. When you grow as old as me, you know when *los huracánes* are coming. In your bones. It was like that." Absorbed in the recollection, he shook his head.

Rafael appeared mystified.

"The animals know," Alejo said sagely. "They know when *los huracánes* are coming. Also birds, snakes, all the creatures. One time a *babalao* tells me it is a powerful spirit in the air." He waved a bony hand vaguely around his head. "The younger people, they think more about the science. Something about the pressures." He also seemed mystified by the concept.

After a time Alejo resumed. "Like a storm of the weather, there can also be a storm of the politics. Now, Ernesto, *mi amigo*, has come to help us through the storm." As if lost in rumination, he smiled to himself. "Like the last time," he murmured.

Rafael studied the idea. They could see the low buildings of the town through the mingled shrubs and tall palms. Alejo began counting, under his breath, "Sugar, coffee, rice . . . ," touching his fingers as he numbered the commodities.

"So, as the great Che created a storm of the revolution," Rafael offered, "this Che is bringing more—"

"—more of a sunshine, *joven*," Alejo interrupted. "And don't call him Che," he grumbled.

13

■

In the days and weeks following *el Comandante*'s stunning declaration in which he dismissed himself from the coming reconciliation with *Tío Sam*, Cuba was a madhouse. What will happen to us now? many people asked. The same crowd will look after things, others answered. Nothing will change. Life will go on. Maybe, they said, our cousins *del norte* will gradually make their way back home and take over things. Even so, things cannot be much worse. Who knows, said the cynics, and . . . who cares?

Yet beneath the surface of confusion, powerful interests were at work. Under the direction of the Politburo of the Cuban Communist Party, now in the process of reconstituting itself as the Cuban Social Democratic Party, the constitution and laws were being rewritten to enable a more or less democratic political process that would include competing political parties, a sort of independent press, free speech for everyone— although there were still very few who wanted to put this idea to much of a test just yet—and open elections. Forerunners and scouts of the Committee for a Democratic Cuba, supported by the recently announced Fair Play for Cuba Committee in Washington, were already in Havana quietly circulating on the perimeters of influential circles seeking intelligence about the new election legislation, the timing of campaigns, the formation of competing parties, and the breadth and depth of a potential network of support. All in all it was a yeasty and uncertain time.

Alfonso Guerrera was one of the people in those influential circles who found himself placed by destiny near the crossroads of this chaos. As the chief political reporter for *La Prensa*, the major daily newspaper in Havana, Guerrera heard and saw most everything that was going on and what he himself did not hear and see was soon reported to him by a far-flung network of "reliable sources." Those sources were by and large the political network of the party, because *La Prensa* was the official newspaper of the party. It printed the stories the party wanted printed and it fomented editorially against the enemies of the revolution, namely *Tío Sam*, almost daily. When Castro announced his new career as international busybody, Guerrera scrambled to secure his position, reckoning that the party would become some other kind of party but, even so, very much in need of its own propaganda arm in the new era of the "free press." To that end, his editor had just assured him that *La Prensa*'s employees would be dipping heavily into the pension funds the party had set aside for them to buy the paper and continue to run it as an "independent" voice of the new Cuban Social Democratic Party. Like his colleagues, Guerrera took note that he had not been consulted about this use of his pension money, but he decided to pretend, at least for the moment and for the sake of the maintenance of his meager weekly salary, to go along.

When his editor told him, ahead of the others, of this plan—they were having a *cerveza* at a tiny cantina where the journalists hung out—Guerrera thought he would reciprocate with a morsel of gossip, the coin of his trade.

"Somebody—I think the regional party boss from Granma province—came in yesterday and told me the wildest story," Guerrera said.

The editor said, "What's that?" somewhat cynically. The whole town was alive with wild stories.

"There's some old man up there preaching some kind of radical doctrine," Guerrera said, puffing on one of his ever-present cheap cigars. "Something to do with 'power to the people.'"

The editor, a very fat man, shook his head in exaggerated disbelief and wheezed in such a way that it could be heard either as a laugh or a death rattle. "He's stealing our rhetoric. But it's a little outdated."

Guerrera said, "This guy says the old man pops up all over the place. The party boss has been riding the circuit from town to town in the province to make sure that everybody's solid for the party—for the Cuban Social Democrats, I mean—and he says that this old man is everywhere. Only he always seems to be a day or two ahead."

The two men finished off the *cervezas* and ordered two more. The editor was breathing heavily and waiting for the punch line. "So what," he said. "Lots of old men with nothing to do but stir people up these days. It's the old man's disease—talking. What else they got to do?" His aged chair groaned in agony as he shifted his considerable weight around.

"Well, the funny thing is, according to the party boss, people are listening to him," Guerrera said. "Apparently, the old man showed up at the town meeting in Media Luna a few days ago, had some other old codger following along, and took the meeting over. The mayor told the party guy later that there was a big fight going on—which, by the way, is going on all over the place—and pretty soon the old man stands up and starts preaching."

"What was the fight about?" asked the editor, bored by stories of troublesome old men.

Guerrera said, "The usual stuff. Our guys, the party guys, saying 'Stick with Raúl' and some other guys saying they're tired of this kind of government. Nothing to eat. Same old problems. That sort of stuff. Then the party people say, 'If we don't keep the government we got, the bastards from Miami will be back and take over again.' When a fight almost broke out, this old man stands up and starts preaching."

"Preaching what," said the editor, "more 'power to the people'?"

"Something like that." Guerrera scratched his thinning hair. "'You can run your own lives,' he says. 'You can take the power yourselves,' he says."

The editor drained half a *cerveza* bottle in a swallow. "Look, Alfonso, get ready for this. Things are going to get crazier before they settle down again. Every town in Cuba is going to have its own prophet, political *loco en la cabeza*, whatever. This is what happens when you have 'democracy.' Everybody thinks he knows something, how to run things. Everybody's got an opinion—about everything. You just got to ignore it until things settle down. Look, we got"—he counted on his fingers— "we got about seven months—less than a year—to go before this wacky 'election.' Let's get through it, get our people elected, then we can go back to normal life."

Guerrera shrugged. "Yeah, but—"

"—but, what, Alfonso? Get used to it. Forget about it. It isn't news. We're not going to put these wacky stories in the paper. So forget about it."

"Yeah, but—"

"But, what, Alfonso?" The editor was slightly drunk, irritated at his persistent interlocutor, and painfully conscious that he himself was a gross, overweight, wheezing gasbag. "I'm getting goddamn tired of your 'but-buts.' "

Guerrera shrugged with resignation. He thought he had a good story to tell and his mercurial boss was mad at him and his story. As he hauled himself down from the bar stool, with considerably more ease than his companion, he muttered to himself, "He says he's Che. That's all."

Struggling to haul his straining belt above the equator of his girth, the editor said, "What?"

"Che," Guerrera said. "Guevara. That's what he says."

"Che Guevara?" spluttered the editor. "The old man says he's Che Guevara?" He uttered a mighty wheeze. Then another.

"Not exactly," Guerrera said. "It's that"—he paused—"it's that *the people* up there are saying that. *They're* saying that he's Che."

The editor shook with emotion. Panicked, Guerrera looked for the exit. He did not even want to think about giving this quaking leviathan mouth-to-mouth. *"Madre de Dios,"* the editor gasped, his head hanging like that of a foundering horse. "Che Guevara." Another round of wheezing followed that Guerrera now recognized as laughter.

"Che's dead . . . now . . . thirty years!" the editor shouted with a gasp. Drinkers nearby turned their heads.

"Thirty . . . two," Guerrera said uncertainly, ever the accurate reporter.

"Thirty-two!" shouted the editor. "My God, we got to send some papers up to those people. They haven't even found out about it yet. My God!" By now the wheeze was merry.

Guerrera said cautiously, "It's like they think . . . like . . . maybe, he possibly *didn't* die."

"Of course he *died*, goddammit!" the editor said, holding his chair with one hand and pounding the bar with the other. "Che's as dead as Oscar's goat. You saw the pictures, stretched out on that table up in Bolivia, as full of holes as cheap cheese. Nobody in the world is deader than Che." The editor shook his lowered head now full of a confused mixture of mirth and wonderment at the scope of human folly.

With an air of trepidation, Guerrera said, "The party boss says it's all over the place up there. The *campesinos* believe it's Che. That he's come back to show them the way."

"Why in God's name would they think such a thing?" the editor gasped.

Guerrera raised his palms to shoulder level. "Because it looks like him and it sounds like him . . . thirty-two years later."

■ ■ ■

"Toil and trouble. Trouble and toil," Shakespeare (or somebody) said. Except for the occasional laugh, that pretty much sums it up. I remember reading, in between all those books on political theory, that book on Zorba the Greek. Who's that author? Kazantzakis. Memory hasn't totally gone. Zorba is talking to his British boss who objects to one of their grand projects on the ground that it is going to cause a lot of trouble. Zorba says, I remember, boss, life is trouble; you got to unzip your pants and go looking for it! That has stuck in my mind.

So it is. Look at this pathetic island. Trouble, trouble, nothing but trouble. They can't get anything straight. Out of one frying pan into another. Fidel did his best. But you can't have common ownership in a place where they don't know what ownership means. At least in Argentina you have some history of ownership—too much by the oligarchy—but ownership nonetheless. You have a more or less European legal system and financial systems. All this doesn't prevent an occasional Perón, for example, or bunch of fascist generals afterward. But it gives a little context for the people to understand basic ideas—citizenship, ownership, responsibility. Things like that.

Then, when somebody like me comes along, preaching some kind of fundamental political theory, the people have some frame of reference to understand what you're talking about. I just pray that some of these poor campesinos *have some clue of what I'm trying to explain to them. I think they do. T. Jefferson thought that everybody had a degree of common sense, kind of folk wisdom. He said it was indispensable to a democracy.*

So now I have to convince them that they can truly govern their own lives. And the time is short. I know what's going to happen. The Havana crowd, my old friends, are going to reconstitute themselves as some jumped-up kind of "social democrats" like all the old Communists in Europe and try to hold on. Our old friends in Miami are going to jump on an airplane, come down here, and try to take over again. The folks out here in these villages are going to be caught in that squeeze and they won't know what to do except stick with the crowd in power.

I have to convince them they have at least one other choice. If I'm able to do that, then this idea could catch on in other places. There isn't any real reason why it shouldn't. Lots of parts of Africa, maybe all of Africa. (Although my time in the Congo doesn't give me a lot of hope for those people. But that was a long time ago. Maybe things have changed.) Everywhere in Latin America—at least the places I've been, and that's almost everywhere. A good part of Asia where they're still struggling, and that's most of Asia. Vietnam. Places like that. Just like Cuba. Hopeless political histories.

The Yanquis had such an advantage. Big middle class of tradesmen and shopkeepers. A raft of landowning aristocrats schooled in Enlightenment theories. Stable families. A history of civil society. Established laws. Orderly procedures. It is hard to imagine the advantages they had. But there was a limit even to their civility. They moved right into the natives' territory. Took over the land. Then they imported those slaves down South to farm it. So much for noblesse oblige. So maybe these poor countryfolk here have a clean slate. Few assets, few liabilities.

Self-government with help from the central government to even things out. Local control of schools, hospitals, transport, environment. National standards in all these social areas and financial help so that no one goes below these standards. Citizen-owned banks with low interest on loans for houses and schooling and little businesses and farms. Ward republics. I like that. Little local countries. People with the power over their own lives.

If these Cubans can't be convinced of this, that they can have the power, they'll stay right where they are. Either the central government guys in Havana or the big corporate guys in Miami will run their lives, tell them where they can live, who they work for, pick their teachers for their kids, give them a minimum wage, tell them most of all who they can vote for. They'll have a choice, of course. But the choice will be so bad that most people, like in the States, will just stay home without some commissar rousting them out.

It's enough to make a grown man weep. Toil and trouble. Well, as Zorba said, we just have to unzip our pants and go looking for it.

■ ■ ■

14

■

Next to the exclusive Bahama Beach and Tennis Club was the even more exclusive Leeward Island Club with its own cove, marina, beach, and discreet bungalow facilities. Carefully planted and pruned island shrubs provide total privacy. Indeed, the only evidence of the Leeward Island Club's existence was a very small brass plaque on the right concrete pillar framing the wrought-iron gate set well back from the road. Just beneath the club's name were the words PRIVATE MEMBERSHIP ONLY. From the sea, the club's facilities were indistinguishable from dozens, perhaps hundreds, of similar private accommodations.

The membership of the Leeward Island Club was indeed exclusive. There were at any one time no more than two dozen members with very limited guest privileges scrupulously supervised by the executive committee of five. Three committee members constituted a quorum and, in fact, those three, also the club's officers, managed all the club's affairs. Aside from hefty membership fees and annual dues, club membership carried few obligations. The club was simply there to be used for relaxation or as a hideaway or to meet with other club member friends. The one exception was the annual dinner.

As was customary, on the night of this dinner, members in attendance wore dinner jackets. The permanent chef, a treasure in his own right, prepared and personally served the elegant meal, then retired to his accommodations off campus. Spouses and girlfriends—for the club was rigidly masculine, if not especially muscular—were treated to an exotic dinner and private floor show at a local nightspot featuring some native Chippendale spin-offs. The Chippendales were paid a bonus to make sure the ladies were amused until at least 2 A.M.

Thus free from the normal cares of the world and satisfied with a dinner fit for royalty, the sixteen club members able to attend the annual dinner finally cast off their dinner jackets, loosened the confining black ties, pushed back from the table, and lit their smokes. According to protocol, the club president offered a traditional toast: "Confusion to our enemies. Fuck 'em all but six, and keep them for pallbearers." "Hear! Hear!" his colleagues said as the brandy snifters clicked around the table.

"All right, here's the deal," the president, Harry Rossell (né Rosselli) said. "The question is our role in the Cuban elections next year. We discuss it thoroughly, then we make a plan, then we carry it out. The goal is Havana in 2000." He smiled a treacherous smile and they all applauded. "Johnny, you been thinking about this. You start."

"Harry asked me to think up some ideas, so I'll toss them on the table and you guys chew them over." He deliberately placed his Montecristo in an expensive ashtray and continued. "Unless Fidel's people get rid of him and the Commies stay on, there are going to be elections next spring in Cuba. The U.S. is going to establish normal diplomatic relations in exchange for the elections. There will be two major parties— the Commies calling themselves something else—we hear it will be something like the Cuban Social Democrats or some such—and a new party from Miami, the Cuban Americans, who are forming a party they call the Free Cuba Party."

"We know those guys," a large man named Maurice said.

"Of course, and we will get to know them better," Harry said.

Johnny continued, "And, whether we like it or not, we're going to get to know the 'Social Democrats.' "

"We'll find out just how social they are," Arnie Amandore said.

"Our goal," Johnny said, picking up the long cigar, "is to know both sides and to be friends with both sides so we have friends no matter who wins. Either way, the island is going to open up to tourism. Even Fidel has built up the tourism to replace the subsidies they were getting from the Russians. Right now, tourism is bigger than anything, even bigger than sugar."

Maurice interrupted, "And tourism means gambling. Right?"

"Not necessarily," Johnny said, "but probably. It certainly will if the Cuban Americans win—the Free Cuba Party. But after we get to know both sides, our next objective is to convince the Social Democrats, the Commies, that they can put their economy back on its feet with casinos. We'll have all the studies, revenue projections, consumer demand, numbers from Vegas, Indian tribes, Monte Carlo, all over the place. The point is, we want both parties committed to open the country up to gambling as a surefire revenue raiser."

Arnie said, "But won't they create some kind of cockamamie gambling board?"

"We're going to recommend that, Arn," Johnny said. "We're going to take the lead and convince both sides that they need some sort of gaming commission to regulate the industry—you know, to protect the public interest. Et cetera, et cetera, et cetera."

Harry asked, "How we going to do this, Johnny? What's the mechanism? What's our base? We can't just be the Leeward Island Club."

Johnny said, "Of course not. Here's what I propose. We create something like a 'Committee for Honest Elections in Cuba.' Incorporate it down here or someplace like Delaware or New Jersey. It's a nonprofit. We use our grown kids as the incorporators and officers. We set up a bank account or a lot of bank accounts down here. We contribute to both parties, heavily if necessary, to make friends. Our charter says we are for free elections, democracy, yatta, yatta, in Cuba. We make it clear to the guys running the two parties that our only interest is to help the Cubans achieve democracy and market economics, and that we believe one quick way to do that is to legalize gambling and license casinos at the hotels." Johnny sat back in his chair and relit the Montecristo. "That's pretty much it."

At the end of the table an older man, greatly respected for his experience and wisdom said, "Harry, that approach is pretty much what we do in the States."

"Right, Mr. Luganis," Harry said. "That's exactly the point. No one can criticize us. We're simply following the process we use in the States. We give to both parties. We host fund-raising dinners for senators and congressmen and governors. We know the regulators, the gaming commissioners. We lobby in the Congress and the legislatures. It's very honest, very open. That's why we like this approach in Cuba. We are contributing to the democratic process down there. Helping them get on their feet."

Mr. Luganis said, "There is enough in our treasury for fairly handsome contributions, is there not? Or do we need to raise a special war chest?"

Johnny said, "We will have to raise an additional small fund—maybe a couple of million. One each to both parties. It's not a big country, so, in theory, the election shouldn't cost all that much. But we hear that a lot of money will be spent there, above and below the table. The stakes are high for a lot of interests. The sugar industry, airlines, banks, hotels, telephones, they're all going to want to have friends in the government. So we believe the spending will be heavy. A couple of million may seem like a lot for a country like that. But we need to be remembered after the election."

Arnie said, "Everybody and his uncle are going to want casinos down there. We have to make sure that the casinos they have are *our* casinos."

Mr. Luganis smoothed his napkin. "What do you estimate the upside is for gambling in Cuba?"

Johnny consulted some notes. "We're having our consultants take a look right now. They're doing some projections. But, based on estimated revenues from a mature tourism industry, cruise ships, targeted advertising in the States and Europe, also by the way the Middle East and Asia—you know those guys love to gamble—our people's early estimate is close to a billion a year in five years, then probably stabilize somewhere around there."

There were respectful nods around the table. A man named Stanley King said, "Take the lid off that two mil. Spend whatever you have to. This is too big to get away. I say we back the Free Cubans, whatever the Cuban Americans call themselves. That's more our crowd. I know some of those people. We all know some of those people."

"You're right, Stan," Arnie said, "but we can't afford to alienate the other Cubans, the Commies. I've raised a lot of money in New Jersey politics, both sides, and there's nothing worse than being on the wrong horse. With these stakes, we simply *must* guarantee that we control those gambling licenses. I say, do whatever it takes."

Harry said, "Johnny, we're going to appoint you to watch this thing over the coming months. Make your contacts on both sides, whoever the party treasurers or finance chairmen are. Set up the new committee. I'll write a check from the Leeward Island Club account to get you started—say a quarter, a half a million. We'll all chip in pro rata to bring it up to two. My son, your son, Mo's daughter, will be the committee officers and incorporators. Let's get going. We should have a meeting every month until the election, just to make sure we're on track."

Maurice said, "Since we're basically doing what we do in U.S. politics, this raises an interesting question. Are we going to have to report all this? I hope the goddamn Cubans don't follow *that* little practice."

Johnny pushed a hand through his coiffed, wavy hair. "Too early to say. I hired a young guy, just on my own, to follow the Cuban Parliament's debate on this issue. Right now, he says there isn't much chance. They have a bill in the Parliament that sets up the rules for the national election. The only thing it says about contributions is something vague about everybody releasing an account of total expenditures after the election."

"*After*," Arnie snorted, "that's keen."

"Right," Johnny said. "My guy, who's a young bright Cuban himself, very savvy on the politics down there, says that the Commies—the 'Social Democrats'—don't want to disclose where their money's coming from either. So they're not keen on opening up that little can of worms."

Mr. Luganis said, "That's good for us. It simply means we can spend whatever we need to, whatever it takes, to achieve our goal. Given the probable stakes you've suggested, Johnny, I would say that we simply must control the process for issuance of gambling licenses in Cuba. A million or two dollars is nothing in such a game. This is a once-in-a-lifetime chance. We simply must take it—and we must win."

Harry looked around the table at the heads nodding agreement. "Any disagreement with Mr. Luganis on this? Hearing none, then that's our policy. We contribute whatever it takes, along the same lines we use in the States—support both sides, make friends on both sides, be direct about our interests with the right people, the people who will have the power—and may the best man win."

"Hear! Hear!" Maurice shouted and, as he stood, the others joined him. "Here's to democracy in Cuba. May the best man—who, of course, will be our best friend—win!"

They all drained the brandy. As they began to drift away, some for private discussions, some to finish their cigars on the beach, some to girlfriends stashed around town, Johnny said, "Oh, yeah, get ready for some real craziness down there. I went down last week to recruit this kid. And the nuts are coming out of the woodwork. Already."

"Like in the States?" Maurice asked.

"You bet," Johnny said. "Let me tell you what this kid told me. He said he had heard a rumor from some pols in Havana that there is some old guy up in the mountains, in the Sierras where Castro started out, who calls himself . . . well, he doesn't exactly call himself . . . who the people are saying is . . . guess who?"

"Jesus?" Maurice said. "The pope? Michael Jackson? Who?"

Johnny laughed and shook his head. "You'll never guess. This old guy is up there in his seventies, wandering around like some nutcase. And the *campesinos*—the farmers, you know, peasants—are saying—" he started laughing—"they're saying it's—Che. Che Guevara."

"Che Guevara!" a couple of the men chorused. "Che Guevara?"

"It's too much," Johnny laughingly said. "He's wandering around these little villages talking some wacky political stuff. He's getting these *campesinos* whipped up. He's some kind of wacky radical." Johnny shook his head. "From now on, they're going to be coming out of the woodwork, I tell you. We just better get used to it—and keep our eye on the ball."

"Yes," Mr. Luganis said over his shoulder as he started for his bungalow. "I wouldn't pay any attention to these people. It's the price you have to pay for our kind of democracy. Look at what we have to put up with in the States. Jesse Jackson, what was that? McGovern, my God!"

As small clusters formed and began to head off into the night, one of the younger men who hadn't spoken said, "Johnny, you thought about the acronym of your committee?" Then he laughed. "The Committee for Honest Elections?"

Then they all laughed. Johnny said, "C.H.E. It's Che." They smacked each other on the back and laughed. Johnny shouted after them as they disappeared into the night, "Maybe we should give him some money too."

1 5

■

Several weeks had passed since Ernesto Blanco had undertaken his mission. Now accompanied on some, but not all, occasions by the faithful Alejo, he was beginning to be a familiar sight in a number of the villages in Granma province. It was not unusual to see him, with or without Alejo, sitting in the ubiquitous town plaza, sipping coffee, and inevitably sooner or later engaged with the locals. His first circle of interlocutors were the old men, who had little to do but reflect on their times and the new political era, the new century, and the new millennium that promised to dawn within the lifetime of most of them. Then, of course, each village and town had its own philosopher, the one who accepted responsibility to step back, aside, or up and look at things less immediately, with more detachment, with more perspective. Ernesto treated each of the local philosophers with respect, whether they always deserved it or not. Though it was not in his nature to suffer fools with equanimity, Ernesto knew that whatever respect they bore from the community at large was fungible if the local wiseperson in turn respected him. So, he spent many hours in usually polite disputation, never seeking intellectual victory or insisting on pummeling his often venerable antagonist. *"Con mucho respeto, señor"* was the watchword.

Sometimes, to his pleasure, Ernesto found himself engaged with the fairer gender. These were sometimes local ladies come to fetch their tardy husbands home for dinner—and Ernesto welcomed this because, more often than not, local custom dictated that he, the stranger, be asked to share in their simple meal of rice and beans. Sometimes the ladies were local shopkeepers or cantina bosses. The rude ones demanded that he move on, that he not conduct his debating society outside their door. The more interesting ones were those who engaged in the discourse. Ernesto, so accustomed in the old days to the patriarchal society, was delighted to see the emergence of these, sometimes not unattractive, ladies with strong opinions and a self-confident manner. Usually, these ladies were possessed of a direct, no-nonsense manner: "*Señor, con mucho respeto*, your idea for local power will never work in a village as populated with lazy men as this one."

For himself, Ernesto had never let his interest, indeed his fascination, with the fairer gender impede his revolutionary mission. On the other hand, there were unique comforts to be sought in the warm gaze, the slight brush of the hand, the lingering squeeze of the handshake, the high color in the cheeks, the finely turned ankle, the ample bosom, the haughty toss of the dark mane, the . . . Here he had to check a temptation toward reverie from totally transporting him into the mysterious and hazardous realm of romance. The mission of revolution took precedence.

One such temptation presented itself on a cloudy day in a lowland town of Dormitorio in Las Tunas province just north of Granma. After their late morning coffee and discussion with the local town fathers, Ernesto and Alejo were shouldering their satchels when the proprietress of the café on the square, noticed throughout the morning by Alejo as evidencing considerable interest in the vigorous discussion, approached from the café door. She was tall and very shapely, the two men noticed, as she swung across the square toward them. She had a fine tangle of black hair and dark eyes and her ample hips rhythmically swung the long full skirt from side to side. For a moment, as her long balletic stride brought her almost to them, Ernesto briefly thought of a fine Arabian mare or a scene from a movie starring Sophia Loren he had seen in a theater outside Quito many years before.

"*Hola, señores*," she said, her voice a symphony of low chimes. "You are welcome for something to eat at my café," she continued, as she gestured behind her. "Unless, of course"—she smiled mischievously—"you are accustomed to finer food. You are clearly gentlemen of the world. So, perhaps, my humble place is not sufficiently elegant for your taste."

"*Muchas gracias, señora*," Ernesto said. His eye had a glint that worried Alejo instantly. "We welcome your hospitality and are honored by your gracious invitation. But we would not take advantage of your kindness. We are perfectly prepared to compensate you according to your standard fare." Alejo rolled his eyes. Of course, they had no money. What was his *compañero* talking about?

"It is strictly business, *señor*," the woman said. "You seem to attract people like flies to a honey pot. If you come to my little place, sooner or later everybody in this town will swarm around my place to see the curiosity. So, as I see it, if I feed you, you will help feed me." She turned and sailed off with an insistent wave of the hand over her shoulder for them to follow. Magnetized by the engine of nature rhythmically driving the skirt back and forth, the two old men, now imagining themselves much younger, dutifully followed like Odyssean sailors helpless before the sirens' call.

"I am Margarita," she said as she seated them in the table near the window of her small *paladar*, where passersby might see them and be drawn in to engage in political dialogue strenuous enough to require nourishment.

Presently two heaping plates of rice and beans and flavorful cups of coffee and a plate of fresh bread arrived. She sat down at the next table, drank her own coffee, and watched them eat. The two men occasionally smiled thanks at her like two grateful old dogs. "*Señora*," Alejo sighed with the pleasure of the first hot meal in three days, "*muchas gracias. You are very kind.*"

"What were you talking about over there, if you don't mind me asking, that had everybody so stirred up?" she asked.

"Politics, Señora Margarita, politics," Ernesto said. "What else."

"Oh, you mean Fidel and the elections and the diplomacy, *sí*?"

"*Sí, señora*," Ernesto said. "I am afraid it is the preoccupation of men such as ourselves who have too much time on our hands. It is why the earliest societies, probably in the caves, invented politics. To give men of a certain age something to talk about. For you, I am sure it is babies and children and things such as that."

Margarita's handsome face flushed and she slammed her cup down. "I know something about politics myself, *señor*. The time has come, *gracias a Dios*, when we women can discuss politics as readily as men. It's you men in Habana who have screwed everything up. Look at this town. Look at this province. Look at this country! Do you think it is the fault of us women? Hardly!"

Anxious to placate their benefactress, and an attractive one at that,

Ernesto said, "*Señora, por favor,* of course you are right. Our achievements cannot be claimed by one gender—but our failures, likewise, cannot be laid at the doorstep of either men or women."

"I am not so sure about that last one," Margarita said. But she shrugged, willing to concede the point. In the background they had heard pronounced banging toward the back of the *paladar.* It sounded like someone with a hatred of pots and pans. Just as Margarita threw up her hands and started to head for the kitchen to quell the chaos, a lanky youth, almost as tall as Alejo, emerged from the back. He wore a tattered apron that, embarrassed, he immediately started to tear off when he saw the strangers.

"I quit, Margarita," the youth said.

"Again?" she said distractedly. "How can you quit when I don't pay you."

"Now I must be paid," he said. "You have promised for a long time."

Margarita scribbled on her order pad "IOU one million pesos," signed the paper, and handed it to her nephew. He folded it, put it in his tattered shirt pocket, and said, "Now it is five million that you owe me. And, when you pay, I will stow away on the next fishing boat from the States and get out of here. You, of course, will stay. You are committed to the great socialist experiment. Not for me, you can have your *socialismo.* I want a car, some clothes, a laptop, a pretty girl, more clothes, a house, another car. Oh, yeah, and Disney World. I don't care if you are the boss of the party here. I quit."

The two senior men's gaze shifted simultaneously and immediately to their hostess. Ernesto said, "Party boss? Señora Margarita, you are responsible for the Communist Party in these parts?"

Margarita tossed her dark mane in affirmation and pride. "You see, we 'little women' are now taking responsibility."

Alejo bowed with respect and Ernesto said, "That includes, then, the responsibility for the success of the Cuban economy." He waved his hand at the decrepit buildings around the square. "You are proud, then, of your great revolutionary achievements." Alejo quickly mopped up remaining morsels of food, knowing from expanding experience that this meal was coming to a rapid conclusion.

Margarita's dark eyes flared. "And you, *venerable señor,* are you then the representative of the bloody-handed gangsters that we chased away some time ago? Those fine *aristos* who raped our people and stole our land from us, those last-gasp colonialists who prostituted our daughters and sold our treasures to the Yanquis, those imperialist lackeys who reduced us to slaves. Are they of your party . . . *señor?*"

"I hadn't realized, that is until you have so brilliantly enlightened me, *señora*, that I had to be either one or the other, either *socialista revolucionario* or contemptible *capitalista*. As a free man, I somehow thought I might be able to have yet another idea."

The young man from the kitchen nervously wiped his hands on his tattered apron. Margarita gestured at him with her coffee cup and said to Ernesto, "Is this your idea? The politics of our new generation, the politics of materialism?"

"Marxism has failed," Ernesto said, "because it promised that the workers of the world would control the means of production and thereby control their destiny. Do you control any means of production? Those guys in the Palacio de la Revolución in Habana don't much look like proletariat to me. You have this"—he swept his hand in a circle—"your *paladar*. But those guys in Habana, so concerned with the proletariat, tax your profits away and make it almost impossible for you to operate. And as for Mr. Michael Jackson here"—he gestured at the youth—"he is the captive of the new global capitalism, the ubiquitous Yanqui popular culture. He is a slave of 'things,' of the baggy shorts, the backward baseball cap, the loud mechanical music, the Terminator movies. Pretty soon, every member of his generation in the world will look and act exactly alike, just like Disney wants them to."

Outside the window, two or three people passed by, noticed the strangers, and stopped to peer in.

Ernesto's words, delivered without rancor or disputatiousness, tamped down a bit of Margarita's fiery temper. But her nature, especially with men, had been honed by experience to a sharp edge. "And you, Señor . . . ?" Ernesto said, "Blanco." "Señor Blanco"—she smiled, intuitively sensing this was somehow a nom de guerre—"your idea for utopia?"

He smiled in turn, taking her aback with the years the smile caused to disappear. "My idea for utopia, Señora Margarita"—he thought, Would be a lifetime with you, but he resisted the temptation to say it—"is to take both the socialists and the democrats seriously. It is to give power to the people, literally. For purposes of the basic conditions of life, this town—what is it, Dormitorio—should be its own country. For purposes of schools, hospitals, local business, land ownership, streets, flowers, and music, it should be La República del Dormitorio. Let Habana, governed by people elected to represent all the local republics, manage—or mismanage—the international affairs and certain national matters. Let the people themselves, however, manage their own local communities, their own local republics. That is my idea of utopia." White teeth glistened beneath white mustache. The people outside the window, joined by two others, shyly came through the door and sat down.

Margarita studied Ernesto to make sure he was not somehow teasing her. She decided he was dead serious. "From your morning debate with the locals, you figure they're ready to run their own republic?"

"As ready as those has-beens in Habana," Ernesto said, "and, besides, *señora*, something tells me *you* will be the first president of the new republic."

She produced a deep blush and turned away to hide it as the young man said, "Politics is a nuisance, *señor*. It gets in everybody's way. No one I know cares anything about your politics. We just want to enjoy our lives. For me, your *república* sounds like more pain-in-the-ass politics."

Three more passersby came in. The *paladar* was filling up.

"That's a very good attitude, *che*," Ernesto said. "You stick with that idea and politics will sure enough bite you in the ass. Who collects taxes, who doesn't pave your roads, who keeps you poor, who isolates this little island from the rest of the world and denies you the materialistic junk you think is the definition of life? Who do you think does those things? Politicians. Those politicians you don't care anything about are making decisions every day that narrow your options to about this." He held a thumb and forefinger about two inches apart. "You keep that attitude, *che*, and I can just about guarantee you'll be wearing that silly apron the rest of your days."

The kid looked at Margarita, confused. "There's nothing I can do about it," he finally said.

"Is that so?" Ernesto asked. "You work for the most powerful politician in town"—he pointed at Margarita—"and you say there's nothing you can do about it? You going to vote next year in the new elections?" He addressed the question to the room at large. Three more people were now standing against the far wall.

The kid shrugged his shoulders, mystified. "I don't know. I don't have a clue about any voting." He looked at his boss. "*Señora* will tell me."

"*Señora* will tell you," Ernesto said with a soft laugh. "*Señora* will tell you. And who will tell *Señora*? The guys in Habana who got you into this mess." He smiled again.

Infuriated, Margarita said, "Wait a minute! Nobody tells me what to do. I support the *revolución* because it brought freedom to these people." She took in the room. "We'd still be slaving for the *aristos* without the *revolución*. When the election comes, I will make up my own mind. But, I can tell you one thing . . . neither me nor any of these people"—she swept the room with both hands—"are going to vote for those bastards who raped us before."

Ernesto said, "What about him"—he gestured at the kid—"and his generation. The bastards in Miami didn't rape them. As he said, he doesn't have a clue about the voting. And, I'll tell you a little secret. Whatever he says, he ain't going to vote like you tell him. The real problem is, he ain't going to vote at all."

Margarita stood up and looked around the room. "You people want something to eat, go back in the kitchen and get it. Go help them, Joséito," she said to the young man and he dutifully marched off to help fill the plates. She studied Ernesto, then the silent Alejo, then Ernesto again. "What are you? Some kind of revolutionaries? *La república!* You don't sound like Yanquis. Where did you come from?"

Alejo gestured southward toward the Sierra. Ernesto smiled again, understanding that it both intrigued and infuriated her, and he also gestured toward the southern mountains.

She shook her head. "Don't give me that. You're no *vaqueros*, at least not recently." She sat down and studied them again, especially Ernesto. "Are you some kind of *loco* prophet? That's it. You like to stir things up, cause a little trouble here and there. You're some kind of prophet."

The dozen or so people began to file back into the room, plates full, and took seats as they listened to the exchange.

The old man smiled again. "Once again, *señora*, your superior powers of observation and understanding of human nature have served you well. I am . . . we are prophets of the new politics. And, *Señora Margarita*"— he leaned forward to gaze deeply into the dark pools of her suddenly wide eyes—"we want you to join our cause." He took her warm, un-resisting hand. "Please join us, *señora*."

She edged back but did not remove her hand. "What kind of cause? What 'new politics'?"

"The politics," Ernesto said softly, "the politics of pure democracy. The politics of the true republic."

1 6

∎

The following communiqué, issued from Washington and Havana simultaneously, was the headline story on the twentieth of August, 1999.

> Tonight, the governments of the United States of America and the Republic of Cuba announce the establishment of full diplomatic relations. Successful completion of negotiations over the past several weeks have led both countries to the conclusion that the time has come to normalize relations and exchange ambassadors. The government of the United States also announces the end of the embargo against trade with Cuba first established in 1961. The government of Cuba announces that President Fidel Castro will become, on the first of January, 2000, the permanent ambassador-at-large for Cuba and will, therefore, hand over the responsibilities of the presidency to Vice President Raúl Castro, who will assume the title of acting President until the national elections scheduled for the first of May, 2000.

During the hectic summer weeks since Fidel Castro's surprise announcement and the United States' surprised response, there had been a turmoil of political activity, almost all behind the scenes and below the surface. The Cuban Parliament, dutifully following the instructions of President Castro, as interpreted by the party Politburo and the parliamentary leadership, had enacted the new election laws. They provided for the registration of political parties, the privatization of the press, nomination of candidates for national office and for parliamentary seats, and the procedures for the conduct of the elections the following spring. The law left many details unanswered because no one was too sure what the answers were.

Within hours of the passage of the new statute, the Cuban Social Democratic Party filed its registration papers. Its founders were key members of the Politburo and the Parliament and its chairman was Raúl Castro. Within a month, the Free Cuba Party registered under the law. Its founders were less familiar, but included names some recognized from more than four decades before. In each case, storefront headquarters of each of the two parties were established in the Vedado section of Havana in the center of the business district. Banners were nailed above doorways, balloons that soon sagged pathetically were released at official openings, and pretty young ladies sat at front desks to sign up visitors. To anyone familiar with urban democratic politics of the 1950s, it all looked vaguely familiar.

But the truly interesting developments, as usual, escaped public notice. The Cuban Social Democrats sent written messages to provincial and local party chiefs more or less demanding their allegiance and outlining their responsibilities in seeing that the local party apparatchiks supported the CSD as before. Same system, different name, went the appeal. The CSD sent out its best circuit riders around the country to rally support. So the Cuban hills were alive with the sounds of politics.

For its part, the Free Cuba Party was equally active. A substantial and growing political war chest of several million dollars had been raised within the exile Cuban community in the States. Several direct mailings had gone out to almost 500,000 U.S. households and the mailing lists were being computerized, based upon the early returns, according to sophisticated categories. The party had been registered under the new Cuban election laws, the headquarters had been opened with much fanfare but little public reaction, and field organizers were being hired and trained. Most important, the FCP had conducted some early polling and was even now planning a media campaign to begin early in the millennial year. Late-twentieth-century "democratic" politics was coming to Cuba with a vengeance.

The FCP's point person, Emilia Sanchez from the Wager-Down political consultancy, had successfully opened the storefront campaign headquarters between an airline office and a movie theater on La Rampa, the central business street of new Havana, and established her own operations center in a suite at the Hotel Nacional. The hotel gardens overlooked the Malecón, the Morro Castle guarding the mouth of Havana harbor, and the monument to the U.S.S. *Maine*, whose dubious demise gave rise to the Spanish-American War. She also could take in the Nacional's two swimming pools and luxurious gardens open only to the foreign guests with hard currency. She broke her eighteen-hour workdays only for dinner at the Monseigneur across from the hotel or La Torre on the top floor of the Focsa building nearby. Then back to the hotel for more phone calls.

"Micky," she said, "we're on track down here. Things are going well." This was her regular 11 P.M. check-in call with the boss. At first they were concerned about their calls being monitored. Then they assumed they were and, except when it simply didn't matter, adopted a vague code. "Office is open and staffed. No trouble from the streets. [No demonstrations or violence.] Sign-ups going well. [A few people drifting in to affiliate with the party or ask questions.] We're doing some leafleting, using some student volunteers and some hires. [Handing out campaign leaflets, in some cases paying people to do so.] We're training people here to help us carry out some preliminary polling. We'll need a couple of weeks at least to get the training done. Then another week or two to do the poll. They'll have to fan out into the countryside and transportation is a nightmare here. Give me thirty days and we should have some numbers."

Micky said, "Any trouble from the top? [Is the power structure hassling you?]"

"No," she said. "Things couldn't be quieter. I think they've got their hands full just making the transition. We may face some trouble when the campaign gets into full swing. But my guess is they think we're marginal. If . . . when . . . we prove not to be, then we have to start being very careful."

"Anything else happening down there?" Micky asked.

Emilia said, "Not really. This is like virgin territory. Everything, including most things we take for granted, has to be invented. It's a weird experience—but kinda fun." She paused, ready to sign off; then she added, "The funniest thing is this rumor going around that Che Guevara has returned." She started laughing and Micky joined in. They were both laughing hilariously at the idea.

Micky said, "Are you kidding me? Che Guevara? That's too much!" He laughed so hard he couldn't continue.

Emilia said, "I tell you, it's true. It's all over the political network here. I don't think it's gotten to the guy on the street. But all the pols and insiders are laughing about it. It's kind of like an escape valve for the political tension. People get uptight and somebody says, 'Let's get hold of Che. Get him down here to take things over.' I tell you, it's a hoot." They laughed for another minute.

Micky said, "I'll get that around to the committee up here—our clients. They'll get a laugh. They may not have Fidel to kick around anymore. But now they got Che! Hahahaha!"

If anything, these vague folk-tale rumors had struck an even funnier bone within the Cuban Social Democratic Party hierarchy. These were all people for whom Che Guevara was an icon beyond iconage. It was hard to turn a corner of any street in any city or town in Cuba without confronting the visionary, beret-topped, chin-jutting revolutionary visage. For those *del norte*, the only way to imagine the image would be, somehow, to combine the premature, death-enhanced charisma of John Kennedy, Marilyn Monroe, Elvis Presley, James Dean, and Martin Luther King, Jr. Even *el Comandante* treated the legend with deference and respect. Che Guevara was not someone to fool around with—even in death.

So, when the *campesinos*, the *guajiros*, and the *vaqueros* of Granma province began to whisper that Che was on the prowl, it was the Cuban political equivalent of the Messiah's return. Except, it was all so preposterous, so clearly connected with Fidel's eschatological departure into history, that you had to laugh. What else could happen?

What else could happen was that Che could come back. And, sure enough, he had. He was back and he had set up his political workshop in the impenetrable canyons, *arroyos*, and caves of the Sierra, consecrated by *los barbudos* a full lifetime ago when *el Jefe*'s beard was black as coal.

In the combination conference room–clubhouse above the CSD's campaign headquarters near the Universidad de la Habana, the jokes abounded. There's good news and there's bad news. The good news is that Che has returned. The bad news is—he's really pissed. How many Ches does it take to change a light bulb? Two. One to put the bulb in and the other to shoot him if he gets it wrong. How old would Che be if he were still alive? Still thirty-nine. He's too mean to get old. What will Che say when he sees *el Jefe* again? Fidel, you fucked this thing up so bad I'm not sure even *I* can straighten it out. And so on, and so on.

When the laughter from the latest joke died down, Victor Pais stared into the urban darkness outside the window. He hadn't been laughing with the others. "Why do you think a thing like this gets started? Why in hell would a story like this start up now?"

No one answered. Then Ricardo Gomez shrugged and said, "Stuff like this happens all the time, Victor. You know how those people are. They're off there by themselves. We're a million miles away. They don't know what's going on. They don't have much else to do but start stories, gossip about who's sleeping with who. That kind of thing."

Vilma Espinosa added, "I have this sister up in the States, in New Jersey. We hate each other. Our politics couldn't be more opposite. She's some kind of greedy capitalist. But anyway, she sends me letters, sometimes we talk. You can't believe the kind of stuff that goes around up there. Elvis is alive. Kennedy's hiding out somewhere with Marilyn Monroe. Martians raping movie stars."

"That's it," Pais laughed. "The Yanquis started this Che story. They're still trying to sabotage us and this is their idea for screwing up this election. Get ready. There will be more."

José Puerta said, "Could be. Those *campesinos* have always believed there are two or three Fidels. Can't convince them otherwise. The story made sense to them. So, no way you're going to get it out of their minds."

Antonio Oliverez said, "We could send somebody up there. Try to track this wacky old crank down."

"Then what?" Vilma snorted. "Bring him down here? Stake him out on the Malecón? Expose him as a fraud?"

Pais shook his head. "You'd make a martyr out of him. Somebody— maybe those *del norte*—would shoot him. We'd have a martyr on our hands. Che's dead again! My God!"

"On the other hand," Vilma said, "it's probably not a bad idea to have somebody—one of our people—track him down and kind of . . . watch him. First of all, find out if he exists at all. Chances are he's nothing but a ghost. A creation of some rum-soaked imaginations. But if there is some old guy, we ought to see what the excitement is all about. You never know, he could be some kind of CIA agent, sent down here to create a diversion, stir people up. I wouldn't put something like that past those bastards. They'd think it was a real joke."

Felipe Morales agreed. "Let's have the party leader in Granma check him out."

Pais shook his head again. "Better to send somebody from here. He'll be more objective. Won't get caught up in the local fever."

"I got a guy," Antonio said. "You know that Osvaldo . . . what's his name . . . that we use sometimes to tap phones and get into hotel rooms?"

"Damn straight!" Vilma said. "I use him all the time. He can pick you clean and you never know he's been in the room. He's slick and he's a killer."

Pais held a hand up. "Easy. Nobody said anything about killing."

"Figure of speech, Victor," Vilma said. "Just means he gets the job done."

"What do the rest of you think?" Pais asked. There were nods around the room. "Okay, Vilma, you and Antonio talk to this Osvaldo and send him out. But he should melt into the countryside. Look like a *campesino*. Lose the city clothes. Become one of the people. Tell him to take his time. We're not in any big rush. He should get next to this Che whatever and develop some trust." He thought a moment. "Tell him to be prepared to stay for a while. If this old man turns out to exist and to have some kind of following up in the hills, we may need somebody next to him all the way to the elections."

José said, "My guess is, he's gone in a month. I've seen this happen before. Some kind of wacky old prophet comes along—*babalao*, whatever—everybody gets excited, then he disappears. We'll see a lot of them during this election. They'll come out from under the rocks."

Pais sighed. "I hope you're right. But, somehow, I can't imagine very many of those crazies managing to get it started that they're Che Guevara. There must be something about this old guy." He looked out the window into the inky night. "Besides, you never know. He might actually have something interesting to say."

Very late that night Vilma sat in a back alcove of a small restaurant near the Palacio de la Revolución used by the party bosses to conduct business over late dinners. Across the table sat a thin, nondescript man nervously fingering a table knife. He had a battered straw hat tilted back on his head. Between the two of them, they were busy filling up a second ashtray. At first disdaining food, when it came he gobbled it up as if starved. A waiter came and absentmindedly filled their coffee cups.

"As soon as you can," Vilma hissed. "None of this, I've got a job that I can't leave. We'll take care of it. This will be your job. When it's over, we'll take care of you."

The thin man blinked nervously. His desperate smile made him look even more uncomfortable. "I'm pretty old to be climbing around in the mountains again," he complained.

"Look, Osvaldo, I don't think you have a choice in the matter. This is what we want you to do and you'll, by God, do it."

The miserable grin faded. "How do I find old 'Che'? Last time I was there—forty years ago—the Sierra was a pretty big place."

"We got lookouts tracking him down. Soon as we hear he's somewhere, we'll get you there. It's up to you after that."

"What do I have to do?" the thin man asked.

"Just like I already told you," Vilma hissed. "Get in with him. Find out where he stays. Find out who's with him. Find out who's behind him. Most of all, *find out who he is.*"

The man's hand shook as he lit a cigarette and sipped the hot coffee. "Who does he say he is?"

"It doesn't matter who *he* says he is." Vilma thumped the table. "What matters is who the *people* say he is. And who they say he is—get ready—is Che-fucking-Guevara!"

The man's eyes, narrowed by years of peering through cigarette smoke, widened. "Che Guevara? Why in God's name would people be saying that?"

"Look, Osvaldo, that's not for you to worry about. That's for me to worry about. Some of these crazy old *campesinos* have been waiting for Che for thirty years. So, why not? Your job is to find out who he really is . . . then we'll figure out what to do about him."

The thin man's knees shook under the table. Vilma's fierce glare hadn't caused this. It was a new problem.

"All I can tell you now," she said, blowing smoke in his face, "is that you should keep your little toolbox handy. We may have to make road-kill out of him if he gets in our way."

■ ■ ■

All politics is a form of seduction. Take that Señora Margarita. She's still trying to figure out if I'm just some horny old man or whether I may really have an interesting trick up my sleeve. I liked her. A lot. She is the very reason this country has a chance. She's strong. She's clever. She's a leader. People respect her. They clearly were listening to her. That is half the equation of leadership—getting people to trust you and listen to you. I can practically guarantee that, when we go back to that place—Dormitorio (what a sleepy name, perfect for that place)—she will have thought about what I said, about pure democracy, about local control, about people running their own governments and their own town business. The true republic.

I got inside her mind. I made her think. It's a kind of mental seduction. You just have to get people to think. That kid—Joséito, she called him— he's a different case. Much more difficult. Because he hasn't learned to think—at all—yet. He is what scares me about this country. Maybe any country. Doesn't care about anything but "things." That's what's wrong with modern society. Nobody—at least the young people—cares about anything but things. When I was his age (I always hated it when older people used to use that phrase—but here I am, doing it myself), I was on fire with ideas—justice, equality, down with the oligarchy, power to the people. Now that I think about it, those are still the ideas that drive me. The only thing that is different is that I've found a new (old) approach.

It isn't about ideas so much as it is about ideals. Ideals—principles, Plato's forms, whatever you want to call them—have driven the revolutionaries of the past and, I suppose, will continue to. More often than not, those ideals are impractical. That's why the "practical" person is never going to be a revolutionary. The revolutionary is a visionary. He sees things other people don't see, the "practical" ones. The "practical" person operates within the boundaries of what is. The revolutionary sees what ought to be. So there will always be a struggle between the "practical" person, even the good one, and the revolutionary.

I liked Robert Kennedy, at least who he was just before they killed him. He quoted that thing about "Some see things as they are and ask why; I see things that never were and ask why not." I like that a lot. He and I would have had a time. Birds of a feather, as they say. He was about as revolutionary as Tío Sam is going to produce. I know this, if he were still alive and down here, he would be on our side of this fight. No question. I can see the two of us, drinking coffee or maybe a couple of cervezas around a camp-fire up here in the Sierra, arguing until dawn. What a time that would have been. Maybe in revolutionary heaven . . . who knows.

Well, now it's time for me to spread out a little. Tomorrow I will slip away—leave Alejo and Rafael here—down to Santiago and then up north and west to Camagüey and then on to Santa Clara. My God, it's been so long. That battle at Santa Clara, the one that decided the revolution. What a time that was. We took the town, had a celebration, then loaded up in the trucks and headed for Havana. A parade, a victory party, all the way. A great experience. We were so young and so sure of everything. Life was black-and-white. The aristos scrambling to get on those airplanes were the bad guys and we, the noble young revolutionaries, were the good guys. Thumbed our noses at Tío Sam, we did.

After forty years, life has become clearer to me again, but in a different way. Revolution is not going to come from the top down. That was our mistake many years ago. You can't revolutionize people who don't particu-larly want to be revolutionized or who are not "owners" of the revolution. This time, I'm trying to help these people become part of their own democratic revolution. That way they have a stake in the outcome. Last time we trans-ferred power from Batista to us, the revolutionary leadership. But we never really transferred power to the people. This time, if we win, the people themselves will have won the power.

But it's up to them. I can only help open the door. The people themselves must walk through it. This is not so much a test of my ideas. It is a test of their courage.

PART II

■

FALL 1999

1 7

■

$\mathbf{S}$tanding in the open door of the VIP lounge of José Martí International Airport, Victoria Savidge breathed deeply, letting the warm Cuban air fill her lungs, and told herself she was a new woman. Free of corporate New York, free of political Washington, free of cynical American politics, and, most of all, free of Marshall Stuart. If ever a human being—especially one who had become almost a study in self–re-creation—had been given yet another chance to start over, it was Victoria Savidge on this spectacular fall day in the Caribbean.

On the plane from New York to Miami, then on to Havana, Victoria carried out a reality check. She told herself that she was on the slide at The Political Network. She rehearsed a career characterized by spectacular but relatively brief tenures as a correspondent at two major networks, an investigative reporter on an evening newsmagazine show, a member of the Washington bureau of CNN, and then TPN—and Marshall. Marshall was the problem. Not exactly Marshall personally, but the Marshalls of the television world. Victoria went through a phase of believing that all women shared her experience. But too many confessionals with women friends, friends who went from wanting this man to wanting any man to wanting no man, had forced Victoria to face reality. Throughout her twenties and thirties she had been drop-dead gorgeous. It had been her blessing—leading to a string of highly coveted on-air jobs—and her curse—leading to a string of affairs with highly coveted, self-absorbed television executives. All jerks. The latest—Marshall—had in many ways been the worst. The epitome of the lot—pseudoliterate in that peculiarly corporate executive way, totally self-referential, incapable of any genuine passion, viewing the quality of life through the prism of his bank account, emotionally adolescent, and possessing the superficial charm of a three-year-old. She shuddered.

Every time she undertook this exercise, repeatedly seeking clues to her own destructive pattern, she shuddered. All Marshalls. All jerks. Now, her biblical reckoning at hand, she realized with the clear steady eye of reality that nature herself was conspiring to break the pattern. Her blessing and her curse, her meal ticket, her looks were beginning to fade. Her choices were narrowing. She could fish for older Marshalls who had fewer choices—she did still have a great body, she thought as she smoothed her skirt and glanced at her reflection in the doorway glass. She could, as some of her more daring friends were doing, launch a series of liaisons with those muscular young hunks who made Marshall seem like Einstein. That brought a different kind of shudder. She had tried that option once or twice and it had brought her to the brink of suicide. Or she could accept reality. She could try one more, one last fresh start.

She knew exactly why she was in Cuba. This was Marshall's kiss-off. And this was her last chance at TPN. The chances of breaking a major story, of hitting a journalistic home run on Cuba's rapprochement with Uncle Sam, were remote. Sure, there was a story here. But it was a real story, an in-depth story, a thumb-sucker for *The New York Times* and National Public Radio, not for TPN's target audience, gen-X yuppies whose idea of serious politics was Monica Lewinsky's life story. Unless she figured out a way to win an Emmy on this story, her days in front of the camera were over. Her sleep-arounds, however high-level, had spoiled her chances of becoming Barbara Walters. And she knew she was not taken seriously enough in her business to become a producer or executive. Cuba was her last stand.

The worried-looking young woman who met her flight arrived with two sweating porters wheeling battered hand trolleys with her ten pieces of luggage. She gestured Victoria toward the waiting car and gave her a running commentary in passable English on the dusty ride into the city. Victoria listened with one ear while she gave most of her attention to the primitive conditions they were passing. Third world, she thought. Reminded her of the run-down condition of many Latin cities she had seen over the years. The revolution hadn't improved things much here, she observed. Pretty much the lot of other scrape-by Caribbean cultures. Though dismayed by the decay, she absorbed the views of *Habana vieja* as they fled past and vowed to set out for the old city after she checked in. Her escort, arranged for by TPN through the Ministry of Information, pointed to a city map unfolded on the backseat between them.

She pointed out her hotel and made an X mark, then drew the rough perimeters of the old city, then indicated key government landmarks and ministries. As they arrived at the stately old National Hotel, a porter approached the car, saw the luggage jammed in the front seat and the tied-down trunk, and waved for reinforcements.

After Victoria had registered, her escort apologetically asked for a few minutes to brief her on her trip. Based upon considerable experience in foreign travel, Victoria had used the influence of TPN to notify the U.S. Information Agency of her visit and ask its help in organizing interviews. The USIA, in turn, found a freelance Cuban journalist through the Ministry of Information and she had intermediated on behalf of TPN to organize the visit. The escort, clearly intimidated by Victoria's notoriety and the importance of her network, nervously referred to her schedule notes.

"This evening you will have dinner with our deputy minister, who will give you the overview of our political situation," she began. "Then tomorrow, you will have meetings with several of our local journalists, who will answer your questions concerning our elections next year, the candidates, and the parties." From the stiff presentation, Victoria concluded that her escort had performed this mission a number of times before and was working from a formula. "Then, in the following days, you may tour outside of Havana to see our country and meet some of our people."

"What about the interview with Mr. Castro," Victoria asked with urgency, "Raúl, Mr. Raúl Castro?" Part of Victoria's strategy was to be the first American reporter to interview the key players, the first to appreciate the political landscape, the first to translate the transformation of Cuba to the American people. If she developed sufficient expertise, or even if she just managed to be the first broadcast journalist identified with the country, half the battle was won. People would automatically turn to her reports—"On our broadcast tonight, Victoria Savidge from Havana on the political revolution in Cuba"—and she would be back in play. Even though this, her first trip to Cuba, was for research and background purposes, she had to see Raúl Castro and try to get him to declare his intentions as part of her strategy to establish her credentials. So far, the Cuban Social Democratic Party had not officially nominated a candidate for president. But it was widely assumed in all political circles that Raúl would succeed his brother as leader of the de-Leninized governing party. No one from the United States had interviewed him yet. He was remaining in the background at least until his brother's long shadow dissipated. "It is extremely important that I see Comandante Castro."

"Not *'Comandante,' señora,*" the Information Ministry woman said. "Is 'Señor Castro.' Our leadership now wishes not to be called by the revolutionary titles of our past. And it is now not possible to assure you that he is available. We are doing our best and I will tell you when we learn something about this."

Suddenly feeling the need to soak off the heat of the day, Victoria stood up and shook hands with her nervous escort. "Thank you. I will see you tonight for dinner. Please tell your minister that it is very important that I meet with Mr. Castro." As the smiling, bowing concierge led her to the elevator, she was already mentally scheming ways to get Marshall to use his influence to get the State Department involved in convincing Raúl Castro to grant her an audience. This was not an ego trip, she managed to convince herself; this story was crucial to America's future.

As she settled into the hot water of her tiled bath in one of the National's luxury suites, Victoria suddenly recalled a Georgetown dinner party two months before when her hostess, a former friend whom Victoria later discovered was one of her nastiest critics on the gossip circuit, had seated her next to some assistant secretary of state for Latin America. He turned out to be a handsome empty suit whose golfing credentials exceeded his foreign policy experience. But he did have a need to impress her with semiclassified shop talk about the private lives of Latin politicians, the kind of secrets that Latins took for granted but that scandalized Washington. By this time, sensing her days with Marshall and therefore TPN to be numbered unless she came up with a big idea, Victoria teased him out on Castro and the political revolution in Cuba. She couldn't get him to shut up.

His knee touched hers, his hand found itself touching hers, and he said, *sotto voce,* "You simply wouldn't believe some of the stuff we pick up down there. Those people are never going to make it in the democratic world. Too much sun, too much rum, too much . . . um, you get the idea," he said, leering at her. "I mean, how can they expect to make a capitalist economy work with all those . . . distractions. You ever been down there? I've heard they've got some nightclub floor shows that would make Hugh Hefner blush." He squeezed her hand. "Of course, sooner or later I'll have to go down there on some mission or other, and . . ."

She didn't want to go down that path. "What do you think will happen in the elections," she asked innocently.

"Those brushed-up Commies will win, but"—he once again leaned closer and spoke in great confidence—"I've heard that certain, shall we say 'unofficial,' support may be going to the Free Cubans, our guys, to give them a chance. Speaking totally off the record, I mean not even 'a high-level administration official,' I've heard some AID money may be going to a certain well-known media group with the initials W-D down in Miami to help them put a campaign together. Whatever is good for democracy is good for the United States, is our motto. Now, you'll forget where you heard that, right?"

She nodded vigorously, having already filed the story verbatim in her head. "But that's the choice," she said with a tone of disappointment, "Social Democrats and Free Cubans? No other parties, no other candidates?"

He shook his head in the negative. "There'll be some upstarts and crazies, but the Cubans will end up with a system like ours—conservatives and lefties." He leaned back and assumed the air of statesman. "Actually, I've studied this a lot. And, when the chips are down, those really are the only choices. A party of business and a party of the handout. That's why you don't have any other real choices. I mean, the Italians, of course, will figure out a way to have about a thousand parties. But that's just for theater. Except for the odd splinter here and there—greens, socialists, whatever—it really does get down to the party of self-reliance and the party of tax and spend." He regarded her smugly. "It really is that simple."

"Sounds very boring," Victoria said disdainfully. "That's not much of a political story."

"Naw," the assistant secretary said, "there'll be plenty of action for the press. You know how these Latins are . . . excitable, passionate, violent. They'll manage to carve each other up trying to learn democracy. There'll be plenty of bloodshed of one kind or another for you to put on the air." He laughed out loud. "One of my people came in today and told me a story that had all of us rolling on the floor." His knee confidently returned to press against hers and he leaned in again. "Seems there is some old guy up in the mountains—ah, Sierra Masters, where Fidel started out—anyway, he's up there telling everybody he's Che Guevara." He made it sound like "Chee Gwee-vay-ra." "I'll tell you, it was a hoot. Che Guevara. Guy's been dead for . . . about a hundred years. Suddenly, he pops up in the middle of nowhere. See what I mean about those Latins?"

Victoria said, "Has anybody seen this 'Che Guevara'?"

"No, and I wouldn't count on it anytime soon," he said. "He's a ghost."

She had not returned the assistant secretary's several calls asking for a date, and now, trying desperately to think of an angle for a Cuban story, she somewhat regretted it. It would have been dreadful, but she might have got another piece or two of the Che Guevara story. She was drying herself off, thinking of that dreadful Washington dinner, one of thousands her job required her to endure, and then considering whether a color piece on the mysterious "Che Guevara" might be the way to lead into a series on the Cuban transition to democracy. It was now after six, so she poured herself a glass of rum from the complimentary bottle sent to her room by the hotel manager and went out on her balcony facing northward across the Caribbean toward the States. She sat on the wrought-iron chair, put the rum on the small glass-top table, and began to put a story together that would trace the troubled island's history and struggle toward democracy. There was just a chance, she thought, if she got it right, if she made it sing, for some serious journalistic recognition. The problem would be her own network. She could run a blackmail on Marshall long enough to give her a chance, but the real hurdles would be Hal Stern and Sam Rapport and then, of course, her bitchy competitor Cynthia Smerlis. They would all do everything they could to shut her out and guarantee failure.

Victoria twirled the rum around in the glass as an idea began to form. This trip she would do solid background work—interviews, research, identify the personalities, get familiar with the territory—then she would find the leaders of the Free Cubans and put them on the air. Then, after she read some books, got some State Department reports, and interviewed the policy makers in Washington, she would come back down and do a series of broadcasts from Cuba, live by satellite, leading up to the election in the spring. But, she smiled to herself, the first hook was "Che Guevara."

That night at dinner Victoria waited until the deputy minister of information had had a couple of *mojitos*, the national rum drink, and a couple of glasses of fine wine she had insisted on ordering; then she told a few funny Washington stories to loosen him up. As the coffee and desert came, he seemed to have gotten over his early jitters and stiffness with this well-known American visitor with the flamboyant dark red hair and the layers of gold jewelry. Victoria said, "Somebody in Washington, a senior government official, told me the most interesting story a few weeks ago. It seems, he said, that there is some old man in the mountains of Cuba who claims he is—"

Before she could finish, the deputy minister straightened up in his chair and started semaphoring with both hands back and forth. "No, no, no, *señora*. No, no. Do not even say it. I know this story—when you said old man in the mountains—and I don't even want you to think about it. You do not even want to think about telling this story to the U.S. people. Please, no old-man-in-the-mountain stories."

"But it's *interesting*," Victoria protested. "People will be *interested* in a story like this more than they will be in just more politics. It's what we call 'human interest' journalism. People love it. They can understand it much more than the usual politics. Please tell me who he is . . . what you know about him. If it is too wild, if he sounds completely insane, then I promise you I will not use the information. Please understand that I am not here to embarrass your country or focus on foolish things. We have enough of that in our own country. I simply want to show the human side of your new politics here, that's all."

Convinced, at least up to a point, the deputy minister reluctantly said, "Well, okay, I will tell you the rumors, stories. But"—he gestured pleadingly—"do not think that all of our politics is like this. We are serious people trying to work out our national destiny."

"I understand," Victoria said as she gestured for him to go on.

"It seems that, some weeks ago, maybe in the spring or early summer, there was an old man, I don't know how old—maybe seventy-two, seventy-five, something like that—who began to appear—it is the correct word, because no one knows where he came from, where he comes from—in the villages in Granma province in the southeast part of our country. He does not give speeches but he simply talks to the people, in the squares, in the cantinas and cafés, he talks to them about politics. I do not know exactly what he says but it is something about how our governing party and the Miami exile party are not capable of governing, how they are out of touch with our times, how they follow old ideas that don't work anymore." He shrugged. "Like that. It is not so dramatic. It's just an old man . . . talking politics. So, I don't know what is so extraordinary, why these stories are started."

Victoria said, "But he calls himself Che Guevara?"

"Not exactly. No one I have talked to nor any of the people in the region has heard him call himself this. It just got started somehow. Che is dead. He is the martyr of our revolution. You will see his picture everywhere here . . . everywhere in Latin America. He is dead now . . . thirty, thirty-two years. Everyone knows he is dead. But, like your Marilyn and your Elvis, he will not stay dead. He died too young, before he was finished. So he becomes a legend, then a ghost, then a reincarnation—somehow." He drank some wine, then shrugged again. "If an extraordinary personality of great energy, great—how do you say—charisma, great style, dies too young, people do not accept it. They must not die. They must not be mortal. They must return."

Victoria studied his face. His earnestness had almost transported him. He seemed ready to believe the myth himself.

"Where can I find him," she asked too eagerly, and the spell was snapped.

"No, *señora, por favor.* Do not even think about trying this." The deputy minister shook his head. "It is folly. No one knows where he stays. He moves about. He is somewhere in the mountains. He does not talk to any journalists. Please, you would not enjoy this effort, believe me." He swept his hand from her coiffed hair to her jewelry to her designer dress and shoes, then shook his head again and chuckled ruefully. "No, *señora, por favor.* No. You . . . it . . . it simply cannot be done."

As he spoke, Victoria's mind flashed across a montage of experiences. The overturned canoe on the Zambezi, the bomb blast in Jerusalem that blew half her clothes off, the Taliban almost capturing her in Afghanistan, the mugging by the Provos in Belfast. This guy didn't have a clue. The Cuban Sierra held no dread for her.

"He doesn't shoot people, does he?" she asked.

The deputy minister laughed, now slightly tipsy. "Only *periodistas, señora, periodistas norteamericanas.* Che, he did not much like *periodistas.* So, this is the way you can tell if it is really Che. If he shoots you." He laughed at his own joke.

*   *   *

She did not after all get to interview Raúl Castro, at least on this trip. There were many promises about the possibility on the next trip. The Cubans had by now become accustomed to U.S. reporters descending on their country, becoming momentarily excited by the experience, and then disappearing for good. She had to settle instead for Raúl's chief of staff, Victor Pais.

As the chairman of the new Cuban Social Democratic Party, Pais assured her at length that his party, even though formed by former Communist Party leaders, was no longer Communist in doctrine or ideology. He insisted that his party would closely follow the evolution of former Communist parties in Eastern and Central Europe and would adopt democratic processes and institutions while tempering the excesses of capitalism and neoliberalism with social programs now considered respectable in Western European countries. Try as she might, Victoria could not get him either to denounce his Communist past or depart from traditional European socialism.

Pais said, "We hold with the Scandinavian model of democratic socialism. We will encourage private enterprise, property ownership, and business investment. But there will be sufficient control by the central government through regulation and taxation to ensure proper distribution of wealth and economic justice. We have had experience with private oligarchies before—economic colonialism—and we will not permit the barons of capitalism to gain control of our country and corrupt our government. We notice," he continued, "that you in the States, after all these years, cannot reach agreement on the proper role for government and the means of financing, for example, necessities such as health care. In our system there will continue to be complete medical care for all people."

Victoria questioned Pais and other CSD leaders at length and found them to have doctrinaire beliefs that seemed to reflect no understanding of a rapidly changing world. She left frustrated. This party, she thought, represented the traditional Left. She was no political theoretician, but she had heard enough political rhetoric in her days, and numerous they were, to know the Cuban Social Democrats intended to break no new ground.

Her efforts to persuade the Ministry of Information to permit her to travel to Granma province and into the Sierra Maestra repeatedly failed. They simply didn't have the manpower available to organize the trip or escort her on it. Every imaginable roadblock was thrown up. She didn't have the requisite vaccination shots, she didn't have sufficient insurance coverage, there were no official cars available, and there were no translator-escorts available. Victoria was legendary for her persistence and ability to get her way in the end. But on this rock she broke her pick. She determined to prevail another day.

On her return to the States, she had prearranged to stop in Miami for background interviews with representatives of the Free Cuba Party. The FCP had expansive campaign headquarters in a modern office complex located midway between Little Havana and downtown Miami. The office furniture was new and the large staff bright and attractive. Modern technology dominated the space, a computer on each desk, an electronic command post, facilities for teleconferencing, and state-of-the-art media centers. It could as easily have been a futuristic bank or brokerage firm as a political headquarters. Victoria was given a tour of the facilities and then had lunch with Angela Valdés and Ramón Heredia, coordinators of the FCP. They laid out the party's strategy for winning the presidential and parliamentary elections in Cuba seven months later. They had considered every facet of the campaign and had detailed plans for each phase of it. They made the effort seem more a corporate marketing challenge than a campaign to win the hearts and minds of the people. In Victoria's view, the FCP intended to bring all the efficiencies of modern U.S. politics to Cuba.

"We intend to make Cuba the model for free market economics in the Caribbean," Angela said, "perhaps in the Western Hemisphere. Every small country in the region is looking for a model to follow. Cuba can be that. We will keep the government bureaucracies small, the taxes at a minimum, and release the energy of enterprise. We're business-people and we've been very successful. We don't want the government telling us what to do, even if it's our government. Government is the problem. It is never the solution. The key to Cuba's future is to keep the government as small as possible."

Victoria tried unsuccessfully to get the FCP representatives to question their own orthodoxy. What will be your policy on poverty? Will the tax system be progressive? What will you do about environmental regulation? But they seemed not to want to address the issues that troubled their closed system.

Victoria reflected, on her return to Washington, how the two belief systems reflected each other and shared the same qualities. Both sides believed they had all the answers. They were closed systems that cultivated disciples not questioners. She saw much of this reflected in U.S. politics, the rigidities, the doctrinal belief in solutions from the past, the inflexibilities, the fundamental lack of imagination.

Based upon the experience of her first trip, Victoria made her plan. She knew she could get Marshall to let her pursue the story. He clearly did not want her around, and this was a solution for him too. She had at least until the end of the year to develop Cuba as a continuing story, her own beat. If she developed the drama of the story, if she could make Cuba a kind of metaphor for the new century, a case study in peaceful political revolution, she could then at least follow through to the election in the spring of 2000. That was as far into her uncertain future as Victoria could see. Just get into the new year, hold on to this island in the stream, and . . . then something else would turn up. For that was the way she had always lived her life.

18

Nick Ferre was nervous. In the eight years since he had graduated from the Georgetown Foreign Service School and joined the U.S. foreign service, he had never been asked to brief the secretary. Because he was bilingual—coming from a Florida household where Spanish was spoken as often as English—he was, naturally, sent to Kenya as his first posting. Then, after two years of filing tedious and voluminous reports for the economic counselor, he had been reassigned to the embassy in Buenos Aires, where he performed essentially the same function for another four years. He had then been brought back to Washington as a member of a new task force on Cuba. Since he was Cuban-American himself, that finally made some sense. The task force had been created in an effort by the administration to forecast Cuba's future and to advise State and White House policy makers on methods to maneuver post-Castro Cuba into the democratic West.

Members of the task force were as surprised as everyone else by Fidel Castro's stunning retirement announcement. In the three months or so since then, the small task force had doubled to fourteen people—economists, political analysts, intelligence personnel—all led by the former head of the U.S. Interests Section in Havana. It was widely believed that the task force members would form the nucleus of the new embassy staff as soon as negotiations on formal diplomatic recognition were completed. That idea greatly intrigued Nick Ferre, for secretly that had been his plan all along. He had gone to school and into the service itself with one goal in mind—to be one of the first U.S. foreign service officers to return to his family's home country.

Nick's father, now dead, had left Havana in 1958, in protest against both the corrupt Batista government and the chaotic revolutionaries he saw as almost inevitably triumphant and inevitably repressive. He had eventually married the daughter of one of the first wave of exiles, a very successful jeweler from the Batista entourage. An only child, Nick had been born in 1967, two years after his parents were married. Growing up, he had heard two different versions of the troublesome island of his parents' birth. According to his father, Cuba was a doomed land, destined always to be governed by outside commercial interests on the one hand or by incompetent local factions on the other. His mother, reflecting the brittle, orthodox exile view of her father, an officer in the Brigade—the 2506—that had foundered on the Playa Girón beaches, demonized Castro as a mad, radical anomaly who had ruined the land of her birth.

Nick had the misfortune to take the ideals of his homeland seriously. In foreign service school his inclination to quote Franklin or Patrick Henry or Jefferson occasionally brought snickers from the back rows of classrooms. In his previous foreign postings he was known to frequent the hangouts of political cadres and firebrands, often engaging in shouting matches just short of fisticuffs with one young anti-U.S. demagogue or another. In Kenya, a Maoist-nationalist group broke into the U.S. embassy compound, lowered the American flag, and burned it. Nick beat the Marines to the spot, stamped out the fire, and raised the badly charred flag back up the flagpole. In Buenos Aires, Nick and some off-duty embassy Marines broke all the rules by setting off fireworks on the Fourth of July from the open-air bar atop the Hilton hotel and hanging a bedsheet over the side with the admonition GOD BLESS AMERICA. Even his most dedicated foreign service colleagues were known to say that Nick bled red . . . and white and blue.

Throughout his early years, Nick had observed the passionate war between his parents, obsessively rehearsing the battle for Cuba's soul, and determined that at some point in his life he would form his own opinion. He would go there, hopefully with some portfolio, and decide for himself what there was about this place that caused his parents and their extended families and claustrophobic network of exile friends to harangue each other endlessly over this otherwise ordinary Caribbean island. What, he wondered, was there about the place that generated this heat, this passion, this love, this hatred, this intensity? As he took the elevator to the secretary's office with the head of the task force, he suddenly understood that he had somehow to answer these questions now for the secretary of state.

The two men, Nick and his older boss, were graciously greeted by the secretary, who walked them across her vast office to a sitting area at one end. "Where do we stand, George?" she asked by way of opening the discussion. Nick's boss summarized the preparation for an embassy in Havana, the staffing and assignments, the key appointments, and the goals. "Most of all, we want to be able to provide complete coverage of the election next year," he said, "to understand the parties and the players and the programs they intend to pursue."

"How far along are you in that regard?" the secretary asked.

Nick's boss George said, "We're in good shape. Our team is complete and everyone is carrying out his assignment. We've got a good handle on the economy. As the system is opening up, data is coming in. They're in fairly desperate shape. We know who the key players are in the Social Democrats and the Free Cubans. Of course, we want to know a lot more about the second and third levels, the people who will fill out a government depending on which side wins." He turned to Nick. "I wanted to bring Nick Ferre with me, Madam Secretary, because he is our political expert. He's spent more time on the parties and the behind-the-scenes people than anyone else."

The secretary turned a laser gaze on Nick. He cleared his throat.

"Madam Secretary, the CSD is heavily favored at this point. It has the political network; it controls, directly or indirectly, the media; it has access to the levers of power. The Social Democrats, essentially the outgoing Communist government, has the upper hand across the board. One of the most important initial tasks our government and our new embassy must play is to guarantee the election is open and fair."

"How do we do that?" she insisted.

Nick said, "With people on the ground throughout the process. Next April in the run-up we'll want international observers, and I think the CSD will go along with that. They'll complain but they won't have much choice. But, frankly, Madam Secretary, the key is to have our people spend time with the two parties from now on and get to know the people and the policies. Obviously, that will be easier with the Free Cubans. The core group are essentially U.S. citizens. But a surprising number of them are planning to apply for dual citizenship, so they can participate in the campaign and vote in the election. We already know a number of those people. The more difficult task will be to infiltr— well, that's the wrong word—not infiltrate, but become acquainted with the Social Democrats."

The secretary smiled. "You show diplomatic promise, Mr. Ferre."

"Yes, ma'am," he said, blushing and bowing his head.

"How would you feel about undertaking that assignment yourself?" she asked.

Nick smiled broadly. "Speaking undiplomatically, I'd love it."

"George and the assistant secretary told me about you some time ago when we were considering how to organize the transition to free elections and full diplomatic recognition and I have even read some of your early political reports. They're rather good." Nick muttered a thank-you as she continued. "We are all agreed that you should go down there as soon as you can. We'll acknowledge you to the interim government in Cuba, so there will not be any misunderstandings." This meant he would go with official credentials so the Cubans would not suspect him of being an Agency plant when he started circulating and asking questions. "And I should think you would want to begin rather soon. Don't you agree, Mr. Ferre?"

"Yes, Madam Secretary," Nick said, somewhat taken aback. "How soon would that be?"

She smiled and said crisply, "Next Monday. All right? Now, Mr.

Ferre, if you will excuse us, I am afraid there are one or two other matters George and I must discuss."

Nick was on his feet, shaking the secretary's hand, and out the door before he felt the full impact. He was going to Cuba. He was being sent by the secretary of state. She had been reading his preliminary reports, which meant that she would be reading what he sent back from down there. He was the point man on internal Cuban politics. This was it. He was on his way both to realizing a boyhood dream and to a big early step up the ladder of a diplomatic career. Ambassador Ferre, he said to himself as he pushed the elevator button.

"A very nice young man," the secretary said, "and so capable. Will he do all right?"

"Yes, ma'am," George said. "I have great confidence in him. He's very bright and very dedicated. He's perfect with the language. His family was not so anti-Castro that he's indoctrinated against the government in power. He seems to have a very open mind on the whole thing, and he's dying to get down there and see what it's all about."

"Can we keep the Agency away from him?" she asked.

George said, "They'll try. They'll certainly want to see his stuff. And they'll want us to task him with some of their collection. We'll have to let some of that go on, obviously without him being witting, but we will have to be careful they don't try to take him over."

"They'll have some of their own people there, I assume?"

"Already do, Madam Secretary," George said, "but they don't have anyone as good as Nick and they know it. They've drawn primarily from the exile community in Miami and New Jersey and those are hotbeds of intrigue. No one knows who is who in those camps. Castro's got people inside those communities. People are spying on each other. It's a political snakepit. We were lucky to get Nick early and get him ready. He's serious about a diplomatic career and, unlike a lot of young people we get, he doesn't want to be a spook on the side. He's perfect for this job and we're lucky to have him."

"Keep me posted," the secretary said as she stood up. "This is going to be important. The president asks me about Cuba all the time. What are we doing? What are our plans? How will we handle the elections and the transition? He's fascinated by it. And he somehow thinks if we're not careful it could blow up in our face and be a thorn in our side for another fifty years. And, George," she said as she showed him out the door, "let me see that young man's reports."

■ ■ ■

Why do some people get more angry when they get older and some get more mellow? I've never figured that out. I was angry as hell throughout my youth and my revolutionary—I guess I should say earlier revolutionary— years. Social injustice, greedy corporations, Tío Sam, poverty, power at the top, they all sent me into a rage. Even when I didn't seem to be in a rage, even when I was supposed to be relaxed and having a good time with los barbudos, I was in a rage. It was like a fire inside me. I couldn't stand it. I hated the time wasted in talk or in entertainment or in screwing around. I wanted to get on with it. I didn't want to waste time. Life is short, I always told myself. There may be no tomorrow. We have to fix everything today. What a joke. Here I am thirty years later and the struggle goes on. Patience and time, time and patience.

In the second half of my life, those three decades on the run, I finally learned that you really don't control the length of your life, only its direction and its purpose. So, when I decided to come back here, I knew whatever I did would take some time. We wouldn't simply storm the beaches and march into Havana. The people had to be won over.

It will be very interesting to see what Tío Sam does here. The U.S. government and the corporations are going to want the exiles to win—what do they call themselves, I heard the other day, the "Free Cubans." But if the Yanquis come on like neocolonialists again, if they overplay their hand, the people here are going to react. They will suspect that the Free Cubans are a front for the CIA, which means the FCP will have to go out of its way to establish its independence from the U.S. This little chess game is going to be very interesting.

If the U.S. was smart, it would support our movement. But I think, down deep, this movement is going to frighten them. It's easier to control a country with one center of power, one set of leaders you can deal with, than it is to influence a country with a thousand or ten thousand centers of power. That's the fascinating thing about T. Jefferson and I suppose the reason he is still talked about up north. If you take him seriously, as I do, he really is radical. He truly is a revolutionary. No wonder he scared Adams. No wonder Madison moved in to add all that stuff about checks and balances and tyranny of the majority. Jefferson scared the economic interests, Hamilton's crowd, to death. That's why T. Jefferson called his election "the second American revolution."

Anyway, I'm not as angry anymore. But I'm still as determined. I still can't figure out why I keep being fetched up here in Cuba. The first time it was simply because I was introduced to Raúl and then Fidel in Mexico. I was a revolutionary, but I hadn't yet found my place. Those guys had the place. They had a plan. They were ready to go. Fidel figured out I had something to offer. So he invited me along. I killed some people in those days. I was full of wrath and justice. Deserters. Shot a few myself. Had to prove a point. My God, it scared those poor kids when I did that. They looked at me like I was the wrath of God myself. I killed a good number of government soldiers, young kids too, in the battles in those days. I've thought a lot about that. It was a war. They were out to kill us. But I couldn't do it again.

Whatever I learned in the second act about patience, I also learned about killing. It's no good. It really doesn't achieve anything, except to terrorize people. And a terrorized person isn't worth much. A person with a sense of his own worth and destiny is a lot more powerful than a frightened person.

■ ■ ■

1 9

■

Johnny Gallagher and Harry Rossell, representing the Committee for Honest Elections, were meeting in the conference room of the Miami headquarters of the Free Cuba Party with Olivero Sanchez, the chairman of the party, Lucia Martinez, the party treasurer, and Diego Falla, the party's principal political consultant.

"Our committee was formed to support free and open elections in countries that are becoming democratic," Johnny said. "We recognize that the United States has an obligation to be a political leader as well as an economic leader. Therefore, we created our committee to raise funds from U.S. business leaders to contribute to free and honest elections in emerging democracies. Since we are a new group, we could not think of a better place to begin than in Cuba." He smiled broadly and held up his hands in the magician's gesture to show there were no hidden tricks.

Harry cleared his throat. "Like Mr. Gallagher says, we think it's important for American businesspeople, who now are doing business around the world, to support the principles of democracy everywhere we go. We give to political parties here in the States, so we should also contribute to political causes where it will support democracy. Simple as that."

Olivero Sanchez said, "Gentlemen, you're a welcome sight. The fact that successful people like yourselves care about good government means a lot. We too are simply businesspeople, obviously of Cuban heritage, who are concerned that genuine democracy be restored in the land of our forefathers. We welcome any support you can give us and we can assure you that, when the Free Cubans win next spring, you'll find our doors open."

Johnny said, "The members of our committee are all businesspeople who'll want to explore the Cuban markets when they open up. So, to have friendly faces in Cuban political circles will certainly mean a lot to us."

Diego Falla said, "Even though Cuba is not a large country and its media advertising costs are nothing like those in the States—even in a state like Florida—it's still going to cost a lot to run this campaign. This is kind of a unique situation. We have to educate these people. They have no background in democracy. They don't know the difference between the parties. So we have to explain the democratic process, we have to motivate them to vote, we have to explain how we are different from the Comm—the party in power—and we have to bring them to our side. All this requires heavy media advertising and that requires a good deal of money."

Lucia Martinez added, "And although we are relatively successful people ourselves, our group cannot afford to finance this whole campaign. So your interest and your support are very welcome." Then she added, "I'm sure you know that we are a probusiness party. Unlike the leftist

Social Democrats, we believe in free enterprise. We'll open the doors of the Cuban economy to investors such as your contributors. We're going to advocate low taxes, less government regulation and bureaucracy, and competition in the marketplace. By the way, what kinds of enterprises are your contributors involved in?"

Harry looked at Johnny and said, "All kinds, really. Our people have all kinds of businesses." He cleared his throat and carefully adjusted his Cartier cuff links. "Actually, I would say that our members are primarily in the amusement and entertainment business. Quite heavily in that . . . those businesses. Entertainment and amusement. Those kinds of things."

"Very reputable," Johnny added. "All our people are licensed, bonded, regulated by various state authorities. No problems." He smiled at the room in general. "Very reputable." Then he looked very serious. "We are concerned, in our line of business, about the quality of the licensing authority where we do business. It must be a very high-quality authority. No politics. No favoritism. No cronyism. You understand? We are for good government. We wouldn't have it any other way."

Olivero gestured, palm out, at the two men across the table. "Gambling. Right?"

"Gaming," Johnny said quickly. "We prefer the word 'gaming.' "

"Gaming," Olivero said with a smile as wide as Johnny's. "You should have said so. So you want to make sure that the licensing authority we set up in Havana for 'gaming' is a friendly one. Is that it?"

Harry and Johnny looked at each other and then nodded vigorously. "No favoritism," Harry said. "Just friendly. Just understanding, you know. Understanding of the importance of gaming to the Cuban economy, to the tourism. You know, people like to come to the casinos. They like to game, gamble, whatever. Cuba is close. It's a new place. Nice beaches, good sun, nice family atmosphere. But they want the tables and the slots and the nightclubs, and the experience of the gaming." Harry looked at them innocently.

The Free Cubans looked at each other. Then Olivero said, "How deeply concerned are your members with 'honest elections' in Cuba?" His gaze went back and forth between the breast pockets of the two suits.

Johnny glanced at Harry, then said, "Very. Very concerned, I would say." He made a scribbling gesture at Harry.

Harry cleared his throat again and reached into his coat pocket. He pulled out a plain white envelope, started to hand it to Johnny who gestured across the table, and then put it down on the table and gave it a short push in Olivero's direction.

Everyone at the table studied the plain white envelope that lay halfway between the two sides. After a moment Olivero reached to the center of the table and retrieved the envelope. "You understand," he said, "that the new Cuban election law requires that all political donations be reported." Then he smiled slyly and added, "After the election."

"After the election," Johnny and Harry both said at once as they nodded in the affirmative.

The room was silent as Olivero unsealed the envelope. He pulled out the check from the Committee for Honest Elections and studied it carefully. His face whitened perceptibly as he handed it first to Lucia then to Diego. Lucia's face flushed slightly and Diego smiled. Olivero coughed, then said, "That's a very . . . generous, I would say, contribution. For honest elections." Lucia and Diego nodded in agreement.

Harry looked out the window at Miami Beach beyond the shoulders of the Free Cubans. Johnny shrugged. "It's the least we can do . . . you know, to help democracy in Cuba. Our members think it's important. And we wanted to be among the first to give you our support."

Olivero studied his thumbnail. "As gentlemen concerned with honest elections and 'gaming,' you have thought, surely, about the possibility, as remote as it is, that we Free Cubans might not win."

Johnny and Harry nodded soberly.

"And, therefore, you will want to make friends on the other side, that is with the 'Social Democrats,' " Olivero said.

Johnny said, "Well, we certainly have considered that. It's certainly something we've discussed."

"Would you suppose that you will want to 'help democracy in Cuba' by contributing to the Social Democrats?" Lucia asked.

"We'll have to consider it, you know, give it some thought," Johnny answered. Harry nodded abstractly.

Olivero said, "Hmmm."

Johnny said, "It's like here in the States. It's important to have friends on both sides. We give to both sides. It's kind of . . . democratic, don't you think?"

Olivero said, "Hmmm."

"Anyway," Harry said, "there it is. We want you to know we're on your side. And, by the way," he said, pointing at the white envelope disappearing into Olivero's jacket, "there's more where that came from."

By early November 1999, not more than a month after the meeting with the Free Cubans, Harry and Johnny made their way to Havana and arranged a meeting with Victor Pais and Ricardo Gomez, the chairman and treasurer of the Cuban Social Democrats. They had used an intermediary in New Jersey who, though himself a Cuban exile, had lately been mending fences in Cuba with the leadership of the new Social Democratic Party. The intermediary had in mind to be a key broker for investors in Cuba after the elections and was busy building a network of friends in both political parties.

"Gentlemen, you are very kind to make time to see us," Johnny began. "As our mutual friend explained to you, our committee is made up of U.S. businesspeople who have an interest in seeing democracy established in Cuba. Clearly, our members want to come here and do some business also. But first, you have to get your new government established and sort things out. When you have the proper authorities established, to license things and regulate things, then we will want to put our investments right here in Cuba."

"What kind of investments?" Ricardo asked skeptically.

Harry said, "All kinds. We're in all kinds of investments. Real estate, hotels, retail, entertainment, amusements. Entertainment and amusements, mostly."

"What kind of 'entertainment and amusements'?" Ricardo asked.

Harry said, "All kinds. Whatever goes along with tourism. Tourism has got to be big here. It'll get even bigger. You got to entertain people—you know, floor shows, nightclubs—and you got to amuse them—you know, like—"

"Gambling," Ricardo shot back.

"Not gambling," Johnny said. "We prefer to say 'gaming.' "

" 'Gaming,' " Victor said.

"Like that," Harry said.

Victor said, "So, what can we do for you now? The election is six months away. Then we have to form the new government." He leaned forward. "Speaking frankly. We didn't have a particularly good experience with 'gaming' under the government we overthrew . . . after the revolution. We threw all those guys out. 'Wise guys' I think you call them. We threw the 'wise guys' out. They corrupted our people. No offense, but we don't want them back. So maybe you should come back after the election and we can discuss it further." He sat back.

Johnny shook his head. "Don't get us wrong, here. We are not here asking for anything. Our people formed this committee to invest in democracy. That's all. We don't want anything. Just democracy. This happens all the time in the States. A lot of businesspeople give money to the parties, both parties, all candidates. For good government. That's what we want. Just good government in Cuba."

"What if we decide to keep 'gaming' out of Cuba?" Ricardo asked. "How will you feel about your 'investment in democracy' then?"

Harry and Johnny both shrugged. "It's okay," Harry said. "Whatever you want. It's okay."

"But," Johnny quickly added, "we thought you might want to see this." He pushed a large business envelope across the table. "This is a little study we had done of the potential gaming industry in Cuba. We had some economists calculate the potential revenues to the Cuban treasury from a gaming industry. Open up there to . . . ah, I think it's about page thirty-seven. You'll see what they project."

Ricardo opened the envelope and found page 37 in the study. He and Victor studied the financial chart down to the bottom line. Ricardo's eyes widened involuntarily and Victor said, "Hmmm."

Johnny said, "See. That's the money the Cuban government will make with a full-scale gaming industry. That's why we think it's important for you to be thinking about this."

"And, of course, you want to run this industry," Ricardo said.

Harry said, "Not quite. We want you to run this industry. We want you to regulate it, create a gaming commission, issue licenses, police it, make sure it's honest. If you don't run it right, you will have the bad boys in here. Then you got trouble."

Victor and Ricardo nodded, thinking.

"So," Johnny said, "while you're thinking about it, we want to contribute to the Social Democrats. To show you how much we care about democracy in Cuba." He gestured to Harry, who pulled out a plain white envelope and pushed it across the table near the open report. "This is our contribution to your party and to democracy."

The two Cuban officials looked at the envelope. This was their introduction to modern democracy. Finally, Victor picked up the envelope and began to open it. "And what do you want for this?" he asked suspiciously.

Johnny shrugged. "Very little. Good government. Democratic government. Your friendship. We know you will remember your friends when you win the election."

The two men looked at the check for a long time. They looked at the numerical figure; then they looked at the written figure. One million U.S. dollars. Finally, Victor said, "It's very hard to forget friends who give you so much money."

2 0

■

While the Committee for Honest Elections was making friends in Havana, Ernesto Blanco, Alejo, and young Rafael found themselves in Pinar del Río province in the western arm of Cuba. They had made their way across the country by a combination of trains, trucks, buses, and assorted vehicles. Alejo never knew where Ernesto got the odd peso for the public transport, but he always seemed to have a few somewhere in the bottom of the ever-present hemp satchel. Accommodations, usually more primitive than not, magically appeared and there always seemed someone willing to heat some rice and beans for them. Alejo had long since given up trying to understand how the whole thing worked. It just seemed to. For himself, Rafael took it all for granted.

But as they traveled throughout Pinar del Río, Alejo saw a new Ernesto. There was an increased animation, a kind of *vivacidad* that Alejo had not seen since the old days. Ernesto somehow seemed thirty—well, perhaps, twenty—years younger. It was as if he were with Señora Margarita all the time. He smiled seductively at the ladies, whether beautiful or not. He responded respectfully to the gentlemen, whether they deserved it or not. He patted the children on the head. Of course, he had always done that. He had a new energy, as if he were animated by some strange internal solar clock that told him when to rev up his engines. Even Rafael, who worshiped him and thought he was capable of anything, noticed the difference.

"Señor Alejo," he said, "what is it? Is he dreaming? Is he drinking some rum? Or, you know, smoking the . . . ?" Here he gestured as though puffing a joint.

Alejo, normally sober and always concerned for the worst, laughed. That alone further shocked Rafael, who had never actually heard him laugh. "*No, joven.* It is a spirit being released. It is a spirit fulfilling its destiny. It is a spirit who has come home." Alejo turned to him with a fierce expression. "You should pray to whatever gods there are that it should happen to you at least once in your life." Alejo looked at Ernesto across the plaza. "He is fulfilling his destiny. He is in heaven."

Ernesto Blanco was addressing a cluster of people surrounding him in the plaza of the town of Los Palacios. Unlike in the early days in Granma province, here he was on his feet. He was not passive. He was not answering questions. He was animated, he was invigorated. "Let me tell you something, my friends. You are going to face the biggest decision of your lives. You are going to decide who will run your lives. You want to continue to listen to the bosses in Habana?"

A few people responded, quietly and almost automatically, "*No.*"

"You want those guys in Miami to come back and tell you what to do?"

This time there was a more vigorous chorus. "*No!*"

"I have only one thing to say to you. *Take control of your lives!*"

Now there was something like a cheer. The number of people in the plaza was increasing and they were drawing closer. "Here's what you can do. You can tell those guys in Miami and those guys in Habana, *no más. No más! NO MÁS!*"

Now there was something like a small roar and Alejo and Rafael ran toward the crowd that now numbered 100 or 200 people. They were flocking in from all around. Alejo could not tell where they were coming from. But, clearly, this was the most exciting thing that had happened in Los Palacios since *el Comandante* visited here some years ago. Alejo could scarcely believe his eyes. He had not seen the like since '59 when *los barbudos* sprang free from the Sierra and began their march to Havana. This was something. A chill he had not felt in years—in decades—raised the sparse hairs on his thin neck. Ernesto had his left hand extended. He was pointing toward the sky. "Here's what you can do. You can rise up. You can create a new *revolución*. You can create a *revolución* of the *campesinos*, a *revolución* of the *vaqueros*, a *revolución* of the *gauchos*, a revolution of the people. You can run Los Palacios. You can run Pinar del Río province. *You can run Cuba!"*

Now there was a full scale cheer that went on and on. Alejo smacked his head. *Madre de Dios!* He swiftly calculated how long it would take the *policía* to get there. He did not look forward to another night in *la cárcel*. They had spent enough nights in the hoosegow because they had nowhere else to stay. And it was not pleasant. Still Ernesto roared on. "Form your own party—a party of the people. You have a choice. This is your town. This is your province. *This is your country!"* There was an even greater cheer. The plaza was now full. People were shouting. They wanted Ernesto to go on. It was, Alejo thought, as if they had waited a lifetime, a century, a millennium for this word. Then he saw them— *quatro policía* coming from the southwest corner of the plaza. Must be near their barracks, Alejo thought. He started to try to push through the crowd toward Ernesto from one side as the *policía* pushed through from the other side.

Then, an extraordinary thing happened. People in the plaza raised the policemen up on their shoulders and gave them a cheer. They moved them toward the center of the crowd where Ernesto held forth. As they descended, one by one, from the shoulders of their fellow citizens, Ernesto shook their hands. He held up his hand for silence. Then he said, *"Compañeros y compañeras*, these men deserve better. They should not work for the state. They should work for you. They should be the guardians of Los Palacios. They are your sons and your brothers. They should not take orders from Habana—or Miami! They should be *la policía de la república de Los Palacios!"*

Now there was a huge cheer and the policemen, suddenly at home, suddenly free of the bondage of the control of the central authority in Havana, suddenly alive with the possibility of their own freedom, threw off their coats and tossed their policeman's hats in the air. There was a tumultuous response. It was as if a great burden was lifted from the people, a burden of oppression and suspicion. These were their sons and their brothers. Now they were home, now they were part of the people. Ernesto, in the midst of this celebration of liberation, started to make his way out of the center of the crowd. People slapped his bony back.

They shook his thin hand. They began to shout, *"Viva El compañero! Viva la revolución nueva! Viva el viejo* [the old one]! *Viva la república de Los Palacios!"*

Waiting for Ernesto to join them on the outskirts of the crowd, Alejo and Rafael stood transfixed. What was going on here? What had their *compañero* opened up? This business was beginning to get out of hand. Alejo, more experienced at crisis and emergency, instinctively studied the turbulent crowd as it shouted and cheered a beginning it did not begin to understand. The faces were happy. They seemed as if cheerfulness had just been invented in Los Palacios, as if they had forgotten how to celebrate life or why it should be celebrated. Alejo's trained gaze scanned and passed face after face. Then there was one face it scanned, went past, then returned to. What was it? What was it in that face? Alejo tried again. Again he returned to the face. He knew it. Where? How? It was a man at least in his late fifties, or perhaps more. It was a still face, an unresponsive face, a watchful face. Perhaps even an evil face? He could not tell. It was not a usual face. The only thing that Alejo knew beyond a certainty was that this was a face to be reckoned with. This was not a face there to celebrate the beginning of a new time. For Alejo, it was an older version of a vaguely familiar face.

Turning down offers of food and shelter, much to Alejo's dismay, Ernesto insisted that they move on. "Remember, Alejo, it's hard to hit a moving target," he always said. Unlike their early operations in distant Granma province, they were close enough to Havana now that their activities would be reported to the authorities by nightfall and a network of agents of the state would be activated to monitor their activities and report on their movements. They had been in the western peninsula almost a week already and had conducted similar meetings in the city of Pinar del Río, in the colorful village of Viñales near the Valle de Viñales with its remarkable *mogotes*, extraordinary geological formations resembling, some said, mushrooms and, others said, elephants strung along twenty-five kilometers in the valley, in the towns of Consolación del Sur, San Cristóbal, Artemisa, and dozens of tiny villages along the way, but none with so much crowd response, none with the vitality and energy of Los Palacios. Now they were on their way to Las Terrazas, after which they would retire to the Sierra to regroup.

As *campesinos* traveled up and down the peninsula to and from Havana, they spread the word of an old man with another old man and a boy who was talking some new kind of revolutionary politics, some kind of self-government, some radical notion of local power. So, when the trio got to Las Terrazas word was around. Still, they came in relatively undetected. The rumors had gotten so big about this little traveling party that people expected some kind of parade with fanfare and music and noise. Three strangers straggling into town on the tailgate of a smoke-belching old truck did not seem nearly auspicious enough for the apocalyptic stories they had heard. Having thanked their driver for his kindness, the three set off up the hillside for the village, a relatively new one built by the Soviets in the heyday of good relations more or less on top of older buildings left by French coffee growers from Haiti in the nineteenth century.

"This place is not called 'the terraces' for nothing," Alejo said as they huffed their way up to the village perched on a hillside overlooking a very pretty high lake. Ernesto was humming some peasant tune quietly to himself. Alejo decided not to mention the strange face in the crowd back in Los Palacios. Like many of the villages in Cuba, Las Terrazas seemed almost a retirement community. True, there were a few young people around, including a pretty dark-eyed beauty Rafael spotted as they passed the visitor center. But mostly the young people made their way south to Pinar del Río City or north to Havana. More opportunity, more excitement. Near the center of the village was an open-air community center that seemed to be the nexus of social exchange. At one end were clusters of mostly older women, sewing, knitting, and engaged in the gossip trade. At the other end were half a dozen or more tables of mostly older men playing dominoes.

The women overtly observed the strangers and commented among themselves as to who exactly they might be. The men pretended not to notice, but they noticed very well. Being a tourist center, the gateway to a United Nations "biosphere" area of thousands of hectares of lush vegetation, exotic flowers, and even more exotic birds and butterflies, the village saw more than its share of tourists of various hybrid hues. But these three stragglers were not *turistas*, at least in any conventional sense of the word. These were Cubans, more or less. Travelers. Castaways? On the dole, or on the lam? Ernesto politely tipped his battered hat to the ladies on the right, which caused a titter, dropped his hemp satchel near an empty chair, and sank down into it. The men continued their dominoes and gave no appearance of noticing.

Presently one of the men at the nearest table looked sideways at the three strangers and said, "You seen Che?"

Ernesto shook his head no, then smiled at Alejo and winked. "I heard they killed him," he said, "quite some time ago now."

The local man snorted. "Apparently they didn't do a very good job of it. They say he's back again."

"That so?" Ernesto said. He could tell, though the dominoes continued, the other men were listening carefully. "Let's see. He'd be . . . seventy . . . seventy-one years old now. Old as me," he chuckled. "Can't imagine Che being nearly that old." He wheezed and coughed. "Besides, he had that asthma."

Several of the men looked over at him. Suddenly, Alejo stood up. In the back corner of the open-air center was the man he had seen in the plaza of Los Palacios. He was staring at Ernesto. Alejo leaned down into Ernesto's ear and hissed, "Let's go. I don't like this place."

Ernesto pretended not to hear. "I don't see how Che could do anything but help improve the politics of this country," he said provocatively.

Now all the men stared at him. Ernesto pretended not to notice that most had now suspended their dominos and had shifted their chairs around toward him. The local man, possibly the mayor but certainly a community leader, said, "Now we have 'free elections,' thanks to *Tío Sam*, and at least two political parties to choose from. It's not very clear what Che could add to that."

Ernesto wheezed and laughed. "He could talk some sense. He could point out that the old crowd in Habana offers more socialism, which nobody in the world, except maybe some frightened Cubans, seems to want. He could point out that the old crowd in Miami offers the same old corporate centralism and some kind of media politics even the people *del norte* are sick of. He could"—here Ernesto stood up and stretched his antique frame—"he could point out that there are more than two choices." One of the older women brought him a cup of thick coffee. He bowed to her and she smiled coquettishly and skittered away. Ernesto sipped the coffee. The birds could be heard to sing in the silence that enveloped the community center. The beauty from the tourist office had left her post and stood near Rafael, who shifted nervously from foot to foot.

"But of course," Ernesto said, "he wouldn't even have to be Che to do that, would he? And besides," he continued, "my friends and I travel around this country quite a bit, and we haven't run into anybody calling himself Che, have we?" He tilted his head toward the wide-eyed Alejo and the foot-shuffling Rafael, both of whom nodded their heads silently back and forth.

One of the men in the back said in a loud voice, "And what kind of another choice could Che point out—if there was a Che—and if he did decide to say something?"

Ernesto shrugged. "I do not want to take advantage of your hospitality. You seemed to be doing your usual business when we arrived. We don't want to upset you with politics."

"Go ahead," said one of the few younger women who, alone, had been playing dominos with the men, "what kind of a choice do you think Che might have in mind?"

Ernesto smiled his seductive, young man's smile at her, the kind, Alejo remembered, that he had used so effectively with Señora Margarita. "This older, wiser Che might say that the people of this place, Las Terrazas, have the power to govern their own lives. He might say that you are smart enough, that you are strong enough, to decide what's best for Las Terrazas without some bureaucrats from Habana or some investment bankers from Wall Street deciding what's best for you, or how to make money from you, or how to have power over you. He might point out that you can form your own party. He might say that the best form of government is *la república*, local self-government, by citizens responsible for their own lives. Democracy, as it was taught by T. Jefferson, is not only about freedom. It is also about duty and responsibility and obligation to yourselves to improve this place, right here, and to leave a better place for your children so they don't want to run away for the bright lights of Habana."

Ernesto walked the length of the community center and returned the coffee cup to the shy elderly lady and bowed to her again. Then he said, so that all could hear, "That's the kind of thing a wiser, older Che might say. If . . . there were such a Che."

No one spoke until the bold younger woman on the men's side said, "We usually have a community lunch here. Do you and your friends care to join us?" With that the tension was severed and chairs were pushed back and queues began to form near plates of cold sandwiches and pans of steaming hot food. Rafael could be seen, red-faced, chatting to the girl from the visitors' center. To his dismay, Alejo saw the man with the strange, oddly cruel face approaching and he stuck a sharp elbow into Ernesto's bony side. This elicited a series of wheezing coughs, which continued as the man stood silently before them.

The man stared at Ernesto, then said, "If Che came back, he'd look a lot like you. Strangely enough, he might even sound like you. Radical and all." It sounded like a blunt challenge.

Ernesto smiled and shrugged. "You knew him, then?"

The man shook his head no. "Not really. I was a kid during the revolution. I ran away from home and went up into the Sierra. *Los barbudos* had me run errands, steal chickens for dinner, steal an occasional weapon from a careless soldier, scout out the territory ahead." He recited all this as if the older men would have already known it, as if he were passing some sort of quiz.

"Che would remember you then?" Ernesto asked.

The man smiled a twisted, crooked-tooth smile. "He might. But I doubt it. I was a kid—on the fringe of things. But then, Che always seemed to have a good memory."

"All this talk about Che," Ernesto said distractedly, looking around the room. "It's kind of foolish. Don't you think?"

"No," the man said, "it makes perfect sense. *El Jefe* steps down. There is no hero. The people need a hero. If they can't find a live one, they'll find a dead one." He laughed the harsh, barking laugh of a heavy smoker. Then he said, "Where do you go from here?"

Alejo straightened up sharply, alert to danger. Ernesto looked sideways at the man. "Here and there. We're not in any hurry to get anywhere."

Unable to contain himself, Alejo blurted out, "Who wants to know?"

The man turned an eye on Alejo as if seeing him for the first time. His grin produced a look Alejo thought malevolent. "Why, just call me Otra Vez. That's what people call me. 'Once again.' Don't you think it fits?"

For the first time since Alejo had met Ernesto, he saw him blanch. Otra Vez was indeed a name from the past. Otra Vez was in the Sierra, one of the youngest of the original revolutionaries. He had always been a controversial character, one that some found sinister and one that few could figure out.

"Famous name," Ernesto said, turning toward the woman gesturing them toward the lunch buffet. The man's hand was on Ernesto's shoulder, restraining him. Ernesto looked at the square fist that held his thin shirt. Under the stare, the man released his grip and said, "I want to join up."

Ernesto looked at him quizzically. Over the man's shoulder Alejo's vigorous sideways head wag threatened to sever his scrawny neck. "Join up with what?" Ernesto asked vaguely.

"You know what," the man Otra Vez said, "what you're doing. Your movement. Your party."

"No movement, *che*," Ernesto said. "No party."

The woman filled a plate and handed it to Ernesto, who in turn handed it to Alejo. She gave a second plate to Ernesto and he turned away.

Otra Vez persisted. "I want to help. I believe in what you're doing. I believe what you said here today. I heard you talk yesterday in Los Palacios and several of the other villages. I've been following you around." Alejo shivered. He had seen the man at Los Palacios. He had not seen him anywhere else. "It's important, what you're talking about. It's exactly what we need, what this country needs. *Por favor*," he pleaded, "let me help." At this instance he seemed ultimately sincere, utterly dedicated, completely committed. "You need more than just the three of you," he concluded.

"There's nothing to do," Alejo said. "Me and the boy take care of things."

Otra Vez smiled crookedly at Alejo again. "I'm sure you do. I have no doubt. But look at the other things that need to be done." He drew closer to the two men and lowered his voice. "I'll find us a printer. I know one already. He'll run off some cheap handouts—for free. He agrees with us. I've talked to him already. He wants to help. You need to leave something behind for these people to read and think about and pass around. Then you need someone to follow up, to keep in touch with the people who agree with you, to give them some idea how to organize their towns and villages. Look," he said, "I've been talking to a lot of people. The word is around. There are a lot of people talking about your ideas. But they don't know what to do. They don't have a clue about politics. Somebody like me can help show them the next steps, how to get ready to vote and get other people ready to vote. Things like that."

Ernesto said nothing and Alejo held his breath. They took their plates and Ernesto managed to sit himself between two local men and strike up a conversation. They animatedly began to respond to his earlier remarks and to ask him questions. Otra Vez drifted toward Rafael and the girl. Alejo slipped unobtrusively around the room asking various people if they knew the stranger there talking with the young people. All shook their heads no. He was not familiar to them. In fact, he had just appeared that morning, only an hour or so ahead of the three of them. Alejo knew the name Otra Vez from the revolutionary times. It was a name attached to a figure who had mysteriously disappeared from the revolutionary ranks. No one had ever been quite sure where he had gone, what he was doing. Yet, here he was. Big as life. Trying to sign up. Alejo didn't like the idea at all.

In the clean, threadbare room Ernesto and Alejo occupied that night in Las Terrazas, Alejo had his say. "Trouble, trouble, trouble." He pinched his long nose. "He stinks. Real bad."

Ernesto rolled over from his position facing the wall on the thin mattress on the floor. "Do you suppose I could interest you in a little sleep anytime tonight?" Then he said, "Around five in the morning is when that truck leaves for Habana. You just plan to talk until that time and walk right out there and get on?"

Alejo sat on his mattress a few feet away in the narrow room with his back against the wall. " 'Otra Vez' he says he is." He spat the name out like a nasty taste. "That's trouble. I know some stories about that *hombre*. If he signs up, we can just call him Señor Trouble."

"What kind of stories?" Ernesto groused, turning back toward the wall.

"Stories about how he became real mean after the revolution. Stories about how nobody sees him around, except when *los jefes* want some dirty work done. Stories about people who he runs into disappearing. Stories about dead people in the ditch after he walks down the road. Stories about—"

"Nothing," Ernesto interrupted with a groan. "Stories are just stories. You don't seem to me to be a man who believes everything he hears."

"Amigo," Alejo whispered, "this is serious trouble. This one scares me to death."

"*Everything* scares you to death, Alejo. Go to sleep."

Alejo sighed heavily. "All right, *compañero*, maybe this will wake you up. My brother in Manzanillo knew a fellow who caused some trouble to the government. Every day he went into the *plazuela* and stood on a bench and shouted about how the government cheated him out of his pension, how the *jefes* were no good, how government didn't care about the people anymore, how the guys in Habana just care about keeping the power. Et cetera, et cetera. Pretty soon people began to see this 'Otra Vez' around town. Sneaking around. Following this fellow home. That kind of thing."

Ernesto gave a snort.

"So, late one night there is a big explosion. Everyone gets out of bed and runs outdoors. This fellow's house down the street has blown up and what's left is on fire."

Ernesto was silent.

"Don't you care about what happened to this fellow?"

Ernesto groaned, "What happened to this fellow?"

"They don't know. They never found him."

Ernesto groaned again. "Maybe he got scared and ran away."

"Maybe. Maybe also he got blown into a lot of pieces." Alejo waited, then said, "And they never saw this 'Otra Vez' around there again."

"Maybe Otra Vez blew himself up," Ernesto offered by way of conclusion.

Alejo said smugly, "Don't think so, amigo. Because some months later my cousin's sister told me they saw him over near Trinidad."

Ernesto whispered, "It is still legal to be in Trinidad."

"Not if you are blowing things up."

"What did he blow up in Trinidad?"

"A car."

"Maybe it was his car and he got tired of looking at it," Ernesto said pleadingly.

"It wasn't his car. It was the car of the editor of the newspaper."

"Who also criticized the government?"

"*Verdad*, amigo. He wrote a story calling for the government to let out of jail another newspaper writer who had written a story suggesting that the Palacio de la Revolución be declared a mausoleum and sealed up."

"If he wrote those things about me—or even if he just kept me awake late at night—I might blow him up myself."

Alejo gasped.

Then Ernesto cackled softly. "Tell you what. Tonight we go to sleep. Tomorrow you start finding out what you can about this bomber friend of yours, and in the meantime we'll keep our eyes on him."

"Who will keep eyes on him while we are sleeping?" Alejo wondered aloud.

"Since you don't seem to need to sleep, you can have that job."

2 1

■

I don't like it a bit, Victor," Vilma said. "Look"—she shook a sheaf of papers—"these are the reports. Granma, Las Tunas, Manzanillo, now Pinar. He's popping up all over the place, goddammit!"

Pais stood up and sighed, "Vilma, it's okay. It's okay. Don't worry about it. He's an old guy. In the next few months, believe me, there are going to be a lot of old guys—young guys—Santería priests—God knows what—running around the hills and the villages. 'Fidel is coming back!' 'Jesus is coming back!' Yes, 'Che is back!' Get used to it, Vilma. Otherwise, you'll have one of these heart attacks about once a week."

"Victor, you're not listening. The people are paying attention to this old fart. They are listening to him a lot better than you are listening to me. These are our people. We are depending on them. If they don't vote for us—if they vote for him or somebody he proposes—it means those madmen from Miami will take this country back. I'm telling you, this is serious."

Pais waved his hand dismissively. "Okay, Vilma, he's serious. So what?"

"So this, Victor. So we do something about it. So we screw him up. So we make him look foolish, or we isolate him—or we throw him in a ditch somewhere. Do you think anybody will remember or care anything about him. In a week it's, Where's that old man? In two weeks it's, What old man?"

"I wish I could be as casual as you are about throwing old men in the ditch, Vilma."

"By God, Victor, I care about Cuba. I haven't given my life to this revolution to see some old crackpot come along and fuck it up. We *have to win this election*! This is serious, Victor. Are you worn out or what!"

Victor said, "I'm not worn out, Vilma. I just can't get as excited by things as I used to. Frankly, I admire your balls—or whatever you women call them."

"We call them balls too, Victor." She pointed at her head. "We just keep them in a different place. All right. Here is what I'm doing, just so there is no misunderstanding later on. We've put one of our people next to him. That's where this stuff"—waving the reports again—"came from. This guy is keeping us regularly informed. This guy will eventually be so invaluable as to be involved in everything. This guy will also be preparing ways of sabotaging this old madman's operations. When the time comes—if it gets down to that—we will be prepared to take him out, that is make him useless—one way or the other."

Pais said, "Unless you insist, I would just as soon not know who you have undertaking this important task."

"No need, Victor," Vilma said. "It's all taken care of. I just wanted to make sure you understood what was going on if the security people turn up some old guy in a ditch who people say is Che himself."

Pais shuddered and turned away.

About the same time, leaders of the Free Cuba Party in Miami were having a similar discussion. Eduardo Pons was having coffee with Lucia Martinez at a small café in Little Havana near the FPC headquarters that the people from the campaign headquarters used for off-the-record meetings.

"I tell you, Lucy, he's a menace, that old bastard." Eduardo stared into his coffee glumly. "He got people stirred up in Pinar the other day. Our guy down there called me up, he was so excited. Said the old man had a regular political rally. People were shouting and yelling and waving handkerchiefs. He said it was like what he had heard about the goddamn revolution."

Lucia laughed. "Eddie, get real. This is some washed-up old has-been. It's Looney Tunes time down there. The lid is off. *El fucking Comandante* has taken a hike and no one's minding the store. Get a life. They're just having fun—for the first time in about a half century. Get used to it. There are going to be about a thousand clowns like this guy before it's over. It's a hoot!"

She punched his shoulder playfully. He didn't respond. "I tell you, Luce, he's trouble. I can't explain it, but you let something like this run loose, anything can happen. I've seen it happen once or twice here in the States. The press and the pundits write somebody off, before you know it, suddenly the public gets interested. Then all bets are off. That's when politics is dangerous. When it gets out of hand. When things take on a life of their own. Then it's dangerous. Anything can happen. Same thing can happen down there."

"Eddie, he's seventy-something, for God's sake! What do you think he's going to do, set Cuba on fire? It's a joke. If you can't laugh about something this crazy, then life's not worth living." She saw her compatriot was still morose, so she said, "What are you going to do, shoot him?"

She wished she hadn't asked. He looked at her for the first time. And he smiled.

"My God, Ed!" she exclaimed.

He still smiled.

"What?" she said.

He smiled and said, "Take it easy. We're just going to kind of 'observe' him for a while."

"Then what?"

"Then . . . we'll see," he said.

"We'll see?" she said.

"Hey, Luce, it's okay," Eduardo said. "Look, we have to win this election. It's that simple. We cannot lose! Do you understand? Politics is not beanbag, as someone said. This is serious. This is the future of Cuba. We cannot let some loose cannon fuck this up. It's simply too important." He looked at her directly, intensely. "Let me ask you something. Are you doing this for fun? Are you putting your life into this to see it blown away? Politics on this scale is . . . *ultimate*. It's the only thing. It's the most important thing. You do not play to lose. You play to win. There is too much at stake . . . to screw around. You must be prepared to do what it takes." He stared at her in a way that she found frightening. She had known him since they both were in school and she had never seen him so . . . determined . . . so monomaniacal. Even . . .

if . . . it . . . means . . . getting . . . rid . . . of . . . something . . . in . . . your . . . way.

"How are you going to do this, Eddie?" she asked. "Will you strangle the old man? Or will you pay somebody to do it? Or maybe you can poison him. Or maybe shoot him? Lots of choices, actually."

For the first time in the evening she broke the spell. Eduardo leaned back and laughed in a way she had seen him laugh as they were growing up. He laughed and laughed. And as he laughed, she was relieved. Because now she knew he had been fooling her, he had been pulling her leg, he had been testing her to see how far she would go. Then she started laughing too, relieved that her lifelong friend was not an assassin.

He looked at her and he had his old schoolboy grin, innocent and free. Then he said, "*We* don't have to kill the old guy, Luce." He said it as if explaining something obvious to a child. "We'll let the press do it for us."

2 2

■

Politics was beginning to infect the Cubans. To a surprising degree, given no contemporary history of democratic politics, large segments of the Cuban society discovered for themselves how it worked. There were lively, down-to-earth discussions of the issues surrounding markets versus command economies, the role of labor and capital, questions of health care, education, and care of the environment, the relative power of local versus national governments, the kind of constitution the country should have, and an almost endless variety of matters that usually did not preoccupy people who have had these things taken care of for them. In Havana particularly the discussion was lively and the impact of the organizing activities of the Cuban Social Democratic and the Free Cuba parties were most evident. Just the presence of headquarters of competing political parties and the street activities of the parties' workers reminded people that an election was coming in the spring.

Now increasingly released from the oppressive paternalism of the state party apparatus, the lively Cuban people increasingly realized they were not constrained by some new two-party paternalism. And interest groups began to form and discuss ways to maximize their political leverage. Those who traveled to and from the countryside also excitedly reported on an indigenous grassroots movement founded by some curious and mysterious old man who called himself—or was being called by others— Che Guevara. This movement was attracting surprising support from a variety of social circles.

Within the past few weeks a new student political union had been formed at the Universidad de la Habana. A new women's tobacco workers union and a *sindicato de los campesinos* were organized. Leaders of all these organizations demanded an audience with spokesmen for the two established parties and required from them their positions on the issues of principal concern. Predictably, the response of the two parties was both doctrinaire and vague. Then, to everyone's surprise, a new Green Party filed its organizing papers with the election commission in the Ministry of Internal Affairs.

"We want to know what you intend to do to guarantee the *campesinos* a share of the economic pie," the leader of the farm workers demanded of the director of policy for the FPC.

The FPC woman said, "In a free market economy, everyone will be able to bargain for fair compensation for his labor according to the value the market places on that labor."

The *campesino* leader scratched his head. "Can we bargain collectively, in your free market?"

"It will not be illegal," the policy woman said, "but we think, in the States, for example, the unions exert a coercive impact on their members and so they insist that the working people participate in making unfair and unreasonable demands on their employers."

"But we are little farmers and farm laborers," the *campesino* leader said. "We cannot bargain individually."

"Farming is the most clear example of free enterprise," the policy woman said. "Each farm worker should be able to go to any farm and demand a wage that the market has established."

The *campesino* delegation could think of nothing else to ask and left, more confused than when they came.

Likewise, when the women's tobacco workers union went to the FPC, they got pretty much the same answers and when they went to see, with some trepidation, their old friends at the CSD, they were told not to worry, the Social Democrats would look after the tobacco workers as they always had in their old days as Communists. But our working conditions have always been primitive, our wages barely support human life, and the sellers of the cigars make a fortune that they do not share with us, the women's tobacco workers told them. The CSD man, a refugee from the state Ministry of Labor, said, "That was all in the old days. Vote for the CSD and things will be much better in the new economy." That was the promise of the CSD.

Both of the major parties issued press releases denouncing the greens as woolly-headed, dreamy-eyed, impractical idealists. The FCP release said: "Environmentalists would destroy jobs to save whales and prevent investments that create economic opportunities." And the CSD's release said: "Everywhere the so-called greens go they put their elitist agenda ahead of the concerns of working people." The green party could not even get an audience to discuss some concessions that might enable them to form a coalition with either the party of capital or the party of labor.

During this time of increasing political and social ferment, a few students from Santiago de Cuba traveled to Havana to meet with members of the new student political union. They reported excitedly on the true republic movement left behind in the wake of the curious old man who seemed to appear and disappear at will. He was, they said, a mystery figure who empowered people and convinced them they could form their own governments and govern their own communities in accordance with the principles of the early city-states in Greece. This idea spread throughout the student community like wildfire. Soon the students were organizing cells committed to the true republic principle and before long they had the idea to make common cause with other disaffected groups.

By the first of December, 1999, the student political union, the women's tobacco workers union, and the farmers-laborers-mechanics union held a collective press conference in Havana. No one was quite sure how to do this. But they printed amateurish press releases announcing the press conference that they promised would make big political news. The press releases went to all the state news organizations and the offices of foreign press organizations. At ten o'clock on the first, representatives of the three unions gathered in a University of Havana classroom. To their dismay only a handful of reporters were there. No radio, no television, no still cameras.

The representatives of the three organizations each delivered awkward and uncertain statements. They criticized the two major parties for their insensitivities and even more for their insistence on holding to orthodox ideologies and rigid old-fashioned economic doctrine. They each said that twenty-first-century Cuba needed new thinking and new principles of government. They were drawn therefore, they said, to support the vital grassroots movement called the true republic that promised to empower the people themselves to govern their own lives with the support of, but not under the dominance of, both the national government and the business community.

They waited uncertainly for questions. The reporters looked preoccupied and bored. Few had even bothered to make a note. Finally, one veteran, Alfonso Guerrera of *La Prensa*, toward the back of the sparsely occupied room, raised his hand. "Has anybody here actually met this old fellow who calls himself Che Guevara?"

The three spokespersons looked at each other uncomfortably. Then the student leader said, "I haven't met this man. But my student friends tell me he does not call himself Che Guevara. He goes by the name Ernesto Blanco."

Guerrera made a note, then said, "This Blanco, did he ask you to join him?"

The women's tobacco workers leader said, "*No, señor*. He did not ask us. We are asking to join him."

Guerrera said, "What makes you think that ordinary Cubans are up to governing themselves in these 'pure republics'?"

The farmers-laborers-mechanics man said, "Ordinary Cubans couldn't do much worse than what we've had."

With that, one of several ominous-looking auditors standing in the back of the room said in a very loud voice, "That's it. This press conference is over. This room is needed for a class. Let's go."

The members of the three organizations searched the few newspapers in vain for days thereafter seeking a report of their announcements. Alas, no reports were printed. For all practical purposes, the press conference and the endorsements of the true republic movement by the students and workers did not occur. This blackout served to anger and energize the three dissident unions and they each set out to print and circulate to their members throughout the country mass-produced handouts setting forth the ideals of the movement and their arguments for supporting it. A correspondent from one of the Spanish language papers in Miami did file a cursory account of the press conference as an instance of the kind of craziness the fledgling Cuban democracy could be expected to produce. This account was picked up by the Associated Press, translated, and carried as a novelty item, with a wry and cynical twist, on its wire.

It was this item that a frustrated Victoria Savidge was given as she sat in her office in the Washington bureau of TPN smoking a cigarette and drumming her fingers as she contemplated her next move. This was a hook, however small, for a follow-up Cuban story. She had her low-paid researcher try to track down any of the three named organizations, but, since they had neither headquarters nor phones, this effort failed. Then, in desperation, the researcher tracked down one Alfonso Guerrera of *La Prensa*, whose name appeared on the original byline. The phone connection was not much better than Guerrera's English, but Victoria made do. She got as much detail and color from Guerrera as she possibly could, thanked him, and rang off.

From these meager morsels, Victoria cooked a feature stew that she was able to persuade her producer to put on the air a few nights later under the tag "Cuba, Welcome to Democracy." The feature piece got little response from a U.S. audience used to much more bizarre carryings-on in its politics. But it was picked up and run on a number of national television networks throughout Latin America, Africa, and parts of Asia. Victoria had not put in almost two and a half decades in television for nothing. She used this fact to convince her bureau chief that there was an audience for Cuban political news in the emerging nations and that, while waiting for the U.S. audience to build in the run-up to the Cuban election, they could market Cuban stories in the emerging nations. Since TPN received a royalty fee for items it fed to other networks, the argument had a certain commercial appeal.

More to the point from Victoria's point of view, it gave her Cuban cause new life. Even more important, Victoria had a big idea. She thought it through, then flew to New York for a meeting with Sam Rapport.

"Sam, I want to interview this 'Che Guevara.' I want to get the first interview with him. I want an exclusive," she said, her eyes shining.

Sam knew the look. He also knew if he turned her down, she would be down the hall banging on Marshall's door. Marshall would, to say the least, not be amused. And he would blame Sam for failing to handle her. "Ah, Vic, who cares? I mean, who really wants to see some old Cuban kook?"

"Sam, honey, he's not just 'some old Cuban kook.' He's an old Cuban kook who claims to be Che Guevara back from the grave. Even somebody with your limited imagination, sweetie, ought to be able to see the angle." She smiled seductively.

Pathetic, Sam thought. Desperate woman. "What makes you think you can find him, Vic? And, let's just say you find him back in the jungle somewhere, what makes you think he will . . . you know . . . talk to you?" He beamed paternalistically back at her.

"Sam, look at the response we got on that last feed," she pleaded. "A lot of third world countries are watching this Cuban thing. And, believe it or not, Che Guevara is still huge in the third world. The old boy will be very exciting to these countries. I'll go down for a few days, track him down, convince him to do an interview from his mountain hideout, we'll put it on the satellite, promote it big time, carry it worldwide. I promise you, it will be gangbusters. What a hoot! You'll get ten times the cost of the trip from the feeds." Her eyes were still shining.

Sam rolled his eyes. He considered the countless times he had lost these taffy-pulls with Victoria. And even the times he had won, she had made him pay many times over. She could be an absolutely 21-carat, ironclad, copper-riveted flaming bitch who would lie in wait for months to catch you at a vulnerable moment—and slit your throat. "Oh, God, Vic. Go find the old bastard, get him on the satellite, and get it out of your system."

To his dismay she leaned all the way across his desk and gave him a very wet kiss.

2 3

■

From the time E. F. Scarlatti went to work for the Free Cuba Party in the Miami headquarters, she was a smash. The head of Wager-Down, Micky Mendoza, said she was the best he'd ever seen. She knew media. She knew fund-raising. She knew events. She knew press. She knew organization. Micky was so blown away, he phoned around to his political consultant counterparts around the country to see if anyone had ever heard of her. They hadn't, but her references, mostly from West Coast public relations firms, checked out. Everyone said she could walk on water. Whatever needed to be done, she could do it. She was one of those high-energy women who always looked great, always was up, always energized a room, and took over the class wherever she went.

Within a week she had been made the head of the political field organization in Cuba. Toward the end of the year, she was flying back and forth once a week. When she went to Havana, she had the same impact there. Energy went up, people got excited, things started popping. She was a whirlwind. By the end of a month, E.F., for Elicia Francesca—no wonder E.F., Micky thought—had a wall-sized flow chart of tasks to be done, assignment of personnel, performance deadlines, and allocation of total resources. Then she did the same thing for the Havana office. Suddenly, the whole campaign began to make sense to people.

Micky had thanked Olivero Sanchez a dozen times for sending her over. Each time Olivero had said, Don't thank me. Thank that guy from the Committee for Honest Elections, Johnny what's-his-name, the big hitter. He referred her to me. To make it perfect, the Committee for Honest Elections even paid her salary, which Micky heard was considerable. So what's another obligation? Micky thought. He had already heard the Free Cubans owed the Committee for Honest Elections about a million bucks in access when they won the election. That was fine with Micky because a substantial portion of the million would be required to pay Wager-Down's fees.

"Johnny?" E.F. whispered into the phone outside the ladies' room in the classy coffee shop down the street from the campaign headquarters, "I miss you, honey."

"Me too, babe," Johnny sighed. "How's it going?"

"Ever better," she said. "We've got this thing rolling. Everybody's up and running. I leave tomorrow for Havana." After a pause she said, "When you coming down?"

"Soon. Not for a while. But soon. These FCP guys know we sent you over there. I don't want them to think we're controlling everything. You know?"

"I know, Johnny," she said, lighting a cigarette. "It's just that . . . it's lonely. You know?"

"Yeah, babe," he sighed again. "Me too. Get your feet down there a little more. Build up the trust. Then you can focus on the real job. Tell you what. We'll slip off for a weekend. Get one of those cabanas up at Varadero, just off the beach. Get room service. Never go out for a few days . . . maybe to the beach in the moonlight. How's that?"

"Oh, Johnny," she groaned. "Don't do this to me."

"It's okay, punkin," Johnny said. "This is a big deal for us. I can't even tell you how big. Tell you when I see you. All the guys expect this thing to go down. They're holding me responsible. It was my idea. When our guys win—whoever wins—we win. Big. Bigger than big. Can't even talk about it on the phone. But you know the idea. We'll be back in business down there. We'll have the equivalent of a license to print money. My piece alone will set us both up for about fifty years."

"That'll about do it, Johnny," E.F. sighed. "Can't wait."

"Okay, sugar," Johnny signed off. "Call when you're back. And keep me informed on phase two."

E.F. hung up the phone, crushed out the cigarette, then muttered to herself, "Crummy bastard."

"I know, honey," said the coiffed, perfumed, bejeweled matron passing behind her, "aren't they all."

E.F. was a contract employee. This was her second contract for the Leeward Island Club. She had gone through the handsome compensation for the first job—she liked to live well—and they had doubled her

$20,000-per-week base salary and tacked on a seven-figure completion bonus for this one. Growing up in Beverly Hills, E.F. had been conditioned to living well, that is until her father took a more than fatherly interest in her about the age of sixteen. She held out until she was nineteen and then fled. She barely met the minimal height restriction for the Marine Corps, but once in she was a terror. She was out in seven years, for two of which she was based at Guantánamo, as a major. Then she went through three marriages fairly rapidly, none more rapidly than the first when she gave her rich, substantially older groom the workout of his life on their honeymoon in Monte Carlo and he, poor fellow, underwent cardiac arrest while she flirted with some French film star by the pool. She figured the marriage game was up when prospective husband number four began to discuss a prenup.

But she hadn't lost her looks and she hadn't lost her charm. And after the Marines, she figured she was up for anything. Then Johnny came along, bless his pathetic heart, and she was back in business. This time business was whatever the Leeward Island Club happened to need done. She had taken a short course in politics from a hotshot Washington political media consultant who taught her everything he knew from a lifetime of campaigns for about half a kilo of magic powder. E.F.'s steel-trap mind absorbed, analyzed, and categorized it all as if she had been doing it all her life before hotshot was halfway through the powder.

This job was interesting, though. She had always wanted to go back to Cuba in civvies. Seemed like an exciting place to hang your hat for a few months, that is until the bozos arrived. Then she'd find someplace else. She heard Beirut was warming up again. And if the Russians could ever get their story straight, St. Petersburg might be interesting, at least in the summer. So many places, so little time. What intrigued her about the Cuban job was the thought of actually meeting some old geezer who thought he was Che Guevara. Every time she thought of it, she had to laugh. Would the human mind ever run out of ways of amusing itself? Che Guevara, for God's sake. Why not Benny Goodman, or Elvis, or JFK? Well, when the time came, she would have to sit down with old Che and work a deal. Here's the deal, Señor Guevara, she would say. My boss wants me to say to you that he has a wonderful little farm fixed up for you in Mexico. You know Mexico, you've been there before. Free of charge, just for you. No strings. What's that, you don't want no stinking farm? Oh, Señor Guevara, how could you say such a thing?

Well, then, my boss he says he will give you some money, in here, in this bag I have with me. You can go where you like. Anywhere in the world. Just not Cuba. *Sí?* No! Oh, Señor Guevara, you don't want the farm, you don't want the money? What can I do, *señor?* Then, come walk with me down this little path that goes way back into the trees. Because, my boss, he says I must kill you. Okay?

She wouldn't look forward to that part. Particularly with a nice old man. But . . . a job was a job. And a girl had to earn her way in the world. One way or the other.

On the flight to Havana later that day, E.F. looked over her list of people to contact to begin checking out this "Che Guevara." People already signed up with the FCP in Havana. Young people mostly, fed up with the Communist system, who wanted to be dealt in early in the new "market democracy." She had the name of one Alfonso Guerrera, reporter for *La Prensa*, who seemed to have picked up the story early and continued to follow it. Then, interestingly enough, there was a new political analyst at the "Interests Section" that was about to become a full-fledged U.S. embassy. Let's see, he's called Nick Ferre. That was enough to get her started. She would ease into it, treat it as a joke, draw people out. She was particularly interested in where the old guy hung out. The Sierra, she had heard, for God's sake. She hadn't strapped on the fatigues and combat gear and done the overnight forced march for . . . ten years. Could it have been that long? Well, at least when she took the job she had done the intensive Berlitz to get her Spanish back to the fluency of the Guantánamo days.

"He's up in the Sierra," one of the most clever FCP staff members told her. "He is now traveling the country, but no one knows how he travels or where he goes. Sometimes we have heard he is two places at once."

"Three places," one of her colleagues corrected her.

"So it is impossible to know where he will go," she continued. "Because you asked us, we have even sent our local organizers out to look for him or asked them to be on the alert. But he comes into the town or village, and then he is gone. Sometimes he has another equally old man with him, sometimes a young man, sometimes both, sometimes . . . he is all alone."

"Always," a young man said, "he seems to go back to the Sierra. And my father said, from the revolutionary days years ago, even ten thousand troops of Batista could not defeat three hundred revolutionaries in the Sierra. They could not find them, so they could not kill them."

E.F. laughed. "This is not the revolutionary days. And we certainly don't want to kill this old guy. We want to talk to him. This is now democratic politics. We want to convince him to join the Free Cubans." She laughed merrily again, and they laughed with her.

A day or two later, E.F. sought out Alfonso Guerrera. "Señor Guerrera," she said in her newly recovered Spanish, "it is such a great pleasure to meet you. I have heard so much about you, that you are the number one political reporter in Cuba." She smiled shyly, fluttered her eyelashes, and looked down at her coffee cup. "You are very kind to see me."

Very kind to see me, Guerrera thought. Are you kidding? Here is a petite beauty in a tight knit sweater talking to me? He assumed he had died and gone to heaven. He was liking democratic politics already. Up to now, the only real sex in Cuban politics had been Vilma Espinosa and she was known to shoot unsatisfactory lovers.

E.F. went through forty-five minutes' worth of general questions about the prospects for the election, the answers to which she already knew. Then she sat back, shook her head merrily, and laughed. "I'm sorry, Señor Guerrera, but I just remembered something I heard in the States. It was a crazy story about some old man. Some old man down here who thinks he is"—then she laughed—"I can't believe it . . . who thinks he is—"

"Che Guevara," Guerrera offered, as if to help her.

"That's it." She touched his sleeve as she laughed again. "Che Guevara. Isn't it too much? I mean, what a wonderful country to bring back Che Guevara." She left her hand on his sleeve. He stared at her hand, mesmerized.

Finally, Guerrera composed himself enough to say, "Well, it's not quite, shall we say, a kind of musical comedy. We didn't 'bring back' Che Guevara like 'Don't Cry for Me, Argentina.' "

"No," E.F. said, her voice low and serious. "Of course I didn't mean it that way. It's just . . . strange."

"Strange, maybe," Guerrera said, "but there he is. And he's making an impression. From what I can tell, from the party apparat, he's more or less everywhere. I've picked up this—what do they call it?—'true republic,' something like that . . . in"—he checked a battered notebook—"in Pinar province, in Granma, of course, in Santiago de Cuba province, in Holguín, in Las Tunas . . . maybe some other places." He looked into her formidable green eyes and said, "I don't know whether this old man is or is not Che Guevara. But the Cuban people are listening."

Once E.F. had peeled Alfonso Guerrera off her, she made her way around to the U.S. Interests Section and asked for Mr. Nicholas Ferre. She had an appointment, she explained. Soon, the very earnest Mr. Ferre made his way out to see her and took her to a nearby conference room.

"Mr. Ferre," she began, "I cannot thank you enough for taking time from your very busy schedule to see me." She quickly decided this young man was too sincere even to know what sex was about. So she played it straight. She introduced herself as one of many, many people in the States who believed so strongly in the Free Cuba Party that she was volunteering her time to help out in any way she could. And her boss had given her the assignment of studying Cuban politics so the movement would know how to get ready for this unprecedented election. Now she was the naïf, adrift, not knowing quite what to do, needing any help she could get. Once again, she hit the right button.

"Mrs., ah, Ms. Scarlatti," Nick stammered, "ah, I don't claim to be any expert. I'll be honest, I just got here myself only two weeks ago. But I'll try to help any way I can."

"It's just . . . confusing, Mr. Ferre," E.F. began, her forehead furrowed. She asked a series of fairly obvious questions about the current state of Cuban politics, the same questions she had asked Alfonso Guerrera a short time ago. Then she got to the heart of the matter, casually as usual. "The thing that *really* interests me," she sighed as if confessing a peculiar obsession, "is this elderly gentleman, the one who thinks he is Che Guevara." She giggled girlishly.

Nick Ferre giggled back. "I know. Isn't it crazy?" Then he resumed being a foreign service officer. "This elderly gentleman. We don't know much about him. Like everyone else, we are trying to find out more. But right now, he still seems a mystery. To us. To everyone. He comes. He goes." He raised his hands in the air and shrugged. "He's a kind of phantom."

E.F. leaned toward him and said confidentially, "But Mr. Ferre, surely our government, the U.S. government"—she made it sound like the Holy Roman Empire—"must know who he is. *Surely.*"

She said that in such a way, Nick thought, that his virility was somehow in question. "Well, Ms. Scarlatti, we're not without some resources. We have people, myself among them, who are looking into the matter. Señor, ah, 'Blanco' has skillfully created a substantial, perhaps even a formidable, political following. He may—let me emphasize *may*—become a political force in Cuba. That being so, our job is to know as much as we can about him and what he is doing." He said this confidentially, giving her the impression that he was giving her inside information.

E.F. nodded wisely and smiled knowingly. "I understand, Mr. Ferre. I completely understand." She stood, smoothing her tight skirt. "I wonder, Mr. Ferre, if I might presume on your very gracious hospitality. I wonder if, from time to time, I might drop around and talk to you about the progress of the campaigns. I might even offer to help you out. I am more than happy to share with you the progress we at the Free Cuba Party are making in our efforts. I can bring you up-to-date on the FCP, and you can help me understand Cuban politics just a little better . . . all in the interest of democracy, of course. Perhaps, next time"—she smiled sweetly into his wide eyes—"we might even have dinner." She touched his sleeve.

Drawing appreciative glances and comments from Cuban gentlemen on the street as she strolled—swinging her handbag—back to the FCP headquarters, E.F. thought, What a bunch of clowns. I know more about the old boy than any of these people. I'll find him, and "interview" him, a long time before any of them do.

■ ■ ■

How age has changed my mind about things. When I first came here, so many years—so many decades—ago, it was almost as if I wanted to conquer these people, to force them to be what I insisted they be. We called it "liberation" of course. But the revolution turned out to be a form of conquest. Because I was a Communist, and Raúl was a Communist, and, even though Fidel was not yet a Communist, we knew, with the help of the Yanquis, we could easily make him one. And, of course, we did. But even that is a joke. Because, for Fidel, communism was always a way to provoke Tío Sam, a way to give the finger to el norte. And how it worked. Why are those people always so predictable. We laughed often because we knew in almost every case what action would provoke what reaction. It is too bad that the U.S., such a powerful country, is not more mature.

But my views on conquest have changed. My youthful radicalism of the left has given way, under the relentless time and pressure of the ages, to a new radicalism, one of the ancient past and the dramatic future. It sometimes surprises me, a man of the late-twentieth-century Latin American jungle, that so few have understood where we are heading, where we must be heading. It is something like the great treasure—such as love—that often can be found right beneath our very noses. If there is some Deity (Him or Her), that One must be laughing right now at human folly.

The only way we—humanity—can survive is to rediscover what the ancients knew—that we must learn to govern ourselves in our communities before we can govern ourselves as nations or whole societies. It now seems to me so obvious. But, of course, the most obvious things are the things that must be learned by each generation anew. Take young Rafael. Even now I look across the campfire at him. He pretends to be reading his book, The Republic, *that I gave him, but he is not reading. He is studying me instead of Plato. He thinks if he looks at me, even out of the top of his eyes, that he will know what I know, what it took me a lifetime to know. Such is youth. Always looking for the shortcut that is never there.*

So now I reckon the forces of the past are mustering. They must protect their hard-won positions. I know how they think. First, they will try to discredit me. "This man is not who he says he is." "Excuse me, señor, who does he say he is?" the campesinos *will rightly ask. That will make the forces of the past very angry. When powerful, established forces become angry, they inevitably seek recourse in violence. That will be the showdown. I just hope these good people—Alejo, Rafael, the* campesinos—*are not injured. It is not their fault. I don't think so. I know something of assassins. They are usually particular, even if they are not successful. Look again at Fidel, for God's sake. From three decades in the countryside, I believe I can hold them off until we complete our mission.*

In three or four months, enough Cuban people will begin to question authority, to think for themselves about their future, to sense real empow-

erment, that they will make it on their own—with or without "Ernesto Blanco" or "Che" or whatever icon they grasp. They will have achieved sufficient maturity that the forces of the old Left and the old Right cannot prevail against them. That is our goal. That is my dream.

■ ■ ■

24

■

"Vilma," Pais said, "get that guy in here. What's his name?"

Vilma studied him, hands characteristically on her ample hips. "Victor, how you managed to rise near the top of the Politburo of the Communist Party of the People's Fucking Republic of Cuba, I will never know. You can't remember your own name, let alone the name of the new head of the State Security Department."

"Vilma," Pais sighed, "if you would keep one longer than two weeks, I promise I would try to remember his name. Last I heard, you were using them regularly for target practice." He made a gesture of casually blowing imaginary smoke from the imaginary gun formed by his index finger.

"That's not what I use them for and you know it," she said in her raspy, nonchalant voice. She motioned to the man at the door and in came the latest head of Cuban intelligence. Pais gestured him into a seat across the desk, next to Vilma, and said in an inconsolate tone, "What's up?"

"What's up, Victor, is a troublesome old man who is eating away at the base of the Cuban Social Democratic Party a village a week. Maybe more." The man sat back and Pais suddenly remembered he had heard that this middle-aged weight lifter had been seen in a back banquette at the Tropicana with Vilma's state secrets in one hand and a *señorita* half her age in the other.

Against his doctor's orders and his own survival instincts, Pais lit a Cohiba. "Well now, what do you think the Cuban Social Democratic Party should do about this old man, presuming we could somehow persuade the State Security Department of the People's Fucking Republic of Cuba to get off its ass at the Tropicana and go find him." He winked at Vilma.

The weight lifter looked at Vilma, who snorted. Then he said smugly, "We found him. We found him a long time ago. We've always known where he is."

Pais sat up, interested. "Really. And where might that be?"

The man studied the manicure given him just hours ago by the *señorita* half Vilma's age. "I'll tell you where he is. He's in the Sierra." He smiled triumphantly.

Pais puffed once or twice on the Cohiba. Then he looked at the head of the State Security Department from the side of his eyes. "The Sierra. Thank God! I thought he might be maybe in the White House in Washington. Or maybe in the Sahara Desert in Africa. Or maybe in the tundra in Siberia. Or maybe . . ."

At this point Vilma took her new pal under the arm and started him for the door. Before they got there, the mild-mannered Victor Pais first threw his Cohiba and then the ashtray he had been recently tapping its ash into and then a sharp letter opener that stuck in the doorjamb just as the weight lifter escaped beyond it. After she had escorted the latest head of the Cuban State Security Department through the door of the outside office, with a whispered promise to see him later at her flat, Vilma returned.

"He's upset, Victor," she said. "You upset him." When she saw the look on Pais's face, she wished she hadn't said it.

"Oh, Vilma," he said, "I am so sorry. Please go fetch him. Bring him back. I'll kiss his feet. I'll kiss his ass. Whatever you want." He looked right through her. "Do not," he said, "do not bring back another one of these Romeos, these hair stickum Valentinos, these *idiotas* whose shoe size is bigger than his IQ to tell me that it has taken the swollen ranks of the State Security Department two and a half months to isolate one little old man in the Sierra." Now the normally calm Pais was shouting. "Fidel hid the entire revolutionary fucking army in the Sierra for over two years!"

Since their days together at the university more than forty years before, Vilma had never seen Pais so angry. She waited a decent moment; then she nodded in agreement and said, "Of course, you're right. We've got to do better. Look, I'll take this job myself. I'll get whatever resources it takes, and I'll find this old guy. Then we'll decide what to do with him."

Pais had calmed down. "Right. You're right. You can do it, even if no one else can. I have no doubt you'll find him. The real question is, What then?"

It was Vilma's turn to blow imaginary smoke from the imaginary gun that was her index finger.

Pais said, "You could do that. You know what you'd have? I'll tell you what you'd have. You'd have a martyr. You want a martyr of the new democracy? I don't think so."

She said, "What then? Victor, everything I can find out tells me this old guy is taking away our political base. Everywhere he goes, he gets *campesinos*, workers, young people, poor people, old people. I'll tell you something, Victor. Ricardo told me, in confidence, that his wife and two grown kids were talking about this guy. The 'true fucking republic.' He thinks if they vote in secret, they will vote for this old fart. José Puerta, just the other day, told me the same thing." She leaned across Pais's desk, her nose almost touching his. "He's a goddamn public menace."

Pais sighed. He didn't like what he had to do. "Vilma, send some of your people, some of Romeo's goons from State Security, and start breaking up this old guy's meetings. We have to do what we have to do." He turned away, hoping the matter was resolved.

Vilma came around the desk and stood almost toe to toe. "Victor, sweetie," she husked, "you're way late. I gave that order a couple of weeks ago. We sent out two of our best people. Ears to the ground. Listening to the jungle drums. And, *caramba!* They stumbled onto one of these little meetings in the village square that we've heard so much about. Guess what?"

Now she had Pais's attention. He shook his head back and forth, eager to know.

"I'll tell you what happened," Vilma said. She paused to make a production out of lighting a cigarette. "What happened was . . . we don't know."

"What happened was you don't know?" Pais was mystified. "What do you mean you don't know."

"We don't know what happened, Victor, for one simple reason," Vilma puffed and said. "They never came back."

"Your guys never came back?"

She shook her head no. "Best we can find out"—she smiled viciously—"they joined the old man."

Pais stared at his desktop for a moment. Vilma was suddenly happy he had no more letter openers. Then he said, "I want you to get a team together. A team of doctors . . . what do you call them? . . . forensic doctors, specialists. The best we've got. Get some outside experts, if you have to, from Mexico, or wherever. Four, maybe six. A respectable number. Send them to Bolivia. Tomorrow. Tonight! I want them to interview everyone there who was alive when Che Guevara was killed in 1967. Then I want them to come back here. I want them to dig up his grave. I want them to dig up his bones. I want them to do that new stuff . . . what do you call it? . . . DNA to his bones. I want a complete, unbiased, world-class, unimpeachable, unquestionable, expert report. I want to release that report to the Cuban press. And if anyone else wants to know, I want that report released to the world press. I want that report to say that Ernesto 'Che' Guevara, originally a citizen of Argentina, a great patriot of the Cuban revolution of 1959, died of gunshot wounds delivered by murderous soldiers of the Bolivian Army, with the aid and support of agents of the Central Intelligence Agency of the United States of America. I want them to say that he died in 1967. And, Vilma"—he looked at her maniacally—"I want them to say that *he is still dead.*"

2 5

■

Nicholas Ferre was nothing if not energetic. The minute he stepped off the plane at José Martí International Airport in Havana, he felt right at home. The language, of course, was no problem. He quickly discovered that the Cuban Spanish that he had grown up with in his

household enabled him to fit in without an identifiable accent. His superiors at the U.S. Interests Section were almost totally preoccupied
with completing arrangements to open the new embassy on the first of
January, 2000, just two weeks hence. After undergoing some rapid-fire
indoctrination sessions to top up what he had learned at the State Department and the CIA about the Cuban political and economic situation,
Nick was pretty much left to his own devices. The head of the political
section understood that Nick had a carte blanche hunting license to find
out everything he could about the rapidly evolving increasingly revolv-
ing, political scene.

Thus, Nick had free range to make up his own agenda. He could go
and do pretty much as he wished. Aside from attending weekly staff
meetings at the Interests Section, Nick was at liberty to decide how best
to achieve his objectives. The only check on his activities was the reports
of his findings that he provided the head of the office, which were sent
on to the Cuban desk at State in Washington. He had two principal
targets, the Cuban Social Democratic Party and the increasingly visible
opposition party, the Free Cuba Party. He spent his first two weeks
interviewing leaders in both parties, visiting their respective headquarters, talking with the principal organizers, and trying to appreciate the
campaign strategies of both camps.

It did not take long for him to grasp the basics—the key policy makers, strategists, and organizers; the policies and programs each party
proposed; and the ideological philosophies each would bring to
government. Before long he felt the need to get out of the politically
claustrophobic capital city and visit the real Cuba. Now just over four
months from the national elections, Havana was beginning to exhibit
the incestuousness and cynicism of Washington. The longer he stayed
in the capital, the less Nick thought he knew about the country. Besides,
there was this curious undercurrent running beneath virtually all of Havana politics that seemed to make everyone he talked to jittery and edgy.
There was an almost preternatural preoccupation with the old man
whom political people were increasingly talking about, the one who either did or did not call himself Che Guevera, the one who had stirred
up this "true republic" movement that he heard about everywhere. Nick
had never experienced anything like it in his life. The less visible and
more intangible the old man was, the more he seemed to insinuate himself into every level of the political fabric.

Nick realized that he would have to travel the island to gauge the strength of the two major parties and even more to determine whether there was anything palpable to this movement. Since the most recent rumors of sightings of the old man were in Pinar del Río province, Nick decided to cross the country west to east and end up in the area of the Sierra in Granma province in the direction of Guantánamo. In half a dozen towns and villages in Pinar, he found cadre for the Social Democrats, primarily members of the old Communist Party apparat; organizers for the Free Cubans, mostly younger people paid to represent the FCP locally; and groups of people discussing the ideas of Ernesto Blanco having to do with local self-government. Old established contacts the CSD had. Young people looking for a shortcut to Yankee capitalism the FCP had. Energy, enthusiasm, and excitement the true republic movement had.

This pattern repeated itself everywhere Nick went in Pinar. He moved eastward past Havana to the north and on through Matanzas and Cárdenas in Matanzas province, then to Cienfuegos in Cienfuegos province, the town of Aguada de Pasajeros, Santa Clara, Trinidad, and Placetas in Las Villas province, Sancti Spíritus in Sancti Spíritus province and the town of Ciego de Avila in Ciego de Avila province, through Jatibonico, Morón, Florida, and Camagüey in Camagüey province, and then down to the village of Amancio and back up to Las Tunas in Las Tunas province, through Holguín and a couple of tiny villages in Holguín province, and finally through Palma Soriano to the city of Santiago de Cuba in the province of the same name. He had bypassed Granma province and the Sierra to the south and arrived at the footsteps to the east of the mountain range.

Nick had traveled by public transport in order to maximize his contact with the people. But it had been, certainly by U.S. standards, extremely arduous. Trains sometimes ran, sometimes didn't, but almost never on time. They were known, sometimes, to arrive and leave early. Buses were even worse. And those that did run were invariably jam-crowded. In many cases his contact with the Cuban people was so intense that he could barely conduct any conversation, not to say a serious one about the 2000 elections. But what he lost in serious political discourse was more than made up for by the perspective he gained of the daily lives of the people—the hardships they were conditioned by long experience to endure, their stoical acceptance of inconvenience, their sense that tomorrow was another day, the basic nature of their everyday existence. As in every country, country and village life was conducted at a slower pace than urban life. Rural life was focused on fundamentals—work, eat, sleep, and small diversions. And, as in every country, the farther Nick traveled from the capital, the less the people concerned themselves with the life of politics.

The one constant, the one common denominator, Nick perceived, was the almost pervasive presence of the old man Ernesto Blanco. He heard the name or a reference to *el viejo* over and over again, in whispered conversations among women standing on a swaying, fuming bus between Placetas and Sancti Spíritus, or among *campesinos* jammed into a corner on a crowded train between Camagüey and Las Tunas, or in a small, intense crowd of young students sharing political revelations in the next booth at a café in Santiago. The more pervasive the experience became, the more even Nick, a novice in the psychology of campaign politics, understood that something significant was at work at the level of the very soil of Cuba.

The resourceful Nick, preparing his assault on the Sierra, sought out anyone who might give him guidance. In all cases he straightforwardly identified himself as an American, a Cuban American, who worked for the Interests Section of the United States and who was trying to understand the forthcoming elections. People he encountered, once they discovered who he was, were eager to render an opinion. In one case, a professor retired from the humanities department of the Universidad de Oriente took the better part of a sunny morning on the fifth-floor terrace of the Hotel Casa Grande overlooking the central part of the city, as well as the Bahía de Santiago de Cuba only half a dozen blocks away to the west, to give his views on the phenomenon of Ernesto.

"When Fidel announced his retirement," the professor said, "it was the signal of the end of the revolutionary era. Actually, the revolutionary era ended after the missile crisis in 1962. Then we settled into the institutionalization of communism and the paternal welfare of the Soviet Union. When Soviet paternalism was withdrawn in the age of Gorbachev, it was essentially the beginning of the end for Fidel. He is still clever enough to understand that. Now the people have nothing and no one to believe in. The two announced parties represent the establishment politics of the Western world—the old Left and the aging Right. The neoliberalism of Thatcher and Reagan is simply a resurrection of nineteenth-century laissez-faire. It appeals for a time to the entrepreneurial youth for whom the god of materialism is sufficient to justify the acquisition of personal wealth and the fashionable impugning of social cohesion. But there is nothing really new in it. Nor will the old socialist model suffice. It is increasingly discredited by its own sclerosis."

Nick said, "But what about the resurrection of Che Guevara? Isn't that simply an exercise in nostalgia?"

"Well, yes," the professor laughed, "certainly to a degree. But keep in mind, the revolutionary ideal represented by Che is still young, because like others who die young, he has not really aged. He is a relatively young and therefore romantic figure for all time. Now comes this senior gentleman."

Nick reflected that the "senior gentleman" would be about the professor's same age.

"This man reawakens all that romanticism even though he himself is not young. And he re-creates an ideal that is much older than the other two. But it seems new because no one living today has really thought about republicanism, certainly not in the pure, ideal form in which he presents it."

Nick noticed peripherally the two men who had occupied the nearby table. He was sure he had seen them somewhere. But not in Santiago. "Is it practical," he asked the professor, "this ideal of a 'true republic' where each village and city democratically selects its own leaders and makes most of its own community decisions?"

The elderly professor chuckled. "Probably not in this age of mass immigration, mass transportation, instant communications, instant, voluminous information. . . . Of course, we Cubans are fortunate in a way that we have yet to 'enjoy' these blessings of the modern age. But we will, soon enough, we will. In the meantime, yes. It is practical. Perhaps except for Habana, we are a nation of towns and villages, much like ancient Greece. Even Santiago de Cuba, our second largest city, could be governed in this way. There could be neighborhood governments and a city-state government."

Nick noticed the two men were smoking, drinking coffee, looking out over the bay. And listening. "I will be very honest with you, Professor," Nick said. "I find the whole idea very exciting. It could really revitalize democracy in the West. To me it's much more interesting than the politics we now have in the U.S."

The professor suddenly looked disturbed. He leaned forward and spoke in confidence. "I agree with you, but I fear for this senior gentleman," he muttered. "I have a sense that the stronger his movement becomes, the more powerful his ideas become, the greater will be the resistance of powerful forces, not simply the two political parties, but also other forces, commercial interests, those who benefit from centralized political power and who know how to manipulate it to their benefit. This is not a big country, but it has the potential, because of its location and its peculiar destiny, to become a rich country. Where money is at stake, people will become unscrupulous." He thought for a moment. "This senior gentleman is very clever to remain obscure. The more visible he becomes, the more vulnerable he will be. I somehow think he understands that."

Later, Nick met with representatives of the two parties locally. They were, as usual, of a type, the CSD people old Communist apparatchiks and the FCP organizers young hotshots on the make. After days of travel and repeated exposure to these people, he understood the professor's notion that neither of the established systems could have much broad appeal. He also kept crossing paths with the two men who had been on the terrace of the hotel. He had received enough basic training from the Agency as a young foreign service officer to know he was being observed if not surveilled, presumably by operatives of the state. He spent time among the students at the Universidad. Given his relative youth and even more youthful appearance, as well as his language ability, he fit in reasonably well. After a day or two he managed to find two young organizers of the true republic movement. He cultivated their trust and soon he discovered they were organizing a meeting in a tiny village called Los Negros two hours away at the foot of the Sierra on the western edge of Santiago de Cuba province. It was to be the following night and the students said that if he would meet them the following evening at six in front of the ancient Santa Iglesia Basilica on the Parque Cespedes they would take him with them to the town meeting. One of them whispered, "*El viejo* may be there."

After a torturous ride in the ancient car of the uncle of one of the students, made tolerable only by Nick's many days of equally torturous indoctrination, they arrived at Los Negros around eight in the evening. Things seemed calm as they fell in with a small file of townspeople headed for the single-room schoolhouse just off the square. Once inside, the mayor droned through a half hour's worth of village business and then said, "We have a *visitante* whom we wish to welcome and who may wish to greet you." He gestured to the back of the room. All turned toward the back, aware of the mysterious comings and goings in the nearby mountains.

"No greetings, *alcalde, muchas gracias*," said an unremarkable old man who looked just like all the other old men in the room until he smiled. Then he looked much younger. "Just this small thing. You people know there is going to be an election in the spring. Great promises are being made to you by the two political parties in order to gain your support and your vote. They tell you what they will do for you. I simply want to tell you what you have to do for yourselves. You have to find your own way. Those guys in Havana, left guys and right guys, want to run this country. I think *you* should run this country yourselves. Starting right here in Los Negros. That's all, mayor, *muchas gracias*." Then he sat down.

Nick looked in amazement as a buzz started across the room. Here he was, the famous Ernesto Blanco, and he was just a simple old man who talked for two minutes and then sat back down next to a young man, almost a boy. That was all? Yet, Nick felt an excitement, a sense of energy suddenly in the room, a feeling that this simple statement had opened up a new possibility. It had all happened so fast. The mayor made some more announcements and then said his cantina was open across the square if anyone wanted a *cerveza*. People got up and started for the door. Nick and the students were near the back and they started toward the old man and the boy who were about to leave. One of the students stopped *el viejo* just outside the door, had a quick conversation with him, then motioned to Nick.

Nick shook hands with the old man, who reminded him of his own grandfather, and spoke to him.

"Ah," said the old man, "I see you are *Cubano. Bueno, bueno*." Then he started off.

Nick quickly said, "I am with the U.S. government." Then he briefly explained his mission.

The old man looked closely at him and said, "I know who you are. I've seen you four or five places in the last couple of weeks. Your government has much to learn about these people. It will be a big mistake if you bring back the old regime." Then he was gone into the night. His wide-eyed young companion went after him.

Within seconds Nick saw the two men from the hotel cross from the corner of the school building toward the direction the old man had gone. They got to the edge of the light from the square, had a whispered conversation, then turned back toward Nick and the students. One of the students took Nick by the arm and got him to their antique car as quickly as they could and they started back to Santiago. The driver said, "He never can stay long. They're closing in on him. They want to stop him. They have been following you also, you know."

Within two days Vilma Espinosa had a report from the State Security Department stating that the new young "political officer," Nicholas Ferre, at the U.S. Interests Section had been all over the island meeting with all kinds of people and asking a lot of questions about Cuban politics. It was clear, the report said, that Ferre was an operative of the CIA and should be watched at all times. What really caught Vilma's attention, however, was this conclusion:

> Subject had a clandestine meeting with the notorious "Ernesto Blanco" a.k.a. "Che Guevara" a.k.a. "El viejo," two nights before, after a town meeting in the village of Los Negros. This confirms the suspicion of the SSD that the U.S.G. is supporting this renegade and the so-called "true republic" movement as a means of dividing the votes of the campesinos and therefore defeating the CSD in the 2000 elections.

Within an hour Vilma was in Victor Pais's office with the report. They called together as many members of the Cuban Social Democratic Party central committee as they could that night to discuss the matter. After heated debate, they decided unanimously to plan an exposé of this man Ferre as the CIA go-between from the U.S. government to the upstart movement. This would be explosive and, given the CIA's notorious history in Cuba, would chop old Señor "Guevara" right off at his creaky knees.

2 6

■

The call from Sam Rapport had sent Victoria Savidge into ecstasy. Typically, he had used few words. "Cuba. Now."

"Why, for God's sake, Sam?" she asked.

"Why? Why? Because you've been driving us all crazy," he spluttered. "Get your ass down there."

"No," she said, "why now? What triggered this?"

He said, "Very simple. There's an interesting old man down there who calls himself Che Guevara. Find out who he is. I just saw a story on the wire about him. That's our story. Go get it. It's great. We already have some people working on some documentary footage on Guevara. We'll wrap it around whatever you come up with."

She blew her cork. "You dumb s.o.b. *I'm* the one who came up with that story. You're feeding me back my own story."

"No, Vic," he said. "It's on the wire. It's hot. Everybody here is laughing his ass off. Che Guevara! It's great! We'll remind everybody under fifty who Che Guevara is, then we'll bring him back to life. What a great story!"

Victoria was beside herself. This was the side of the business that drove her around the bend. Someone, in this case her, breaks an improbable story. Inevitably, that person's superiors yawn. If our reporter found something new, then it can't be too important. If the competition's reporter finds a story, why in God's name didn't we get it first? "Sam, are you listening to me? This is *my* story. *I* found Che Guevara. He's *mine*. He's ours. *I've* been trying to sell you this story for four weeks!" She was shouting, her least productive tone.

"Okay, Vic, okay," Sam said. "You win. It's your story. It's our story. Now, get off your ass and go get it." He said this very slowly so she would understand that he was serious. Then he said, "Look, here's how we've decided to play it. You get an interview with this old nutcase.

We'll show the real guy . . . back in the sixties. We'll have a bunch of experts come on and they'll say, He's dead. We know he's dead, 'cause we shot him. Full of holes. So, see, we'll expose this old guy for the fraud he is. It's a great exposé, our kind of story."

That had been almost a week ago. Now Victoria was in Havana, and she was making little progress at finding old Che Guevara. She was sure of one thing. The old codger was not in Havana.

Actually, he was, but Victoria didn't know it. The Free Cuba Party didn't know it. The Cuban Social Democratic Party didn't know it. For sure, the State Security Department didn't know it. But Ernesto Blanco was meeting with some students at a bar frequented only by university students near the Universidad de la Habana. He had been doing this now from time to time, on the principle that the way you brought down the system was not to attack the capital but first to surround it and then undermine it.

Nevertheless, Victoria's best efforts to find guides to take her into the Sierra had all foundered. One very sincere man her local contacts had sent around to her had taken her to a very nice *paladar*, a family restaurant, then to a floor show, then tried to get into her hotel room. Most important, he had convinced her he grew up in the Sierra, had family all over those mountains, knew it like the back of his own hand, and would take her and her cameraman right to the man. In fact, he had leaned very close over the dinner-table candle, his eyes soft but aglow, and said, "I've seen him myself. Walked right up to his camp. They were so surprised, they had me in for coffee." He leaned back smiling and snapped his fingers. "Like that," he said.

It seemed, though, that he needed an advance. Travel money. "Gratuities." He rubbed his fingers together under the table. "You understand, I'm sure," he said. Actually, she did understand. She had gone through the selfsame process in half of Africa, a third of Latin America, and too much of Asia. She sighed and, as much as anything to keep him out of her hotel room, she slipped him a couple of hundred. Half of what he asked for. He'd need more, he said. There'll be more when we're under way, she said. He said he'd be back with the approval in two days. That was almost a week ago.

Now Victoria found herself for the fifth night in a row in the bar on the veranda of the Hotel Nacional. The same crowd every night. Unlike her first trip, this time there were possibly a dozen and a half reporters, half of whom she knew from the States. My God, she thought, is this place going to become the next Saigon, the hangout for every journalist on the lam from an editor, a wife, an alimony lawyer, a subpoena of some kind? A place to live better on a "hardship" credit card than you could ever live in the States. Please, do not let this place become fashionable to the journalistic world, she prayed over her second *mojito*, at least until I get my story and get out. Right now she was in no hurry to get out. She actually liked it here a lot. What she wanted to do, most of all, was to find that old fox who thought he was a revolutionary. And most of all, she wanted to find him before anyone else did. Looking around the room, she knew every reporter there had the same idea.

Suddenly, a simply dressed young man sat down at her table. Cute, she thought. But his look was too sincere for him to be a gigolo. "*Señora, por favor. Señora*, are you Señora Savidge?"

She lit a cigarette and said, "Who wants to know?" in her most worldly voice.

"*Señora*, please, that man coming to our table, he is going to throw me out of this hotel unless you tell him it's okay. I am from *el viejo*."

The maître d', who had also tried three nights in a row to get into her room himself, said, "Señora Savidge, I am so sorry. This young man, he came through the kitchen. I am so sorry." Then he turned to the young man and rattled off a string of Spanish words Victoria somehow knew were not polite. He started to lift the young man roughly by his arm but Victoria said, "*Señor*, it's all right. He is here for me. I sent for him." These last two sentences she said slowly, her voice low and very suggestive. The maître d' stepped back as if scalded. He looked at the underfed student and suddenly understood. She liked them young and skinny. He shrugged as if to say, There is no accounting for taste, and stalked off, his nose in the air.

"Okay, young man," she said, "what is it?"

"*Señora, por favor*," he stammered, "my cousin he works in the kitchen and our network told me you are here. I am so sorry. But we know who you are and we know you want to see our *jefe*. I can help you with it, if you wish. And," he said both politely and firmly, "and if you do not wish to do him harm."

Victoria held her arms up to suggest the absence of weapons. She frisked herself, a provocative gesture in itself, and then shrugged. "I promise you. . . . What do I call you?"

"Pedro," he said. Somehow she knew every Latin who didn't want to use his name was called Pedro. Actually, she fleetingly remembered a "Pedro" down in São Paulo. . . . But that was another story.

"Okay, Pedro. I have never hurt anyone in my life. I'm a journalist. A famous journalist, more or less. I work for an important network. It's called The Political Network. TPN."

"*Sí, señora,* we know all this," he said. "We know very well who you are."

That's a relief, she thought. She reached into the ample purse at her side and said, "How much do you need?"

The young man looked confused. "*Señora?*"

"How much does it cost? My network will pay . . . up to a point." Then she looked around the room and noticed other reporters looking at her. They'll assume the worst anyway, she thought.

The young man looked horrified. "*Señora.* Pay? *Por qué?* You do not pay. There is no pay."

"Sorry, Pedro," she said. "I was just used to another system. All right, what's the deal? Where do I go? When do I see your . . . *hayfay?*"

Pedro held a finger to his lips. "Please understand. I cannot promise you a—what do you call it?—interview. I can only take you to the place where our *jefe* is. Then it is up to him, after he has talked to you a little, to decide about the journalism."

Suddenly, Victoria was suspicious. It was in the genes. "Why me? Why not one of these other bozos?"

"*Posos?*" Pedro asked.

"Journalists. Reporters. Why did your 'network' pick me?" she persisted.

Pedro shrugged. "*Señora,* I do not know. I think perhaps *el jefe* himself may have decided. He will have to explain this to you. My job is only to take you to him. If you wish."

"I wish," she said urgently. "What do we do?"

Pedro gave her instructions for the following morning. Where to go, what to do. The directions were complex, so she wrote them down. Better to be sure. He stood to go. "*Gracias, señora.* You are a very kind lady. Now, I must ask if you will walk me past that man. Otherwise, he will grab me and beat me up."

She put her head back, grabbed the young man's hand, and they walked together out of the dining room, all eyes following them. My God, she was thinking, wait till *this* gets back to Marshall.

As Victoria made her way out of the hotel early the following morning, her giant handbag swinging as if she were off on yet another shopping tour, she could not know that a woman from the CSD picked her up and discreetly followed her toward the Plaza de la Catedral. Since her phone was monitored by the State Security Department employee at the hotel switchboard, both the intelligence service and the party knew she was trying to find the man known as Ernesto Blanco. On the crazy off chance that she might get lucky, they both decided it was worth one or two people, of which they had more than enough, to keep a tail on her. Absolutely loving the intrigue, Victoria stopped at just-opened tourist stalls along the way leading into and around the cathedral square. Although she smiled happily, inside she fumed and plotted violent revenge at the leers she got from several fellow journalists at the breakfast buffet. After the appropriate number of minutes, she checked her watch, then entered the cathedral. While her eyes were adjusting to the sudden darkness, a hand took her arm and pulled her quickly into an alcove. A finger pressed to her lips kept her from protesting. In a few seconds a middle-aged woman burst into the darkness through the main cathedral entrance. She too took a moment to adjust to the sudden loss of light. "She is following you, *señora*," a voice whispered into Victoria's ear. They remained silent. Confused, the second woman turned and left.

Quickly, Victoria was handed off to yet a second unidentifiable person who took her through the cathedral and out a very small back exit. Just outside, a car waited. She was thrust in and the driver immediately sped away down the narrow alley. At the end of the alley he stopped, blocking the street. Her door opened and an attractive young woman silently took her to a second old car and got in with her. They drove through *Habana vieja* to a ferry. The young woman motioned for Victoria to get out. They got on the ferry just as it prepared to cast off. They were taken across Havana harbor to a landing near the community of Casablanca. When the ferry docked, the young woman had Victoria by the arm and off the ferry among the first passengers. She was then taken by two young men who put her in another old car, which then sped off into the territory east of Havana.

It had all happened so quickly that Victoria didn't know whether to be frightened or exhilarated. From time to time she wondered about kidnapping but refused to pursue that because she did not want to have to calculate how little Marshall might pay for her. Mostly, she loved the drama. As they drove through the countryside, she felt in the giant handbag. As instructed by Pedro, she had brought an extra blouse, skirt, and underwear. She had thrown in the usual makeup, aspirin, and so forth. But that was all. She had no idea how long she would be gone.

By nightfall, the car began to climb. It also began to overheat. Presently they reached an intersection and she was handed off to another car. This one was occupied by two rather serious-looking men who had probably never been students. Victoria began to worry again for her safety. They drove for miles over a combination of four-lane highway, two-lane older highway, and rougher roads that would never be highway. They passed through a few towns, bypassed other cities whose lights could be seen in the evening dusk, and through village after village in what she believed to be an easterly direction. After a number of hours during which she alternately dozed and came wide-awake, the car rolled into a large city. The sign on the outskirts read Santiago de Cuba. They had driven over half the length of the country during these arduous hours. The car wound its way through the outskirts of the city in what seemed to Victoria to be a circumferential direction so that after more than a half hour they had come back very near the western part of the city where they had first arrived. Finally, they pulled up next to a small cantina in a poor, crowded neighborhood. Houses and shops were mixed together in a tight jumble. As the two silent men opened the back car door and handed the weary, stiff Victoria out onto the sidewalk, she momentarily reflected on the possibility of escape and how difficult it might be to find her in this jam-packed suburban neighborhood.

Now the two men, who had said very little to her in the preceding hours, seemed at ease and even friendly. They invited her inside and quickly ordered what seemed to her to be a lot of different dishes. A kindly proprietress showed her the way to a tiny restroom. When she returned, food and a bottle of rum were being placed at her corner table. Victoria suddenly realized it had been hours since she had eaten and she was famished. The lady who ran the place also seemed to be the cook and the waitress. She smiled as she poured Victoria a glass of rum and gestured for her to eat. Victoria tried the *"moros y cristianos,"* the basic rice and black bean dish, the *tostón*, and the *palomilla* steak and found them all delicious. She looked at her watch and discovered it was almost ten o'clock. The only other diners were a large family on one side of the room and two elderly men drinking coffee and playing dominoes on the other. Within minutes the noisy family group drifted off into the night. The two men nearby seemed totally preoccupied with their dominoes. She ate hungrily and quickly. As the waitress poured her second rum and removed the dishes and plates, she began to feel much more like a human being again and began to relax for the first time in hours. Her concern for her safety was outweighed by her excitement at the possibility of meeting the elusive rebel.

Her reverie was broken by one of the men at the next table who smiled at her, bowed slightly, and asked politely, *"Americana, señora?"*

She nodded in the affirmative and smiled back, not anxious to disclose her identity or her mission.

"Turista, señora?" the smiling man asked again.

"Sí," she responded. *"Yo no habla español."* She had virtually exhausted her Spanish and hoped that might put her interlocutor off.

Then he said, in heavily accented English, "I hope you like our humble country."

She assured him that she was thoroughly enjoying herself and apologized for not being able to speak Spanish with him.

"It's okay, *señora*," he said, "many of us here know a little English." He hesitated, then said, "Are you following our very interesting politics?"

She said, without thinking, "Yes. I am trying to understand it. But it is *muy complicado*." Then, her reportorial instincts took over. Why not conduct an interview while waiting for her next move. "The thing *más interesante* is this mysterious figure 'Ernesto Blanco.' Does anyone ever see him?"

The two men laughed. "Of course, *señora*. He is seen all over Cuba. How else can he be doing his job? He must meet the people and discuss with them his ideas. He simply chooses not to be part of the chaos that is Habana."

"But surely he must meet with *periodistas*. He must give his ideas to the reporters and the press," she said. "It is necessary in a democratic system."

The two men laughed heartily. *"Por qué?* According to whom, *señora?* Who made this rule? Was it *Jorge* Washington?" one of them said. "I don't think so."

Victoria was nonplussed. The idea of politics outside the media arena dumbfounded her. "Look at your match," she said, pointing at the dominoes. "How will anyone know who wins if no one reports on this contest?"

"If I have many friends in Cuba," one of the men said, "and I tell this lady who is the victor"—he gestured at the beaming proprietress standing in the kitchen door wiping her hands with a towel—"very soon all of my friends in Cuba will know."

"But no one outside of Cuba will know," she answered.

"It is hard for us to believe that people outside Cuba really care for our politics," the smiling man said. "Certainly not in *el norte*, they have not cared about us for a long time." Then he leaned closer to her as if to study her face. *"Señora dolorosa,"* he said, "could it be that you are one of these *periodistas?"*

She put the glass of rum to her lips as much as anything to cover a blush. She imagined what an exposed spy must feel like. *"Sí, señor,"* she said. "I am from American television. And I am here, frankly, because I want to talk with the famous Señor Blanco."

The men sat back as if stunned. Finally, one of them said, "What do you want to know, *señora?* Perhaps we can find out for you." The other one, who had said little, said, "I have seen him. I have heard him speak."

Victoria turned her chair toward them, feeling the combination of fatigue and rum. "I want to ask him one thing—where did he come from?"

The men looked at each other. "Do you not care even more, *señora*, where his *ideas* came from?" the smiling one asked.

She looked perplexed. "People—our viewers—care more about the personalities of our leaders. They think that ideas . . . well, that ideas are . . . too complicated." She seemed to be testing the validity of her own assertion. "They seem to believe that if they know someone and trust someone, then his ideas must be all right."

The two men looked at each other and raised their eyebrows. "Can it be so?" one asked. "Perhaps some politico may be very charming and engaging, but perhaps his ideas may be very wrong—even perhaps dangerous." Then he said, "Let us say that you met this 'Ernesto Blanco,' and that you make an interview with him. How can you know that he will not be very charming to you and enchant you and those who see your movie? And perhaps his ideas will be very bad for the people." The other one said, "Or the other way. Perhaps he is not so charming, but his ideas create good for people and liberate the people."

"I . . . I don't know," she said. In all her television years, she had not seriously questioned her industry's orthodoxy—personalities are fascinating, ideas are boring. People want exposé, not discourse. "It is what works in the United States, that's all I know."

One of the men leaned closer to her. "*Es verdad, señora?* Does it truly work in the United States?" He looked at his companion and said, "I have heard that not so many people are voting in the north, that maybe half of the people who can vote are not voting."

"Or even more than half," the other man said.

By now she was much too tired to argue. "Look, *señores, por favor,* if you know how to find him, please tell Señor 'Blanco' that I want to talk to him, to do an interview for U.S. television with him, so that our people will know who he is. If he wants, he may discuss his ideas. Whatever. I simply want to have the interview." She leaned wearily forward as if to plead. "I will be honest with you. I want this story. The first interview with this man. It . . . it will . . . it will help me. It will make my boss happy. If he is happy with me, he may let me keep my job." Then, head down, she added something that surprised even her. "This man may help me. He may help me keep my job." She sighed deeply, close to tears. "He may help me keep my life."

The shorter of the two men signaled to the proprietress of the cantina. As she came forward, the two men stood and helped her up from the table. "This lady will give you a place for the night. You will be very comfortable. She will look after you. *Buenas noches, señora.*"

Suddenly, Victoria was confused and concerned. "What will happen to me? How do I return to Havana? How can I contact the camp of 'Ernesto Blanco'?"

"Do not worry. It will be taken care of. You will be contacted tomorrow," one of them said as they turned to go. The shorter man hesitated and said, "*Señora,* what would you do if Señor Ernesto required you to spend time in his camp . . . to become acquainted with his work and his ideas? What if he required this of you before making your movie?"

Feeling now lost and alone, but with a sense of little left to lose, she shrugged. "Why not? Of course, why not? It is only fair that I try to understand him and his movement. Of course I would do it, if that is the requirement."

"*Gracias,*" the two men said as they moved toward the door. "You will be looked after and then you will be met tomorrow."

Suddenly, Victoria realized that the two men, whom she had first believed to be mere bystanders and coincidental figures, were in fact part of the elaborate network that had scooped her up very early in the day—it seemed now days ago—moved her across more than half of Cuba, and deposited her here on the outskirts of Santiago de Cuba in this tiny cantina. They were part of the game, among the complex series of gatekeepers through whom she had to pass to meet Ernesto Blanco. The men were almost through the door and she through the kitchen door when she turned and called, "Tell me your names. What do I call you?"

The tall thin one in the door said, "*Mi nombre es Alejo.*"

The shorter smiling one said, "*Mi nombre es Ernesto.*"

2 7

If there was one part of his job Micky Mendoza really disliked it was strategy sessions with clients. He and his senior team were previewing their media strategy for the Cuban national elections for the finance committee of the Free Cuba Party at its headquarters in Miami. Many of his people at Wager-Down knew the key leaders of the Cuban-American community and often socialized with them. Nevertheless, this was a client-consultant relationship and the FCP had already advanced several hundred thousand dollars to its media consultants and would, at the end of the day, pay several millions in fees by the election in the spring. So, Wager-Down had to perform, to sing for its supper, and convince its client that the campaign it had put together, a media blitz, represented a winning strategy. Every time he prepared a presentation, Micky Mendoza thought political heaven must be big fat fees from anonymous clients.

"Angie, why don't you kick things off?" Micky said as seven members of the FCP finance group and four members of the Wager-Down team got their coffee and took their seats at Ollie Sanchez's large corporate conference table.

Angie pointed a laser beam at a series of flip charts. "This first series shows our placement schedule. As you can see, we have planned a classic high-low-high intensity strategy. That means, as you see here, that we will open right after the first of the year with about six weeks of heavy radio and television, and as much print as we can get, then back down for another six weeks with about half that size buy, then close the last six weeks with a full-scale blitz leading right up to election night." Her young assistant threw over a chart. "Here we show the size of the buy. We'll dominate in the early phase, we'll at least match the other side in the middle phase, and we will clearly dominate in the third phase. Now—"

"Excuse me, Angie," Olivero Sanchez said, "what do we know about the other side, the Commies? Do they know anything about this stuff? I mean, it's not like they been running democratic campaigns all their lives."

Micky said, "We're busy collecting information on that right now. It's tough because their system is still pretty closed. But we've got some people . . . well . . . let's just say we've got people making friends in high places down there. I don't want to say more than that."

Ramón Heredia of the finance committee snorted. "So do we, Micky. That's no great secret."

"What do you hear then, Ramón?" Angie asked.

Eduardo Pons said, "We hear that the Commies don't know their ass from second base about how to run a real campaign. Apparently they've been shopping around up here for somebody like you guys to help them out."

Micky said, "So far no good. Nobody here in Florida will touch them. But if the price is right, I know quite a few New York or California outfits they can pick up. Look, let's be honest. This is a business. Our clients are people with causes—campaigns for office or promotion of beliefs—but, don't hate me for saying this, for us it's a business. When we sign on, we adopt your campaign or your cause. But we're business-people. Every week we send out paychecks, and every quarter we have to show a profit. All I'm saying is, somebody out there is going to help the CSD."

Lucia Martinez, secretary of the committee, said, "Let's get to the important stuff. Show us what you're going to say—what's our message."

Micky said, "Angie . . ."

"All right"—she pointed at the next series of charts—"here are our themes. Freedom. Opportunity. Cooperation. Freedom to succeed. Opportunity to win. Cooperation with our neighbors. The whole idea is that individuals have the freedom to create their own prosperity if they cooperate with us. See, you get the democratic ideal, the capitalist ideal, and re-creation of the Yankee-Cuban partnership. The whole idea is that people can become rich by becoming partners once again with U.S. investors, companies like yours." She ran through a series of storyboard pictures portraying happy Cuban children holding hands with Uncle Sam walking, presumably, into the future, smiling *campesinos* working on, possibly, Yankee-owned sugar plantations, dignified Cuban doormen greeting elegant tourists at luxury hotels.

Micky said, "The themes are simple and the message is clear. Partnerships for prosperity. The dawn of a new age of wealth for the Cuban people. Our success is their success." He had been watching the faces of the client committee. It was important that they like it. Wager-Down had put a great deal of effort into these glitzy pictures.

Finally, Ollie Sanchez said, "Hmmm. I like it. I . . . really . . . like it. I like its subtlety. It tells a great story. It's the story of free enterprise. And it's the story of capitalism. It's what makes us great. It's what will make Cuba great." Slowly, he began to clap. Then quickly the others joined him and they were all clapping happily. There were smiles around the table.

Striking while the iron was hot, Micky said, "Emilia will tell us about the placement and the buy. This is where the story gets complicated."

Emilia, the electronic media expert, stood up. "In addition to myself, we've had a couple of our people in Havana meeting with the Ministry of Information—the media are still state-owned—about buying time. They've assured us that we will have at least equal time with the CSD and, if we're willing to pay a premium for it, they'll make additional time available. In other words, each side is guaranteed a certain block of time. Then there is a pool of time that goes at a prime rate."

Olivero Sanchez said, "Will there be enough time available to get our message across?"

Emilia said, "Yes, we'll have to pay a little more for the final burst. But we'll have enough time for the complete placement."

Sanchez looked around the table, twisting a diamond-studded pinky ring, and said, "Look here, I got an idea. Let's put a company together and buy one of the television stations and a couple of nationwide radio stations. Can we do that, Micky?"

"If we . . . no, *when* we win the election, you betcha," Micky said. "In fact, it's a great idea. Those properties will all be privatized, I assume, under a Free Cuba government. That's our philosophy. And I have to believe those media properties will be great investments. You own a TV station, a couple of radio stations, a major paper, you'll have a lot of influence. In fact, the FCP ought to make sure the major media outlets are in the hands of friends of yours."

Lucia Martinez looked around the table at her old friends, political allies, and business partners in a variety of enterprises and said, "It looks to me like those of us on the FCP finance committee can pretty much form a new media company among ourselves and pick up the best media outlets. It'll be a damn good business and it'll support our political agenda down there."

Micky said, "Let me know when you put that company together if you're looking for investors. I'd like a piece of it. First, though, we have to win the election. Now, in addition to the TV and radio ads, we'll be doing the full load of print stuff—newspapers, billboards, brochures, and handouts, whatever we need." He gestured to the shy Pinky, who stood up and displayed his own set of charts and storyboards all built around the Freedom-Opportunity-Cooperation themes. The colors, designs, and pictures all replicated those used in the television ads. The red, white, and blue colors dominated, but there were graphics using pictures and bright, clear colors of an idealized Cuba woven through all the glossy materials. They were eye-catching, vivid, and professional to the point of slickness.

"This stuff is great—for a U.S. political campaign," Ramón Heredia said, "but how do you know it will work down there? I mean, the Cubans have lived pretty grim lives for forty years. They don't have slick TV and advertising, so how do we know they won't be turned off by this stuff?"

Micky smiled and pointed at Emilia. She said, "Focus groups. Same thing we do up here. We don't create any spots or run anything without talking to focus groups. We find out what they're thinking about. We put some ads together around those concerns. We take the spots back to the focus groups and ask them to watch. Then, if they like what we show them, we keep it and if they don't, we change it. So we end up showing the people exactly what they want to see."

Angela Valdés, who up to now had been uncharacteristically silent, said, "That's what we pay you the big bucks for." They all laughed, the Wager-Down group somewhat nervously. "Speaking of which, Micky, when do we see the budget for all this? Or, since we are all engaged in an errand of mercy here and are on the side of the angels of democracy, why don't you just donate your services?"

There was an awkward titter around the table. It was as if Angela had dumped a highly odious substance in the middle of the conference table. "Well, Angela," Micky muttered, "that's a . . . a . . . that's a complicated suggestion. Of course we want the FCP, your party, to win. It's important for Cuba. It's important for us. But, ah, we're in a business. These poor people here have to make a living. We just can't . . ."

Angela had a hand to her mouth. She suddenly let out a hoot of laughter and the others joined her. "Just kidding, Micky. Just kidding. Don't look so serious. Of course, you'll get paid. We all know, and the people we represent all know, that winning this election is going to open up pretty sizable business opportunities in Cuba and all of our contributions to the FCP—to pay your bills—will produce a business payoff. It's an investment for us. You win this election for us. We'll be taken care of. Now, how much?"

The Wager-Down group seemed collectively to exhale. "Don't do that, Angela," Micky said. "We believe as strongly as you do about winning this thing. But we're in a competitive business here and we're giving up other campaigns—particularly lucrative campaigns—to do this job. Now, let's see." He stood up and yet another set of flip charts appeared. Each chart contained separate budgets for TV, radio, print advertising, billboards, even leaflets, pins, and bumper strips. It was a full-scale campaign budget fit for a large state or a small country. The last chart Micky showed totaled up all the others. The total figure was $29.7 million, a figure that included a 10 percent management fee for Wager-Down, a time-buying fee of 10 percent of the total TV and radio placement costs, and a separate consultancy fee for Pat Patton for designing and analyzing the polls and poll results. Wager-Down's fees came to just under $5 million.

This was the moment of truth. If the finance committee was going to balk, they would do so now. Micky's practice under such circumstances was to remain silent and let the client absorb the figures. If they signed on now, then there would be no complaining later.

Olivero Sanchez looked at his committee colleagues. "Any problems?" No one said anything. "All in favor?" They all raised their hands. For most of them, $29.7 million to win a country seemed a pretty good bargain. The thought had crossed more than one mind in the room that those who put up the money for this campaign would be in the enviable position of deciding who got what in the next Cuban government. That was the rough equivalent of a license to print money.

Angela squinted at the last chart and said, "What's that down at the bottom of the chart? It looks like an asterisk. I can't see it from here."

"Standard," Micky said. "Ten percent contingency. We do it in every campaign."

"Contingency?" Ollie asked. "What kind of contingency?"

Micky stood up and hooked his thumbs under his bright red suspenders. "Ladies and gentlemen. I've been in this business twenty-seven years and I have learned one lesson. Something will come up."

There were a lot of handshakes all around and a sense that this team was on its way. Victory. And Cuba would be theirs. Olivero and Angela remained behind until the others had left.

"What about this old creep . . . our 'Che Guevara' nutcase?" Angela asked. "What do we do about him?" Then she rendered a cackling laugh. "Is that your 'contingency' fee?"

Micky motioned them down the hall toward Ollie's office. Once inside he said, "I didn't want to talk about this in front of all your people and my people, but I understand that certain steps are being taken to 'expose' the old fraud."

"Expose him, how?" Olivero asked.

Micky shook his head. "You wouldn't want to know the details. But just to prove that he's not Che Guevara. You know how dumb these poor people are. They gotta have some hero of some kind. If they don't have one, they make one up—you know, some superman character—or they go dig one up from the grave."

Angela said, "So the idea is, prove he's not really Che, and this 'movement' behind him will just wither away?"

"That's pretty much the idea," Micky said.

"How do you do that?" Olivero asked.

Micky said, "Look, you don't particularly want to know the details. But Che Guevara was killed in Bolivia in 1967. He was dug up and reburied in Cuba in 1996. His grave is some kind of national monument or something. We've got people interviewing people in Bolivia who saw him dead. We've found the people who shot him. And, if it comes to it, we'll dig him up in Cuba and do a little DNA."

"Cubans won't much like that, Micky," Angela said.

"We don't intend to ask them," Micky answered.

Olivero said, "You're serious about this."

"Serious as cancer," Micky said. "We don't have a choice." He pulled a folded sheet of paper from his jacket and unfolded it. "We did a little poll down there. It's not a cross section of the country, mostly Havana, but that makes it even worse." He showed them the sheet that had only a few numbers. "Essentially this says that we have about twenty-five percent, the CSD has about the same, about a quarter or more are undecided, and the so-called 'pure republic' movement has over a quarter. We get mostly people in the city who want to own a business and make a lot of money. They get the old Commies. 'Che' gets young people, old people, women, all the greens, and almost anyone who feels left out. That's the *campesinos*, workers, truck drivers, all those people."

Angela said, "Look, hotshot, get that thirty-million-dollar TV campaign going and turn them around."

Micky shook his head. "Doesn't work that way. We've found out in the past that you can't peel off the true believers from this kind of committed base with advertising. I hate to admit it. These people are dedicated. Unlike the two parties, this movement has depth."

Olivero asked, "What do you do?"

Micky said, "I'll tell you the only thing you can do. You have to destroy the messenger. It's called a negative campaign. You destroy the other guy's credibility. If you can't do that, you destroy his character."

Angela said, "What if that doesn't work? What if these dumb *campesinos* stick with him?"

"Then we have to destroy *him*," Micky said.

2 8

■

Have you heard anything from him?" Vilma Espinosa asked.

Victor Pais said, "Only that he is in place and has his eyes and ears open. He'll keep us informed as things develop. We think we've set up a pretty secure system of communication."

"Is that all he's had to say?" Vilma persisted.

Pais said, "The only other thing is that he's surprised at how strongly these people feel about this thing—this movement, they call it."

"Is that a surprise?" José Puerta asked.

Pais said, "I guess we all thought at first that this might be some kind of a joke. You know, an old guy pops up, says he's Che, gets everybody excited, and says, 'Surprise!' "

Vilma said, "I thought from the beginning that we ought to take the old fool more seriously. Any country that can keep Santería going for three hundred years is capable of anything." Vilma's well-known agnosticism was catholic.

"Well, we took him seriously enough," Pais reminded her, "partly because of your insistence, to put your man right in the middle of his operation."

Vilma ran her fingers through her hair. "Good job, too. If this comedy turns out to be serious, we'll at least have some information to go on when we have to do something about it." She left little doubt that something would have to be done about it eventually.

"We can't do anything until we know more about it," Pais said, "and you let us know when your contact reports in. Right now, let's deal with what we do know." This was the regular meeting of the steering committee of the Cuban Social Democratic Party, more or less a reconstitution of the Politburo of the Cuban Communist Party. This meeting, coming at the end of the year, was for the purpose of assessing their strategy and the progress they were making, and it was intended to lay the groundwork for the big push after the first of the year toward the spring elections. It had been understood from the beginning that the basis for the CSD victory would be its superior network represented by the indigenous political structure built and perpetuated during four decades of Communist rule. It was well understood that the so-called Free Cubans, the hated *batistianas* in Miami, would spend a lot of money on a slick advertising campaign to overcome the natural organizational advantage of the party in power.

Ricardo Gomez had been given the responsibility of converting the old party structure into a new campaign organization. "It hasn't been easy," he reported, "but we're making progress. The cadres are having trouble understanding the idea of competition. They think this election in May will be like all the others. Just march the people to the polls. We've been holding meetings in all the provinces to explain that it's more complicated than that, that there is another party, that they'll be advertising on television like they're selling Coca-Cola, and that people can make a choice." He rubbed his forehead. "Frankly, they still don't understand it. They want Fidel to give a speech, tell everyone to vote for us, and that's the end of it. So, right now no one is very excited by this business."

Vilma snorted. "Ricky, baby, take me around to these meetings. You're being too reasonable. Too polite maybe. Let me talk to them. You got to get in the face of these cadres," she said with her nose about a foot from his, "and you got to say, 'Look, dumb-ass, get with the program. I want every one of the regions in this province, and every one of the towns and villages in these regions, and every one of the people in these towns and villages to understand one thing . . . if they don't vote for the CSD next May one, their ass is grass. Understand?' That's the way I would help them understand our program."

Ricardo shook his head. "The time may come, Vilma, when your, shall we say, direct approach is necessary. And we've already used it with the party bosses in the provinces. But when the *vaqueros* and the *campesinos* begin to understand that there will be more than one party on those little pieces of paper, and even more when they realize they can vote in secret, I'm not sure the 'direct' approach is going to work."

Antonio Oliverez, a hard-liner like Vilma, said, "This is not exactly rocket science, this election. My understanding is that there was a time in the States when mayors of the big cities could produce just about as many votes as they needed to win. No more—no less. Seems to me like that's all we have to do. Get them there. And get them to vote for us. It's a great democratic tradition."

Pais gave a deep sigh. "Those were the days also, as I understand it, when certain 'encouragements' could be offered. They got jobs. They got coal in the winter. They got ice in the summer. Anybody with a problem got some help. The 'machine' took care of its people."

Antonio said, "So what? Can't we do that? That's what the party has been doing for these people for forty years. No complaints. That's the way the system works."

Ricardo said, "We are working with the cadres on the 'encouragements.' We've got some bright young people at the campaign headquarters who are figuring out how many votes we need in each province and in each district and in each village to win. We're giving the local leadership those quotas. And we're giving them some money. Pretty soon people are going to figure out if they want to get their grandmother in a good hospital, they have to support us. If their kid wants to go to the university, they got to support us. If they want a better job, they got to support us. If a young couple wants to get married and needs a place to live, they got to support us. Like that. The way to solve your problem is to vote for the CSD."

Vilma smacked her hands together. "That's our slogan, motto, whatever you call it. 'The way you solve your problem is to vote for the CSD.' " She grinned. "See, I understand this 'democracy' pretty well after all." She looked at José Puerta, whose portfolio included the Ministry of Information. "You going to use that on the television?"

José had been struggling to master the complex dimensions of campaign advertising and had made little progress. "Sure," he said, "why not? All this stuff, this 'media,' is based on slogans anyway. We'll have to get some help. I've got our office in Washington asking around about some of these consultants"—he said the word with disgust—"who are specialists in selling politics like soap. We may have to hire one of them."

Pais said, "I think they're expensive."

"You bet," José said. "They charge a fortune. It's a real racket what those guys do." He gave a resigned shrug. "But I don't know how you do it." He looked around the table to see if anyone volunteered. Even the ebullient Vilma was silent. "So we may not have much choice." Then he added, "The good news is that we control the stations."

Ricardo said, "So that's our big advantage over that other crowd."

José said, "Yes and no. We'll try to reserve the best times to put on our programs. But apparently we have no choice but to sell radio and television time to the other side."

"Who says so?" Vilma asked defiantly.

José said, "*Tío Sam* got the Organization of American States to create this 'observer group' that intends to make sure we do everything their way. They sent us a letter the other day with a whole list of conditions for conducting the election. One of them is equal access to the media at the same cost to all sides. They're appointing this 'observer group' to make sure we follow their guidelines."

Vilma asked, "Who the hell are the 'observers'?"

"Don't know yet," José said, "but it'll probably be a bunch of out-of-work politicians."

Pais said, "We don't have much choice but to cooperate. I saw the letter. They impose trade sanctions if we don't."

Vilma shouted derisively, "So what? We had an embargo from Sam for forty years and we're still alive."

Pais shook his head sadly. "No more. That's why Fidel made his choice. Those days are over. We've got to be part of the game now. So we're going to have to play it their way."

"The good news is that we've got a political organization all over this island," Ricardo said, "and no one else does. Not the damn 'Free Cubans' and not that old quack who thinks he's Che."

"He may be a quack," Antonio Oliverez said, "but he's beginning to show up all over the place. I've met people here in Habana who say they've seen him—here in the city."

Several heads nodded. Felipe Morales said, "My son at the Universidad told me he's been meeting with students over there. They're all talking about it."

José said, "The cook in my house said her husband's brother was driving his truck back from Pinar the other day and gave the old fraud a ride."

Vilma pounded on the table. "Goddammit!" she shouted. "I thought it was just rumors." She looked up and down the table. She lowered her voice to a hiss and said, "I heard he had lunch in the cafeteria of the Ministry of Agriculture. Goddammit!" Her face was red and accusing as she looked at Pais. "What are we going to do?" He understood she meant what was he going to do.

His own face uncharacteristically red, the taciturn Pais said, "You reminded me a few minutes ago, we have someone next to him. We're trying to find out what his plans are. We—"

"His plans are to fuck up this election!" Vilma shouted. "I don't need somebody next to him to tell me that."

Pais was controlled but angry. "What do you want to do, Vilma, shoot him? He hasn't broken any laws that I know of. He—"

Vilma was standing. "It wasn't too long ago that we didn't wait for someone to break a law. We just locked them up for disturbing the peace. What do we need, a riot?"

"Sooner or later," Pais said in a measured tone, "he will step over the line. When he does, we will know about it and we will deal with it." These last five words were said with enough firmness, and a touch of menace, that even Vilma calmed down. "But, in case you haven't noticed, there are journalists from other countries, not just *del norte*, but other places, gracing our island kingdom. They are beginning to hear about Señor 'Ernesto Blanco.' If he were to be tossed in jail, do you know what would happen? I'll tell you what would happen. They would make him a martyr and an international hero overnight. Do not forget that."

"Better a dead hero," Vilma muttered, "than a live one."

Pais said, "Let us not even think about such things on the eve of a new century."

2 9

■

Nick Ferre sat in the corner of the large office of Wallace Turner, the head of the U.S. Interests Section in Havana. Occupying more prominent positions facing Turner's desk were the head of the economic section, the head of the political section, the head of consular affairs, and the chief's secretary. It was widely understood, though not discussed, that the consular man, ostensibly responsible for visa and immigration matters, actually ran the local Agency station. This was the last monthly meeting of the group in 1999. After the first of the year, they would begin to meet every other week and then once a week up until the election. For this was the subject that brought them together. Since arriving almost sixty days ago, Nick had been expected to listen and learn. This would probably be the meeting where he lost his political virginity, and he was not looking forward to it. He instinctively knew they would not like to hear what he had to say. But his turn was coming, and it couldn't be avoided.

"Nick," Turner said, "why don't you tell us what you've found out. Who's up, who's down, and—most of all—who's going to win. I want to get my money down." There were chuckles around the room.

Nick cleared his throat and pulled his chair tentatively toward the semicircle in front of the chief's desk. "I'll give you the headline if I were writing this story. 'CSD One Third, FCP One Third, Populists One Third, and One Third Undecided.'" There was another, this time more uneasy, chuckle.

Turner raised his hands palms up. "Whatever they're teaching you people in foreign service school these days, it isn't math."

"It's called 'political accounting,'" Nick said, "and, since every party always claims more than it actually has, the sum of the parts is always greater than the whole. That I learned from my uncle in Miami."

He had, he could tell, broken some ice. He continued, "Some of these numbers I got from a very interesting consultant with the Free Cubans." He checked some notes. "A woman named Scarlatti. She, of course, says they're going to run away with the thing when they start their TV ads."

"When's that?" the head of the political section asked.

"Early next year," Nick answered, "second or third week of January."

"My God," the head of the economic section gasped. "Surely, they're not going to follow our horrible example and create these interminable political campaigns."

" 'Fraid so," Nick said. "In fact, before it's over, this Cuban election is going to look a lot like late-twentieth-century U.S. politics. At least the FCP campaign is."

"How so?" Turner asked.

"According to this Ms. Scarlatti, the FCP is using a Miami-based political consultancy, the largest and most expensive in the Southeast, and their campaign is going to be almost entirely media."

"My God," the economic section chief said again in dismay.

"Look at it this way, Liz," the political section chief said, "it'll be a huge boost to the Cuban economy."

Nick added, "I think you're right. Scarlatti didn't exactly say how much, but I think they're planning to spend at U.S. levels."

"That's in the millions," the political man said.

"Tens of millions," Nick answered.

Liz, the economic specialist, said yet again, "My God. These Cubans will be blown away."

The political man said, "Or they'll laugh their asses off."

"Whatever the tune," Turner said, "they'll figure out how to dance to it." There was a knowing chuckle. "What else, Nick?"

"The Social Democrats, the incumbents, are also following the U.S. model," Nick said. "Chicago in the fifties—or maybe the thirties. They are planning to base their campaign, according to the *La Prensa* reporter"—he checked his notes again—"Alfonso Guerrera, on their existing political organization. Just convert the old party structure into a campaign structure. They expect their provincial, district, and local cadres to turn out the vote just as they have over the past forty years—and they expect them to vote for the same ticket."

The political man rolled his eyes toward the ceiling. "Has anyone told them this is going to be a *secret* ballot?"

Nick said, "They know that. But they also know the ballots in Chicago in the old days were secret. Somehow Daley's man always won."

"Yeah, but Jimmy Carter wasn't counting the ballots in Chicago," the political man huffed.

Nick said, "I guess they'll worry about that matter when the time comes. Anyway, that seems to be what they're up to. I gather they will do some advertising. But it will be about as dated as their organization."

Turner rubbed his hands together, leaned forward over his desk, and smiled conspiratorially. "One third undecided, I also can understand. Let's get to the good part. What's up with old 'Guevara'? And how in hell can he have a third?" The question the others in the room knew was cast in a tone of voice suggesting Turner would not believe a word Nick said on this subject.

Nick shrugged, a little defensively. His increasing uneasiness with the meeting's tone caused him to make a snap decision. He would not report, at least not yet, on his brief encounter with Blanco. "This is pretty . . . intuitive, I have to confess. It's just a feeling that I'm getting. I can't really back it up with any data. But whatever the old man is up to, it's resonating. His ideas are moving around this country on some kind of jungle-drum network. Now, Scarlatti laughs at him, says he doesn't even show up in their early poll numbers. But, I think . . . I think she's lying. She pushed the issue too hard. She came down on the old guy like a ton of bricks, laughed at him, said it was the funniest thing she's ever run across in years in politics, a lot of stuff like that. But, she . . . she protested too much. She talked too much about an old character she claimed to think was a wacko." He thought momentarily and looked at his notes. "Then this reporter Guerrera, he said the Social Democrats claimed to think the old man ought to be locked up. But he said he thinks they're worried about him. He couldn't say why, but he said he knows it. Finally, Guerrera tried to get his editor to let him do a story on the old man. The editor, who's in the pocket of the CSD Party bosses, told Guerrera they'd do a piece on him all right, closer to the election when it might do some good. Guerrera said over some *cervezas* that his paper was going to make a fool out of the old man. But he didn't sound to me like a guy who was looking forward to the assignment."

"You give the old guy a third on this kind of stuff?" the head of the political section asked derisively. He turned and addressed himself to Turner. "I've talked to my sources and they agree with the two parties.

'Che Guevara' is the joke of Havana. Up in the States, between Letter-
man and Leno he'd be gone in a week."

Nick blushed. He had effectively been slapped down by his superior.
He studied his notes and played his last card. "There is press interest in
the States. I don't know whether the press office has mentioned it to
you, Ambassador, but some reporters are beginning to come down for
background on the election. And word's out up north about this 'Guevara.' I only mention it so you don't get blind-sided by a press question."

The consular man said, "Reporters? You mean Savidge? Victoria Savidge started on the downhill slide about ten years ago. She's out of gas
and everyone's afraid to tell her. My friends in Washington say that
TPN keeps her on because Marshall Stuart is"—he glanced at Liz,
straightened his tie, and said—"well, let's just say he's getting the last
few miles out of that model before trading it in." His colleagues laughed
raucously at the joke.

Though far from prudish, Nick was brought up to resent slander on a
lady's virtue. "I've talked to her," he said, "and she intends to find Señor
Blanco and interview him. She claims they have found worldwide interest
in him from the few times they've mentioned him. He strikes some kind
of spark in the third world especially. And, by the way," he added, "Blanco
may be the joke of Havana. But don't tell the university students that. I've
been spending time over there and he has a following."

"Students?" the consular man snorted. "Those the same students that
scared everybody in the States in the sixties until they all got mortgages
and potbellies?"

Turner sensed the session turning ugly at Nick Ferre's expense and
decided to bring him into the club. "Look, Nick, let me explain our
position here. Obviously, this isn't to go outside the room, but it does
represent what I think we can call 'administration policy' on this election. This country is important to us. We've still got Guantánamo and
that's a vital part of our Western Hemisphere defense network. This
country has been outside our sphere of influence for almost half a century, and we need to get it back. We want U.S. companies to come here
and invest. We want a very large and solid U.S. business establishment
here to provide economic stability, jobs, opportunities. They will require
a solid, probusiness political base, the right kind of investment, tax, insurance, and partnership laws. They'll particularly want the right kinds
of laws on foreign ownership of local assets, protection against repatri-

ation, all that stuff." Turner stood up and walked to his window facing out on the broad Malecón and thence to the sea. "The only way to ensure all these things happen is"—he scratched his head thoughtfully— "well, to see that the Free Cubans win."

Nick watched him and seemed to see a dim picture beginning to emerge against a dark background.

"There must not be any of Uncle Sam's fingerprints on this process," Turner mused. "This must, above all, be an open, honest, fair election. But, after that open, honest, fair election, the Free Cubans *must* have the most votes." He turned to look at Nick, as the others in the room did, and said gently, "It's just that simple."

Nick was remembering stories he had heard in school and in the foreign service about government money being funneled into political consultancies in foreign elections, assistance given to the "right" parties and the "right" candidates, about companies with huge investments in foreign countries visiting the State Department and the White House and explaining the importance of their plant, their facilities, their money in a country with an election coming up and then hearing that certain financial assistance made its way through complex cutouts and offshore banks to the parties and candidates who had given guarantees to protect those investments and assets. Nick felt embarrassed now, not only for himself but also for these people in the room who may have had at one time early in their diplomatic careers some notion of idealism and for Turner whose job required him to initiate young foreign service officers into the brutal fraternity of *realpolitik*. He tried to think of what he might say to them by way of an apology for his naïveté and he could think of nothing.

Finally, he said, "Well, now at least I understand the program." He shook his head and laughed with a slight note of bitterness. "If all of this had just been explained to me up in Washington, it sure would have saved all of you a lot of trouble."

Turner spoke deferentially, as if to a student. "We felt you would understand things better after you had a chance to see things down here firsthand. We needed you here. You had the skills we needed in addition to the language and family history. The great personnel computer at Foggy Bottom tossed your name to the top of the heap, and we didn't want to scare you off by making you think the deck was totally stacked."

"What I hear you saying is that the deck may not be stacked yet, but that we intend to stack it before it's dealt," Nick said.

"That's a little harsh," the consular man said. "We have a favorite that we intend to help in deniable ways and frankly in ways that have very little risk of even requiring deniability. It's an easy choice for us. The so-called Social Democrats are the same old warmed-over Communists with somewhat brighter smiles. In exchange for recognition and lifting the trade embargo, we don't intend to let a gang stay in power that started this whole thing."

"The Cuban people will thank us, Nick," Turner said.

Nick said, "What about the old man? What about the true republic movement? What's wrong with them? They're not Communists."

Turner said, "They're not viable, Nick."

"They might be with our help," Nick countered too quickly. He was becoming a quarrelsome advocate.

The political man said, "The U.S. treasury isn't big enough to make them viable. 'Ernesto Blanco' is a joke." He barked a laugh and lit a cigarette.

"How do we know that?" Nick asked, trying too desperately not to sound desperate. "Why not give them a chance to prove they're at least worth talking to?"

The economic counselor turned halfway around to look at Nick squarely for the first time. She was a greatly overweight chain-smoker who had given up years ago any effort to do anything with her hair. Although she did not address him as "young man," that was distinctly her tone of voice. "We are talking here about Che-fucking-Guevara. If you want to try to sell that to this Congress, let alone corporate America, be my guest. You will deserve an Oscar, an Emmy, and quite possibly the Nobel Peace Prize."

Nick's deference to seniority and authority crossed its fragile boundary. "I'm not trying to 'sell' anybody anything. I came down here apparently under a mistaken impression that we were here to help encourage and possibly oversee the first democratic election in modern Cuban history. Nobody explained to me—until right now, that is—that the foreign policy establishment of the United States of America had set itself up to pick the winners in emerging democracies. That being the clear case, I now understand considerably better than an hour ago what I'm expected to do here."

Turner shook his head sadly. "That's putting it a little strongly, Nick. That characterization has a . . . shall we say . . . *colonial* connotation to it."

Nick strayed ever nearer the bounds of diplomatic—and career—propriety. "It wouldn't do for Uncle Sam, the last and only superpower, to also be the last colonialist, would it? Particularly in the service of Corporate America." He smiled benignly around the room. "I know none of us would want it on our résumés that our real master was the East India Tea Company."

"All right!" the consular official said. "That's enough." He pointed at Turner and said, "If Mr. Ferre wants to work for the other side, that's his business. I'm sure there are those in Washington who will be interested to know his true loyalties. But I don't have to waste my time listening to this adolescent horseshit." He stormed toward the door, turned, and looked at Nick. "Radicalism in America isn't dead after all. I'll confess, I find it surprising . . . maybe even shocking, to be honest. But what I didn't know was that it had crept back into the U.S. foreign service. *That* is significant."

Nick had enough experience to know that the CIA station chief in Havana was headed for his office to file a report on the dubious loyalty of the hotshot young Cuban-American political analyst sent down by the State Department to observe the Cuban election. He further knew that this report was doomed to haunt him for the rest of his diplomatic career. Don't touch Nick. Old Nick, the lad, is radioactive. Went back home and turned native. Never send a hyphenated American back to the old country. They always go over. And so forth, and so forth. But this last five minutes had gone by in five seconds. It was one of those rapid-fire exchanges that could, and under the right conditions of heat and pressure would, define a lifetime. Nick had a clear sense he had just defined his in a way any reasonable person would judge to be unhelpful.

The room was silent as Turner sought a diplomatic resolution. "Them are the rules, folks. We don't make 'em, we just play by 'em. I served under an ambassador once in"—he mused—"maybe it was in Salvador . . ."

Nick thought, God save me from ever becoming a nostalgic old codger.

"Salvador it was. He said, 'Young man, if you don't like the policy, your place is not in the foreign service. Your place is in Congress or the White House where the policy is made.'"

Nick knew this was for his benefit, but he waited before responding. "It seems to me the politicians look to us to advise them on what our policy ought to be in any given country. We're supposed to be the experts. We're supposed to know these places. Is it too naive to suppose that we could advise the secretary to advise the president to advise the Congress that there is some kind of new force at work here that might be worth giving a chance?"

Liz, the economic chief, had had enough. She struggled to her feet, waved to Turner, and left. "Nick, I am afraid this has already been resolved way above our pay grade. The president and the congressional leadership are united behind it. There are a lot of U.S. companies queued up to get in here. To a large degree our future policy in Cuba is dependent on their willingness to invest here and support a future government favorable to us and favorable to their investment requirements. Quite honestly, this train has left the station. Even if this old guy called himself Abraham Lincoln, I don't think anything would change."

Nick sensed the meeting was over. The political counselor stood up, waved to Turner, avoided Nick, and left. Turner studied some papers on his desk. Nick badly needed to get out of this office, out of the Interests Section, and into the fresh sea air on the Malecón. He headed for the door, then turned and said, "What should I do? Pack up? Seek another assignment? If the fix is in, I don't think I have much of a job here."

Turner studied him, his eyebrows raised. "Of course you do. What are you talking about? We still need to know what the other guys are doing. We still need intelligence on the Social Democrats. We still need to know about the undecideds. We still need to know about the campaigns, the strategies, the polling, what everybody is up to. Of course you have a job to do. So go do it."

Nick opened the door and Turner said, "And most of all we need to know about Ernesto Blanco. If he really has created a network, if there really is any kind of groundswell, if there really is any kind of movement, we need to know that. It is important to our duties. I think you're overestimating his reach. But what do I know? What if he does become a factor? What if he takes votes away from our friends, the Free Cubans? That's crucial for us to know. So, if I were you, I would not do what you're planning to do based on this meeting, that is, ignore him. Just the contrary. If I were you, I'd get as close to that operation as ever I could. I'd get to know Señor Blanco. I would get to know everything there is to know about the True Republic movement. It may prove crucial to us in the endgame."

■ ■ ■

I don't claim to know much about economics. I never did. I never had the patience for it. It's much too scientific. Besides, even in the old days, I never believed in "economic man." What a bloodless, demeaning goddamn idea. Men and women are humans. They have souls and spirits. We Communists made the same mistake as the capitalists. And that is to believe that all that was important was work, food, and shelter. Important? Of course. Essential? Obviously. Definitive? Not a goddamn chance.

Men have souls and spirits and crazy human dreams and hopes. Mostly hopes. I haven't met an economist yet who can quantify a hope. Maybe it's because none of them have any. They wouldn't know a hope if it jumped up and smacked them in the face.

So I guess it was the emergence of this so-called neoliberalism, together with Fidel's predictable departure, that brought me back here. It was a clear shot at something new, some new approach, based on the ancient ideals. Neoliberalism is a fancy-sounding license to steal. Reagan and Thatcher simply resuscitated the corrupt and discredited theory of laissez-faire—leave me alone. I'm all right and to hell with everybody else. Nothing new in that. It was discarded a long time ago when societies developed a social conscience. Along came the neoliberals and said, It's okay. Who said you had to have a conscience. This is a dog-eat-dog world. So, every man for himself, and the devil take the hindmost.

Unless you end up on top of the heap, or started there with a silver place setting in your mouth, it's not particularly attractive economics. And it sure as hell isn't a very attractive outlook on humanity. Look at what's happened to the countries that went back to this laissez-faire. Communities torn up. Families torn up. High divorce rates, alcoholism, crime. Part of the social policy that inevitably goes along with laissez-faire is incarceration. You don't have to be a genius to know that people without work and without any hope of work and without any help from the society are going to figure out a way to feed their families. Of course, they follow the example of the "successful" people and they become capitalists. That's after all what they're told to do. And the most efficient economic investment of their labor is selling drugs.

It's capitalism. Why do the capitalists get so upset? It's laissez-faire, for damn sure. Leave us alone. Don't tell us to become capitalists and then throw us in jail for selling what gives us the biggest return on our labor investment. They've got over a million people in jail del norte. *What did they expect? It's exactly what anyone who had even an ounce of sense about human nature could have predicted. Economic theory at war with social values. Economics wins every time. Laissez-faire!*

Up to now my little experiment has been a lot of fun. A lot of work, but also a lot of fun. In a few days it will be the new year, the century year, the millennium year. I have a sense things are going to get a lot more serious. Four months to the election. We've got the campesinos, *the students, the women, the greens excited. We've got a lot more support than the parties suspect. But they'll find out soon. When they find out, they will try something. One or the other or both. They'll try to make me look old and foolish. That will fail. Then the serious stuff will start. They'll send somebody after me. No question in my mind. The only question is who, and when, and how. I can't really tell Alejo. He would have either a heart attack or a nervous breakdown. Maybe I will find a way to put this woman to use. For someone in her line of work, she really doesn't seem too bad.*

I never liked journalists. Always hated them actually. Unless I could find a way to use them. I don't want to use her in the bad sense. I want to use her in the good sense. And I have a feeling she wouldn't mind that. When we met her that night, she was not what I expected. She's a human being in an antihuman enterprise. Talk about capitalism! But she's like a lot of them. Used up. She thought she would be a professional, someone who had to train and be qualified and carry out serious professional duties. And they've used her. You can see it in her eyes. And they've used her up. And you can see that in her eyes. She's closer to the end of her rope than even she understands. It's really sad. Look at that jewelry and that hair. That's really her problem. She's coming to realize that she sold out her life for thirty sets of gold earrings.

What if I find a way to get her to help me and it helps her at the same time? Maybe I can buy some time by using this television to talk about the idea, the true republic ideal. Not much, just enough to get people interested. If you get too near the eye of that camera, it will steal your soul. The Indians are right. To take your picture is to steal your soul. So I'll give her a chance to try to understand the movement. Then we'll let them turn on the camera. She'll know the right questions then. She won't waste the opportunity with the silly stuff. Who are you really, Señor Blanco? Were you not killed in Bolivia in 1967? If you were killed in Bolivia in 1967, señor, how is it that you can be back here in Cuba more than thirty years later hiding out in the Sierra like some barbudo revolutionary?

No, I hope she will say, Señor Blanco, what do you mean by this "true republic"? How can these poor dumb campesinos possibly understand ancient Greece? Are you not expecting too much from poor illiterate people? Do not these people need some smart politicians and businesspeople to organize their lives and tell them how to live? These questions she should ask. And, when the time comes, if I am correct that she is a misused decent human being, I believe she will. Turn on the camera. Make the questions. Make the answers. Turn off the camera. Back into the rocks and the trees.

What will then happen to her? It is impossible to know. Should I care? She is after all a grown-up woman who seems to be able to look after herself. Should I care? Of course I should not. We can get her to Santiago and then back to Havana exactly as she came. She will have sent her interview across the airwaves. Everyone will see I am just a harmless arthritic, asthmatic old man. Maybe the Communists and the capitalists will leave me alone to do my work.

No way. Then the hard work just begins. This woman, this Victoria, will be gone and we can then move our camp quickly and quietly as we must. Our inevitable tormentors will not be able to find us from the clanking of her many bracelets. That is for sure. She will be gone. Me and Alejo and the boy Rafael and Otra Vez if he chooses will disappear only to emerge one night within sight of the gates of Guantánamo and the next night in Pinar and the next night in Matanzas. We will strike like the true revolutionaries that we are. Strike and move on. We will bedevil their flanks and trick them. We will strike and melt away. We will disappear in the sunlight and materialize like ghost warriors in the moonlight. We will scare them witless. We will be everywhere at once. We will have the energy of hundreds. They will think there are surely several Rafaels, dozens of Alejos, and hundreds of Ernestos.

There will be no place for a woman with clanking bracelets and hair like the Medusa among our ranks.

PART III

■

JANUARY–FEBRUARY 2000

3 0

■

On New Year's Day, 2000, the people of Havana, Santiago de Cuba, Matanzas, Pinar del Río, Santa Clara, and every other major city of Cuba awoke, somewhat later than usual, to find that the doorways of churches and cathedrals, of schools and hospitals, of city halls and administration buildings, of libraries and cantinas, of lobbies in apartment buildings, of many shops and stores, all were plastered with a flier crudely printed on paper of the cheapest quality. Everywhere it appeared it bore the same message:

People of Cuba

Soon we will decide our fate. If the powers permit, it will be done openly and fairly. We can choose to let the state run our lives. We can choose to let wealth run our lives. Or we can choose to run our own lives.

The Movement of the True Republic believes in the common sense of the people of Cuba. We believe in each community governing itself and contributing to the self-governance of the whole society. We believe the will of the people is greater than political authority or concentrated wealth.

We are ordinary Cubans of neither the Left nor the Right. We are neither Communists nor capitalists. We believe in education for all. We believe in medicine for all. We believe in jobs for all. We believe in private ownership of land by individuals, not corporations. We believe our government should be run by the people not by career politicians.

Our Movement advocates the creation of strong local governments in each community. Everyone should participate in selecting the leaders of these governments. The leaders should serve at the will of the majority, but should protect the rights of the minority. Local taxes should be used to build the schools, clinics, parks, and all local facilities. In communities with fewer resources, the national government should provide additional resources so that every community in our country has an equal chance.

In the True Republic, no child will go without food, no old person will go without medicine, no worker will go without a job, no person will go without adequate shelter. As much as possible, the local republic will have the power to help meet these needs.

Our Movement is one of radical democracy. All can and should take part in government. Power will not be bought—or sold. Neither the state nor wealth will own the power. Only the people will.

The Movement of the True Republic asks for your help. Bring your friends and join us. The parties of power and wealth have their support. We need your support. Join our Movement.

Viva la república auténtica!

Viva Cuba!

As the morning grew mature and the fumes of the celebration rum gave way to strong coffee, people began to gather around the fliers. They read them several times and they discussed them. In some places, local officials of the ruling party or supporters of the Free Cuban Party tried to tear down the flimsy leaflets pinned to the doors with tiny thumb-tacks. But in every case they were shoved aside and told to mind their own business. In many places there were lively, usually heated, discussions. Local people had no way of knowing at the moment that tens of thousands of their fellow Cubans were repeating their experience in thousands of public places throughout the country. Everyone had his own view that this was an odd local phenomenon carried out by some isolated true believer. But within days, certainly within a week, when people had talked to their neighbors, traveled from town to town, or talked to a sister in the next province, it became apparent to all that something worth considering was at work here. Suddenly, the Movement of the True Republic was the talk of every village square, every workplace, every cantina.

Now the myth of the ancient Che who had returned to stir up yet another revolution took on a complex reality. *El viejo* could not himself have planted all these leaflets. He might be a ghost but even a ghost could not be everywhere at once in one night. *El viejo* clearly had some friends. A lot of them. And they were all over Cuba. Overnight, the mere fact of distributing thousands and thousands of these little manifestos made the movement a social force to be reckoned with. People looked sideways at each other wondering, Is she with the movement? Did José put up that manifesto? Is it my neighbor or the schoolteacher? Or, *Madre de Dios,* perhaps it is my daughter or my husband. It became a new and sometimes exciting social game to guess who was the leader of the local cell. But those who knew or thought they knew—based upon the sly wink or the furtive disappearance—would not tell. The local leaders of the party in power and the Free Cubans were themselves too eager to know. There was fear of retribution. So, almost without even thinking about it, tens of thousands of Cubans became coconspirators of the movement. If they knew or thought they knew who was with the movement, they would not tell those who seemed to want to know the most.

Thereafter, routinely but not regularly the same fliers were found by kids in their classrooms, by soldiers in their barracks, by *campesinos* in the fields, by shopkeepers in their produce boxes, by patients in hospitals, by patrons in movie theater seats. They were taken home and discussed. They were passed around and debated on the streets and in the shops. In surprising numbers the debates involved someone who just happened to be able to discuss the principles of the movement, to answer questions, to explain how the true republic might work. Little explanation was required, however, to demonstrate the difference between the ideals of the true republic movement and the politics of the old Left and the old Right.

The phenomenon took a new twist one day in early January when the door to Victor Pais's office in the Palacio de la Revolución burst open and Vilma Espinosa charged through waving a thin sheet of paper. "Goddammit, Victor! This shitty thing was in the chair at my desk. It's that goddamn what-do-you-call-it . . . 'movement' . . . propaganda. 'Pure Republic' shitty thing." She threw the helpless leaflet on the floor and tried to dance on it before it even hit the carpet. The leaflet skittered across the floor, making her look even more distraught and helpless.

"Goddammit!" she shouted as she tried to stamp out the movement with her high heels.

Pais was torn between the comedy of her helpless dance and his horror at the audacity of the movement in penetrating the holy of holies of the Cuban Social Democratic Party, né Communist Party of the People's Republic of Cuba. "Sit down, Vilma." The first step was to end the comedic flamenco. He picked up the leaflet and shook his head at the mystery of it. "This thing was brought home by my grandson—from his school—two days ago. He wanted me to explain what it was. Then my wife found one in the food shop," this being the special store available only to government officials, Vilma knew. "Now I can't drive down the street without seeing people who should be working standing around instead discussing this thing." He wadded it up and banked it off a wall into a wastebasket in the far corner of the room.

"How did it get in my office, Victor?" Vilma demanded to know. She was making the obvious point that, if it was in her office, it was, for all practical purposes, everywhere. Her tone was sufficiently accusatory to suggest that Pais himself might have put it there.

Pais shrugged. "No idea, Vilma. I expect when you cool off you'll find out that it was José or Ricardo having a joke on you."

Vilma sighed. That explanation hadn't occurred to her and it gave her a sudden wave of relief. "They are all over the place, you know."

Pais nodded, feeling helpless. "Look," he said, "you have to expect stuff like this. I told everybody in our group when this thing first began that it would get pretty crazy." He pointed at the wastebasket. "This is just somebody trying to rattle our nerves. It's a kind of guerrilla warfare . . . like we used to do. Psychological warfare. Rattle the other side. Keep them off balance. Maybe they'll do something crazy and you can take advantage of it. Che taught us all of this. . . ."

Suddenly the impact of his rambling observation hit them both. There was a silence that neither wished to break. Pais finally said, "It's common guerrilla tactics. Don't worry about it. I've heard this kind of stuff happens in every election *del norte*."

Voices were heard coming down the hall. Pais looked at his watch. He had forgotten they had their weekly campaign meeting—the first of the new year—right now. He and Vilma joined the others in the adjoining conference room. The dozen or so leaders of the Cuban Social Democratic Party got their coffee and came to order. Pais said, "José, weren't you going to tell us something at this meeting about this 'polling' that we have to do? Public opinion . . . that stuff?"

José Puerta nodded affirmatively. "We decided a few weeks ago that we had to conduct some public opinion polls about this election. So I looked around." He pointed at Ricardo Gomez—"Ricardo helped me . . . and we found this outfit in California that does this kind of stuff. They had a lot of experience in U.S. elections and they seem to know how to do this. So we hired them and they did their surveys before the holidays. They pick out some 'sample' they call it that is supposed to represent all the people and they ask them a lot of questions. About the parties. 'Who will you vote for?' 'If you don't know, which one do you like?' that sort of thing."

Ricardo said, "Then they analyze all of these interviews and they tell you what is going to happen."

"Not quite," José said. "It's more like what would happen if the election was right now. But they tell you when they give you these numbers that a lot can happen in the next few weeks—sixteen weeks—before the election."

Vilma was, as usual, impatient. She didn't care about the scientific mumbo-jumbo. "So what does it say, this poll?"

José smiled as he reached inside a manila envelope. Dramatically he withdrew a thick sheaf of papers, possibly thirty or forty pages. Those next to him could make out columns and columns of closely packed numbers. They were distributed so neatly and uniformly that only a computer could have produced them. José straightened his shirt cuffs and cleared his throat, enjoying the moment. "Here is what they say. Free Cuba Party . . . eleven percent. Ten percent undecided. Cuban Social Democratic Party"—there was a dramatic silence—"seventy-nine percent!"

The room erupted into cheers. Vilma jumped up and down and shouted, "I knew it! I knew it!" She circled the room hugging everyone and giving José a locker-room whack on the butt. There were handshakes and high fives and pounding on the conference table until the coffee cups rattled.

When the racket quieted down, Pais said, "José. This 'movement' that puts out all these little manifestos, what do *los californianos* say about it?"

José laughed. "I really don't know, Victor. They said it wasn't even worth asking about."

*   *   *

Shortly thereafter, the steering committee for the Free Cuba Party held a similar session in its Miami headquarters. Routine campaign business was now conducted in Havana where the party headquarters was the command post for day-to-day operations. Despite the routine use of sophisticated electronic detection gear to sweep for bugs, however, party officials still did not trust the integrity of their offices and hotel rooms in Havana and instead chose to fly key organizational people, like E. F. Scarlatti and a few others, to Miami for top-secret strategy discussions. This particular meeting was to review plans to kick off the media campaign in one week, a campaign designed to peak on the eve of the first of May election.

Micky Mendoza led off. "We've reached agreement with the Cuban government regarding our demands for purchasing television and radio time. In the end, greed overcame all barriers. The Communications Ministry realized it could make a lot of money selling us time for political advertising. We got virtually everything we wanted—thanks particularly to the good work of Emilia and E.F." The committee gave them both enthusiastic applause. "So, we'll start running our radio spots next week at a high-intensity rate. A week later we'll start the TV spots and increase those throughout late January and early February. Then we'll reduce both buys somewhat in late February and early March. Then in late March we'll come on strong on both television and radio with a saturation buy that will carry right up to election eve. High-low-high. That's what's worked for us in all our campaigns, including the one we did—very successfully, I might add—for the tobacco industry in '98."

The lights went down and a screen came down at the far end of the room. "Here's what we're opening with." They watched as an ordinary-looking Cuban woman walked down a brightly lit Havana street. There was bouncy salsa music in the background. The camera panned slightly ahead to show her approaching the headquarters of the Social Democratic Party. As she started to enter, she looked inside and saw rows of heavy-jowled, Soviet-looking commissars and aging, seedy-looking *barbudos* sitting behind bureaucratic desks stamping papers. The woman paused, put a hand dramatically to her mouth and looked around. The camera panned across the street to the Free Cuba Party headquarters. She paused momentarily, looked at the brightly lit rooms full of eager, enthusiastic young people singing and dancing. The salsa music came up to a crescendo as the woman dramatically crumpled her Social Democratic leaflet and crossed the street to enter the Free Cuba offices. The last still frame superimposed "Join Free Cuba—Now!" on the scene.

Committee members applauded vigorously. They watched a half-dozen additional spots of equal simplicity and then, with the lights back up, they listened to the radio spots that consisted largely of a mellifluous male voice seductively suggesting there were limitless possibilities in a Cuba governed by the Free Cuba Party. "That's the first flight of ads," Micky said. "We'll run attack ads in the middle. Go after the other guys." He chuckled. "Wait'll you see the thuggy-looking guys we've lined up to play the old Commies. They're a hoot. These guys'll make Karl Marx look like Tom Cruise."

After answering a series of questions about the frequency of the ad placement, the location of radio and television stations, the possibility of genuine national saturation, Micky said, "We've got a little bonus surprise for you. He gestured at Pat and said, "Pat's completed his first in-depth poll in Cuba. I think you'll be interested in the results. And keep in mind these numbers predate any electronic media advertising. Pat."

Pat hauled his bearlike figure to its feet. He snuffed out a cigarette in an ashtray conveniently placed next to the NO SMOKING, PLEASE sign. He rubbed his eyes and frowned. "You got to understand, Cuba isn't like any place on earth. This place is somewhere back in the political ice age. By comparison, Russia today is a flourishing democracy. These people have been shut out of virtually all modern media flows." He shook his head in wonder. "Polling down there today must be a lot like the early days of Gallup. We had to completely rework our standard questionnaires to make the whole process much, much simpler. In some ways it was an educational exercise. In most other ways, it was a nightmare."

Micky and other Wager-Down people who had worked with Pat over the years understood this was part of the shtick. You had to make the job seem impossibly difficult to justify the huge fees. "In some ways," Pat continued, "the hardest part was the training program. We always use local people offshore, and we have to train them. I mean, these people were really nice to work with—but they didn't have a clue what we were trying to do. We did some test runs and it was a disaster. Our local interviewer would end up spending the morning over coffee. Get one interview done in the time it was supposed to take to do about four. Can't motivate these people." Pat rubbed his salt-and-pepper beard. "You win this election, all I can say is you're going to have a hell of a time running this country."

Micky made a circle with an index finger. Speed it up. "The other thing," Pat said, "was the sample. What demographics the Cubans have are primitive. Either that or they're not giving us the sophisticated data. Either way, it was really tough to create a sample. We did our best. But I'd have to say, compared to the four percent margin we use up here, down there you got to have a six to eight percent margin of error."

"Give us the numbers, Pat," Micky urged.

Finally, Pat smiled. "Okay. During the period December eighth to December seventeenth, we carried out"—here he checked an unruly stack of papers scattered in front of him and found some handwritten notes—"four hundred sixty-five in-depth interviews with adult Cuban men and women eligible to vote and most likely to vote. By the way, given the traditions created by the Commies, expect a spectacularly high turnout in May." He looked at the numbers again. "Well, I'll spare you all the break-outs—although they're really interesting—and get to the bottom line. We got for the Social Democrats . . . twenty-two percent. For the Free Cuba Party, we got"—he looked around the room and lowered his voice—"seventy-eight percent."

There was stunned silence. Then the party chair Olivero Sanchez said, "Yes!" and they all began to clap and cheer. Pat signaled to one of his young aides at the door and in came waiters with champagne bottles and glasses and trays of expensive canapés. Free Cuba Party balloons were brought in with paper streamers. A boombox was put on the table and a tape with the party anthem began to play. It was as if they had just been declared victors in the election campaign. The celebration replaced the remainder of the discussion agenda and went through a number of bottles of very fine champagne. As the noise began to subside, Angela Valdés cornered Pat and said, "Let me ask you something. You didn't give any numbers for undecideds."

Pat stared over her shoulder. "That's because there weren't any."

"There weren't any undecideds?" Angela asked incredulously. She had been a candidate for the Miami city council and had lost in the final days of a close campaign when most of the 18 percent of the undecided voters went against her.

"None," Pat said. "They're against the old Commies and they're overwhelmingly for us."

She shook her head in disbelief as a waiter filled her glass. "One other thing. What about this 'movement,' 'republic' whatever. You know, the old guy who says he's Che. Do they really not show up?"

Pat made a face. "He doesn't say that he's Che. Other people say that he's Che."

"Well, surely they have some support," she persisted.

"Maybe so," Pat said lighting a cigarette. "But I didn't even include them. It's an insignificant political cult and it's not going anywhere."

Angela said, "Did you hear that story about the leaflets? E.F. said somebody put up a lot of leaflets on New Year's Day."

Pat admired E.F.'s figure in its tight dress across the room. "Hype," he said. "We did that kind of stuff in some early campaigns I was in. Hire some kids to spread these leaflets around. Creates the impression of a huge movement. Lots of people. Dead of night. You never see them. They're everywhere. We call it 'The Wizard of Oz.'"

"Wizard of Oz?" she asked, mystified.

Pat said, "You know. The movie. Dorothy and those other guys . . . tin man, cowardly lion . . . finally get to the Wizard and they hear this terrifying voice telling them to go away. And the little dog—Toto—pulls the curtain back and it's a little old man with a megaphone. Smoke and mirrors."

Confused, she shook her head and walked away. People merrily began to clear the room. Micky stayed behind until the others had gone off into the night and, as Pat crammed his scattered papers into a battered leather briefcase, said, "Pat, let me ask you something. I won't tell the others. But I got to know. What were the *real* numbers?"

Pat laughed and crossed to shut the door. He studied his handwritten notes. "Last week I found out who the Social Democrats are using. It's an outfit in California—Public Opinion Research—run by a friend of mine. We exchanged numbers." He noticed the shock on Micky's face and waved a dismissive hand. "Get over it, Mick. Happens all the time. You know that. Anyway, here's what he gave his clients." He looked at the numbers again and began to splutter with laughter. It took him a while to gain control. "Free Cuba—eleven percent. Ten percent undecided. Social Democrats—seventy-nine percent."

Micky was stunned. "Almost the reverse? Pat! What the hell is going on? That's crazy! You can't have numbers that far apart!"

"Oh, yes, you can," Pat laughed.

"How?" Micky pleaded. "How is it possible?"

Pat said, "I'll tell you how it's possible." He brought Micky around the table with a beckoning finger. Then he whispered, "They're lying. People are lying. They're lying to pollsters. It's happening up here more and more. Between us? You can't trust any political polls anymore. All my numbers are phony now. People don't trust pollsters any more than they do the politicians or the press. Politicians, press, and pollsters. We're the problem. They know if they tell us what they really think, we'll just run to our client-politicians who will say exactly what the people want them to. The only chance people have now to get a straight answer is to lie to us as a means of smelling out the politicians who are just following the polls. When they hear the lie coming back to them, they know they're dealing with a phony."

Micky stared at Pat. What he had heard was not exactly news to him. He knew his business to be corrupt and corrupting. "But," he said, "the Cubans? How could they have figured this out already? They haven't even been through a democratic election."

Pat put a paw on his shoulder. "Look, pal. These people may be behind, but they're not stupid. They've had to trick a centralized bureaucracy for decades. For all they know, one of my people shows up on their doorstep asking a lot of questions, could be—probably is— someone from party headquarters." Pat laughed until he coughed up processed nicotine. "They told us exactly what they thought we wanted to hear. Frankly, I'm surprised we got twenty-two percent for the other side."

Micky shook his head at how complicated it was all becoming. Then he said, "Okay. What are the real numbers?"

Pat looked at his scribbled notes. "The real numbers? Let's see." He hummed to himself. "Actually, it's quite interesting. Social Democrats about twenty-five percent; we're at about the same. Maybe twenty-four percent. Then we got about twenty percent undecided."

"That leaves . . . about thirty percent unaccounted for, Pat," Micky said.

Pat laughed again. "Oh, yeah. That thirty percent. That goes to the 'Movement for the True Republic.' You remember. Our old friend Che."

3 1

■

Routinely contacting his sources around the island from the hotel suite that doubled as his office high atop the Hotel Nacional, the Associated Press wire service reporter picked up enough pieces of the New Year's Day mass leafleting incident to file a feature piece about the bizarre and mysterious true republic movement. It ran in the second section of those few U.S. papers that chose to carry it. This story triggered a decision by *The Washington Post*'s chief investigative reporter, Woody Robertson, to knock down the Che Guevara myth once and for all. Things were slow politically in the States anyway and it seemed like a chance to put the upcoming Cuban elections in some kind of perspective. The *Post*'s editors saw it as a public service to help the Cubans get rid of nuisance political baggage from the past.

As he had on repeated occasions in the past, the *Post*'s man started with the CIA. He found out all he could about Che Guevara from his sources at the Agency. They were only too happy to cooperate. Che himself was long dead and it was not doing the Agency any good in establishing a new network in Cuba to keep running into his ghost. They had an interest in seeing the old fraud claiming to be Che exposed and gotten rid of, if for no other reason than that the CIA itself had played a role in tracking Che down in the Bolivian outback and expediting his execution. It was uncomfortable to have that subject revived by a character pretending to be the victim of the execution. Besides opening virtually all of the voluminous Che files from the mid-fifties, when the Agency picked Che up in its routine surveys of Latin American rebels, to his death in Bolivia in 1967, the Agency put the *Post* reporter onto a number of retired agents who had chased the revolutionary throughout Central America, Africa, and other parts of the world during the 1960s and two or three who had direct experience with the events that led up to his demise in Bolivia. In part for its own amusement, the CIA was even kind enough to provide the reporter with a computerized version of Che as he would look more than thirty years later—had he lived.

Woody Robertson tracked down Felix Rodriguez, the better known of the two CIA-recruited Special Forces officers sent to Bolivia to stop Che Guevara in 1967. Rodriguez had gone on to serve the Agency in Vietnam and Central America, among other places. He had finally surfaced as a key operative for Ollie North during the Iran-Contra affair and his role in tracking down Che finally came to be known in the congressional hearings that resulted. To Robertson, "Captain Ramos," as Rodriguez had been called, generally confirmed printed reports of his role in the capture of the notorious revolutionary and his personal interrogation of Che. He proudly showed Robertson the framed picture of himself, in a Bolivian officer's uniform, with the filthy, disheveled, pathetic-looking Guevara. Against his strong urging, Rodriguez told Robertson, Guevara was indeed executed by one Mario Teran, Bolivian sergeant. Rodriguez hadn't actually witnessed the execution, he admitted, but along with many others he had viewed the riddled corpse with the coup de grâce bullet in the throat. No question at all—it was Che himself.

Robertson tracked down the second CIA man. Even though many of these sources were anonymous, he had always followed the "two source" rule. He believed in "deep throats," so long as there were two of them. The anonymous CIA man told a lurid story. Although the lowly Bolivian sergeant had always taken credit for killing Che Guevara, that was far from the truth. He had accompanied the CIA man into Che's tiny room in the primitive schoolhouse near the village of La Higuera and, as the CIA tried to interrogate Che, the Bolivian soldier opened fire in a drunken rage over the death of three of his comrades in the final firefight with Guevara's ragged guerrilla force. Wounded, but not mortally, Guevara sank his teeth into his own wrist to keep from crying out. Panicked, the CIA man pulled his service .45 and put the final shot into Guevara's throat. He wanted to make sure Guevara's face was not disfigured to confuse identification. Guevara, he said, had drowned in his own blood.

Robertson wanted to know why, now, in his early seventies, the CIA man hadn't told his story publicly. It was a fascinating, never-before-told story. His account was worth a book. It could be a great success. To himself, Robertson was fashioning a coauthorship role when the CIA man shook his head no. No way, he said. Why not? Robertson wanted to know. The elderly man smiled wryly. They're still out there, he said. Who's still out there? Robertson insisted. The friends of Che, he said. They tried to get Rodriguez on more than one occasion, he said, and they have never believed the story that this ridiculous drunk little sergeant killed the great Che Guevara. They were still out there and they were still looking. He walked Robertson to the door and, smiling, he said, You can use the story . . . so long as you protect me. He gave Robertson a final pat on the back. You use my name . . . and I will kill you. Then he gave a friendly wave good-bye.

Robertson reviewed all the files once more, read the account of Che's death in the three recent biographies, made some more phone calls, then filed his story. The following Sunday, the *Post* carried it on the upper-left-hand side of the front page under a two-column headline: CHE STILL DEAD. The first three paragraphs highlighted quotes from the two on-the-scene CIA veterans, then gave the context of the story. In the first post-Castro Cuban election, fear and loathing had permeated Cuban politics. Most notorious, there was an antique character claiming to be Che Guevara. Given the great-martyr status of the famous revolutionary, he had created a grassroots stir. On behalf of the *Post*, Robertson justified his story as a service to the Cuban people. The theme of the story was that democracy would come to Cuba when Cuba dismissed its romantic attachment to its revolution. The story concluded with the assertion that the so-called true republic movement was not going anywhere anyway and confidently asserted, based on leaks from Pat, who gladly gave Robertson the phony poll numbers, that the Free Cuba Party had a commanding early lead.

Official Washington got a kick out of the story. It was the kind of wackiness that turned up in the post-Communist world as backward countries struggled to emulate the more sophisticated Western democracies. It was the kind of story that alleviated the boredom of the nation's capital while making it feel good about itself. Besides, Woody Robertson was a favorite on the Georgetown dinner circuit and the Sunday morning chat shows. The State Department liked the story because it helped reduce its fears of an uncontrollable, unpredictable populist uprising that conceivably might get out of hand. In the post–Cold War world, State had learned that independent "democratic" states could be every bit as unmanageable as a predictable ideological "enemy" with whom a detente had been negotiated. Besides, the White House had put its money— literally, it turned out—on the Free Cubans. Nothing must be permitted to get in their way. Woody Robertson had once more done official Washington a favor.

Not long thereafter, *The Flag,* a counterculture monthly published in San Francisco, carried a long story based upon extensive research performed over the past three months by a Spanish-speaking, freelance investigator from El Paso who had spent many weeks in the wilderness of Bolivia, in the state records of Argentina, and in the archives of Cuba. He had interviewed all the survivors of the Bolivian debacle. He had particularly spent time with the aged villagers in La Higuera and surrounding villages who had witnessed the 1967 guerrilla uprising and the subsequent demise of the revolutionary chieftain Guevara. What began to pique his interest were the several people who remembered seeing Che in two different places at the same time. Trained as an interrogator and fluent in the language, the reporter knew how to draw the poor elderly people out and separate their dreams and wishes from their memories and recollections.

In the villages of central Bolivia, the clean-shaven man who had come to Bolivia as Adolfo Mano Gonzalez let his hair and beard grow back until, even with a frame made fragile by asthma and a scavenger's diet, over the months of 1967 he came to resemble the still little-known revolutionary hero of far-off Cuba. But so did the other man, the old people said, the one who came to join them sometime in April . . . or was it May? This man, they recalled, was clearly Bolivian. He used none of the Cuban euphemisms with the Argentinian accent. Spanish might be Spanish, but it still had national, regional, and even local inflections and peculiarities. And the second man, the one who seemed a twin, was different only in the language. Throughout the summer and fall of that year, there had been a Che here at the same time there had been a Che there. Memories were clarified by bullets. There had been skirmishes and firefights between the rebels and the militia and later the *federales.*

Those one could remember. Bullets were flying. The death of a mule or a goat from a stray bullet was an event to remember, an event whose date would be precise. If this man Che was involved in that shootout on that date when Jorge's goat was shot, how could he then have been some forty kilometers away outside a village near the border of the province on the same date when the *campesino* José lost his wife?

The Flag investigator understood he might be on to something. He pressed and pursued until finally a poor *campesino* in his forties offered, for as much money as he could earn that whole year, to take the reporter to his mother who had a story to tell. For thirty years, frightened for her very life, she had never told her story. But now she was old and the money was necessary for them to hold on to their small plot. She had, she related, been the cook for the rebels whenever they passed through the area. As a younger woman she had accepted the Communist dogma and had helped the local cadres plan the resistance to the Barrientos regime. Then came the Cubans and she had helped them even more. She scavenged and prepared their food and on more than one occasion she had been sent into the nearest town with a *farmacia* to get medicine for the lungs. She pointed to her bony chest and coughed to imitate the *comandante*'s travail.

She knew he was Che Guevara. The Bolivian cadres had told her in secret to motivate her to get the food and the medicine. He was a hero. He would lead the liberation of Bolivia, he would help drive out the greedy oligarchy, as he had in Cuba eight years before. And she knew the Bolivian one very well. There was a remarkable resemblance. They could have been twins. And the real Che kidded the other one incessantly about his look-alike beard and mustache. The Bolivian Che had understood all along that he was there as much as anything else to confuse the enemy, to multiply Che's presence, and, if need be, to act as sacrifice. She knew that, she said—her son out of her mud-walled room—because she was the lover of this twin Che. He knew if Che were captured, he would carry on as Che. He knew if he were captured, he also would have to carry on as Che. And that, she said, beyond a doubt was what he had done.

The Flag reporter flew to Buenos Aires and, with a carpet of bribes and dogged persistence, found the ancient functionary who had been responsible for Argentinian state security fingerprint files. When he heard the name Che Guevara, he laughed. Him again, he chuckled. Is he still dead? Maybe not, the reporter said. The man nodded. Could be, the man said. Over a steak dinner and a second bottle of wine, he had confessed that his department was not nearly as efficient as his own government and the Bolivian government had led people to believe in 1967. They had sent Che Guevara's hands, severed after his execution and before his summary burial in an anonymous grave, and asked for a match with his fingerprints on file in the man's department. The man laughed ironically again. It was a joke, he said. Even if they had had Guevara's fingerprints, as the Argentinian government—eager to please the United States and the Bolivians—quickly claimed, there was simply no way we could have found them in the chaos of that place, the man admitted ruefully. To tell you the truth, the man said, I don't think we ever had them.

The reporter sat stunned. You're saying you didn't identify those hands as Che Guevara's? he asked incredulously. Of course I did, the man replied. That's what I was told to do. That's what the government expected me to do. If I had said anything else, I would have been sacked or, even worse, disappeared. So I told them what they demanded to hear. These are Che Guevara's hands all right, no question about it. I made a press statement and signed all kinds of official oaths and affidavits. But I didn't have a clue, he said. I was never able to find any fingerprints that belonged to Che Guevara.

Thirty days later *The Flag* ran the story. The headline was, DOUBTS CAST ON CHE GUEVARA'S DEATH. The publication went into several press runs and caused a sensation. It was reprinted in Spanish and circulated throughout Latin America. It was translated into every major European, Asian, and African language. It ricocheted around Washington. And the first pirated copies to reach Cuba went from hand to hand until they literally fell apart. For every one person that actually read the piece, ten or twenty more heard about it. Suddenly, from Havana to Washington to Miami and throughout much of the world, the possibility seemed to exist that *el viejo* might be something more than a ghost.

Besieged for a response some days after *The Flag*'s story ran, *The Washington Post* issued an unsigned statement that said the paper was reviewing its sources.

3 2

■

The five days E. F. Scarlatti had with Johnny near the Leeward Island Club in the Bahamas had left her both refreshed and motivated, if also somewhat lonely for her beloved, as she packed her bags in her South Miami condo. The campaign staffs in both Miami and Havana knew that she had been called away to advise, on an emergency basis, a gubernatorial campaign in distress in California. Even though she might be gone for some time, there was little concern. E.F. had, typically, trained her subordinates well. Assignments had been made and deadlines established. Micky's deputy, Angie, had been assigned to see that goals were met. The Free Cuba Party now had coordinators in every one of Cuba's provinces and local organizers in every major city. Within the next six weeks—by the end of February—they would have a representative in virtually every one of Cuba's villages and precincts. It was important to show presence and organizational outreach, even though everyone at the top of the party hierarchy knew that the real campaign was just beginning to be waged on television and radio. For E.F. had chosen the week of the launching of the media campaign to make her, hopefully temporary, departure.

An observer might have been puzzled to see E.F. cast aside her high-style pantsuits and print silk blouses and scarves for more serviceable garments whose colors uniformly ran to greens, blacks, tans, and khakis. For her garments she chose washable cargo pants with numerous pockets, work shirts, long-sleeved, lightweight turtlenecks in black, camouflage T-shirts, one pair of black sneakers and one pair of thick-soled hiking boots, a thin black balaclava, a crushable bush hat and a thin black stocking cap, black cotton gloves, a folding pocket seventeen-in-one tool, a pair of shooting goggles, insect repellent, a small pair of 8-by-40 Leica binoculars, a small infrared night scope, and a few camouflage undergarments. Virtually all this wardrobe came from a military surplus store or from her Marine Corps days. The few remaining items E.F. needed for her next assignment would be waiting for her when she arrived, placed in hiding by a loyal and trustworthy supporter of the cause with a fast boat. E.F. was indeed returning to Cuba. But this time she would be going native.

Finished with her packing, all contained in a single, durable camouflage duffel, E.F. spread towels in front of her vanity table, put a towel around her shoulder, and, with a sigh, sat down. She studied her coiffed crown of dark, wavy, shoulder-length hair, then took a pair of shears and methodically chopped it off about three inches from her skull. The effect she wanted was quickly, if crudely, achieved. Without makeup, her usual figure-hugging clothes, and high-style coiffure, E.F. would not have to worry about the knat-swarm of men usually hovering around her. She could, in fact, use her language skills and rough country appearance to melt into the Cuban countryside. Which is exactly what she intended to do.

The short flight to Havana, processing through customs, and departure on the crowded, fuming bus were all accomplished without notice. The same languid airport guards to whom she had given a provocative hip-flip on her departure a week before—just for kicks—didn't even pay attention. Pretending to sleep in her corner seat on the last row of the bus, she went through her plans over and over during the seemingly countless hours it took to traverse almost two thirds of the island's length. When, exhausted, she finally pulled into downtown Santiago de Cuba, she could have gone through the drill, with all its contingencies, in her sleep. Rather than take a taxi, and risk a later recognition, she hitchhiked her way to the city's outskirts even though it took much longer. She finished by walking the final mile and a half to the tiny isolated house that would be her headquarters for the indefinite future. It was the farmhouse of a widow who had accepted a handsome stipend to move in with her daughter in the city for a while.

As arranged, she found the key to the back door above a nearby windowsill. It seemed largely unnecessary. A swift karate kick would have opened the door just as easily. Once inside, she lit the candles and oil lamp and inspected the place. Though ancient and decrepit, it was swept and dusted. Thin, worn sheets and towels were there. And the basic necessities of coffee, beans, rice, and a few other staples were stockpiled by her nameless, faceless advance agents. She noticed that all the curtains in the three small rooms had been tightly pulled and that they were new enough and thick enough to prevent anyone outside from looking in. She unpacked the duffel and arranged her clothes in two drawers of the antique dresser. She washed her face in a basin provided next to a pitcher of fresh water, then studied her face in a small cracked mirror whose mercury was thin and flaking. From the stress of the last thirty-six hours, her eyes were hollow and dark. A little spooky, but more in line with the daily arduousness of life in Cuba. After she had examined every nook and cranny in the place, she turned finally to the single worn bed bowed under the weight of years of nightly occupation. It was covered with a thin blanket which hung almost to the bare wood floor. E.F. carefully raised the blanket edge and laid it back on the bed. She reached underneath and, with a smile, felt the edge of a cardboard box.

She pulled the box from under the bed, placed it on the bed, then carefully slit the tape that sealed it with a razor-sharp spring-blade knife. She lifted out several heavy items wrapped in old rags. She carefully unfolded the wrapping and found a ten-shot 9-millimeter Beretta and two boxes of shells. Then she unwrapped an ordinary, worn *campesino*'s machete whose blade broke the skin of her finger at the slightest touch. The longest and heaviest item in the box was a black carrying case with a shoulder strap and a snapped flap at the top. She unsnapped the top cover, turned the case up, and let its contents slip out onto the bed. As she did, she heard the shells packed in the base of the case rattle slightly. It was a .30 caliber long-barreled bolt-action rifle with a folding metal frame stock and a long, thin sniper scope. She unfolded the frame stock, hoisted the weapon for balance and weight, then sighted through the scope. She could tell nothing about the latter until she took it out for a test drive. But she knew enough about weapons from her military days to know this piece was not off the shelf. It had been custom-made by someone who knew what he was doing. She examined it carefully. It bore no serial numbers or manufacturer's markings. This was a once-in-a-lifetime, use-it-and-lose-it item. Too bad. Then she smiled. She would cheat—just a little. She'd bury it and come back and dig it up for a souvenir after the election when Johnny's crowd took power.

E.F. carefully rewrapped each item but one in the rags, packed them back in the cardboard box, then shoved it back under the bed. She loaded ten shells into the Beretta, racked one into the firing chamber, set the safety, and put the pistol under her pillow. For many years now, it had always made her sleep more comfortably. Before finally taking off all her clothes in preparation for sleep, she carefully examined two maps in plastic folders still in the bottom of her duffel. One was a standard tourist map of Santiago and the adjoining two provinces. The other was a picture from a low earth orbit satellite taken a few years before of a particular section of the Sierra Maestra mountains. She carefully studied the meticulous markings and notes of specific locations, roads and trails, and distances superimposed on the photograph. She shook her head in wonder, once again, at the incredible precision of the picture. Within three minutes of restoring the maps, she was sound asleep, her left hand on the Beretta under the thin pillow.

At the same time, somewhere in the area covered by the satellite picture, the old man sat on the ground, his back against a large log and his feet toward a pile of glowing embers. With him were his shadow Alejo, the boy Rafael, the man who called himself Otra Vez, and the woman Victoria. This was Saturday night, so the old man permitted himself and his companions the joy of a small portion of rum which they drank from cups so cracked they could barely hold the liquid. Very soon, as was the established practice, Alejo would take the woman Victoria to the house of a dependable *campesina* less than a quarter of a mile away where she would spend the night. Then he would return to wrap himself in a blanket and stretch out as the other men did on separate piles of leaves near the glowing charcoals. When they broke their camp the following Monday, the old man Ernesto and the boy would leave for a town near the border of the Guantánamo military base. They would do their usual Sunday morning coffee sipping in the town square and engage in their usual colloquy with the local people on behalf of the true republic movement. The woman Victoria would sleep little this night. For tomorrow they were taking her with them on her first campaign outing.

Otra Vez broke the peaceful silence. "You must expect more people now . . . with this sensational journalism."

Ernesto shrugged and sipped the warm rum. It matters not, his gesture said.

"It is true, *compañero*," Alejo said, permitting himself his only familiarity. "Rafael says this thing is all over the place."

The boy nodded agreement. "I have visited several technical schools in the Habana area, as well as those nearby. Everyone is talking about this journalistic story and saying, 'See, I knew it. It really is him.' They are saying this about you, Señor Blanco."

Ernesto shifted from one bony buttock to the other, his knees creaking slightly. "I can do nothing about it. If they talk, so they will talk."

"Señor Blanco, if I may say so," Victoria offered, "pretty soon you will have to go into the cities, surround yourself with your friends and supporters. For your own safety. Your movement is spreading and getting stronger. Believe me, there will be powerful people who will do anything to stop you."

Otra Vez said, "She is right, *Comandante*."

"I told you not to call me that . . . never!" Ernesto said heatedly. "Do not call me that. I am no '*comandante*.'"

Otra Vez put his hands up defensively. "Okay. But she is still right. Now they're after you, for sure."

" 'These are desperate men and they will stop at nothing,' " Ernesto said with a cackle. "It's a line from an old Yanqui gangster movie I saw many years ago in a tiny cinema outside . . . Bogotá, I think." He chuckled at the memory.

"Would it not be safer in the town, *señor*?" Rafael asked politely.

"You're just thinking about all those pretty girls, Rafael," Ernesto laughed. "That why you are in such a hurry to get into the big city?"

The boy's blush could be seen even in the firelight's glow. He looked down and shook his head no.

"Let me tell you something," Ernesto said as he drained the cup. He was tempted to go for another drop, but he had a rule. "If someone wants to kill you, they will kill you. Or at least they will try to kill you. If they know what they are doing, they will undoubtedly kill you." He set the cup down and stirred the embers with a long, straight stick. Sparks shot up into the night sky. He pointed behind Otra Vez's back. "Right now there could be someone out there, really good outdoorsman, knows what he is doing. He has a rifle. He spent the last hour or two getting close. Really patient. Didn't break a stick. Coming on hands and knees. A few feet. He waits. Then a few more feet. Then he waits. You ever see one of those panther cats—*panteras*—stalking?" He pointed the stick at Otra Vez, who shook his head no. "Just like that. They get close enough, you don't even know he is there. Then . . . he jumps.

Raghhhhr!" he snarled. Victoria jumped and slapped a hand to her mouth to cover a squeal. Ernesto looked delighted with his scary story. "That's the way they can do it. Even up here."

Otra Vez said, "But in the city there are many people around. No one can creep up on you like that."

"Someone probably also told President Kennedy this," Ernesto said. "But it is not the point." He looked at Victoria and smiled. "That kind of assassination has now become old-fashioned. Now, *del norte*, the new style is to assassinate them but leave them walking around. It has the advantage of being legal. No one pulls a trigger. No one fires a bullet. But someone is assassinated. He is no longer politically alive. For political purposes he is dead. Who cares if he walks and moves and breathes? It is all the better. No crime, no trial. But your enemy is dead. He is gone. He is no longer a threat to your political interests. *Es verdad, señora?*"

Without thinking, she shook her head yes. "No!" she suddenly said. "No, it is not *verdad*. What are you talking about? You mean the press? The media? That's not assassination. That's reporting the news. We . . . they . . . the press doesn't *make* the news. They . . . we . . . *report* the news. That's not 'assassination.' If it's the truth, how can it be assassination? I hope that's not what you're talking about." She drank the last of her rum and unsuccessfully looked for the bottle. It was behind Ernesto's back.

Ernesto smiled again at her confusion. "I am making no accusations, *señora*. I am merely 'reporting' to you the case. Unlike anywhere else in the world, if someone—even a political enemy—says that one of your national leaders may have had a romance with some lady to whom he was not married, it is enough. He is finished. You call it a 'scandal.' He is assassinated. You say that he has a flawed character . . . that he is too impure to lead." He stirred the fire again. "It is possible to be 'factual' and not be totally accurate. It is possible to be accurate and not be telling all the truth." He looked evenly at Victoria. This time he did not smile. "Who gave you the right to judge another person's character? The person who gives you the camera and the microphone? The one who makes the money from your 'news'? And who is he? What about his character?" Victoria winced involuntarily and looked away. "Who gave that man, whose job it is to make money, the authority to judge anyone else's character?"

Ernesto alone saw tiny reflections from the sudden moisture in Victoria's eyes and he saw that his argument had found a raw spot somewhere near her heart. "I don't mean to debate this point with you, *señora*. I simply mean that with this new politics now coming to this country, with the democracy comes the 'free press.' And with that comes the new forms of more sophisticated and subtle cruelty." He pointed the stick into the black night beyond the back of Otra Vez. "That *pantera*—panther cat—out there. He would not kill me just to be killing me. He would only kill me if I interfere with him. In the city there are men like this. But they are too clever to use bullets."

He slowly shifted sideways to his knees and then with a hand on the log helped himself to his feet. He bowed to Victoria, *"Buenas noches, señora. Hasta mañana."* He gestured to Alejo, who took Victoria's arm. She started to say something to him but saw that he had turned toward his blanket folded nearby. She permitted Alejo to take her down the trail to her shelter. He had picked up a thick piece of wood, one end of which was burning brightly, for a torch and they set off. The stars and moon were bright and she could make out the donkey trail even with the natural moonlight. But she was glad for the fire and for Alejo's companionship.

"How did you come to be his . . . how do you say it? . . . compan-yer-oh?" Victoria asked.

"It was my destiny, *señora*," Alejo said. "I was put on earth to make a revolution against injustice. But I had the good fortune not to have been created a leader. So, people like me, we wander the earth waiting for the leader . . . the one who will show us the way to go."

Victoria said softly, "Did you know the leader would be this man?"

Alejo's long head wagged up and down in the moonlight. "Indeed. I knew when he left before, that the work was not finished. I always knew he would return."

"All these years? How did you live? What have you been doing all these years?"

Alejo pressed his long thin arms against the sky. "Lifting and carrying. Carrying and lifting."

"And waiting?"

"And waiting, *señora*. And waiting."

"It has been a long time, Alejo, to wait."

She could see his crooked, fractured teeth as he smiled. "Not so long.

When you make a revolution, it takes a long time. You must learn the patience. But I always knew we were not finished here . . . that my *compañero* would return."

They walked in silence. Then Alejo said, "He was not angry with you, *señora*. He was merely telling the truth. He understands the danger. But for now he believes the danger is greater in the city than here in our camp. If you wish, *señora*, we may take you to the city tomorrow. You would be more comfortable there."

She shook her head vigorously in the dark. "No, Alejo, I don't want to go to the city. I simply want Ern . . . Señor Blanco . . . to be more careful. He seems not to care. Believe me, this will get rough. Now powerful people on both sides will hate him. They will try to do something to him." She stopped and tried to see Alejo's face. His torch lit them both. "I know this. I know how things are becoming . . . how really evil some people who want power can be." She could see in his eyes that he understood her and shared her concern.

They walked further in silence. Then Alejo said, "It is a mission for him, *señora*. He is doing what he must do. Come whatever may. That is why he is at peace. He has found a very rare thing, *señora*. He has found something he never had before . . . in the old days. He thought he had, but he had not. Now, he has found his destiny."

"His destiny will not do him any good, Alejo," she whispered, "if he is not alive to carry it out."

"But you see, *señora*," Alejo whispered back, "he knows one other secret."

She took several steps and listened. Finally, hearing nothing, she asked, "A secret which is what?"

Alejo's voice was soft, almost like a lullaby. "If he is killed, he becomes a martyr. He learned this secret from the previous time. If he is killed, his movement becomes eternal."

3 3

■

There was a baseball game in Havana that Sunday, an annual contest of old-timers, former national stars and heroes who came out to play a few innings as a kind of national celebration. Several thousand people came to the stadium for the shortened game. But many more watched the national television broadcast. They remembered the aging stars, the ones who had run and thrown and batted so gracefully and beautifully and had kept the game near the front of the national imagination year after year. So people watched not only out of enjoyment, they watched out of respect for the aging athletes who could no longer run so fast or throw so well or hit so far.

The studio announcer said he was turning the broadcast over to the ballpark announcers. But first there was a brief message. Cubans in general and *habanistas* in particular were by now becoming accustomed to television advertising. They knew that in the new age of commerce, Cuban television would become much more like *Tío Sam* television. There would be all these announcements—"commercials" they were called—for hair products and toothpaste and deodorant products and certainly for *cervezas*. But for the first time in any of their lives they saw, as they waited for the old-timers baseball, commercial politics.

They heard one of the latest catchy Cuban salsa tunes. They saw coming toward them on their small and mostly old television screens a handsome young couple leading a small boy and a small girl. All four were smiling and skipping a bit to the bouncy music. Then a voice came on and said, "Here comes Cuba's future." And behind the smiling, skipping family were superimposed pictures of nice houses, then nice new cars, then beach resorts, then nightclubs, then a new hospital, then children entering a new school building, then an elderly couple relaxing on a porch with their feet up. And the laughing family continued to skip forward, threatening to burst right into the tiny sitting rooms and crowded kitchens of the mesmerized audience. Then the voice, a calm deep voice much different from the strident tones of *el Jefe*, said, "Here comes the future of Cuba. On the first of May, you will have the chance to vote for the future. You will have the chance to vote for"—the music became like an overture crescendo—"the Free Cuba Party!" Cheers, as if from the throats of thousands, more than even those at the baseball stadium during the Cuban national championship series, lifted and soared and rushed to lift the skipping family skyward. And then it was over and the picture shifted immediately to the ballpark.

People in flats and houses and cantinas and public places all over Havana, all over Cuba where television could be seen, looked at each other with amazement and stupefaction. What had they just seen? Was this the government telling them to vote for the Miami crowd? Surely not. There must be some explanation for this. And very soon there was. After they had seen the same little televised vignette several times that day, even as they went to turn off the television before going to bed that night, it had begun to seep into the public consciousness that this was part of democracy, that this was to be expected in elections involving parties contesting the government in power. Indeed, it would not be long before the government in power, in the form of the Cuban Social Democratic Party, would itself be offering announcements before sports events and news events. They would never, ever be so artful and so theatrical as those of the FCP. They would in fact be boring and dull and usually involve some political heavyweight from the Palacio de la Revolución simply instructing the people to vote for their friends who had given them so much already. As frothy and surreal as the FCP commercials would seem, so the CSD commercials would seem always to convey a hidden message that a vote against the government would not be forgotten.

It would be early April before most people caught on that the other group, not a party really, more like a movement, the true republic group, the one led by *el viejo*, was not offering these commercials and would not be offering these commercials. The televised contest for the hearts and minds of the people would be waged by the FCP and the CSD. And all the while *el viejo* and his growing band of enthusiasts would continue their grassroots efforts to reach the people one by one. And even as the happy family in the first political commercial in the history of Cuba skipped into the nation's living rooms if not into the nation's heart, *el viejo* was sipping coffee on the narrow porch of the only cantina in the village of Baracoa, separated from the Guantánamo naval base to the southwest by the Sierra de Purial and near the easternmost point of the country. Columbus, it was believed, made his first landing in the Western Hemisphere only a few hundred yards to the north over five hundred years before.

Ernesto had joined a table of people drinking their coffee at the cantina on the Parque de la Victoria. On the park was the Centro de los Veteranos and the occupants of this seniors' residence frequented this cantina as the venue for their discussions of current affairs. As Rafael and Victoria took a small table nearby, and the boy began to provide a *sotto voce* interpretation of the discussion, she briefly wondered whether Ernesto was demonstrating a sense of irony in choosing a park with this name as the site of her first campaign stop.

"He is saying that one side will simply keep the power in Habana and continue to share the shortages evenly, while the other side will bring in the big money and some will become very wealthy by owning the land and the factories but that most will still be poor and powerless. That woman is saying," he whispered, "that the second way at least gives a few people a chance to do better and, anyway, the power will stay in Habana where it has always been. There is nothing little people like us, she is saying, will ever be able to do about the power."

As Rafael spoke, Victoria studied Ernesto's expressions. She sensed he was more alert to everything going on around him, more even than in the camp. He puffed a small cigar and occasionally touched his mustache abstractly. Most interesting, he listened. He listened with an energy that was itself palpable. She had never seen anyone listening with such intensity. It was as if he were willing the person to whom he listened to express her feelings. His eyes never left a speaker. His gaze was like a warm laser, soft yet intense. To show he understood, his head nodded often. It was a receptive and encouraging gesture. It said, Please continue. When someone used a particularly insightful phrase, he would smile. It was easy and natural without being condescending. It caused Victoria to reflect briefly on how smiles might sometimes be used as weapons in her culture. Remarkably, his smile brushed away decades of wear from his face. It was easy to imagine what a magnet to ladies that smile must have been. Even now still was, she thought uncomfortably. A few times he chuckled and once he laughed out loud, something she had never heard him do in the days since she had been watching him.

"*Con mucho respeto, señor,*" a very elderly lady had just said, "as refreshing as it might be to have some wisdom in government for a change, are we quite ready to replace one *view* with another?" That had brought the laugh from Ernesto.

"*Señora,*" he chuckled, "some old people are older than other old people. And some young people"—he tapped his brow—"are older than some old people who are much younger," again tapping his head. The circle of retirees shook their heads in agreement. "Besides," he continued, "I do not intend to replace the present *Jefe*. There is a *profesor muy interesante* from the Universidad who had announced his candidacy for the presidency of this republic on the platform of the local power. If it is the will of the people of Cuba, and good people like yourselves vote for the movement of the true republic, then he will become our leader."

Victoria quickly made a surreptitious note in the small notebook in her lap. "What shall we do about the ownership of the land?" asked one man. "If your movement—"

"Your movement," Ernesto insisted quickly.

"—our movement succeeds, how will the ownership of the land and the houses and the shops be decided?"

"This is, of course, a decision of all the people," Ernesto said. "But a lively possibility is that put forward by the *profesor* who is to lead the movement. He has said that the new government of the people in each town can create a citizens' bank that will make funds available at very low rates to those who wish to buy their own farms and houses and shops. These loans can be paid back over a long period of time. And these same banks all over Cuba, owned and managed by the local people themselves, can loan money to students for the university and to your children for improvement of their homes and for financing of all kinds of local projects."

One woman said, "We cannot know about the money. It is for the power to own the money. We are too poor and too ignorant."

"This is wrong," Ernesto said, pointing a finger in her direction but smiling as he did so. "It requires no special genius. This has been told to you always by those who want to keep the power, that there is some magic about the money. It is no great magic. Your children and their children are intelligent enough to manage these banks of the local republic." He drank his coffee and puffed the cigar. "The main point is whether you trust the people or whether you think that the government power and the money power are too complicated for the people. If you trust the people, if you believe they have the intelligence to know what is best for them, then you must also trust they will find the proper means to make their villages the best place to live."

Victoria watched him speak. It seemed so natural to him. He was like a teacher surrounded by thoughtful, sometimes skeptical, students. He spoke to everyone simply but with respect, respect that was clearly returned. She noticed one stocky man standing in the doorway of the cantina. He had been silently watching every move but saying nothing. As a new coffeepot was passed around the table, he said, "*Señor*, it cannot be that you are making all this trouble for the politicians in Habana and the bankers in Miami and still that you are not intending some position of authority in the new government. It is being said that you are traveling all over this island, that you have had perhaps hundreds of discussions of this sort, that as a result this movement you speak of is breathing and growing, that men and women are putting themselves forward for the important elected positions on your platform. Yet, you say you have no ambition for yourself. If those who follow your ideas are elected to power, surely you will have some position as the stage manager behind the curtains of the drama directing the actions of your followers." His words were heavy with skepticism and obvious distrust.

Perhaps more than any of those present, Victoria absorbed Ernesto's response. "No"—he nodded his white head back and forth—"I do not wish to govern, even behind the scenes. I have no talent for it, nor do I have the tolerance required to negotiate the necessary agreements with the other politicians. It is the job of a person much more patient than me. In earlier times"—everyone seemed to lean forward at once, waiting for a clue—"in earlier times I was close to some who gained the power. It did not interest me." He chuckled. "There was always more talk than action."

The stocky man said, "Were those earlier times with the *barbudos*, *señor*?"

As Ernesto studied the man, cars pulled up at each end of the small triangular *parque*. Victoria became aware that both cars were full of men

and about the same time she realized that a lone guitar player had positioned himself a few moments earlier at the far end of the plaza and
was strumming a vaguely familiar tune. At first she did not place it and
then suddenly recognized it as "Guantanamera," the tune from the 1940s
that had become a popular anthem of Cuba. Then Ernesto said quietly,
*"Con los pobres de la tierra, quiero yo mi suerte echar; el arroyo de la sierra,
me complace más que el mar."* Rafael breathlessly whispered to Victoria,
" 'With the poor of the earth, I want to play out my destiny. The mountain stream suits me better than the sea.' *Señora,* it is the last verse of
the song. Quickly, we must go."

Suddenly, Victoria found herself lifted by Rafael's thin hand under
her arm. He was pulling her through the door into the cantina. As she
brushed past the stocky older man who had asked the last few questions,
she saw that two young men who had not been there the previous moment blocked him out of the way and then closed the door behind her.
Before the door closed she looked back and saw that Ernesto was no
longer there. As Rafael pulled her quickly through the long, narrow
cantina toward the back door, she saw the back of a figure that looked
like Ernesto disappearing out the door ten yards ahead of them. Once
outside the dark cantina, she was momentarily blinded by her rapid entry
into the bright sunlight. Then she looked both ways up and down the
narrow alleyway and saw no one. A door suddenly opened into a garage-
like structure two buildings down and across the alley. As Rafael pulled
her inside, she heard shouting and the vigorous protest of elderly voices
in the front of the cantina where they had been less than a minute
before. Once again she found herself in total darkness. She heard only
breathing behind her. Since Rafael was standing between her and the
closed garage door, she knew someone—Ernesto?—was there with
them. She whispered, *"Señor?"* before Rafael's hand was placed firmly
over her mouth.

Outside, running feet pounded up and down the alleyway. Rafael carefully placed a wooden board into the latches on both sides of the door.
Within seconds hands pressed firmly against the doors making them
creak. But they held. Minutes passed in the darkness. Presently Victoria
thought she could hear car doors slamming out on the plaza and tires
squealing. Then more minutes passed. Soon there were three light taps
on the door and Rafael lifted the bar. Rafael helped her step aside as
the figure behind her said, *"Hasta mañana, señora,"* and the thin white-

haired figure of Ernesto Blanco slipped past her and out into the sunlight.

As they made their way westward down José Martí Street, which ran the length of the long narrow town of Baracoa, Rafael said, "Such things are happening more and more where we go. It seems more often these days that the authorities are aware of our meetings and they arrive regularly and more quickly to try to frighten people away or to make some excuse to bring Señor Ernesto into their headquarters. If such a thing should take place, then who knows what 'accident' might happen to him in their keeping." They walked the dozen blocks or so to the end of town and the small bay called the Ensenada de Miel. There they located the antiquated bus station where Rafael checked his watch then negotiated tickets on the bus to Santiago leaving in an hour. The two-hundred-kilometer trip would take until nightfall. "Someone told the authorities?" Victoria asked as they waited.

"*Claro que sí, señora*," Rafael said. "The only question is whether they told them *while* Señor Blanco was making his discussion or . . . *before*."

Victoria said, "How did he get away so fast? How did you get me away so quickly? Who were those young men? How did you know what we should do?"

"Señora Victoria," Rafael said, "we have come now to have plans everywhere we go. Our network of supporters know that they are to be prepared for anything."

"But I didn't see them at all," Victoria said, "until we started to move and then they seemed to be everywhere."

Rafael said, "They make sure that they do not appear too much during our meetings. They do not want the local people to think that Señor Blanco needs protection. Most of the time not even he knows that they are nearby."

"What was the verse that he said just before the excitement?" Victoria asked.

"It is a poem by our national hero José Martí," Rafael said. "It became the words to the famous song called by the same name as the province where we were."

"Yes," Victoria said, "I know it well. It is known everywhere. But, Rafael, I know I heard that song just when those men came. Then Señor Ernesto said those words. It is incredible that there should be such a coincidence."

Rafael stirred the dust underfoot with one worn boot and studied it. "Señora Victoria, it is no 'coincidence' as you call it. Here I am instructed to explain to you—since you will be with us for a time and such things may happen again—how our protection for Señor Blanco works." He leaned toward her, his voice low but his eyes slightly wider. "When you hear that song, you are first to make sure you are not in the way and then be prepared to get away yourself. Our first duty is to protect Señor Ernesto. But we also must look after you. Señor Ernesto insists that you be protected also." Here he pursed his lips and softly whistled the melodic tribute to the provincial girl from Guantánamo. "It may be sung or played or even sometimes we whistle it. But, whatever the means, it is our signal."

The bus eventually arrived and they took the battered carriage to Santiago and then spent the night in the humble house where Victoria had first stayed on her arrival in the Sierra. The following day they were taken in a fuming truck to the small village of Bartolomé Masó, a gateway to the mountains. There they undertook to make their way on foot into the region where they had made their last camp. After months in the mountains with Ernesto Blanco and as a native of the region, Rafael had learned the intricate codes and tricks the movement had developed to mask the location and movements of its leader. On this trek Victoria was once again grateful that Alejo had returned from the nearby town of Bayamo, shortly after she had arrived, with a pair of plain but sturdy native walking shoes and a few pairs of thick, unglamorous, but comfortable socks. She was even beginning to feel excess pounds fall away and strength restored to her legs and body for the first time since travel forced her to abandon her exercise class years before. She had, in the meantime, given up on her luxuriant hair. After a week in the mountain camps, lacking her customary hairdresser and the vanity drawers full of sprays, brushes, conditioners, and shampoos, she had made what was for her the ultimate sacrifice. Rafael had come to collect her from the tiny cabin and, tears pouring from her eyes, she had insisted that he hack away with his sharp brush knife at the thick flowing tresses that had been her television signature for twenty years. To see them fall to the worn wooden floor was to see the symbol of a lifetime career collapse in a forlorn sigh.

With her amateur hairdo, plain shoes, peasant dress, and sun-darkened skin, the Victoria following Rafael up the narrow donkey cart trail was scarcely recognizable as a famous television reporter and might even have passed as a native. Ahead they could make out a widening in the trail marking a crossing. They were still a hundred yards away when they saw a figure enter the clearing from the hiking path that crossed their road. Instinctively, Rafael reached back, grasped Victoria's shirt, and pulled her with him into the thick shrubs bordering the road. From behind thick foliage they could see this figure unfold a paper that appeared to be a map. At that distance they found it difficult to make out the person's gender. Whoever it was was dressed for the mountains. The clothing blended with the natural grays, browns, and greens. The person wore a bush hat and carried a small bedroll and a black carrying case over his back. This person knelt down, spread out the map, and appeared to consult a compass that he laid on the map. Quickly the figure reoriented the map, turning northward, and then took sightings with the compass to establish a bearing.

After a moment the figure rose, folded the map and stored the compass, slung a bundle over each shoulder, wiped his face with a kerchief, and set off to the southeast up the road Rafael and Victoria were on. Rafael checked Victoria's Cartier watch and held a finger to his lips. They waited ten minutes and then Rafael gestured them back on the road. As they followed the road now winding steeply upward, Rafael whispered, "Could you tell what kind of person it was, *señora*?"

"Your eyes are better than mine," she answered, "but it seemed to be a rather small person, almost petit. It didn't seem to me to be someone from around here. The clothes looked too 'military' somehow. Do you get very many tourist hikers who come up into these mountains?"

Rafael still spoke quietly, looking ahead as they went, "Some, but almost always in groups. And almost always they have a guide from Cubatour to show them the mountain trails—especially if they are planning to camp outside. There are a number of very simple mountain cabins here for tourists. But somehow this one looked prepared for the outdoors."

"I thought so too," she said. "And this person seemed to be looking for a particular place rather than simply to be trekking through the outdoors."

Rafael looked at her sideways and blushed, "Could it be one of your rivals, *señora*, a *periodista* looking for Señor Blanco?"

She stopped, dumbstruck, in the middle of the road. "Dammit! That's it! Why didn't I think about this? Of course that's who it is. Probably some freelance out to make a fast buck or a name with a sensational exposé. 'I found Ch . . .' Sorry, but you understand, don't you? That's what's going to happen now. They're all going to start showing up— first a trickle . . . then a flood. Goddammit!" She started forward at forced march speed.

Rafael trotted a few steps to catch up. "What are you doing? He will see you."

She quickened her speed as she turned to him, "We have to get to Ern . . . to Señor Ernesto. We have to warn him. And"—she glared at Rafael, competitive instincts as fiery as her glance—"I am not enduring this 'Outward Bound' experience to be scooped."

"Scooped?" Rafael queried. "What does it mean, *señora?*"

She strode purposefully forward. "Beaten. To 'be scooped' is to lose a story to someone else."

Rafael trotted with her, then said, "Is that your purpose, Señora Victoria, to get a story?"

She stopped and looked at him. "Yes. No. I mean, it *was* my purpose. That's why I came here. But now it's more than just a 'story.' It's important. It's not just important to me. It's important to him . . . and to you . . . and to the people of Cuba. People outside have to know who he is . . . what he stands for. They have to hear his ideas. This is important, Rafael, this movement, not just to Cuba. It's important in other places." Her voice was low but quick and intense. "If he is right about what he says, that people can run their own lives, make their own decisions, govern themselves in their own communities, that's not just a Cuban idea. It's a universal idea. The world has to know this idea and he has to be the one to tell them. I'm going to see that he has at least one chance to do that—before the vultures show up and pick him apart."

"Vultures, *señora?*" Rafael's eyes were wide. "You mean like that man on the trail?"

Victoria restarted her fast walk up the mountain. Over her shoulder she said, "That was no man. That was a woman."

3 4

■

At sunset that evening Rafael and Victoria arrived at their agreed rendezvous and found only Otra Vez who reported that Alejo had gone to meet Ernesto Blanco and that they were due back the following evening. They recounted to Otra Vez the events in Baracoa and all agreed that their two *compañeros* must be taking the long way back to ensure against detection. Early the following evening *los hombres viejos* arrived, Alejo fatigued and Ernesto bright and vigorous like a young boy who has just won a hiding game. They shared their adventures, and then, over their usual dinner of rice and beans, Victoria described their encounter with the strange figure on the trail. She insisted that it had to be a journalist who, due to his—or her—stealthy methods must be up to no good.

"But, *señora, por favor*, are you not also a *periodista*?" Ernesto asked in a serious tone. Even after more than three weeks on what approximated a campaign trail for the True Republic movement, Victoria still could not tell when Ernesto Blanco was serious and when he was being mockingly ironic.

"More or less," she said. "Yes. Of course, I am. But this is different. I believe I understand much better what you are doing . . . what you stand for . . . what you are trying to achieve." This she now realized had been his purpose all along, to indoctrinate, if not to recruit, if not to seduce her politically. It had happened to her in earlier campaigns as a young idealistic reporter. On the rare occasion she covered a candidate who had ideals and ideas and seemed genuinely committed to public service ahead of career, her stories gradually and usually unconsciously began to swell the crowd size and inflate its response, to glamorize the candidate and make him or her a more profound leader, to promote rather than critique. Then came the era of exposé and scandal and the thought of such softheartedness became laughable. The whole role was to disclose the fraud, out the scoundrel, undress the packaged careerist, test the boundaries of public humiliation. As she sat with the others at the raw wooden camp table, she realized how far she had regressed—and how good it felt.

"If I may say so, Señora Victoria," Ernesto mused, "you are perhaps most concerned that a rival may appear on our doorstep before you have made your broadcast?"

"No. Well, yes, I guess I am," she said. "But for a good reason. Look, I don't know how much experience you have with the media these days. My guess is, little or none. There's a popular saying in the U.S. that we're all famous for fifteen minutes." She was interrupted by one of Ernesto's rare hearty laughs. The other men snickered obligingly. "And if your fifteen minutes is used to make you look foolish or fraudulent, there will be no other chance. You must speak for yourself. You must tell the audience—and, believe me, it will be big—about the true republic idea, about how people everywhere can have the power to govern their own towns and villages. It is . . . it is . . . well, it is . . . revolutionary."

Ernesto smiled. "How can something twenty-five hundred years old be revolutionary, Señora Victoria? It is not my idea. It is the earliest idea of democracy. It has simply been forgotten—at least since the age of T. Jefferson."

"You can remind people then," she urged. "You can remind them of the true ideal and you can tell it to people in Latin America and in Africa and in parts of Asia that have never heard it before."

For the first time since they had met, Victoria felt that she had said something important enough to make him think. It was clear he did not want to be bothered with the press, that the possibility had not really occurred to him until she had shown up, but that he was shrewd enough to understand that what she was saying was true. He would have at most one chance to state his case before the deluge and before the monster static of the modern media began.

"Señora Victoria," he said after some moments, "I am not out to revolutionize the world. I do not want to discuss these ideas with *periodistas* who, in any case, are scarcely interested in them at all. And I most emphatically do not want to be famous—even for fifteen minutes. If I do as you suggest, if I speak to the television as you propose, how does this end rather than start a kind of madness? How can I deflect the focus from the messenger to the message?"

"You simply state that purpose as forcefully as you can," she responded, "and I will help you. After all, it was your idea to have me here. I suppose now it was to get me to this place where I believe your movement is more important than any leader. I can say that firsthand as my conviction and my testimonial, if you will. It is not much, but there are still a few people who remember who I am."

"Will that then be the end of *los periodistas, señora*?" he asked.

Victoria looked him in the eyes. "Honestly? No. You are going to be a big attraction, at least until this election. Then they'll have some other warehouse fire to cover." She thumped her fist softly on the table to emphasize her point. "But you will have the defining moment. You can make your case first . . . and hopefully to the largest audience. You make the contrast with the other political parties. You show how your movement is so different. The reporters will then go to the others for a reaction. You will set the contrast between your politics of the future— even the future of the ancient past—and they will be left with the worn-out politics of the recent past."

Ernesto looked out of the window of the small cabin into the darkness outside. He briefly wondered if the figure Rafael and Victoria had seen along the trail were somewhere out there. Then he studied her momentarily and nodded his head up and down.

The following day Rafael took her down to the nearest village and they got a donkey cart, then an old truck, then a bus into Manzanillo. There, on a hill on the outskirts of town, they located the Hotel Guscanayabo overlooking the sea. It had a telephone guests might use and Victoria convinced the manager that her call to her U.S. company would bring business to his hotel. Her physical appearance did not encourage any belief that she could have any positive influence with any reputable firm. But, for a ten-dollar tip, he relented. Pursuing company policy, she placed a collect call to Sam Rapport in Washington. He was at a National Press Club lunch and his assistant promised a call back within an hour. When his pager showed the call was from Savidge, he got her number from his office and responded immediately. This was her first contact in almost a month and TPN had considered filing an insurance claim on her life until its comptroller reminded them she had been written out of their corporate policy at its latest renewal.

"Vic, have you got him?" Rapport shouted down the line.

Typical, Victoria thought, the story before her personal well-being. "Assume we have company," she cautioned. "Get H.F. down here with his superportable. Tell him to check into my hotel and he'll get instructions. How long will it take?"

Rapport had been through this drill enough years to know she was warning about auditors on the line, that she used the initials of her cameraman, Harry Ferris, so listeners would not know his name when he passed through immigration or checked into the hotel. She assumed Rapport would be clever enough to get the name of the Hotel Nacional from her office. The superportable was broadcast equipment developed by Ferris that, through miniaturized technology, permitted a single person to establish a viable satellite broadcast signal. The equipment could be carried in two medium-sized suitcases.

"Done, Vi . . ." He didn't use her name again, realizing he shouldn't have done so before. "When do you need it?"

"Tomorrow," she said, meaning as quickly as you can.

"Done," he said. "Give us seven to ten days. H.F. is on assignment, so we'll have to round him and his equipment up. Work out the transport and reservations. All like that."

"Quick as you can, Sam," she said. Then she used the magic words guaranteed to stimulate action. "We've got competition. I'll start checking in a week."

"Do my best. It's a big story now. Everybody's talking. Are you in the capital?" he shouted.

"You don't need to know, Sam," she said. "And, Sam, get time on the bird. I need all you can get but at least fifteen." The connection was suddenly cut. She looked at the phone, then Rafael said urgently, "Señora Victoria, we must go."

Victoria's call was paralleled by one more or less on the same subject during the same hour between Olivero Sanchez, chairman of the Free Cuba Party, in Miami, and Johnny Gallagher, the director of the Cuba gaming initiative project for the Leeward Island Club and liaison with the Free Cuba Party, in the Bahamas. Sanchez was eager for a progress report on a contingency campaign project known only to the two of them plus Angela Valdés of the FCP and Johnny's boss, Harry Rossell, the Leeward Island Club president.

"He's a nuisance, Johnny," Sanchez said.

"No question, Mr. Sanchez," Johnny replied. "We're on the case. Our guy should be in place pretty soon now."

"Don't screw around, Johnny," Sanchez said. "Get it done. We screw around any more and it's just going to get tougher. He's getting too much attention. Everybody's talking about him. It's incredible. We wait any longer, it'll get too much attention."

Johnny said, "Couldn't agree more, Mr. Sanchez. Our guy's good. It'll get done."

"There are a bunch of reporters headed down there," Sanchez said. "They're going to make a hero out of that old son of a bitch."

"Already there, Mr. Sanchez," Johnny said. "Don't think we ought to talk much more about it. You never know who's listening in these days." He was appalled that Sanchez had even suggested the age of the subject. And he was afraid he would want to know specifics about the agent hired to do the job. Of the four who knew about the project, he was responsible for hiring the gun and seeing that the job got done. He alone knew his choice was also his lover and that she was even now within a hundred miles of this old fraud "Ernesto Blanco" and probably, since she was so good, probably much less. With more assurances that a report on the success of the project would be made to him first, Sanchez terminated the call. Johnny thought, You're gonna see it on TV before E.F. has a chance to call me. He regretted that she would have to lie low for a while before he could get her back to the Bahamas for a little "reunion."

Victor Pais, the chairman of the Cuban Social Democrats, and his principal deputy Antonio Oliverez went for a drive outside Havana. They let the driver go and Antonio drove around Havana harbor and out toward the Ernest Hemingway house thirty kilometers to the east. On the way they reviewed the progress of the campaign and the plans for the remaining eight weeks. But the real subject of their discussion would wait until they arrived at the Hemingway property now preserved as one of Cuba's most popular national sites for tourists. Once the car was parked at the foot of the steps leading to the rambling open-air house looking out on the Caribbean where Hemingway loved to fish, the two political leaders shook hands with the curator and requested privacy. She disappeared and permitted no visitors or staff to follow them. They made their way around the main house to a small adjacent structure that had served as a combination staff residence, writing studio, and, on the third floor, a lookout to the sea. Even if Hemingway had not been able to see the great fish from that distance, he could surely see when the fishing boats were going out.

On the lookout floor Pais said, "Okay. Where do we stand?"

"Our man has established himself," Oliverez responded. "He's on the inside. He is waiting for us to instruct him. He can act when we say."

Pais stared at the gleaming sea and understood Hemingway's fascination. "I don't want to do it, Tony. It doesn't seem right."

"We won't, Vic . . . unless we absolutely must." Oliverez was no more comfortable with their contingency plan for Ernesto Blanco than Pais was. "We'll wait until we have no other choice."

"He may simply go away," Pais said hopefully, "or his movement may just collapse. A lot of things can happen. There's still a lot of time."

"I think it's like a novelty," Oliverez agreed. "There's a little mystery. Where is he? Who is he? All that 'Che' damn craziness." They both chuckled.

"I still can't believe that magazine in the States that said he didn't get killed," Pais said ruefully. "I was there when they brought his bones back from Bolivia and Fidel buried him, for God's sake." Pais shook his head at the absurdity. He turned to his old friend and ally. "Tell your man not to hurt him in the meantime. He's an old guy and—aside from getting in our way—he really hasn't done anything wrong. Leave him alone until . . . until we have to do something."

Oliverez said, "It's agreed. He won't touch him or anything. Our guy won't make the decision anyway. He knows we make the decision. He knows we don't like even thinking about this."

Pais said, "What does he say—about this old guy? What's he like?"

"He likes him, Vic. He says he's a smart, funny old guy. He likes him a lot," Oliverez responded. "He shouldn't have said so, but he said he actually thought the old guy's ideas are . . . what did he say? . . . 'interesting.' He said the old guy, Ernesto, has read a great amount, that he has thought about this stuff for years."

"Where did he do this stuff?" Pais asked reflectively. "Where was he all this time?"

Oliverez said, "All over Latin America. Just about every country in South America and Central America. He's been everywhere apparently."

"Doing what?" Pais asked.

Oliverez said, "Teaching, Vic. He's a teacher."

"Why is he over here screwing around in our politics?" Pais asked. "Did your guy tell you that?"

Oliverez said, "He didn't really say, but it's just like the old guy felt he had to do it. He seems to be on some kind of . . . I don't know what you'd call it . . . like a kind of 'mission' I suppose you could say."

The two men looked out to the sea one last time and then left their lookout post, walked past the boat shed containing Hemingway's fishing boat, around the main house and to their car. As they were getting in, Pais said, "Tell your guy to wait till we have tried everything else. Don't do anything unless we have no other choice."

Oliverez shrugged, then shook his head affirmatively.

■ ■ ■

I suppose I should say why Cuba. It had to be a small country. And this is one I knew—and loved. Over all those years, I could never get the old days out of my mind—the people, the places, the combat, the terrible bad times, then the victory. Mostly the people. Not that they are any different or better than people in other places—people anywhere—just that they had been colonized and victimized by everybody who passed by. I guess I always wanted to come back and see how things turned out and whether there might be another revolution to begin. It could have been Guatemala, or Nicaragua, or maybe Salvador, or Honduras. But Cuba was for me something unfinished. I had to come back.

Now I'm trying to plant some seeds. Ideas are like seeds. Inside them is their own life. But they need the soil, and the water, and the sun. The soil is the people, and the water is open debate, and the sun is the energy from the mind. One thing new growing things also need is time. What I can tell about the wealthy societies now is that they don't have time for anything. Particularly ideas. They live their lives so fast that it crowds out the time a new idea needs to put out its roots in the soil, among the people. If everything is about selling a product, what they call the "commercial," it must be quick, right now, immediately. No time can be given for the idea to grow its roots and then start to push up.

What the idea of the true republic needs is time. It has the people. They are ready for some idea like this. It is now being discussed among the people. It is receiving the water. And the young people like Rafael are providing the energy from the sunlight of the mind. We may not succeed this time. It is really very soon—and there is so much resistance from the forces of the status quo—that it may not win the victory so soon. But it really does not matter. It matters that the roots go down in the minds of the young people of Rafael's age. Then the idea cannot be crushed. Then it will live forever. The idea of self-government began with somebody called Pericles—or someone before Pericles (it doesn't matter). Then the Greeks started making these wars— Peloponnesus, Sicily, and so on—and they lost the idea. The Romans had it. Then they gave it up for an empire. Then the whole idea got lost. That Machiavelli—an unlikely character—brought part of it back, I guess mostly because he thought the Florentines shouldn't be ruled by the church and the feudal princes. Then later they had this "enlightenment" also to break free of superstition, and here came people like T. Jefferson.

So an idea that got planted in a small town called Athens grew, then was lost, then sprang up, then was crushed and stayed underground for centuries, then sprouted back up in Italy, then was scattered around and lost again, then sprang up again in the eighteenth century. Now here we are. We picked up some seeds and we are planting them here. Whatever Great Spirit there is should just give these seeds a little chance. Let Rafael and his friends water them and provide some sunlight. And they will grow. And they will finally make these poor Cuban people free. And they can maybe even make poor people in Somalia, and in Ecuador, and in Vietnam free. Who is to know?

Now I am thinking of something else. Why does this happen to me— now? Here is this woman. It was pretty damn dumb to let her come here. What was I thinking about? Other than that she clearly needed some help, and maybe even that she was pretty in a kind of phony glamorous way, I cannot imagine why I did this. Now here she is. This business we are doing is going to get dangerous before this election comes around. She shouldn't be here for that. Even we old guys, me and Alejo and Otra Vez, are going to have to be able to move fast when they send the bad guys around. (If they aren't here already.) What can we do with her? She'll just be in the way.

Well, she's right, I believe, about this press-media thing. I guess I have to show—at least one time—that I am not totally crazy. I have to state what the true republic is—clearly—so the lies don't catch up. Then that's it. She leaves. I don't talk to those people anymore. And we have stated our case. She's done her job. She can go back and join those glamorous TV people again. Everybody is happy. We have our election. And we move on. The seeds are planted. Simple plan.

Why would she want to go back to that phony life I cannot imagine. But it's her life. She is a grown-up woman (most of the time). And she can live her own life. It's not my business. If she wants that kind of life, she can have it. It makes no sense to me. But it's her life. I wouldn't interfere with it if I could. And I can't. But what a crazy life it must be. "Images," she keeps saying. Everything is an "image." It sounds like some kind of Santería, some kind of tribal voodoo, to me. Who wants to live in a world of "images"? Not me.

First thing she does, I am sure, is to get her fancy hair back, all that hair she showed up with. Lots of hair. So, I guess they go to some shop. I've seen them in Caracas, and in Quito, and in Mexico City. Always in the rich part of town. Poor women can't go there. It's sad. Poor women must care about glamorous things as much as rich women. Hair must be just as important to them. But they can't go to those shops. Too much money. But she'll go to one of those places right away when she gets back to el norte. Wouldn't want her fancy TV friends to see her as she now looks. It makes me laugh to think about it. What a sight that would be. Right now she looks like an honest poor woman more every day. She can't do that where she lives and how she lives.

But it's her life and I don't even worry about it. I'll just be glad when we get this TV over with and she gets out of here. She'll be safe and she'll be famous again and—she can grow her hair back. It doesn't make any sense to me—but there it is.

The main thing is making sure those politicians don't find a way to crush the true republic before the election. The people need a chance to vote. This TV business makes me realize the importance of making sure people have the simple manifesto that summarizes our movement, what it's about, what it wants to do. We'll put it up around the country again about the time of this TV business. People can read it again and they can hand it around. That way people will have their own understanding of our idea. If the others try to lie about it, then the people can say, No, here it is, here is the idea of the true republic. It is not as you say.

We'll print more next week and send them around the country when the TV thing happens. Then the woman will be free to go back al norte. *I will move my camp. And she can live her own life, as she wishes.*

■ ■ ■

3 5

■

Over the weeks that he had been "observing" the run-up to the Cuban national elections, Nick Ferre began to realize that, contrary to his orders, he was spending a disproportionate amount of time trying to solve the mystery of the true republic movement. Despite the warning from the head of the Interests Section that the fix was in—that the U.S. government was doing all it could to pull the Free Cuba Party through—the intrigue of this novel movement continued to draw him. He continued to file his reports on the CSD and the FCP. But, because of the blinders his superiors in the Interests Section wore, he alone appreciated the growing power of the movement's undertow.

Because he was tuned into their thinking, Nick made a point of building a personal network among university students. They were the ones who, after developing their own level of trust, tipped him off when a public meeting of the movement was going to take place or when key organizers were gathering to plot strategy. Only minor and often distracting references to the true republic movement appeared in his reports. He was aware that he was both operating outside his mandate and deceiving his superiors into the bargain. But the secretary herself had ordered him to Cuba to find out what was going on, not to rig the election. His plan was to gather as much information as he could about the movement and its potential impact on the election, then send that—outside channels—directly to the secretary. That course was guaranteed to get him either fired or promoted, but he was committed to doing his job.

His student contacts knew he wanted to understand their leader better. But he did not press. He knew he had to continue to prove himself to them. When the time was right, the occasion would arise. He visited a number of small towns and villages within driving distance of Havana when the movement held public meetings. He knew that eventually, if he showed up at enough of these, the man himself, Ernesto Blanco, would pop up again— unannounced. The meetings were always pretty much the same. There would be a small group of regulars gathering over coffee or *cervezas*. Then one or two local movement organizers would arrive. Then more local people would show up, anticipating action. Then a couple of out-of-town strangers, usually young, would appear. Then everyone knew what was up. It was the true republic—and Ernesto himself might be nearby.

Nick had felt the electricity these meetings generated. Nothing like the perfunctory lectures given by the local Cuban Social Democratic functionaries or the glitzy, now familiar, television advertising of the Free Cubans. The very idea, the remote possibility of a sighting of the mysterious Ernesto now made every true republic event a happening. But because there were now as many as a dozen local rallies a night all over the country, it was impossible to focus on any one or to estimate at which one, if any, the leader might appear. Nick had given up planning. The Ernesto sightings were always somewhere else. His pleas to his student friends collected only a shrug.

One afternoon he piled into an old car with six students from the Universidad de la Habana and they drove out to the town of Consolación del Sur in Pinar del Río province. Since it was Saturday, workers would be coming in from the countryside to visit the markets and have a meal in town. The dusty central square was crowded as the students handed out leaflets promoting the true republic's cause. One of the local CSD officials challenged the students' leader. "Do you expect the people of this town to trust some old guy they've never even seen?"

A small crowd began to gather. "This 'old guy' you speak of, *señor*," the student responded, "has never asked these good people to trust him. He has merely asked them to trust themselves."

"They don't need some old foreigner to tell them to trust themselves," the man answered, rising to the bait. "They already know very well how to do that." The circle around the two men, one young, one old, was now three deep.

The student said, "If that is so, *señor*, then why do your friends in Habana make all the decisions—where they shall work, what they shall be paid, where they shall live—for them? If they are as intelligent as you say, surely they do not need a small group of big shot officials in Habana to tell them how to live." There was a murmur of approval from the kibitzers. More people crossed the square to observe the fracas. They were not used to high-spirited politics and they were coming to appreciate the drama of it. For, had the young student come to their town talking like this only a few months ago, he would have been disappeared.

The party boss turned to the crowd. "Anyone here seen Señor Ernes-to Blan-co? Anybody met this *hombre viejo extraordinario*? You people here want to have the responsibility to run this town . . . this 'true little republic'?"

"Why not?" wheezed a voice in the back of the crowd where the evening light was dim. From his spot on the other side of the circle, Nick Ferre tried to make out the interlocutor.

"Why not?" said the party boss. "Why not is because it is a heavy responsibility. You people"—his hand swept the crowd—"have to work hard all day. You don't need the heavy duty of worrying about things like schools and roads and water systems. That's what you have a government in Habana for. We have experts that know about these things."

"If they know so much, these 'experts,' " said the wheezing voice, "why are the roads and water systems and the schools falling apart?" There was a strong round of approving applause.

"They're better than they used to be," the boss said defensively. "Nobody can deny that they're better than in the bastard *batistiana* days." There was polite applause from a crowd that now numbered well over a hundred.

The student leader said, "I don't remember the *batistiana* days. I am more concerned with the future. What is this country going to be like in the twenty-first century?" He motioned to the back of the crowd. "*Señor*, what do you think this country should be like?"

The crowd made way and a slight older man made his way forward. He coughed several times as he pushed forward. A few of the older people near the front whispered to each other. As he entered the inner circle, his hand swept around the crowd. "You know as well as I do what this country should be like." Nick immediately recognized the reincarnated revolutionary and was struck by the clarity and power of the old man's voice. "That's the point. Why should 'experts' in Habana know more about your lives than you do?" He looked intently at the skinny student almost a foot taller than he was. "It's going to be his country . . . and your children's country . . . pretty soon. Not this man's." He gestured with a thumb over his shoulder at the party man. "Don't you think the young people of this country have a clearer picture of the future than the 'experts' this man gives his trust to?" The crowd, still growing, applauded warmly. "The folks in Habana should have plenty to do making sure the monopolies and the rich people don't take over this country."

The party man raised his hand for silence. "You're some kind of stranger here, I think. I've lived around here all of my life and I haven't seen you before. Why do you come here to tell us what we should do?"

The white-haired old man put up both hands palms out. "Did I tell anyone what they should do? I don't remember saying such a thing. It is not my business to tell these people here what they should do. They know enough what they should do. That is my point."

Nick had been edging closer both to listen and to study Ernesto. Beneath his thick white eyebrows, his dark brown eyes glowed. Beneath the thick white mustache, white teeth gleamed when he spoke. The older man had clearly established some harmony with the crowd. He seemed to ask the very question in people's minds. Nick looked across the crowd and noted with concern the sudden presence of three ill-kempt local policemen. They had not been there a moment before. They seemed to be watching the party boss for some kind of signal.

"*Señor*," the party boss said, "most of the people of this town are strong supporters of the Social Democratic Party. Where do you yourself stand on this coming election. We hope you will be on our side and not with the oligarchy *del norte*."

The old man showed the strong white teeth. "I suppose I believe this young man here has a better argument than either party. It seems to me he is concerning himself with distributing the power to the people. And he seems to believe that if the central government will support the strong local governments of the people, then we should have the proper balance in our public affairs." He looked off into the gathering shadows from the large palms overhanging the *parque*. "It is an old idea from a long time ago."

To Nick, Ernesto seemed fragile, almost frail. His hair, though somewhat receded and thinning on top, was still thick white on the sides and back. Blanco occasionally combed it back with his fingers. His eyebrows and mustache were equally thick, white, and unfamiliar with trimming scissors. He was not a big man. He was well under six feet and, though covered with simple peasant clothes, it was clear his limbs were thin. His gestures as he spoke, especially when he turned his head, were rendered stiff by arthritis. He drew his breath with effort, the lifelong asthma still a plague. Every few minutes he coughed softly and his sentences often ended in a breathless wheeze that sounded like a small leaky bellows.

Yet there seemed to Nick the tension of an old jungle cat about him. His skin was taut and the muscles in his thin neck were wiry. Despite the stiffness, he displayed a seasoned actor's degree of elegance in his movements. He appeared both ready and at ease. He was a man enormously at home in himself, Nick thought. A casual glance suggested just another old *campesino*, a figure of little note in a crowd. A moment's study revealed instead a figure who had taken life on fiercely and had given little quarter. Nick wondered how many men—deserters, betrayers, spies, outright enemies—he had himself killed and whether any of them still troubled his sleep. He wondered where he had been and how he had lived during three and a half decades of rambling exile. Wherever he had been, Nick thought, he had found an identity he could live with.

The old man suddenly looked at him and said, "*Tío Sam* is watching this country. He is trying to decide whether to take us over again— maybe not so openly as in the past—but moving in down here with all his money and his power. Maybe he will, maybe he won't. The old crowd in Habana will probably keep him out for a while. The old crowd in Miami will let him in sooner. But you"—and here his eyes swept the crowd as he turned a complete circle—"you can decide how much power over your lives you're going to give him." His eyes came back to rest, penetratingly, on Nick.

Nick was startled. His eyes were those of a young person. The eyelids and the skin around the eyes were wrinkled with years of nature and combat. There was a deep furrow between the eyes separating the thick, bushy brows. But the dark brown eyes themselves were clear, almost translucent. They betrayed no age, no combat, no defeat, no death. Then Nick was stunned to see Ernesto smile hugely—his white teeth gleaming against the dark skin—and wink.

The party boss said, "You got part of it right, old stranger. Our party, the Social Democrats of Cuba, will not let *Tío Sam* take over this country ever again. That's the reason why the people of this town and this island are not going to let the Miami crowd come back."

During the several minutes Ernesto Blanco had been engaged in the debate in the center of the crowd, Nick noticed people murmuring to each other and occasionally pointing at *el viejo*. They were gradually beginning to suspect that this stranger might possibly be the legendary Ernesto. Finally, a weathered *campesino* at the back, energized by a few *cervezas*, shouted out, *"Ernesto! Viva el movimiento! Viva la república auténtica!"*

Quickly the party boss raised two fingers and pointed at the man. Two of the ragtag policemen moved in on each side and, a hand under each arm, began to drag him away. The man continued to shout, *"Viva Ernesto! Viva la república!"* The crowd turned toward the fracas and several people shouted in protest at his removal. Several local young people blocked the policemen and tried to rescue the shouting man as he struggled to get free. The third local policeman moved in and swung a fist at one of the young men pulling at the arm of the other policeman. Two young people in turn pushed him back. Suddenly, the struggle grew in size and intensity. Shouts went up throughout the crowd and people moved toward the struggle.

Nick felt a hand at his elbow pulling him in the opposite direction toward the edge of the square. He looked for Ernesto but couldn't locate him. Skirmishes were breaking out and the square was in turmoil as deep dusk began to settle. One of the students from Havana led Nick around behind the buildings on the square. He was quickly shoved into the ancient car that had brought them down. Its engine had been running and it immediately sped off in the direction of the Havana highway. As Nick turned back from watching the town lights recede, he was shocked to find himself sitting next to Ernesto Blanco.

"You see," he said, smiling broadly again, "we are creating some excitement. Even more, we have the old boys in the Palacio worried. They don't know anything about this idea of democracy." He twisted the corner of his mustache and studied Nick out of the corner of his eye.

"You're from the States, right? You're the young man from the Interests Section who is supposed to be studying our little experiment here. I wouldn't imagine that you're too happy with your government helping out that Miami crowd."

Nick was shocked. The old man was also a mind reader. "I would be very interested to know," the man Ernesto said, "what you think of our election . . . what your government thinks of our election." He shrugged as if to say, It really doesn't matter to the outcome. "It is a matter of curiosity to me and my friends."

The car swayed and clattered onto the central highway to Havana. Nick said, "I don't know that my government—the government of the U.S.—has an opinion." He averted his eyes, uncomfortable with the lie. "I mean, there are probably lots of opinions. If you know anything about how our country works, you must know that. On the politics of other countries, we're almost always divided."

Ernesto smiled. "I know something of the way your country works." Absentmindedly he fingered a couple of scars—wounds?—on his chest. "I have had some personal experience with that. But rarely have you not had some opinion of Cuba. This island is like a comb of honey and you are a swarm of bees. This place is a small flame and you are a big moth." He bugged his eyes and flapped his hands.

Nick now looked squarely at him. "How did you know who I was . . . am? How did you know I was from the States and worked at the Int . . . for my government?"

Ernesto patted his shoulder. "My friends here"—he gestured at the two students in the front—"know a lot of things. They figured out who you were even before you told them. They're pretty smart." The student leader in the passenger seat turned and smiled. "And besides, I think I knew something about your family—many years ago."

"What?" Nick blurted. "You knew my family?" His parents had told him little of the old days.

Ernesto looked out the window on the driver's side. "They had a lot of land down in Oriente—Granma—province. I was with a bunch of guys that landed in a boat there a long time ago." He was silent for a moment as Nick pondered the overwhelming irony of the story and the circumstances that now brought them together. "I think they sent some people to shoot at us. Or maybe they just told the *batistianas* where we were." Then he laughed. "Good thing they couldn't shoot straight. Anyway, I never got to meet your family. They ran one way and I ran the other." He looked at Nick. "They okay now—up in the States?"

Nick nodded affirmatively. "Look, I'm not a spy. I've been following all the parties. . . ."

"We're not a political party," Ernesto said, "we're a movement."

"But you've got a candidate for president and candidates announcing for the legislature," Nick countered. "That sounds like a party."

"About that, you are right," Ernesto observed. "But the main thing is the idea—the true republic—the community making most of the decisions. The party should serve the idea, not the idea the party. That's the difference between us and the others. They have no idea—or maybe a worn-out idea—and all they know about is the power—getting their party into the power."

Nick thought for a moment. "You frighten them, you know. They're scared of you."

"They are not frightened of me," Ernesto said. "They are frightened of the idea."

"That's even more dangerous," Nick said. "They don't know how to get rid of the idea. It's popping up all over the place. But they think if they get rid of you, they get rid of your idea."

Ernesto laughed softly. "For them, that's a big mistake. It's not my idea. It's some early Greek—Pericles, or somebody—it's his idea. I just blew a lot of dust off and brought it to Cuba. Now, I think, it is too late to kill this idea." The students in front nodded vigorously. "This idea is beginning to enter the soul of the people. That's what makes it dangerous. It took more than thirty years, but I learned this truth. You cannot kill the soul of people."

Nick said heatedly, "You and I may know that, but politicians hungry for power may not know that. Both sides are focused on you. You're the one thing that unites them both." He studied the road ahead. "It wouldn't surprise me if they didn't find some way to get together on the project of getting rid of you."

In the darkened car space Ernesto shrugged and raised both palms. "You know something. It doesn't matter much." He pointed to the front seat. "These are the ones they should care about. They are the ones whose safety concerns me. I am not the future of Cuba. They are the future of Cuba." The two young men laughed softly, embarrassed. Ernesto turned in his seat and studied Nick full on, his eyes reflecting the light of passing vehicles. "They would not be so stupid as to kill me. Then they have an old martyr to deal with."

3 6

■

Later that night Ernesto transferred to a fuming truck loaded with produce that was making its way across Cuba back to the Sierra. The students returned Nick to Havana and, according to instructions given by Ernesto, gave him directions to the same safe house used by Victoria Savidge on her first rendezvous with Ernesto and Alejo almost six weeks before. He was to go there in five days and wait to be picked up. He was being invited to visit the guerrilla politicians in their mountain hideout. Ernesto thought it might be an interesting idea for a representative of the government of the United States of America to see that the organizers of the true republic movement were ordinary law-abiding citizens. And he thought Nick should also be present for his first, and probably only, interview he would give to any journalist.

Before leaving for the town meeting in Consolación del Sur, Ernesto advised Victoria that she should make contact with her cameraman and prepare for the interview. While he was in Pinar del Río province, she was escorted down to Matanzas, where her cameraman had been instructed to meet her. While there she contacted Sam Rapport and, after a series of vaguely worded phone calls, they had agreed on a satellite time at eight in the evening three days later. The time was the product of a violently negotiated compromise between Sam's insistence on prime time and the cameraman's need for natural light. The two suitcases of miniaturized equipment needed to beam to the satellite were heavy enough. There was no chance of hauling lights and even a small generator up the narrow, almost impassible ravines of the Sierra. As it was, the cameraman had to use every trick imaginable to convince Cuban customs that the equipment was for the new Havana TPN bureau to use for interviewing officials of the Cuban government and the Cuban Social Democratic Party.

Alejo took twenty dollars U.S. from the cameraman to hire a donkey from a local *campesino*. They used the donkey to pack the heavy suitcases up the mountains from the parking place where they had to leave the car. Precautions were taken to guarantee that the car and driver rented by the cameraman in Havana had not been followed to Matanzas. When the cameraman first saw Victoria at the hotel in Manzanillo from which she had made the first phone call to Sam Rapport, he didn't recognize her. "My God, Victoria, what have you done!" They had worked together often on bizarre assignments around the world and he was accustomed to her notorious divaesque demands, regardless of the hardship circumstances, for hairdo, makeup, and designer clothes. Cigar crammed in his mouth, he stared at her. "My God," he muttered again. "What have they done to you?" Suddenly protective, and suspecting the worst, he gestured angrily at the frail Alejo. "Have you guys made her a hostage?" And looking back at Victoria, "Have they . . . you know . . . done anything . . . like . . . bad to you?"

Turning to a mirror in the alcove of the hotel, the first she had seen in weeks, Victoria clapped a hand over her mouth. The thick red mane, chopped off weeks before, was growing back into a bird's nest nightmare. Mouth agape, she plucked some pine needles from it and touched its sprouting ends gingerly. She hadn't used makeup since the first few days in the mountains when she had exhausted her supply. Her face and arms were sun darkened. She wore an open-necked, ankle-length brown hemp dress brought to her by Rafael after her city clothes had become ripped and torn through constant relocation in the mountains. She wore peasant huaraches and she blushed when her self-examination revealed how rust colored her feet were. Harry, the cameraman, eyes wide, handed her his comb and she shook her head no. Glancing in the mirror again, she said, "This comb . . . the job overwhelms it."

As they followed the donkey up the mountain path, Victoria explained the procedure that was to take place. Ernesto would be waiting for them in a new camp they had recently established. Harry could use the evening light to find a spot and study lighting and angles. He could use whatever time he needed the following day to set up and test his equipment. She would go over some of the questions she intended to ask in keeping with her original agreement with Ernesto. There were no pans or establishing shots that might give away their location. There were to be no surprises. There were to be few specific references to his background or years, presumably, in exile. He had made it emphatically clear that he would answer no personal questions. He had insisted that the questions must relate to the true republic movement and the forthcoming elections in Cuba. Lady, he called her, like a title. "Lady, if you try some journalistic trick while the broadcast is under way, you must understand that I will stroll into the forest and leave you by yourself. But before I leave, I will explain to your viewers that you have broken your promise to me and are not trustworthy." His usual soft tone and his hand on her wrist took the edge off the guilt she felt. Countless times in planning the interview, she had been tempted to go for the on-air home run—"Are you or are you not . . . ?"—When the thought now occurred, it embarrassed her. She still wondered at the loss of her journalistic instincts.

Rafael and Otra Vez were waiting for them after the long, hot trek and, after greeting the stranger, Rafael offered him some coffee. Harry was stunned to see that the hideout of the vaunted revolutionary was a simple outdoor camp hidden in the trees. Indeed, they had come within twenty feet of it before he even realized that this was it. He looked in vain for the old man of past and current legend. He was not in sight. There was a fire for the coffee and the evening meal. There were a few heavily patched tents with mats and sleeping bags inside. Logs had been rolled up for seats and backrests near the fire. The smell from the warming pot of beans and rice suddenly made Harry hungry. With Rafael's help, Harry unloaded the two specially built metal suitcases and a duffel bag of clothes and put them in a tent he would share with Rafael. Every chance he got, Harry raised his eyebrows and rolled his eyes at Victoria. Where's the old man? he silently asked. She smiled and turned away.

Harry studied the layout, marked the direction of the setting sun, checked his watch—for it was near the time they would broadcast the following evening—and looked for a spot to locate Victoria and old Blanco. He put his back to the setting sun and saw the light falling through the thick pine trees suddenly illuminate a nest of mountain flowers punctuated by dramatic vines of orchids climbing several new trees. He squatted and studied the angle. He got a Polaroid camera from his duffel bag and took half a dozen quick shots. Then he got a small pocket scope that gave a sense of what the television camera would see and studied the spot through that. Perfect. Suddenly he realized how utterly dramatic this interview would be. After he cleared Cuban customs, TPN had been running spots hourly promoting the interview. They featured clips of Victoria from various war zones and historic interviews with news-breaking figures. They told how she—alone—had bravely ventured into the wilds of Cuba to track down the now world-renowned Ernesto Blanco, who, as everyone was quickly discovering, was on the verge of revolutionizing Cuba—possibly, once again. Violating Victoria's understanding before her departure, they showed film footage of Che Guevara from the 1960s and even the stunning still pictures of him dead on a table in a tiny village in the jungles of Bolivia. The interview would be carried live on the TPN network worldwide and the audience was going to be huge.

Rafael invited Harry to sit down on the logs with them for something to eat. "Where is he?" Harry hissed at Victoria, seated next to him. She pretended not to hear as she pushed the food back and forth on the customary paper plate that required no washing, was easy to pack, and could be burned after use. Harry looked behind him at the site he had selected for the interview, and as he turned back, he suddenly realized that a frail-looking white-haired man had silently joined them. It was spooky how he just materialized without a sound, yet with a plate of food on his lap. The old man nodded at him pleasantly. Victoria said, "Harry, this is Señor Blanco." The old man smiled when he saw half of Harry's dinner slide off his plate.

They turned in early. Harry was exhausted and Ernesto and Otra Vez were leaving early for a trip to a cabin halfway down the mountain from which they would send some messages by courier to various movement leaders throughout the country concerning plans for the final push. They would also pick up the young diplomat, Nick Ferre, who was being escorted from the safe house at the base of the mountains by trustworthy supporters.

Except for Ernesto Blanco, the odd collection of people in the camp slept little that night—especially Victoria Savidge. She would have to find some way, she thought as she stared at the low canvas roof of the frayed old tent, to try to make herself look presentable by tomorrow evening. But, much more important now, she had to find a way in no

more than fifteen minutes of airtime to permit this man for whom curiosity had given way to respect, and respect to admiration, and admiration to affection, and affection to . . . To what? she asked herself with
a shock. What am I thinking about? We have nothing in common.
Nothing. He's thirty years older than I am, for one thing. Well, perhaps
not quite thirty. But, I'm old enough not to get swept up again in revolutionary fever. She reflected ruefully on an earlier tendency, before
she discovered the comforts of wealthy, highly successful media executives, to form passionate attachments to earnest candidates or campaign
workers zealously pursuing a noble cause and needing the warmth and
comfort she might offer in her hotel suite. Pondering the problem of
how to compress Ernesto Blanco's cause—a cause that was turning her
life upside down—into the bite-sized canapés demanded by her hungry
medium, Victoria fell asleep.

As usual, the imminent sunrise awakened the birds and the birds awakened those in the camp. And as usual, Ernesto was off before the dawn
trailing Otra Vez, who seemed never to require sleep, in his wake. Victoria and Harry spent the day preparing and testing the portable broadcast system and rehearsing her introduction and questions. As Rafael
watched with excitement and Alejo with mystification, Harry set up the
two panels that transmitted the signal and electronically oriented them
to the azimuth where the satellite would be that evening. He explained
to Victoria that visual clarity had been sacrificed to portability and that
inferiority of the picture, broadcast at 18 frames per second, as opposed
to the 30 frames per second of standard video, would be distinctly no-
ticeable to the viewer and would also not lend itself to action or rapid
movement. But, since the interview would involve two talking heads and
minimal action, they agreed the slower transmission speed really
wouldn't matter. Indeed, visualizing the effect, Victoria thought it would
convey a quality of cinema verité. Harry tested the two 64-kilobit-per-
second satellite phones, as he had dozens of times before leaving the
States, and found them to be operating perfectly. Likewise, the video
compression module, the cigarette pack–sized wireless transmitter, and
the camera itself were all in tip-top shape. Finally, the heart of the
system, a specially designed magnesium-aluminum-rubber-encased computer that had proved itself on an Everest climb, beat with authority.
"There it is," Harry said, gesturing at the exotic equipment spread out
on a couple of flat rocks and a log over a two- or three-square-meter

area, "a full-blown field television broadcast station, a tribute to the age of miniaturization."

Humbled by this display of modern techno-sophistication, Alejo stared at it, his hat worriedly twisted in his weathered hands. "Does it, *señor*, make the people whose pictures you take also seem very small?" Alejo's confused expression and Victoria's snort convinced Harry that the old man was not, intentionally at least, making a political observation.

While Rafael guarded the expensive equipment with his life, Victoria took Harry on a walking tour of the rugged mountainside. In the early spring season, the air was clean and decidedly crisp at the two-thousand-meter elevation. Flocks of noisy, colorful birds competed with florid displays of mountain flowers for attention. After years of working together on assignments around the world for a variety of networks, Harry was astounded to see how this urban creature, a child of the age of televised glamour and sophistication, seemed so at home in this primitive mountainscape. Despite, or perhaps because of, the backward environment, she seemed years younger. Her frequent laugh was spontaneous, almost childlike. She paused to study orchids or flamboyant birds that she would have passed without notice had they been growing in Central Park. The transformation, in a matter of a few weeks, was so remarkable even the world-weary Harry could not help but speculate about the role the soft-spoken elderly man with the intense gaze had played in it. It was as if Victoria, this quintessential creature of the age of television, had returned to nature.

Just as they were turning back for the camp, Harry saw movement behind a rock outcropping fifty yards away. While Victoria strolled ahead, he stopped momentarily to try to make out what kind of animal it might be. He briefly wondered if there were predators in the area and made a note to check it out with Ernesto. He saw the movement again, a brief flash of light on glass, and what seemed to be a glint of metal. He called to Victoria, who stopped and turned back. Together they studied the area, then Victoria called out. There was no response. Harry started toward the rocks, but Victoria pulled him back by the shirt sleeve. She silently waved her hand no. They heard the breaking of a dead branch, then silence. After a further wait, and hearing nothing, they returned to the campsite. When Alejo suggested any one of several harmless natural creatures at work, Harry silently dissented. None that

Alejo named would be carrying glass or metal. Rafael's reconnaissance of the rocky area found nothing.

By late afternoon Ernesto and Otra Vez had returned with a wide-eyed Nick Ferre, as excited as a child at the adventure of finding himself in the inner cell of the true republic movement with its notorious leader and his loyal band. He was introduced all around, including to Victoria, whom he had already met, and bonded immediately with Rafael, a younger version of himself. His greeting of Ernesto contained a warning. "*Señor*, the place down below"—meaning the area surrounding Santiago—"is crawling with journalists and fortune seekers. I saw many people I recognized from Havana. Some I would not trust at all. I am sure some are from the Palacio, the Social Democrats, and I would not be surprised if the Free Cubans don't have some agents down there also. Apparently, word got out about this man"—he pointed at Harry—"and they all know from Ms. Savidge's network that an interview is scheduled for this evening. All the journalists in Havana are coming this way and I fear others as well who may have a more sinister agenda."

Ernesto nodded and thanked him. He seemed neither surprised nor dismayed. But he was even more quiet than usual. Preparations for yet another peasant dinner were begun. Ernesto wanted dinner over with and all gear packed. He wanted to be able to move out after the interview. He had some intuitive sense that the sending of electronic signals back and forth might be detectable and that their location might be found by some kind of sophisticated equipment. Harry concurred and explained how it might work. His instincts verified, Ernesto instructed Rafael to go down the trail to the cabin where he had been earlier in the day and to return before eight in the evening with one of their loyal local guides and donkeys for the gear. They would be packed up and ready to move out the minute the interview was completed.

Forgoing dinner, Victoria went to work in her tent with a broken hairbrush, a small compact mirror, and the remaining stub of a lipstick. The hair was the worst. There would be viewers who would legitimately doubt that it was her, and her many critics would get a stupendous laugh at her appearance. Her signature hair looked like a rat's nest. Screw 'em if they can't take a joke, she thought wryly. Just proves I'll still do anything it takes to get the story. And what a story. The return of a legendary revolutionary.

But, she reminded herself yet again, that was not the story. For the first time in her long career, she knew this story to be more important than her future, the fortunes of the pathetic Marshall Stuart, or even the success of The Political Network. If she would ever be remembered for anything, she thought, she wanted it to be this interview, this broadcast that introduced the most honest leader she had ever met. She did not completely understand herself why she believed letting Ernesto Blanco speak to the world was so important. But believe it she did. During her weeks in the mountains trailing the elusive rebel on his rambling excursions throughout the region, she came to conclude that he possessed an extraordinary understated magnetism, that he had a mystical ability to alter the human environment just by his presence. Though she did not claim to understand how the byzantine byways of politics were ordered, she knew beyond a doubt that if Blanco's approach worked in Cuba it could also work in Vietnam, or in Hungary, or even in the United States. Recycling throughout her mind since Harry had arrived in Matanzas and the full reality of her project had finally struck her, that thought accounted for a degree of nervousness she had not experienced since the first time she had asked a question at a presidential press conference.

Harry stuck his head in her tent. "Ready?" She looked at her watch. It was twenty minutes until airtime. She went outside and noted immediately how calm and beautiful the evening was. The sky was cloudless, a few evening birds whistled to each other across the forest canopy, and she noticed that the spot Harry had picked for the interview was lit like a studio. Although Ernesto was not in sight, she could smell the cigar that he alone occasionally smoked. She saw him at a distance from the campsite, his back to them, staring into the sunset in the west. He seemed to be concentrating on something in the distance. Victoria suddenly realized he was looking in the direction of the rocky outcropping where Harry thought he had seen some movement that afternoon. Suddenly, Ernesto turned back, took a puff on the cigar, and smiled at her grandly. She felt a rush of emotion she could not begin to identify.

Harry shouted, "Let's go. Get in position." He held up one of the phones. "We've got the bird. We're on in ten."

All around them the activities of striking tents, stuffing bags into the donkeys' panniers, and snuffing out the campfire heightened the tension surrounding the exotic equipment that would magically broadcast the antique Ernesto Blanco to a vast audience spread throughout the Americas, Europe, Africa, Asia, and who could imagine where else.

Even without the bustle and the tension, it was doubtful that any of the handful of preoccupied people would have sensed the wiry, taut figure now settled into a niche in the rocky outcropping to the west, the one Ernesto had been studying moments before through the haze of his cigar. The figure's gray, tan, and khaki camouflage clothing blended perfectly into the rocks. The dull matte black barrel of her rifle drew no reflected sunlight. The sun now directly behind and slightly above the outcropping would blind anyone looking directly that way in any case. The bill of the figure's fatigue hat covered the special 8-by-40 combat binoculars now focused on the campsite and the area covered with high-technology gear just beyond. The range finder on the binoculars put the distance at just under 175 feet. The figure checked her watch. Five minutes to airtime. Between five and ten minutes into the broadcast, the falling sun would be directly behind the rocks and would prevent anyone from detecting any movement whatsoever from that spot.

Victoria directed Ernesto to a spot in the brightly lit clearing marked by two crossed twigs. She stood just to his left with the microphone. Alejo and Rafael led the pack donkeys a couple of hundred yards down the mountain trail so that their brayed complaints against their burdens would not make their way into the broadcast. Harry had a satellite phone to one ear and was tweaking dials on the transmitting panel. He held up a circled forefinger and thumb to signal okay. Laying the phone down, he flashed ten fingers five times. Less than a minute. As he held an index finger in the air, a breathless, wide-eyed Rafael staggered back into the camp. "Señor Blanco," he rasped, "a big mob is coming up the main trail." He pointed to the other access trail slightly to the east. "They will be here in . . . I don't know . . . maybe fifteen or twenty minutes. It sounds like half of Santiago," he hissed.

Harry dropped his finger. They were live by satellite to the world. Victoria looked into Harry's camera and said, "From somewhere high in the Sierra Maestra mountains of eastern Cuba, this is Victoria Savidge for The Political Network." She turned slightly to her right and said, "And this is Señor Ernesto Blanco. Welcome to this, ah, somewhat unusual broadcast, Señor Blanco." Ernesto showed a row of bright white teeth and nodded. Despite her years attached to television microphones and cameras, Victoria's hand and voice trembled slightly. "You have started a political movement here in Cuba that has gained surprising strength and that has worried the two traditional parties. Why?"

Ernesto's eyes widened slightly. "Why are they worried? Or why did the movement gain strength?"

Rattled, Victoria grasped for clarity. "First, why the strength of your movement?"

"The true republic is for the people of Cuba a chance, maybe their first chance, to gain control of their destiny," Ernesto said. "They should not have to have a political party run their country. They should be able to decide for themselves in their own communities what they will do—about their children's education, about their hospitals, about their homes and jobs, about their air and their water. It is as simple as that. So when this idea is explained to the people, they like it and give it their support." He smiled. "It is not really so complicated."

"Then why," Victoria said, "does this simple idea create such opposition from the Social Democrats, the former Communists, and the Free Cubans, the previous ruling party?"

Ernesto shrugged. "You must ask them, I think. It must be about the power. The more power have the people, the less power have the politicians."

"Señor Blanco," Victoria said, looking right and left, "you choose to operate from this rustic mountain, ah, retreat, I suppose you would call it. Why here? Why not Havana or a major city?"

"A campaign for the people," Ernesto said, "should be where the ordinary people are. I know these mountains. It is comfortable for me and my friends here. We are with nature and do not have the noise and distractions of the city. Besides"—he winked at the camera—"as we now are proving, it is possible also to communicate with people from here as well as in the city."

Harry wagged his index finger in a circle. Time was running. They had less than ten minutes on the satellite. Victoria's voice became more urgent. "Could the idea that you call the 'true republic' be used in other countries besides Cuba? Do you think that other people—in Africa, or in Asia, or even the States—could use this idea? Could it become some kind of new politics . . . ?"

Suddenly Ernesto became animated. "Of course," he said, "that is the whole point. This is not a Cuban idea or a Latin idea. It is a human idea. It is an idea about restoring the dignity and the authority to people. So that they are not talked down to from above. They are not told what to do by some boss or some politician. It is about their ownership of their own lives."

"But won't politicians in power . . . political parties . . . interests with access to those in power . . . won't they resist this idea . . . try to stop someone like you who pushes it?" Victoria insisted as she watched Harry from the corner of her eye. He held a satellite phone to one ear as he balanced the camera on his shoulder. He briefly put the phone down and wound his finger in the hurry-up circle again.

Ernesto smiled and shrugged, as if to say "of course." Then he said, "But once the idea of self-government, of the people themselves owning the power, is free, then no force can stop it."

Victoria's brow was knitted with the tension of the moment. "Are you not afraid? What if someone tried to harm you?"

"It is, *señora*," Ernesto said, "but the problem of one man. No one can kill an idea. It is too—"

There was a sound like a slight cough over the hill to their left, a whispered sigh, and simultaneously a soft whack on a tree just behind Ernesto's right shoulder as bark and wood chips flew out to reveal a cone of fresh wood six inches deep and almost a foot across in the tree trunk just behind Ernesto's head. There was an eternity of silence while a thousand singing birds at once grew silent, trying to identify the unfamiliar sounds. Victoria looked at the red light on Harry's camera and tried, reflexively, to frame a new question. Stunned, she turned toward Ernesto only to see him hauled down and away from camera range by Nick Ferre. She turned slightly back to her left and thought she heard the distant slide and click of metal on metal as Nick, now aided by Rafael, almost carried Ernesto into the trees and out of sight down the back trail.

As a distant loop in one hemisphere of her brain told her that someone had just tried to shoot—perhaps had shot—Ernesto, the dominant hemisphere said the show had to be wrapped. She turned back to the still-registering camera and saw Harry's index finger make a half-dozen fast rotations then reach down for the satellite phone while he continued to focus on her. Dumbfounded, she stared at a reflection of herself, wide-eyed, in the lens.

"All right," she blurted. "He's all right. He'll be all right. He's safe. He'll be safe." Then she was overtaken by a frenzy. "We'll be all right too. I'll be all right." She pointed into the lens. "You'll all be all right." Then a dazed smile framed her mouth. "Or will we? Are any of us safe from assassins who would stalk a harmless elderly man in the mountains of Cuba? Who wants to kill this man for preaching democracy? Who could be frightened by his idea . . . his idea of political power for ordinary people? Who can be so afraid of that that they would kill someone?" Clutching the microphone so hard her knuckles were white, she ran her free hand through her thick uneven mane. Her voice panting, her eyes still wide, her hair wildly askew, she scared the hell out of Harry as he knew she would the watching world. She took a pace toward him and he involuntarily backed up.

"Our job in the media ought to be to find out who's so afraid," she insisted. "Could it be someone in the White House . . . or maybe the CIA? Could it be the people in power in Havana . . . or maybe the exiles from Miami who want to come back and take over?"

Victoria stared intently into the lens. "Perhaps there are powerful people in the media afraid of radical democracy . . . power to the people." Rows of mesmerized heads in the TPN control room in New York involuntarily swiveled to look at the chairman of the network, Marshall Stuart.

"Who tried to kill this man tonight?" She pointed into the lens. "The people of the world will want to know. The people in Cuba and around the globe who support this decent man will demand to know." The picture was now beginning to break up slightly and the focus was unsteady. It had just occurred to Harry that whoever took the shot was still out there and might want to terminate this broadcast even before the satellite did.

"Let's hope," Victoria said, as she looked sideways into the lens, "let's hope there is still at least one journalist out there who cares enough about the truth to track it down. It won't be me." She now seemed almost to be speaking to herself, her image jerking and dancing. "I've done this job long enough. I think my job, my network, political journalism, and the whole political process is corrupt." She turned back toward the camera. "Take this microphone. I don't need it anymore. I'm doing the first really honest thing in my life. I'm going to find that good man and try to help him find the true republic." The last picture several hundred million people saw from the Cuban Sierra was Victoria Savidge thrusting the microphone at the camera.

3 7

■

Get off me, *joven*. I can't breath." Ernesto wheezed and hacked, struggling for air. Reluctantly, Rafael got off his back and Nick, backed up against the two of them, moved away. The old man and two young ones were piled in a heap behind a giant boulder on the side of the mountain about a quarter of a mile below the camp from which Ernesto had just spoken to the world—and where he had almost been killed.

All were panting for breath, none more so than Ernesto. Their flight down the hill had been pell-mell, tripping and falling, scrambling and tumbling. They had no idea where the shooter was or whether there might be more than one. They fully expected any minute to be confronted by an assassin emerging from behind a rock or tree along the trail. But as breath returned, so did reason. Whoever had taken the shot was very likely headed, undoubtedly more efficiently, down the other side of the mountain.

"Let's go back," Ernesto wheezed. "We have to help the others."

"They are coming, *señor*," Rafael panted. "They will join us soon."

Nick added, "We . . . you shouldn't go back up there. We don't know what's going on. I'll go back and see." He got to his feet, look quickly around, and brushed the leaves and dirt from his jeans.

"Get that woman out of there," Ernesto said. "That Victoria. Alejo and that camera fellow can take care of themselves." He struggled to his feet and put his hands on his knees, still struggling for air. Rafael brushed him off. Though grateful for their concern, Ernesto was furious that the two young men had hauled him out of the camp like a sack of turnips and left the *Americana* there all by herself. He considered it a breach of courage on his part.

Nick headed back up the trail and had only been gone a minute when the two others heard running feet and hushed noises from above. Ernesto looked around the giant boulder and saw a mad dream. First came Nick, then Victoria, then farther behind, Harry the cameraman.

All Ernesto could see was Victoria's dress flying, her red hair spreading out like wings, hands waving for balance. She was, at that moment, a vision. What a sight, he thought. She was simply the prettiest woman he had ever seen in his life. In an instant, the wave of adrenaline driven by flight was transformed into relief and passion. As naturally as the dawn, the onrushing Victoria threw herself into Ernesto's outstretched arms. Their embrace lasted long enough for the surrounding, panting men to search for reasons to study the trail above them.

Moments later, the odd band regrouped and started down the trail in a more orderly fashion. Victoria and Ernesto walked some steps behind. "I was surprised at how happy I was to see you," Ernesto finally said.

Victoria took his hand, squeezed it, and smiled. "I gave a hell of a speech after you left—after they pulled you away."

"I gave those boys some grief for jerking me out of there," Ernesto grumbled. "It was not very polite of us to leave you there."

"Politeness becomes less important when bullets are flying," she said. "Besides, they were shooting at you, not at me."

"What did you say to the people on the television?"

"I quit my job—quit the television," she said. She smiled again and said, "I told them I was joining the revolution—your revolution."

"*Madre de Dios,*" Ernesto breathed. "You cannot join my revolution."

"Why not?" Victoria exclaimed loudly enough for the advance guard to look back.

Through gritted teeth, Ernesto said, "For the very simple reason, *mi amiga*, that it is not *my* revolution." Then after a moment he said, "Besides, it is dangerous—in case you haven't observed. This business is becoming serious now." He nodded backward toward the camp. "There will be more of this—this kind of thing."

"And what will you do when . . . if it happens?" Victoria asked.

Ernesto's lungs rasped as he breathed. "Against me, I will do nothing.

But against you . . . if they do anything against you, then I will put on the old beret, sling on the rifle and some grenades, and go get them." Despite his age, and the obvious fact that he was a respiratory disaster, Victoria believed unquestioningly that he was serious.

Suddenly Victoria began to laugh. She threw her arms in the air and made several twirling revolutions in the middle of the trail. The others, now pushing forward down the hill to the rendezvous point with the vehicle Otra Vez had procured for them, were too far ahead to hear or see. Mystified, Ernesto exclaimed, "Are you *loca*, woman? Are you making a joke at my manhood?"

She shook her head no. "No, Ernesto, it is just that I am free. And I am happy. I have never felt so free and happy before. Then she fell in his arms again. And then he began to laugh also. "We were almost killed, Ernesto, and now we are alive." Then she began to laugh again. "You came within inches of death, and now you are alive." Then, caught in the spirit, Ernesto started to laugh. He laughed and wheezed and laughed and wheezed. He had not been heard to laugh like this since he became very drunk one night in a small village in Ecuador some months before. It was the night when he realized his destiny was to return to Cuba to lead this new revolution.

Gasping for air, Ernesto shouted, "Almost dead by a couple of inches."

They both started laughing again. "I will never forget," he whispered, "the sight of you—running like a madwoman down the trail—hair and dress and arms flying in all directions." Then they both started laughing like children again. Ernesto leaned forward, hands on knees, gasping for air as Victoria resumed her mad twirling and finally fell in a dizzy heap into a clump of tall grass from which flowers exploded. Ernesto looked at her and thought, This is the most beautiful creature I have ever seen.

■ ■ ■

No one was more surprised than I was when they decided to take their shot, or should I say their first shot, in front of more people than I have ever talked to in my whole life. I knew it would happen sooner or later—maybe not bullets, but maybe poison or a knife or maybe a bomb—but not in front of a television camera. If they were smart, they would have just let me talk and maybe the television would have done the job.

What made me the angriest was leaving that woman there all by herself. It wasn't very courageous on my part. But by the time I got free of those guys, Rafael and that American boy, she was coming down the trail after us. She told me that night, after things settled down, that she had made a speech on worldwide television quitting her job right there. Came over to our side. That must have shocked a lot of people del norte. I guess she is, or was, pretty important up there. I'll bet they're still talking about it. I don't know much about television. Never cared for it while I was wandering all over South America. But the way she told me that night, the whole thing—what I had to say, the potshot, her tantrum—must have really lit up those tubes, or whatever it is they call them.

However many years I have left I will never forget how she looked—all right, how good she looked—tearing down that trail. She was a vision all right. What a sight she was. And when we caught each other, I really didn't care about those two young guys. I just wanted to hold her. Here two minutes before we both came within a couple of inches of being dead and all I could do was laugh. And she laughed even more. We just stood there laughing.

Then Rafael sobered us up. For all we knew, the shooter, or maybe shooters, was still up there. We heard noise ahead of us—it later turned out to be Alejo and Otra Vez with the donkeys—so we took off. They caught up with us halfway down the mountain at the rendezvous point. The excitement wasn't over by any means. But what I remember most was that woman, Vic-tor-i-a, coming down that trail, waving her arms, coming into my arms, throwing her arms around me. And laughing.

The only thing I could think about—besides how pretty she looked and how good she felt—was that I hadn't laughed like that in many, many, many years. It seems pretty crazy. Someone tries to kill you, almost succeeds, with a lot of people watching. And two minutes later there you are in the middle of a forest with a beautiful creature laughing at it all.

I wonder if it's too late for me. I wonder if it's possible to have that laughter, to keep that laughter. I wonder if people really do that, really keep that. I've seen some poor raggedy-ass campesinos sometimes after work on Saturday or maybe in the evening on Sunday when they've had a chance to relax. And they have a good woman and some kids around. And they're piss-poor. But somebody says something—and they all laugh. It seems to me the most wonderful thing. In the middle of that simple life with none of the things, the material things, they have del norte, to have a family and to laugh. It's a way of saying to God, it's okay. You didn't give me much. But I've got these people. I've got this family. And I can laugh.

I don't have a family. I guess there is Alejo and Rafael and some others who have helped me so much. Everything I've got—some books, some papers, some pictures—are right here in this bag next to me. Now this woman doesn't have anything. She doesn't have a job. Where she comes from they won't let her work again. In a few weeks this election is over. What will she do? Where is she going to go? She doesn't have a family either, I think. What will happen to her? Yet, there she is over there by the fire. Sound asleep, with a smile on her face.

But we have work to do now. Everything comes down to the next few weeks and days. We have to keep this movement going and building. We can't let it stall now. Too many people have given too much, have sacrificed too much. I fear some of them may be hurt. I am afraid that those out to stop the true republic will try some dangerous stuff. I don't want these people, particularly these young people, to get hurt. This country doesn't need any more martyrs. It has enough. We have to carry this movement down to the finish as safely as we can.

Yet I worry about the young people and the candidates for the legislature and for the national leadership and all the simple people who are passing around our manifesto and defying the authority. They must not be endangered. It is their country and their children's country. They have earned the right to run their own country. They should not be required to shed more blood for that right. If I could pray for them, I would. But instead, I can only work.

PART IV

■

MARCH–APRIL 2000

3 8

■

When Ernesto Blanco and his followers abandoned the rocky redoubt, they made a dash down the steep trails of the Sierra pushing some donkeys and pulling others. Rafael and Nick had excess baggage slung over their shoulders. Alejo had lingered behind to evacuate the distraught Victoria. Her even more confused colleague Harry had taken considerable time packing satellite phones, transmitters, transmission panels, computer, and camera into their specially designed cases. Even as he did so, he kept one eye over his shoulder toward the rocky outcrop whence the silenced shot seemed to have come. Whoever had tried to get Ernesto had failed at the principal task but had surely succeeded at truncating the broadcast. He hoped the shooter did not have a separate bounty on cameramen.

Harry had not cleared camp carrying his two heavy metal cases fifteen minutes before the abandoned campsite and outdoor broadcast studio was overrun by a boiling herd of journalists. They clawed and shouted their way into the area stirring up the recently dampened dinner fire, thrashing wildly in the underbrush for laggard revolutionaries, searching behind trees for the famous television interviewer who had scooped them all, and generally falling about in comic disarray. None was aware of the dangerous drama that had transpired until a stringer for the *Chicago Sun-Times* saw the rounded, conical scar in a nearby tree, speculated regarding its nature, and stirred the pack into a frenzy with the thought that "somebody just tried to kill somebody here." The moments taken to evaluate and reevaluate this proposition provided the escaping political rebels additional lead time to reach the rendezvous point halfway down the mountain and link up with a fresh group of rescuers.

The original plan, before the assassination attempt and the appearance of the press mob, had been to meet their four young escorts, overnight in two rough-hewn *campesino* cabins, then make their way to a political

meeting with true republic supporters in Holguín the following afternoon. Now things were in disarray. Otra Vez said, "Look, the rest of
you go to the cabins. They're about a mile and a half from here. I'll go
down the trail to Victorino and get us a truck to take us into Santiago.
We got to get away from that mob. They'll be down here on us pretty
quick if we don't get out of here. And God knows where that shooter
went."

Ernesto nodded agreement. They were all too winded to talk. Otra
Vez took off with his own satchel over his shoulder. The young people
who had come to meet them took their hand luggage and pulled the
mules farther down the trail as Ernesto, Victoria, and the others followed.

It was now well after nine o'clock and the spring sun had made its
departure. To the east, a full moon lit the way. The moonlight through
the trees and rocks made eerie shadows on the trail. Holding Victoria's
arm as they made their way at a rapid pace down the trail, Ernesto could
feel her shiver. She shrugged off his attempt to throw his own jacket
around her. It was fear, not the cooling evening temperature, that made
her shake. The adrenaline rush of the previous moments suddenly
stopped as the full impact of the attempted assassination struck her. She
instinctively understood that the bullet represented the instantaneous
change of the true republic effort from incipient political movement to
endangered political revolution. One of two established political orders
now felt itself sufficiently threatened by the sprightly white-haired man
at her side to have tried to kill him. Having failed in this instance, there
was little reason to believe that other efforts would not be made. She
pulled her arm with his hand in it close to her side.

Ernesto whispered to her, "It's okay. Clearly, they cannot shoot
straight. Besides, it was probably one of your journalistic competitors."
She shook her head and smiled in the darkness at his roguish good cheer.

Within half an hour they were at the primitive shelters built for local
herders in the area. They left the donkeys packed, but they pulled a
blanket from a pack for Victoria to wrap herself in. Two of the young
people went back up the trail two or three hundred yards to listen for
anyone—journalist or assassin—who might be following them. They
could not light a fire for fear of attracting attention. They would have
to wait for Otra Vez.

As they huddled on the floor, Nick looked at Ernesto. "Who did it?" he whispered.

"*Quién sabe?*" Ernesto shrugged. "Somebody who didn't like one of my speeches maybe."

"Look, Señor Blanco," Nick whispered, "this is serious. One of the two parties, or somebody supporting them, wants you out of the way. They won't give up. There will be other efforts."

"What do you want me to do, Señor Ferre," Ernesto said. "Give up? To do so would also give them what they want. One must follow one's destiny and not surrender to a fate dictated by someone else."

Nick wondered if Rafael, Alejo, and the others could tell how close Victoria was now sitting to Ernesto. "Let your friends carry the message now," he said. "You can still direct the campaign from a safe place. There are only . . . a few weeks till the election. This thing now has a life of its own. The worst possible thing that could happen is if they were to . . . elim . . . you know, do something to you. Your followers might then give up."

"These young people," Ernesto said, "and the others, the women, the *campesinos* and *vaqueros*, even the government workers risking their jobs, they all will continue on regardless. This is now their movement and their cause. It is now their future and their destiny. If I were to hide, if I became frightened and disappeared, this is far worse. You cannot become more concerned for yourself. This is a form of assassination. If your enemies can make you disappear, then they have killed you already."

Sensing the failure of his plea, Nick said, "At the least, let us get you some bodyguards, some security protection."

Nick could see Ernesto's teeth gleam in the faint moonlight through the open windows. "Who is 'us'? Are you speaking for *Tío Sam*? That would be a great irony. Maybe the CIA can now protect me. There would be those who would fall down with laughter even to hear such an idea."

One of the young escorts appeared at the door and hissed for silence. They all listened keenly. They could hear nothing. Time passed and Victoria's head fell on Ernesto's shoulder. More time passed and they then clearly heard noise coming up the trail from below. A donkey brayed softly and a murmured conversation took place. Presently one of the young people stuck his head in the door. "*Señor*, it is Otra Vez. He has got a truck down below. It is perhaps two miles this side of Victorino. We should go now."

The small, disparate band, exhausted by the tension and stress of the previous two hours, now got to its feet and followed the guides outside. The donkeys were pulled from their nearby grazing and the troop organized itself to go down the mountain. Otra Vez said to Alejo and Rafael, "There is a truck at the crossroads of this trail and the road into Victorino. It is parked by the roadside. Drive it to the safe house outside Santiago and I will meet you there tomorrow morning."

Rafael asked, "And you? Where are you going?"

"Back up the trail," Otra Vez answered. "I will make a diversion for the journalistic mob. They will be coming this way soon. I can occupy them for a while and you will be safely away."

Rafael's efforts to stay behind were rejected by Otra Vez. "You need to stay with *el jefe*. Besides, you are probably the only one who can drive the truck. Here is the key. It is a green truck from a nearby collective. I 'liberated' it. They won't miss it till tomorrow morning. Get going."

As Otra Vez headed back up the trail, the group started down. At Ernesto's insistence, they put Victoria on one of the donkeys with him on one side and Rafael on the other to keep her from falling off. They still had a two-mile hike to get to the crossroads and she was clearly near exhaustion. Ernesto held her hand tightly as they walked.

The farther down the mountain they moved, the less steep the trail became and the more quickly they could move. Still, it took close to another two hours to get near the junction. Once there, they all helped transfer broadcast cases, camping and cooking equipment, and personal bags and satchels from donkeys to the truck that, as Otra Vez had promised, awaited them. After much grinding and rasping of aged starter and generator, Rafael got the truck engine running and Victoria and Ernesto joined him in the cab. Alejo, Harry the cameraman, Nick, and the young supporters piled into the back. There was barely room for everyone together with all the gear. There was also what appeared to be a wooden toolbox in the rear with Otra Vez's own satchel on top.

Driving by moonlight only, Rafael turned onto the dirt road toward the village of Victorino. Once there, they would pick up a paved road through the town of Guisa heading northward toward the city of Bayamo. They would then be on the plains north of the Sierra and would join the highway leading southeastward toward Santiago. Even if all went well, it would be well after midnight before they reached the safe house where Victoria had first stayed on her way to meet Ernesto Blanco. Now, here she was, more than six weeks later, asleep next to him in an ancient belching truck with her head once again on his shoulder.

By now it was well after ten o'clock and they saw few lights in Victorino as they approached. Rafael turned several knobs and tested a few switches before he found the truck lights. As they passed through the deserted village square, the truck backfired twice, setting off a dozen neighborhood dogs. Those in the front and the back winced at the noise and Victoria, half dreaming of gunfire, jerked awake with a gasp. Ernesto squeezed her hand in reassurance. Just as they picked up the road leading to Guisa, they saw two vehicles approaching rapidly from the north. Ernesto waved his hand downward to slow Rafael's acceleration. Two heads appeared through the window separating the cab from the truck bed.

Ernesto put his hand on Victoria's head and pulled them both below the level of the dashboard as the cars approached. The two vehicles slowed as they passed and Rafael reported that they were both full of people. They were either Cuban security forces or more reporters. It was impossible to tell. But the cars were new enough that they could not belong to poor local *campesinos*. Gradually, as he monitored the other cars, Rafael gained speed. To his horror, a quarter of a mile behind he saw the cars stop, then begin to turn around. He reported to Ernesto that they were being followed. Ernesto watched them himself through the mirror on the passenger side. They were both now coming behind and gradually closing the distance.

Ernesto studied the road ahead. He turned to the open window into the back truck compartment. "When we get to the next narrow place in the road," he shouted, "Rafael will turn the truck sideways to block those cars. Everybody has to jump out and head into the trees. We will get separated. But you should all go back to Victorino. Make sure you are not being followed. There is a small cantina just off the square. It belongs to one of our people. The back door will be open. It will be dark in the back but make sure no one sees you. We will meet there and make our way out in the morning." Ahead he saw a single-lane bridge overpassing a small stream from the mountains. He gave quick instructions to Rafael, whispered to Victoria "stay with me," then said to those in the back, "Good luck, pals."

Rafael approached the small bridge hesitantly, then quickly twisted the wheel throwing the truck into a slow sideways skid, and jumbling the flailing group in the back. Victoria was pressed hard against Ernesto. Even before the truck stopped, Ernesto had his door open and was helping Victoria out. Behind them they could see people scrambling out the back and heading into the trees close to both sides of the road. The following cars were now two hundred yards behind and slowing, confused by the maneuver. Ernesto pulled Victoria after him as he used the cover of the truck to shield his quick dash into the nearby trees. She remembered later being surprised at his wiry strength and agility in covering the ground. They made it twenty-five yards into thick trees and underbrush as Ernesto audibly counted people that he could see scrambling across the road in front of them. Rafael was the last out of the truck as the two cars hesitantly approached.

Rafael was coming their way and was just at the treeline, and the cars were screeching to a halt and doors opening, when the truck erupted with a massive explosion. The vehicle lifted into the air, the bed blowing one way and the cab another, when the shock wave hit the escaping passengers in the trees. A thick fireball lifted skyward and lit the surrounding area like daylight. The people emerging from the two cars were blown backward to the ground, barely escaping injury from the flying shrapnel of the truck parts. The windshield of the nearest car was shattered. After the blast, there was eerie silence.

Then, those in the two cars, shouting and cursing, jumped back in their vehicles. They gingerly made their way forward through the debris, the two halves of the truck now burning at the roadside. The road to Victorino was a dead end, so they had to go north to Guisa to get out of this hellish battle zone. The passengers in the forward car kicked remaining shards of the windshield out with their feet and drove forward with the wind in their faces. Those in the trees heard the shouts and curses continue as they disappeared from view around a curve.

Rafael had been driven into the ground by the blast. Led by Ernesto, several of his people dashed forward as he slowly got to his hands and knees. Miraculously, he had not been struck by flying metal and glass and, though temporarily deafened by the blast, would recover. Now alone on the road, the group magically materialized from the trees lining the road. There was utter silence from the shock. Stunned faces were eerily lit by the burning truck remnants. With one arm around Victoria, Ernesto organized them to march back down the road to Victorino and shelter. Less than a mile away, lights could be seen coming on in the small village. Inhabitants of the remote village were sleepily wondering if this was some new CIA bombing or artillery signaling a rerun of the Bay of Pigs.

As senses gradually returned following the second attempted assassination of the evening, confused murmurs moved from straggling person to person. They moved, zombielike, down the road toward the lights, some wondering vaguely whether ninjas with assault rifles might erupt from the thick underbrush nearby. The combat veteran Ernesto, familiar with the confusion of warfare, sought to lift their spirits. "Look at it this way. Tonight we have only used up two of our nine lives. We still have seven left."

He ruffled Rafael's thick black hair as the others managed a chuckle. He still held Victoria with his other arm. He looked sideways at her and gave his familiar wink. Shaking her head at his unflappable composure and good cheer, even she managed a vague smile. There were pine needles in her hair and great black smudges on her face. Ernesto hoped there would be no mirrors in the simple houses where they would now spend the night.

He could see a few of the townspeople coming to investigate and to meet them. They would be curious, but when they discovered the identity of their temporary boarders they would ask no questions. Some in the group would be awake most of the night trying to fathom who might have planted an explosive with a timer in the truck. Over time, most would reach the inevitable conclusion. For Ernesto, it was an easier proposition. When they had loaded the truck earlier at the crossroads, he had noted with curiosity—not enough as it turned out—that the satchel belonging to Otra Vez lying atop the toolbox was empty.

3 9

∎

"Let's agree we have a problem on our hands," said the assistant secretary of state for Latin America. The Cuban task force was meeting in the national security advisor's White House office and the eight people, representing State, Defense, the National Security Council, the CIA, and Treasury, were not amused by recent events. Their collective equanimity had not been improved by a blunt message from the president, delivered by his national security advisor, that the task force had to produce a "creative and constructive" policy toward the "true republic" movement and its founder, Ernesto Blanco, and it better do so quickly. Circumstances, largely in the form of the now famous TPN interview, had overtaken administration policy.

"Do we have any idea what the audience was for that interview?" the assistant secretary asked.

The national security advisor said, "The press secretary estimated about forty million in the U.S. and something north of four hundred million worldwide."

A voice murmured, "Someone say Oscar night?"

"It isn't just the interview," the Treasury man said. "Here you've got an incipient folk hero—who may or may not be the ghost of a long-dead radical revolutionary—narrowly escaping a goddamn assassination attempt on live television followed by an on-air resignation by a somewhat faded television personality in favor of the hero's revolution."

The CIA representative added, "Some jerk in Hollywood has already announced plans to make a full-length feature film about this story."

"It's a lot worse than just show business," the security advisor said. "This thing is blowing back on us." He stared at the CIA man. "There is a chance—just a chance—the shooter might be traced to 'interests' here in the States." Someone groaned and several heads shook in disbelief. "Walt, your people better talk to the Bureau and find out what the exile groups are up to." The CIA man made a note and nodded. "Then there is the political problem here at home. We're getting reports of the formation of so-called true republic committees on dozens of campuses. Even worse, we just learned that airline ticket sales—apparently to students also—for Cuba have jumped into the high hundreds. They're flocking down there to help this Blanco character in the last weeks of the campaign. The point is, this isn't just a Cuban issue anymore. Thanks to this infamous interview, this is now an issue for us."

The assistant secretary said, "Worse than that. We're getting cables from most of the Latin countries that students in South and Central America are forming 'true republic' committees. A lot of them are also trying to get into Cuba." She consulted a yellow pad. "As I was coming over here, my staff gave me similar reports beginning to come in from our embassies in Europe, Asia, and Africa. Posters with this Blanco's picture are going up all over the place. Not just on campuses, but around labor, women's, and green groups."

The Political Network broadcast had indeed created a sensational tidal wave, the early ripples from which were just beginning to splash up on the political shores of Washington. Virtually overnight the true republic cause swept across the United States and much of the rest of the world. Thanks to TPN's massive advance promotion, an extraordinarily large international audience had witnessed the dramatic appearance of the white-bearded, white-thatched nonviolent revolutionary—who might or might not be a ghost. Topping it all had been the confusing termination of the interview and the dramatic defection of the interviewer. Only after reports filtered out from the late-arriving press mob did the sensational possibility arise that someone had tried to kill him on live television. That possibility gave the story a second life that preoccupied investment bankers at Park Avenue cocktail parties as well as sidewalk rug merchants at souks in Ankara.

The lure of a Pulitzer Prize attracted flocks of journalists to Miami—looking for anyone connected to the Free Cuba Party—as well as to Havana—similarly targeting officials of the Cuban Social Democrats. There may have been others with motives to kill the reclusive senior citizen who called himself Ernesto Blanco, but his biography was so thin that the most logical assumption available was that one or the other of the two major parties was responsible, directly or indirectly, for the attempt on his life. One of the many fascinating facets of the mystery, however, was why the shooter chose to take his chance before a world-wide television audience. Either he didn't know that a television broadcast was in fact going on or he wanted the verification of success that a multitude of witnesses could provide.

Efforts by "high-level administration sources" to suggest that the assassination attempt had been staged backfired badly. The look of dismay on Blanco's face in the seconds before he was violently pulled from the scene was enough to convince viewers that no charade was at work. Then when word came that hours later a second attempt, involving the bombing of a truck carrying Blanco and his party to safety, had been made, it served to prove beyond doubt that powerful forces were out to destroy the aging revolutionary. Not only were True Republic committees springing up on university campuses around the world, but the media were providing heavy coverage of groups picketing the White House demanding that the United States government take all steps necessary to guarantee the safety of the old hero.

At TPN, network officials tensely viewing the static-riddled, battlefield-authentic interview were initially outraged at what they considered to be Victoria Savidge's hammy and ham-handed defection. "Well," Marshall Stuart said, "what can you expect from a broad who never had good taste anyway. The least she could have done," he sniffed, "was to find some cheap Communist hairdresser down there to make her look respectable." Later, in the men's room, he told Sam Rapport, "What I ever saw in that woman, I'll never know. She wasn't even that good in bed. And, God, all that cheap jewelry."

Within hours, however, ratings numbers began to come in and the corporate switchboard was deluged with demands for reruns of the interview and further coverage of the Blanco-Savidge drama. The same network officials, heading home after a tense and disappointing evening, suddenly began to get calls on their car phones that something big was happening and ordered their limos to return to their corporate tower. By midnight, attitudes were changing. Suddenly, plans were under way for a one-hour Cuban election special, the truncated interview was to be rerun in every hourly newscast, and Sam Rapport, swept up in the giddy euphoria of the moment, even whispered to Marshall Stuart, "Let's get somebody down there fast to give Vicky a new contract with a big signing bonus. Look, if we don't, somebody else will. She's hot. We could promise her a personal profile . . . summarize the highlights of her career . . . let her pick her own assignments. I'm telling you, Marshall, I always said she'd do us proud." Marshall briefly tried to recall ever hearing such a prophecy.

Within forty-eight hours, the vice president for government affairs at American Airlines got a call from headquarters asking her to find out from State or Treasury the permits needed to schedule charter flights to Havana. Students and political activists from around the country were flooding ticket offices and travel agencies for seats on the few flights from Miami to the Cuban capital. "I don't even need to ask," she said. "It's legal. Travel restrictions were lifted when we granted diplomatic recognition and exchanged ambassadors last year. Same rules apply as with charters anywhere. We just need to file papers with the FAA letting them know when we plan to depart. Everybody's on his own getting back—unless, of course, the same groups want to schedule a charter coming back. My guess is, given what's going on, most of these kids are going to stay through the election on one May. Then they'll take a few days to celebrate and party. So Suzie's old man is going to cut off her credit card about five or six May. I'd keep at least a couple of planes available around then. Besides, don't they have to take exams anymore?"

The United States Senate convened the following Monday. Events in Cuba dominated floor speeches and debate. The common theme of the speeches was "do something." The Left, reflecting the view of the students and the protesters surrounding the White House and the Capitol itself, demanded that the administration guarantee Ernesto Blanco's safety. Democratic spokespersons called on the president to disavow rumors that the CIA might be somehow involved in the assassination attempt. The Republican whip demanded that the president dispatch the Marines at Guantánamo to capture "this jumped-up Commie who calls himself 'Che Guevara.' " Never mind, as his staff quickly whispered, that Ernesto Blanco had never claimed to be anyone but Ernesto Blanco.

At least one message from the Tower of Babel in official Washington concerned Guantánamo. The Defense Department representative ordered troops at the base to prepare plans to intervene militarily if the forthcoming Cuban election disintegrated into civil war.

Sunday morning network pundits dissolved into total confusion, yet again, as they struggled to force Blanco into one of their two convenient ideological boxes. "Hiding behind his phony commitment to local government and something called the 'true republic,' " the conservative virtuoso sniffed, "is an out-and-out liberal who wants to destroy the natural order of things and who continues to hint—too cutely for my money—that he is Che Guevara risen from the grave." "What troubles me," the escapee from the current administration sighed, "is that he hasn't really declared himself a conservative or a moderate centrist. Clearly local governments won't work, especially in a backward place like Cuba." The guardian of journalistic ethics rendered her considered opinion: "For a seasoned reporter like Victoria Savidge to let herself be caught up in a story she is supposed to cover objectively is a black eye for all of us who are serious journalists."

In Havana, the central committee of the CSD held an emergency meeting. "Did we have anything to do with this?" Victor Pais asked as his eyes searched those around the conference table. He looked particularly hard at Vilma Espinosa. "This isn't one of your 'special projects,' I hope, Vilma," he said. She nodded in the negative, but he noticed that, as she did so, she looked vaguely out at the Plaza de la Revolución not at him. "When we discussed keeping this old dog in his kennel," Pais continued, "I don't believe we actually discussed doing away with him. Or am I mistaken about this?" Once again, he looked at his colleagues around the table.

"He's getting out of hand, Vic," Vilma said.

"He's taking our voters and our support away," José Puerta added.

Antonio Oliverez said, "We got just a month from the election, Vic, and we're not doing so good. Those hotshots from California—the ones who tell you about public opinion—they say we're losing the people . . . the working people, *campesinos, vaqueros* . . . that should be for us. What do *you* think we ought to do?"

Pais hesitated. He knew for a fact that his two children, one a student and one a nurse, were probably going to vote for the true republic and he wasn't even sure about his own wife. "Not kill him, that's for sure. He just became a hero. We sure don't want him to be a martyr. Look, I been thinking about this. We're known as the old Commies—the lefties. Apparently nobody wants to go back to communism. What if we started the word around that he really is Che Guevara—that this 'true republic' business is just a scam to bring communism back. I know it doesn't sit well with most of you. But we've got an election to win here. If everybody thinks he's Che, then let's make him the old Che, not some new Che."

There was silence around the table. Then Vilma said, "I wish he was the old Che. We could use him now."

Felipe Morales said, "No, Vilma. Victor's right. People don't want communism now. I know it seems strange, but maybe we can be the ones to scare people about this old guy—to say that he's just an old radical Communist in disguise."

The more the Social Democratic Party leaders discussed the idea, the more most of them liked it. They even laughed at the irony of themselves, the heirs of the forty-year Communist regime, being the agents warning the people against turning to some outdated old Communist for leadership. Achieving a consensus behind their last-gasp strategy, their chairman Victor Pais gave instructions to their nationwide political network, the legacy of the fading Communist Party of Cuba, to disseminate the message that Ernesto Blanco was in fact Che Guevara come back from three decades of exile to establish some subversive form of communism in the fancy guise of something called the true republic, that he was engaged in perpetuating a trick of historic proportions on a people who had been tricked throughout their history.

After the meeting, Victor signaled Vilma to stay behind. She was visibly offended by the decision. "Why were you so vague about the shooter?" he demanded.

"The shooter's not ours," she assured him. "But . . ."

"But what?"

"But the bomber was."

Meanwhile in Miami, the scene was even grimmer at the Free Cuba Party headquarters. Outside, hundreds of protesters demonstrated against the FCP and anyone else who might have tried to kill Blanco. Inside, a debate raged about who might have ordered the attempt. Fingers were pointed in a circle around the conference table. Everyone denied complicity. The worst news was delivered by Micky Mendoza of Wager-Down. "You're down by twelve to fifteen," he declared, "and continuing to sink. Those numbers come from before the interview. I expect they're a lot worse now. This'll boost the old guy big time."

"Goddammit," Lucia Martinez shouted, "we're paying you big bucks to tell us what to do—not just to tell us what's wrong." Nerves were strained.

Pat the pollster said, "I've been telling you all along—go negative.

Go after this seedy old bastard. Destroy him. Blitz the airwaves with this message: He's a fake messiah, claiming to be somebody he's not, and—here's where it gets interesting—that the so-called true republic is a smokescreen for a right-wing takeover."

"We're the right wing," the titan Olivero Sanchez screamed. "What are you talking about?"

Pat rolled his eyes heavenward and gave a deep sigh, as if to say "you dummy." "You and I know that, Ollie, but we don't want the Cuban people to know it. You're the party of opportunity and freedom from government regulation. See, we have to make this Blanco character—just for the purpose of the election—look like he's fronting for a bunch of mysterious fat cats."

The fat cats around the table looked dubious. "You mean make him look like some kind of extremist," Angela Valdés asked, "like a nut of some kind?"

"Not exactly," Micky interjected. "Just cast some doubts about who's behind him, what's the hidden agenda, that kind of thing."

Pat said, "But whatever you do, don't try to shoot him." The room erupted into a shouting match.

At the White House, the task force was starting to break up when the press secretary came in and handed the security advisor a note. "Oh, for God's sake," he said after reading it. "Some history professor at Montana State—McLarty or McLemore or something—has just announced for the U.S. Senate on a True Republic ticket. Where in the hell is this thing headed?" he said exasperatedly. Pointing at the assistant secretary of state, he said, "One last thing. We have some Agency data that suggests one of your people . . . some young guy named"—he consulted his typed notes—"Nicholas Ferre, a Cuban American, is becoming too chummy with the Blanco crowd. We can't let that happen. You better check into it and have the ambassador down there rein him in. Matter of fact, why don't you just order him home for the duration. Give him some desk work until the election. Then send him someplace else."

The assistant secretary of state later that day prepared a cable to the Havana embassy to instruct Nicholas Ferre to return to the United States to assume duties in the department in Washington pending reassignment abroad. Pursuant to this instruction, the American ambassador in Havana summoned Nick to his office.

Nick checked into the embassy two days after the two dramatic assassination attempts and was told to return to Havana immediately for consultation with the ambassador. The tone of the secretary's voice was stern. Concerned, Nick caught the first bus from Santiago, where the Blanco inner circle was reconnoitering, back to Havana. The trip took most of a day. The following morning, freshly scrubbed and shaved, Nick appeared in the ambassador's office fortified with notes of his activities he had prepared on the long bus ride the previous day.

"Well, Nick," the ambassador began, "it seems you've been keeping yourself pretty busy monitoring this election, especially this 'new republic' thing." His long forehead wrinkled. "Our station chief suggested you may have even been around for this bizarre assassination plot."

Nick said, " 'True republic.' Yes, sir, I've been trying to cover all the bases. And most recently I did make my way into the Ernesto Blanco headquarters—such as they are." He looked at his notes. "I persuaded them to let me observe their campaign from the inside starting five days ago. Then two days ago, someone did take a shot at Señor Blanco and then, someone else apparently, tried to blow up a truck we were all riding in. Luckily, we all got away safely."

"Sounds pretty risky, Nick," the ambassador said. "It wouldn't do to have you—you know—get blown up or something while following this strange character around. Wouldn't look good for me or for the embassy or, for that matter, for our country. We just can't get involved that way, you know."

"Yes, sir," Nick said. "But the secretary herself said she wanted to know everything there was to know about this election. And everybody here had pretty much agreed that I could go into the field and observe all the campaigns. I was just trying to do what I thought were my instructions."

The ambassador said, "Well, a lot has changed since then. We made clear to you that we heavily favored the success of the Free Cubans and now this Blanco character has come on like gangbusters. I mean, this interview—with you right there on the scene—has boosted his chances even more. With you that close to these events, someone might conclude we've changed sides in this thing."

"Yes, sir," Nick said uneasily, "I appreciate what you're saying . . . although I think you're aware I don't agree with the U.S. taking sides and I've repeatedly reported on the popularity of the true republic movement, even before others did."

"Nick, see, there you are," the ambassador said. "You're not part of the team and now, even the powers that be in Washington—I mean, even in the White House—have taken note. They've heard about you and, frankly, they think you're on the other side. This assassination episode . . . well, that just took the cake. I'm afraid you're being sent home. I've been instructed to send you back to Washington. You'll work there for a couple of months. Then you'll get a new assignment." He shoved an envelope across his deep desk at Nick. "Here's your ticket. The plane leaves in the morning at ten."

Weeks of tension, the pressure of developing three new sets of sources, the stress of the previous seventy-two hours, all fell on Nick like a rock slide. He slumped in his chair. The diplomatic career he both coveted and treasured seemed to slip away before his eyes. He was too drained to make sense of it all. He had tried to do the job they had wanted him to, in the country in which he had wanted to work. He had tried to be as objective as he could. But he couldn't fall into line behind a corrupt old oligarchy when he knew his government was missing the mood of the Cuban people, when to perpetuate colonialism, even in a modern, sophisticated form, was beneath the ideals that had so attracted him to public service.

The following morning the ambassador found the ticket on his desk with a letter from Nick. "Dear Mr. Ambassador: I cannot leave Cuba right now. There is an important revolution going on. It might give the Cuban people their first chance at democracy and self-government. Please accept my resignation. Please tell everyone I'm grateful for the chance and I'm sorry for letting them down. Sincerely, Nick."

By the time the ambassador was reading this letter, Nick was on a crowded, fuming bus headed back to the Sierra.

■ ■ ■

Politics I understand only a little bit. Women I understand not at all. Never have. And given the length of my lifeline, I guess I never will. This lady, this Victoria, is now somehow in my soul.

I've had a couple of wives and some children, now grown. I've been "in love" and I've been out of love. It's a complicated business. Makes politics look simple. Ideas are much easier to deal with. The true republic is an idea. You can explain it and discuss it. Of course people get passionate about political ideas. They quarrel and argue. They debate. Sometimes they throw things. Occasionally, they even start wars and kill a lot of people. But this thing you sometimes get for another person—sometimes it makes you feel very good and sometimes it makes you feel really awful.

I'm too old to be having these romances. It does get the blood circulating in interesting ways and it makes you feel a lot younger than you are. But if you're not careful, it can mess up your mind. You get distracted and you can't do what you're supposed to do. Then you get angry at the person who's distracting you—like it's their fault you're making a fool out of yourself. That's the thing—you can't let this love thing make a fool out of you or keep you from doing what you're trying to do, if it's important. A lot of what we do isn't very important. But this true republic is important. And I've got just a few weeks more to see it through here.

Then what? This lady? Quién sabe? *I don't think so. She'll wake up some morning and see that I really am an old guy. Very old. I've got maybe ten years. She's got three times that. It's not a fair deal for her. Besides, I can't really provide the meaning of her life. She has to do that for herself. That's really what she's doing down here. And I think it's working. She's been transformed in the past two months. She's much calmer and more settled. She's more at peace. She's found out what really is important. It's not being famous and rich and important. It's causing other people to have something to hope for. It's having a belief that's bigger than you. It's helping to lift people up and giving them a chance at a better life. Not much else matters.*

But this lady is a really fine person. When she shed that jewelry and cosmetics and phony life, underneath was a very fine human being. She's compassionate and she genuinely cares about things—ideals—and human beings. I've seen her hold these poor kids and talk to the campesinas. *She has a very good heart. I have to confess—at least to myself—that I care a lot for her.*

It makes me angry at myself that I didn't protect her better. I knew that shot was coming. I just didn't know when. It never occurred to me they would try it while we were on television. I've tried to keep some distance between us just for that reason. But there we are with that microphone and they take their shot. Then that damn truck. I should have been more careful there too. That was close. We're just going to have to search better from now on. I'll just have to make sure Rafael and Alejo keep her away a little bit. We'll also have to bring in some guards, particularly at night.

These people here are right on the edge of winning their freedom for the first time in their history. We have to help them stay focused on the main point. "You can choose your destiny. This is your country. It doesn't belong to anyone else. Communism had its chance. You've had the money rule. Now it's your turn."

■ ■ ■

4 0

■

Ernesto stirred the fire and watched it deposit another layer of carbon on the pitch-black coffeepot. High, wispy clouds drifted across the three-quarter moon and played hide-and-seek with the bright white constellations. An owl hooted softly three times, listened vainly for an answer, then repeated its lonely call.

"How would you think if he were to join us? Because he is a Yanqui, I mean." Ernesto handed Alejo a cracked cup full of fresh hot coffee.

Embarrassed to have his *compañero* serve him, Alejo started to get up, then settled back against the large log backrest and coughed. "Not all Yanquis are bad, amigo."

"Not all Yanquis resign from the service of *Tío Sam* and want to throw in with a band of old Cuban revolutionaries."

Alejo knew Ernesto was merely testing his opinion and was flattered to be asked. "Then he has asked to join us?"

"Not exactly," Ernesto mused. "He is too polite and he does not wish to be suspected of spying on us for his government."

"Then how do you know, *compadre*?"

Ernesto showed his teeth. "I did not live such a long and hazardous life without knowing these things." He touched his nose, suggesting a keen sense of smell.

"Then you think he is a spy?"

Ernesto stirred the dwindling fire with a long stick and looked through the spark shower at his gaunt companion. "What do you think?"

Alejo drank the coffee. "I think he may be worse than a spy. I think he may be one of those idealistics."

Ernesto wheezed, cackled, and wheezed again. His lungs sounded like an ill-used concertina. "Idealist, you mean, amigo." A cough rattled through his throat. "And is it so bad to be an idealist? What harm is there?"

Alejo could never tell when his clever old pal might be amusing himself at his expense. "You know from much experience—as do I—that harm is in the heart being crushed beneath the falling dreams. He should listen to experience—yours and mine—and not to dreams."

"So your 'experience' has made you more realistic," Ernesto offered. He saw the scarecrow figure nod knowingly. "And this—your experience of the realities of life—this is what brings you here, back to these mountains, sleeping on the hard ground with those old bones, instead of in a bed under a roof?"

Alejo shifted awkwardly, pierced by the insight of his leader. "This young Yanqui does not know how tragic things can be."

"Some great prophets and leaders, amigo, have understood both idealism and tragedy," Ernesto said wistfully. "The great trick is to accept the tragedy without letting yourself become cynical."

The flickering fire made a shadowy grid of Alejo's furrowed brow. "This 'cynicism.' It is like a distrust?"

Ernesto nodded. "More like a bad expectation—a belief that everything will turn out bad because everyone is to be mistrusted. It is a kind of distrust of the spirit."

Alejo's long, old-pony head shook up and down, ridding itself of the buzzing horsefly of cynicism.

"Now in this little revolution we are making here," Ernesto continued, "our greatest fight is with this disease. Our enemies—of the old power— they will spread this disease so that the young people, like this Yanqui Nick and Rafael, will have no dreams of better things."

"So our fight is with this . . . disease," Alejo ruminated to himself.

"Claro, amigo." Ernesto smiled, a successful teacher. "If we prevent this sickness from spreading among the young ones, they will have their dreams—their ideals—and they can try to make this—this crocodile of a country—a better place."

Alejo raised a spectral hand. "But this *joven*, Nick, the Yanqui, he is not of this country."

"Nor am I, *che*." Ernesto grinned. "Have you forgotten? Despite years of revolutionary hell-raising in these mountains and through these cane fields"—he swept his arm widely—"I am still a foreigner, an intruder. This Nick, on the other hand, has his blood from this land." He raised a handful of dirt and let it sift through his fingers. "He came back here— he was pulled back here by something unfinished—and he has found out that blood is the strongest politics."

Now caught up fully in his leader's drift, Alejo said, "So . . . Cuba is his destiny."

"Now, amigo, you are becoming a poet"—Ernesto wheezed and coughed—"as well as a revolutionary."

The ridiculousness of this notion caused Alejo to give one of his rare laughs, a sound like the closing of a rusty gate.

The fire flickered lower. Again the owl overhead rendered three mournful hoots, unanswered. Ernesto yawned. "This Nick feels as I do for this land, these people. They deserve better than to be the Caribbean doormat for every 'ism' looking for a home."

Alejo also now yawned, then smiled crookedly. "So you believe he is not a spy for *Tío Sam*?" He sounded relieved.

"Just the opposite, amigo. He can become a bridge between us . . . between you and Sam. He does not have the anger of his fathers, their hatred for Fidel, their wish to restore the old power. If there is to be any kind of friendship between our . . . your people, the Cubans and Sam, on any kind of fair basis, it will depend on the daughters and sons of those exiles. They are Cuban Yanquis. They will be the bridge."

Seeing his *jefe* roll over onto his knees, then struggle wearily to his feet, Alejo joined him. Their respective grunts, groans, and popping joints commingled with the hisses and pops of the lowering fire. They both reflexively kicked loose dirt onto the embers.

As always inspired by his leader, Alejo delivered a short speech, a rare event. Ernesto listened respectfully. "I have lived as long as you, *mi amigo muy grande*, but not as much as you. I have not seen the world as you have. I have never left this poor garden of an island." He sighed deeply. "And it looks as if I never will. But I know some things. Some things about the sad creatures of humanity. I know who is true. I feel in these very old bones who is to be trusted. This *joven*, this Nick, is a spy only in the service of his own soul."

Ernesto studied a remaining blinking coal. "You would have him join this merry little revolution?"

Alejo said, "I do not possess the wisdom to know how to keep him out." He kicked dust over the coal. "Besides, he can help us cure this disease—this cynicism—that kills the dreams."

4 1

■

All across Cuba the warm spring air of early April was filled with the cacophony of campaign rhetoric. Candidates for the new legislature peddled their wares in the squares and markets of the cities, towns, and villages. Every town of consequence had small offices on the main square for each of the two regular parties—the Cuban Social Democrats and the Free Cuba Party—and throughout the neighborhoods there would be small placards in house windows signaling the commitment of the inhabitants to the True Republic cause. The True Republic followers rarely had offices because they could not afford them. The radio and television stations were saturated in the final months before the vote with advertisements for the two established parties and their candidates. Increasingly these pronouncements attacked the party's competitors. The Social Democrats preached solidarity of the masses and the urgency of marching arm-in-arm into the future. These advertisements also proclaimed the Free Cubans to be *batistiana* robber barons out to steal Cuba from the masses and plunder it once again. The Free Cubans shouted for the opportunity provided by laissez-faire and the liberation of the spirit of entrepreneurship through the marketplace. Their advertisements blasted the Social Democrats as closet Communists interested only in retaining power in the Politburo of the past.

But both sides reserved the greatest vitriol for the True Republic movement. For the Free Cubans, the True Republic was a snare and a delusion, a sham front mounted by the far Left to cloak its perverse intent to collectivize all property and create a pure Maoist state that would grind all under its massive heel. The shady character "Blanco" was but an agent for sinister totalitarian interests too cruel to show their faces. For the Social Democrats, the True Republic was a shadow right-wing conspiracy out to reserve ownership of the emerald of the Caribbean for the Mafia, and the mysterious "Blanco" was a front man for a Miami-based authoritarian cabal that intended to prostitute Cuba's daughters and enslave her sons. From Punta Cajón in the west to Punta del Quemado in the east, every available frequency and licensed airwave was awash in glowing promise one minute and mad invective the next. Beneath the surface the worst practices of democratic politics flourished. Unsigned circulars bearing the fingerprints of the state-owned printing shops claimed that Ernesto Blanco was financed by Mafia interests using Bahamian bank accounts and that, win or lose, he was set up for life. Crude pornographic pamphlets produced in back-alley Miami sweat-shops purported to show pictures, conveniently blurred, of Ernesto Blanco disporting among a bevy of underaged girls all free of the confines of clothing. Word-of-mouth stories circulated from the Free Cuba offices held that Ernesto Blanco was the younger brother of the butcher of Nicaragua, Anastasio Somoza, conveniently redesigned by the best plastic surgeons in Miami to resemble an aged Che Guevara to trick the people. Likewise, the state *nomenklatura* network got it about on the streets of the towns and villages that this Blanco character was no fake; he was in fact the real Che Guevara back to establish a dictatorship of the far Left so cruel as to make Pol Pot seem benign.

For Juan and Jorge on the streets of Cárdenas or Sancti Spíritus or Las Tunas, Cuban culture had transformed democracy into a circus of stupendous proportions. Never had they seen a soap opera of such intricate claims and contradictory counterclaims. In one ear came a truly dumbfounding story and in the other a claim even more fantastical. At first it was frightening. Then it became merely amazing. Then, as the destructive barrage assumed overkill proportions, it all was transformed into rich fodder for folk mythology. Juan told his wife that Ernesto Blanco was truly the devil, that he had three male organs and fourteen wives, and that he was out to impregnate every Cuban female over the age of fourteen. Jorge told his girlfriend that he had it from the *alcalde* that Blanco was really John Kennedy, who had been hiding out in Ireland all these years and now wanted to govern a small, warm country in his remaining days. If anything, the Cubanas were even more interested in the flamboyant Yanqui journalist, Victoria, who they themselves transformed into a soap opera heroine of Amazonian dimensions. She was seen everywhere in the markets shopping for food for the band of revolutionaries in the Sierra. She was preparing to host a Yanqui-style chat show on Cuban television that would expose the secret sex lives of the politicians as they did on the television *del norte*. She was Blanco's mistress, who would dictate styles and fashions once she took power in Havana. She was Jackie Kennedy, who had not died but had gone into seclusion awaiting the return of her husband from his long sojourn in Ireland.

It was as if Cuba had become a great train junction for the excesses of late-twentieth-century politics. It became impossible to separate truth from fiction, fact from fantasy. Politics mingled with sex, and sex mingled with sensation, and sensation was overtaken by fantasy. And television magnified it out of all proportion to any conceivable reality. As the train of ideology approached the junction at high speed, so did the train of political power, and the train of the media, and the train of rumor and innuendo, and the train of history. And they were all scheduled to arrive at the station of decision on the first of May.

Beneath the surface of this mayhem, events of real consequence did, however, take place. One such event involved the reestablishment of contact between Johnny Gallagher of the Leeward Island Club and his sometime inamorata Elicia Francesca Scarlatti. E.F. had not had time to curse the tiny insect that had spared Ernesto Blanco's life by peering into her sniper scope at the moment she squeezed the trigger. She was too busy retreating down the hill behind her rocky outcrop hiding place dragging her shoulder bag and handcrafted sniper rifle with her even as Rafael and Nick pulled Ernesto away. Years of discipline and training, together with the knowledge that the odd radical band on the mountaintop would be in total disarray, gave her the clarity of thought necessary to abscond safely. The motto of her profession was, First get away: there will always be another day. As the Blanco troop made its way down the southern mountain slope and the madcap press pack came in from the east, E.F. retraced her more arduous northern ascent. After collecting her carefully hidden pack at the mountain base and finally hitching a ride on a slow-moving farm truck, she made her way cautiously back to Havana. She had changed from her camouflage fatigues to simple city clothes in the trees and had brushed out her hair before approaching the highway. Given her sun-darkened skin and perfect Spanish, she had no trouble melting into the passing scene. Anyway, she looked much more like an attractive shopkeeper than an assassin.

Ditching unnecessary clothes and camping equipment in a trash heap outside Havana, she found a nearby giant palm with a cracked trunk. After noting nearby landmarks, she placed the canvas-wrapped dismantled rifle and scope, 9-millimeter pistol, and combat knife into the hollow where it could not be seen. Then, carrying only a travel duffel, she took a taxi to José Martí International Airport and joined a noisy crowd of Mexican tourists on the next flight to Cancún. After checking into the Cancún Sol Melia hotel, she placed a call to Johnny from the hotel pay phone.

"It's me."

There was silence. The thought of mixed lust and anger coming down the line excited her. "You okay?" he asked.

She knew this was as much a question concerning her escape as it was her well-being. "Yeah, all things considered."

"Where are you?" he foolishly asked, then quickly followed with, "Don't answer that."

"I hadn't planned on it," she said. After a pause, she continued, "It was a goddamn bug . . . in the sco . . . in the spotter. Just enough to throw me off. Next time."

"We gotta discuss next time," he said.

"When and where?" she quickly asked, seeking her orders.

There was a pause. "If you're clean, you can come here."

That signal was lust, she knew, triumphing over anger, and caution. "I'm clean," she said. "Besides, I need a couple of days' rest . . . and . . . you know . . . 'relaxation.' It was tough down there. Or maybe I'm getting too old."

"You're not too old, baby," he said. "Believe me. I remember the last time." Lust now reigned. "Come on down. Call me when you get here. I've got a place we can go away from the club. Make the next plan. And . . . you know . . . 'relax.' "

The following day she caught a small island hopper from Cancún to the Bahamas and, after a few hours of "relaxation," they talked, sweaty sheets thrown back and daiquiris on the night stands. "We got less than thirty days to get it done," he said. "You up to it—one more time?"

Curled inside his hairy arm, she nodded affirmatively. "I don't think I can get him in the outback again. Next time, it's going to have to be out in the open. In a crowd, or maybe moving around. Problem is, you never know where he's going. He knows. But no one else knows." She paused. "He's smart, you know. He expected this. And he'll know we're coming again."

"Can you get close?" Johnny asked.

E.F. said, "Sure. Problem is to find out where he's going to be. Get there first. Get in position. Most of all, plan a withdrawal."

He put a hand between her legs. "Always easier gettin' out than gettin' in," he laughed.

Fingers stiffened, she gave a short, sharp thrust into his lower rib cage that emptied his lungs, doubled him up, and made him gasp. "Don't do that," he wheezed. It always troubled him that she could kill him in a heartbeat.

"The money's still there," he finally said. "The guys are pissed. But I made them understand that it ain't easy."

She reached up to kiss him as a peace offering. "We need the money, hon, if we're going away. I'll get it done." This time she reached between his legs, gripped, and pulled. "And, believe me, I'll figure a way to get out."

At roughly the same hour, the phone on Sam Rapport's desk at TPN international headquarters rang and the operator said, "Accept a collect call from Cuba?" Sam yelled, "Yes."

"Sam, it's Harry," the cameraman said from the phone booth at the Horizontes Casa de Valles motel a few kilometers west of Matanzas on the north-central Cuban coast. Nick Ferre had booked several rooms for the traveling party using his credit card and they were there for two days of rest before the final campaign push. Built atop a sulfur mineral spring, the motel provided baths for the treatment of Ernesto's asthma and for reducing the stress the others felt from the previous days' traumas. "I've got Vicky here. Do you want to talk to her?" He shoved the receiver at the reluctant Victoria.

"Hi, Sam," she said. "We're okay. I know you've been worried." Her tone was only slightly ironic.

"Vicky, Vicky," he shouted, "what a close call you had. But such ratings! You won't believe it, doll! Off the charts! We're still doing reruns around the clock. This place has been a madhouse." Then, remembering her sign-off, his tone changed. "What do you mean pulling a trick like that. Dramatic, okay. But everybody here believed it! Now, I've known you long enough to know when you're hyping. So, I says, 'Marshall, she's hyping.' But everybody here believed it."

"Believe it, Sam," she said. "It's true. I'm done. But you better get somebody else down here. This is an important story. I don't mean just the assassination stuff. What's going on here is important. And people need to know it."

Sam shouted, "Vic, it's *your* story. Do you think anybody can touch this story after that closing shot of you . . . with a big bullet hole behind your head . . . saying good-bye to the world?" He said, "Doll, we got to have *you*. Only you can tell the people what's going on."

"Can't do it, Sam," she said. "You weren't listening. I've gone over. I've signed up. I'm a partisan now. Journalistic credibility all gone."

"Okay, Vic, whatever," he shouted. "Then let's do it this way. You be campaign spokesperson. Give us feeds from inside the campaign. Act like a campaign press secretary."

There was silence as she thought it over. Her mind flashed across the dozens of political flacks and hacks she had witnessed spouting nonsense and propaganda, most of which they knew to be only marginally true, over the years. Not her. Totally contrary to what she now believed. On the other hand, she uniquely now had the opportunity to communicate Ernesto Blanco and the true republic to the world. She herself had said, This is an important story. People need to know it. If she let her former colleagues in the press corps have the story from now on, they would butcher it and butcher him.

"Sam," she said, "let me talk to Ern . . . Señor Blanco about it first. But I will give you this." She knew Sam had a recorder going. He always taped all his calls. "Señor Blanco is alive and well. His campaign for the heart and soul of Cuba is marching forward. He is gathering strength every day. The ordinary people here—not the bosses in Havana, nor the bosses in Miami, nor for that matter the bosses in Washington— the ordinary people are behind him. They understand his idea. They understand this chance they have to redeem this nation for themselves and for their children. They will not let this chance get away. And if the true republic works in Cuba, it can work everywhere in the world." She paused, looked at the phone, and then hung up.

"Vicky, Vicky," Sam was screaming. "Don't go away! When can we talk? Call again! Please. . . ." Then he looked at the receiver and smiled. The beat goes on. Within an hour, the last minute of Victoria's call, minus the reference to Washington, was on the TPN hourly news report with a glamorous backdrop picture of Victoria in combat fatigues. It was promo-ed as an exclusive report by the award-winning TPN political reporter Victoria Savidge from inside the Ernesto Blanco True Republic campaign somewhere in the wilds of Cuba. Sam Rapport was betting her racehorse journalistic instincts would take over again soon and she would call in yet another piece. All he had to do was keep this going another three and a half weeks. TPN's ratings were already at record heights. And then, of course, there was also the matter of TPN's stock going north 4½ points.

Pollsters for the CSD and FCP waited a full week after the negative ad and the contradictory rumor campaigns began before going back into the field to sample their effects. Pat reported to the Free Cuba steering committee three weeks before the election. "We've stopped him," he began as the overhead projector threw a series of charts and numbers on the screen on the far wall of Olivero Sanchez's conference room. "See this trend line?" He pointed a red laser dot on a chart that showed the True Republic favorable ratings over the previous six months. From October 1999, when the polling first began, the number started near zero and then climbed gradually until early February 2000, when it started to go ballistic to an astronomical 72 percent favorable and 49 percent most likely voter support. Then the last week's tail made a plateau.

"Stopping isn't enough, Pat," Sanchez huffed. "Stop him there, hold the election, and he wins in a landslide still."

"You have to stop him," Pat said sarcastically, "before you can turn him around. What is happening is that people are beginning—for the first time—to have doubts about this old fraud. What we're after here is destruction of trust. That's what negative campaigns are all about. If your opponent is able to build up trust and you don't challenge that trust by destroying his credibility, then he wins. So you first have to destroy people's trust in him, then you can begin to make people really dislike him. Now that we've got people's attention, I strongly suggest we put on a television blitz that will tear him apart. Mock him. Make fun of him. Question who's behind him. Make a lot out of this relationship he's got with this wacky television type—Victoria what's-her-name. . . ."

"We don't know if he's even got a relationship," Eduardo Pons said.

Pat rolled his eyes in pain. "Doesn't matter, does it? Let him explain. The main thing is to put him on the defensive about his personal life. That's all people care about anyway. Make him a sex maniac. Make him gay. Make him impotent. Make him a womanizer. I don't care. *Just make him the subject!*"

Within forty-eight hours, radio spots raising all sorts of personal questions about Ernesto Blanco began to play on Cuban radio, and within seventy-two hours there were television spots doing the same. The Free Cuba Party turned virtually its entire advertising budget to an attack on Ernesto Blanco's character.

The Social Democrats were not far behind. Their slick California political consultants had given them much the same analysis as Pat had given his clients. That was in large part because Pat and the California "competitor" had been colluding all along, sharing polling data and discussing comparative strategies. It was standard practice in any campaign in the States where they shared a common enemy. So, right behind the FCP came the CSD with an all-out barrage against Ernesto Blanco. He was demonized, he was mocked, and he was pilloried shamelessly. The television spots, lacking real photos, featured simple cartoon caricatures. They were crude and they were blunt. Half of them had Blanco as an aging rooster chasing a flock of squawking hens down a dusty road, catching them, and jumping them all. Another version on the same theme had the aging rooster catching the hens and then scratching his head, unable to perform. Following the pattern of the more advanced democratic neighbor *del norte*, the first Cuban free election was becoming a travesty of democracy.

Refreshed after two days of mineral baths, Ernesto led his eclectic troop out from Manzanillo to undertake the final battle. The cause of the true republic had just three weeks in which to resist the most virulent assaults the two traditional political forces could make and to raise the banner of a new and different kind of politics and government, as old as civilization but forgotten in an age of concentrated wealth and power. Ernesto knew the next twenty-one days would tell whether his odyssey of thirty years and his search for an enlightened form of self-government for the forgotten of the earth would die on the ramparts of the established power structures or whether, somehow here in this land left behind in the march of twentieth-century "progress," a different story might be told, a new beginning might be forged.

4 2

In 1514, Diego de Velázquez founded seven cities on the island that was to become Cuba as the urban network of his empire of gold. The fourth of those cities was Trinidad in the southwest corner of what would become Sancti Spíritus province near the southern port city of Casilda, a doorway so inviting that fanatical pirates throughout the sixteenth and seventeenth centuries could not resist it as a convenient portal to the wealth—real and imagined—of Trinidad. The conquistadors, shortly to include Hernán Cortés, dropped their settlement on the heads of the resident Taino Indians who had the spectacular misfortune to be discovered by the Spanish panning for gold in the nearby Río Yayabo running down the Valle de los Ingenios later to be dotted with sugar mills built to pulverize the flourishing regional cane that would, inadequately, replace the gold. Old Trinidad was to become, by twentieth-century consensus, the "crown jewel" of colonial Cuba.

It was to Trinidad that Ernesto Blanco's last national political tour came in the closing days of Cuba's grasp for democracy. Following the Matanzas respite, Ernesto headed eastward to Cárdenas, then along the northern coast to Caibarién, then through Morón to the main highway eastward, through the cities of Diego de Avila, Las Tunas, Holguín, then to the city of Guantánamo and a turn eastward back to Bayamo and a long stretch westward to Sancti Spíritus and south through the province of the same name to Trinidad. Leaving Sancti Spíritus, Ernesto had pointed eastward toward the area called Arroyo Blanco—"not after me," he assured Victoria with a laugh—where the young Winston Churchill, while covering the War of Independence in 1895 for the *London Daily Graphic,* had heard the uncomfortably close whirring of a rebel bullet and delivered his famous pronouncement: "There is nothing more exhilarating than to be shot at without result." To her somewhat nervous laughter, Ernesto added, "I guess I could have said that myself, yes?"

Aware only vaguely of the concentrated vitriol emanating from increasingly frightened competing campaigns, the Blanco tour had been a turbulent triumph. Ernesto's attempt to perpetuate his sedate town plaza coffee debates disintegrated before the swirling, surging, antic crowds wherever and whenever he appeared. Mobs materialized by magic in his wake and they were far from sedate. Though overwhelmingly strong and supportive, each crowd contained the seeds of its own destruction. There were mercenaries of the FCP and partisans of the CSD bearing banners and placards, suspiciously well printed and uniform, denouncing the True Republic as a scheme of unnamed foreign interests and Ernesto Blanco himself as a fraud of garangtuan dimensions. Predictably, proximity to the Blanco supporters led to friction, then to confrontation, then to imprecation, then to assault and mayhem. This pattern, of course, played into the hands of the protesters who had in mind any way to disrupt True Republic rallies and prevent Ernesto Blanco from making his appeal.

Down the winding, twisting cobbled streets leading into the Plaza Mayor of Old Trinidad, purposely made labyrinthine to confuse the ambitions of vagabond pirates, came trickles, then floods, of humanity. The workday was ending and they poured past, through, and around the Museo de Arquitectura, the Museo Romántico, the Museo de Arqueología y Ciencias Naturales, and the Museo de la Lucha Contra los Bandidos, all housed in the exquisite mansions of the golden colonial age of the eighteenth century, past the Galería de la Arte Universal and through the triangle-shaped Plazuela de Segarta, and around the simple Catedral Santísima Trinidad rebuilt on the eve of the War of Independence. Some came from new Trinidad on the awful camel buses from Hungary and the Chinese bicycles imported by *el Jefe* when the Soviet oil tap was shut off. They were young and old, they were of almost every skin hue and wore brightly colored clothes. Save the dour professional protesters, they were eager, laughing, and excited.

Around six in the evening, Ernesto had stood holding his ubiquitous coffee cup near the Catedral in the corner of the majestic Plaza, one of Cuba's most beautiful. Surrounding him were a handful of proprietors of nearby tourist stalls and shops eager to meet and touch the white-haired, white-bearded old *caballero*. He was saying, "A French writer called Hugo once said, 'One thing is stronger than all the armies in the world, and that is an idea whose time has come.' That's what I believe and that idea is power to the local communities, people like yourselves governing your lives." Then, when he looked up, there were suddenly dozens of people around their small circle and dozens more coming in behind them. He looked up a street called Fernando Hernandez Echarri and saw it full of people all headed his way. He briefly struggled to remember if it was some traditional festival day. But soon he realized, they were for him. According to a pattern developed over the months of the campaign, rail-thin Alejo stood close by, while young Rafael stood slightly farther away; Otra Vez, now disappeared, had normally circled another tier away, and the newcomer Victoria, true to her former profession, stationed herself at a respectable distance to observe. Three days before, while standing on the steps of the cinema on the Parque Martí in the depressingly Leninist city of Guantánamo, Ernesto had peered over the heads of the crowd to see a familiar young Yanqui face. It was the grinning Nick Ferre freshly liberated from his biased duties and yet to feel the full professional consequences of his recent decision to join the partisans. Now in Trinidad he had assumed the widest-ranging scout position.

As the crowd grew, Ernesto raised his voice in an effort to be heard. The crowd pressed him back toward the steps of the Catedral. He mounted the steps and shouted, "Wait for the politicians to come here for speeches to be given. Not being a politician, you will get no speech from me." There was a robust cheer. At the far side of the square a chant went up. "Che, Che, where've you been? You're still a Commie, just like then." The crowd of several hundred now hissed lustily. "Besides," Ernesto said, "this election isn't about politicians anyway. This election is about"—and here he pointed at individuals throughout the crowd—"you . . . and you . . . and you . . . and"—he pulled a small girl

in a tattered dress from the front of the crowd up the steps with him—
"you, *niña mía*. Which of several futures do you want for this *muchacha*
and your own *hijos*?" The crowd began to clap rhythmically and chant,
"*La república auténtica . . . la república auténtica.*" Ernesto raised his hands.
"You vote for '*la república auténtica*' and you will have the duty to govern
your communities well. You will have to take the responsibility for making your own towns the best they can be." Now in the spirit, the crowd
chanted back, "We will! We are ready! *Adelante! Adelante, Ernesto! La
república auténtica!*"

Ernesto shouted, "You must vote *el primero de mayo!*" The crowd
chanted back, "*El primero de mayo! El primero de mayo!*" Across the
Parque another claque of protesters set up a counterchant mocking the
phony "Che" as an agent of the CIA. "Che, Che, you're our man. If
you can't do it, the CIA can." Ernesto held up a hand and pointed across
the crowd at the noisy claque. "Amigos, you want the CIA, you vote for
the so-called Free Cuba Party." The crowd erupted into a roar drowning
out the noisemakers. "The CIA is done in Cuba, amigos. We don't need
the Free Cubans to provide another Playa Girón in this century." A
huge shout erupted from the crowd now almost filling the Parque.

Ernesto started down the Catedral steps, hesitated, then returned to
the top step. "This isn't about who I am or who any other person is,"
he shouted, his antique voice cracking. "It isn't even about who one
political party or another is. It's about who the Cuban people are! It's
about who you are! You are going to have a chance *el primero de mayo*
to tell the world who you are." He raised a thin finger skyward. "You
are free people! This country belongs to you! You tell the world, Cuba
belongs to us now! Now, *we* are Cuba!"

There was a great roar from the crowd and the chant, "We are Cuba!
We are Cuba! Now we are Cuba." Few noticed, in the moment of
delirium, that the white-thatched *caballero* had stepped into and then slid
out of the crowd. By the time the crowd surged forward to slap his back
and try to lift him on its shoulders, he had been deftly pulled to the side
of the steps and then toward the side wall of the modest Catedral. With
Alejo leading interference and Victoria and Rafael close behind, the
small group climbed a wide cobbled staircase leading to the Casa de la
Música and then, Ernesto wheezing badly from his shouted remarks and
rapid climb, they continued behind the music museum to the Casa Particular on the street called Juan Manuel Marquez where, fortunately,

their student supporters had a car waiting and the runaway Nick Ferre linked up with them. They made their way through the narrow streets to the north and then the west of town and took the road along the southern Cuban coast into Cienfuegos province. By nine o'clock they had arrived at the house of the local leader of the true republic movement in the historic section of Cienfuegos city.

Once the group had settled into two small houses next to each other on a darkened street, Alejo wisely suggested that Señor Ernesto might enjoy a quiet dinner with Señora Victoria. The fatigued couple was taken to a local *paladar* called Romeo and Juliet. They were seated when Victoria looked at the handwritten menu with the name of the *paladar* at the top. For the first time in days, she gave a hearty laugh. Ernesto wryly joined her.

"You are thinking perhaps, Señora Victoria, that a great drama will occur here tonight," Ernesto chuckled.

She observed him thoughtfully for a moment as their *cervezas* arrived and Ernesto ordered a simple meal in rapid-fire Spanish. "Do you mind, *señor*, if I ask you a question that might seem personal?" she finally asked.

"Having been shot at—more or less together—it is not seemly now to call me *señor*," he protested. "Having lived through the extremes of modern politics—from international live television broadcasting to outdoor living to having a very menacing bullet buzz just between us—I think it is now permissible for me to be known simply as Ernesto and you, if you don't mind, as Victoria. *Es posible?*" He moved his brown weathered hand a mere foot across the small table and placed it on hers. "What is your question, *seño* . . . Victoria?"

She studied his hand, then said, "Were you afraid? I mean . . . when the bullet came? Were you frightened? I want to know"—she hesitated—"I want to know if you think about dying . . . if you are afraid of dying."

Ernesto's white teeth gleamed; then he became more serious. "Once I was a warrior. I sought political authority at the muzzle of a gun. I have known war in all its aspects. And, Victoria, war is a violent teacher. I did not renounce war as an instrument of revolution simply because of its violence. Over many years of thought, I came to renounce it as an instrument that defeats its purpose. People cannot be made peaceful by war. They cannot be made civilized by war. They cannot be made democratic and self-governing by war. Instead, it works the other way.

Violence destroys the instinct for peacefulness, and civility, and democracy. Your own leaders should have learned this lesson in Vietnam. I learned it in the Congo and here in Cuba and in Bolivia." He gazed out into the dark night. "I lost fear long ago. I renounced it. My life has been full and eventful. I do not need to live forever."

Victoria shivered, hugged herself, and rubbed her arms. "Your fatalism frightens me. There are so many people here—Alejo, Rafael, all of your supporters—who believe in you. Even if they don't entirely understand your ideas, they believe in you. They trust you and depend on you."

"I have no plans to leave right away," he said, smiling. "It is just that every danger cannot be—and should not be—avoided. If you go in harm's way, if you challenge authority and power, you should know the possible consequences. Sometimes they are not happy consequences. But if you live your life in fear, you do not live. You merely survive. To speak up, to try to open new doors for people, it can be a risky task. Besides, as you know, I do not want people to believe in me. I want them to believe in themselves and their own possibilities." He gestured at the food that had been brought. "Please. *Bon appétit.*"

They both found themselves suddenly hungry and devoured the simple food before them. "Were you surprised by Otra Vez?" Victoria asked.

"I am surprised by very little," Ernesto answered. "I have learned that trust is a tricky proposition. I have a sense of who is worthy of trust. But I do not believe anyone, including myself, is worthy of absolute trust. I trust Alejo and I trust Rafael. I even trust that young Yanqui, Nick. Otra Vez is an angry man, a frustrated man. I would guess that life has not treated him well. He does not like himself. So he cannot like others. To me, he is like a dog who has been beaten. He himself was probably beaten by a cruel father or even by a prison guard. He does not trust, so he cannot therefore be trusted."

He smiled hugely at her. "Then there is you, Victoria." He reached for her hand again. "From the first night I saw you in the little cantina outside Santiago, despite your . . . shall I say . . . elaborate appearance, I liked you and trusted you. I don't quite know why. You seemed, beneath the surface, like a wounded creature, a creature tortured by your life. Beneath your ambition, you were so . . . vulnerable. You required care."

As he spoke, tears filled her eyes then slowly descended down her now much thinner face. She did not try to brush them away, but simply leaned forward and softly kissed Ernesto's weathered cheek and grasped his hand as if to prevent herself from being swept away by a powerful current. In the kitchen, pots and pans banged together and the lights in the room dimmed as a signal to the lone diners that this refuge was closing down. After a moment she said, "In a few days this adventure will end. What will happen here, I do not know. For you, I suppose you will be called upon to help lead this country. What will happen to me, I cannot imagine. Though, for the first time in my life, I do not worry. When I was young, there was a song that seems now to fit—"Que Sera, Sera." I will not go back to my old life. I cannot. They would not have me back, even if I wanted to return. I have a little money. Perhaps I will find a small place here and stay and write a book about this whole odyssey. Someone should try to get it right."

Ernesto said, "That you should do. For me, I will not stay. I cannot govern. I do not understand the art of politics. I have ideas. They are simple. They are, for me, fundamental. That is, I cannot compromise them the way those in politics have to do with their programs. So I suppose I will look for somewhere else to sing my song. For me, it is also easy. I know only one song." He studied her. "You should stay here. This place agrees with you. Learn some Spanish. Write your book. It is important that the story be properly told. It is historic. A record should be made." He smiled. "When I am at the campfire writing to myself in this old book"—he pointed down at his ever-present hemp shoulder bag—"I also see you writing some observations. So I think you have some material for your book."

"This book," Victoria said, "it must be about you."

He shook his white hair vigorously. "You do not listen, woman. This book is not about me. This story is about the Cuban people's struggle for freedom and it is about an idea. I will go away. The idea and the ideal will never go away."

The dim lamps in the tiny dining room went dark. Victoria leaned forward once again and kissed him on the lips. This time he leaned forward to meet her.

■ ■ ■

Tonight I have come as close to being in love with a woman as I have for many, many *years. The more I became a revolutionary of ideas, the less I believed I could afford to get entangled in the demanding web of such feelings. In my exile years, I knew many women, some of them good, some of them not quite so good. I enjoyed the company, sometimes the companionship, of all of them. In my later years I have learned not to go with the ones you will regret soon after or the ones who try to make you feel guilty or despise you.*

I have had wives, at least two, and children, several. After this struggle, I will try to find the children to see if they might, after all, want to know me. I hope so. I have missed them. They will be grown with their own families. Because of me, because of all that I have done, I understand how they might want to try to be invisible. Still, I think of them often. Of my many regrets, the failure of my fatherhood is the greatest.

I have rarely seen anyone transformed before my very eyes as I have seen this Victoria. It surely means that she is now simply who she always was, that the woman she has let others see, probably for many years, was not the real woman. That's the intriguing thing about causes such as this. If they are just and if they are right, they can transform people even in the very performance of their drama. Indeed, if a political cause produces bad people it cannot be a just political cause. The just political cause is about more than politics and power. It must be about the transformation of the lives of people. First, there was Alejo, drifting around without a purpose but knowing he had some role to play. Then came young Rafael, knowing that things were not right in his own country but, in his inexperienced youth, not having an idea what he could do. Then there is this young Yanqui, Nick. His life has already been changed. I hope he will not regret the price he is paying to give life to his patriotism and idealism. Then, to see how this outlandish experience has transformed this lady—maybe liberated is better—is, for me, proof that we are doing something right.

I worry for her—afterward. Is she strong enough to be on her own? Does she need someone to lean on? Will she, as I fear she has done before, pick a man not suitable for her goodness? But enough of this. She is a mature woman. Far be it from me to govern her life. It would be easier to try to govern a country and that I know I cannot do. To try to govern a woman— or for that matter anybody else—is a hopeless task. Sometimes, when I am honest with myself, I think about what life would be like, despite my age, with this lady. But then I think, my mission will not let me stay in one place. And she cannot be expected to live this life that I now have.

The effect of this idea, the true republic—the real democracy—on these people here tells me one thing. It is a universal idea. It is an idea for the Latin world, for the African world, for the Asian world, as well as for those del norte. *Each group of people will impose its own culture upon it. But its light can shine everywhere. It can sweep away some of the old politics of favoritism, of corruption, of dictatorship, of oligarchy. It can give people without the smallest plot to stand on the chance to own their lives, to prepare a legacy of freedom and confidence for their children.*

So I have no choice. It is now my destiny. I have become now a missionary of this idea. I would not be happy living in a house and being a passive observer. God made me an actor, a creature of passion, a meddler and a troublemaker. It is in my soul. I can do no other. Once a revolutionary, always a revolutionary. I see the space between what is and what ought to be. It will never be completely closed. There is no utopia for mankind. It is a sad truth, one that those of us swept up in utopian socialism in another age have had to learn. Thanks to God my learning began sooner than that of some. But the knowledge that there is no utopia, no ideal society, achievable is no excuse for not trying to close the space between what is and what ought to be even just a little. To accept injustice, to ignore human misery, to tolerate poverty, is to admit corrosion into the soul.

I have set myself upon a road that has no end. There is no house at the end. There is no gold watch. There is no happy retirement or golden contentment. (Goddamn the thought!) There is only holding up the tiny light that says to the oppressed, Things can be better.

This lady has seen that light. For her it has meant shedding the weight of wealth as measured by the "successful" world. It has meant returning to her true and natural self and learning again to sense the needs of others. She has been subject to the revolución *and she is now the* revolución.

Now that I think about it, I do love her. But I don't intend to talk a lot about it.

■ ■ ■

4 3

■

As the campaign for Cuba clambered toward its ineluctable final station, in the fashion of late-twentieth-century democratic elections, all stops were pulled. What had previously seemed excessive began to seem merely quaint. While the True Republic movement and its candidates for national office pursued their nonmedia, grassroots campaign, the two "major" parties, under the lash of their professional consultants, pulled every possible cat out of the bag.

From its glitzy headquarters in every city and town in Cuba, the Free Cuba Party unleashed a get-out-the-vote drive worthy of the most sophisticated election campaign in the late-twentieth-century United States. Every vehicle imaginable was rented for election day to drive voters to the polls. In exchange, those who accepted were told that it obliged them to vote FCP. *Campesinos* in the fields were seen wearing new FREE CUBA black-and-gold baseball hats. Political stalls in markets, plazas, and *parques* all over the country were handing out, in addition to the hats, FREE CUBA buttons, banners, posters, potholders, aprons, yardsticks, cheap ballpoint pens, key chains, tiny Cuban flags, and every imaginable kind of junk upon which the FCP's gold giant palm logo could be fixed. Rumors circulated throughout the island that cash rewards were available for Free Cuba voters and that the party had a way of knowing who voted for the FCP and who didn't. Throughout the final days of the campaign and this commercial barrage of political paraphernalia and promises, the intense media artillery assault against Ernesto Blanco and the perfidious True Republicans rained down.

For its part the Cuban Social Democrats determined not to let the FCP steal the show. Their great strength, the established political network led by the *nomenklatura* left over from the waning days of communism, was mobilized down to the block level in the finest traditions of mid-twentieth-century Chicago in the age of Richard J. Daley, Sr. There were CSD block captains in every community in the country and it was their job to identify every CSD vote—and recruit them where they were too thin—and bring them to the polls on election day. CSD block captains were given "walking-around" money to help solve the immediate financial needs—a chicken here, a bottle of rum there; a new car battery here, a wedding present there—of both dedicated and swing, or undecided, voters. What the CSD lacked in Free Cuban fluff and merchandise, it more than made up for in meeting daily needs through its old political network. Local party officials who had disappeared for years suddenly emerged with matching straw hats with the red band of the CSD and the familiar symbol of the alligator, representing the outline of the island, affixed. Though the FCP had rented most of the private vehicles on election day, the CSD's ace in the hole was the public transport fleet. Though the buses and other public vehicles were theoretically available to all, the block captains were to see that only CSD voters would have access. And, like those of its established competitor, the CSD's attacks on the defenseless Ernesto Blanco hammered on over such airwaves as were not dominated by the Free Cubans.

Despite this onslaught, however, various Juans and Jorges in various fields and on various street corners around the country carried out variations of the same conversation.

"I see you have the new baseball cap," Juan says.

Jorge says, "*Sí, amigo*, everyone in the town is wearing them. And I see you have the banner of the CSD in your back pocket."

"So you will vote for the FC candidate?" Juan asks politely.

Jorge answers, "It is very difficult for me and my family. You see, the boss of the SDs in my neighborhood presented a nice ham for my daughter's wedding."

"Well then," Juan says understandingly, "you must follow the one who gives you the ham, not the one on your cap."

"Perhaps," Jorge says, "perhaps. And you, Juan, you will be voting for the SDs, because you have their banner in your pocket?"

Juan says, "It is not so easy to know, Jorge. Because, you see, the FCs are giving me a ride in a very nice car to the voting place. It requires some respect, *verdad?*"

"It is so difficult," Jorge sighs, "there seem to be so many friends everywhere these days making gifts, helping the grandmother across the road, patting the little children on the head." He reaches in his pocket and hands Juan the fine cigar he extracts. "Things like this."

"I cannot take such a fine cigar, Jorge," Juan protested.

"It is okay, Juan," Jorge says, "the FCs gave me two. But now, you see, if you smoke the cigar you must vote for the FCs."

Juan says, "Jorge, how can I vote for either one? They are now being so good to me. If I vote for one, then I will make the other angry for my ingratitude."

Jorge scratches his head. "I think I have a solution to this difficult problem, Juan."

Juan nods sagely. "I think I know of your solution, Jorge."

They turn and walk down the road arm in arm, laughing as they go. Each has placed the small white mariposa, sometimes called the butterfly jasmine, in his shirt pocket. It is the symbol of the True Republic.

All across Cuba, the white mariposa is everywhere. It is in the buttonhole of a lady's blouse and the gentleman's shirt. It is in the straw hats of the *campesinos* in the fields. It is stuck in the belts of students in the schools and in the shirt pockets of their teachers. Young soldiers and policemen place the fragrant flower in the barrel of their guns. It is found in the fruit and vegetables in the markets. It makes its way between the pages of the official newspapers and into the FC baseball caps and gifts from the SDs. It is found in the corner of the windows of many shops and in the windows of passing cars. It was in the buttonhole of the TV news presenter—until a hand shot out from outside the camera range and snatched it out. It is in the back pocket of the cart pusher on the street and in the hair of street vendors. It is wrapped up in the packages of souvenirs purchased by tourists and it is on the plates of steaming dishes in the *paladars*. It is placed on the altars of the now-opened churches. It appears in the folded hands of the deceased as they lie in state. Everywhere one looks, the white mariposa is there.

In the closing days of the campaign, it is becoming increasingly clear that the suave entreaties of the two traditional parties, the savage attacks on Blanco—the missionary of the true republic—the presents of cheap junk and giveaways, all are having little effect. Pollsters for the FCP, the Wager-Down group, and the slick Californians contracted to the Social Democrats are both reporting the same results within a few percentage points: one quarter of the voters for the Free Cubans, one quarter for the Social Democrats, one quarter for the True Republic, and one quarter undecided. The last one quarter was driving everybody—with the possible exception of Ernesto Blanco—absolutely crazy.

Sophisticated analysts for the two mainstream parties reasoned, based on experience in other "emerging democracies," that it was not unusual for people emerging from the fear of authoritarianism to exhibit reluctance to reveal their true preferences. Indeed, it was to be expected. One never knew who this person was at the door asking these intimate political questions. What if one gave an undesirable answer? Rations might dry up. Jobs might be lost. Children might find themselves without medicine. So, given this choice, it was always easier—and safer—to say, Undecided. There was also the strong likelihood, the analysts argued, that this one quarter were simply the least likely voters, the ones evident in great quantities in every electorate who simply didn't want to be bothered. But each of the two big parties had a thorough list of these "undecided" voters and they would be the focus of the closing days of the campaign.

Because he had met face-to-face enough of the Juans and Jorges over the weeks and months, something the other parties could not claim, Ernesto thought that something different was at work. Ernesto thought that these so-called undecided voters supported the ideal of the true republic and, if fear and reluctance could be overcome, would represent the margin of victory in the looming national election. As the Blanco group made its way back eastward across Cuba to sanctuary in the Sierra to await the final campaign results after the completion of the nationwide tour ending in Pinar del Río and Havana itself, Ernesto reasoned as much to the worried Alejo. "It's natural, my friend," he said, "these people are just beginning to breathe the oxygen of democracy."

A deep furrow of worry between his eyebrows, Alejo shook his head sideways. "How can you be so sure, *compañero*? What if they do not even go to vote?"

"Oh, Alejo, *mi amigo*," Ernesto said, patting him on his bony stooped shoulder, "these are our people. They are our friends. Most of all, they want a future. They know the others offer only two different versions of their past."

"Sometimes the past," Alejo sighed, "even an unfortunate past—because it is at least known—may be more appealing than an uncertain future."

Ernesto said, "You are very wise, *compañero*. An equally wise Russian once wrote about bread and freedom. He had the great authoritarian of all human time—one called the Grand Inquisitor—say that, given a choice between bread and freedom, men would choose bread every time."

Alejo smiled his crooked, cracked-tooth smile. "You see? I could not have put my idea better myself." Then, considering the implications, he again looked worried.

"But one must have faith, Alejo," Ernesto said, "faith in humanity, faith in some common instinct for freedom from power and wealth, for equal justice for all. We would not have undertaken this quest—would we?—if we had not had faith in our brothers and sisters here in Cuba."

"We certainly would not," Alejo agreed, always flattered when the man for whom he had such respect treated him as an equal and especially when he addressed him as "*compañero*." "That is the one thing we have always had . . . that faith."

"Having this faith then," Ernesto said, "can we have any other choice than to go forward in our quest to offer a small portal through which these people might pass to their own destiny?"

Alejo shook his long, sad head in agreement. "You are right, *Jefe*. Forward we must go. Right now," he said, pointing ahead through the windshield of the coughing antique car, "right now I am seeing the finish line of the race. I am seeing us reach our goal. I am seeing a new land where people—my people—can own a little land, can say what they think, can go where they please, can believe what they want, can be part of the government of their own lives. As always, you are right. These people will choose that destiny, as uncertain as it is."

An exhausted Ernesto once again put an arm around his *compañero*'s thin shoulder and patted it. Then his own head slid sideways in sleep.

He would not see Victoria, huddled in the backseat between the two dozing figures of Rafael and Nick and gazing out into the black Cuban night, wipe the tears from her face.

44

■

On the veranda only the candles treated to create a negative aura for the colossal menagerie of insects could be seen burning by anyone with the courage to test the impressive security arrangements of the Leeward Island Club in the Bahamas. Cigar smoke, produced at considerable expense, drifted from the four figures seated in the darkness. Only a low murmur and an occasional clink from a brandy snifter meeting a tabletop disturbed the silence. "What happened, Johnny?" someone murmured. "Just tell us what happened."

Johnny Gallagher snorted. "Our guy missed. It's that simple. Look, this is rough country. Getting in. Getting out. Getting the right equipment in . . . you know . . . the piece. It isn't easy. Got to climb back into the mountains. Got to find the old guy. Got to time the thing just right. Take the right shot. Got to have a way to get out. That's important. We made it a condition that our guy not get caught. Wouldn't do to have to explain who set up the job . . . who paid for it. That kinda thing."

"Johnny," Mr. Rossell rumbled, "we don't need to hear all the problems. The details don't matter. Results matter. We didn't get results. All we want to know is, when do we get results?"

Johnny had not been looking forward to this personnel review by the officers of the club and, in effect, his employers. Johnny had been doing the heavy lifting for the handful of club members for a number of years and this was one of the few times he had let them down. As satisfying as his passionate reunion with E.F. over the past seventy-two hours had been, this after-action report was the polar opposite.

"We still got time," Johnny said, playing his hole card. "Our guy is going back down tomorrow. This time, it'll be done different. This time, it'll be a crowd approach. Either in close—which has the best chance of success, but the toughest problem of getaway—or a sniper takeout—little tougher to make work but a lot better chance of getting out."

Stanley King said, "We don't need to know details, Johnny. That's your business and your guy's business. We need to know results, like Mr. Rossell says. We just don't need any more screw-ups."

The raspy voice of the venerable Mr. Luganis sawed across the night. "As part of the deal, Johnny, you got to take out the guy after the job. I thought about it. There's no other way . . . you know . . . to protect ourselves. The old guy down there, he's gotten too big. If we take him out, there's gonna be hell to pay. They'll come lookin'. There can't be anything coming back to us. You understand? Like what we had to do with that casino guy in New Orleans. You get him taken out, then you take out the guy that took him out."

Johnny downed a large swallow of brandy, grateful for the darkness that hid his grimace. He couldn't do that. He couldn't take out E.F. She was the wildest thing in a bedroom any man ever dreamed of. What a waste of a resource. What a squandering of an asset. Besides, she was a great hit guy. As always, the club officers had followed the practice of leaving the identity of their contract employee to Johnny. The less they knew, the safer they were. They didn't care who did a job, so long as the job got done according to the terms of the contract. They would not care whether the employee was man, woman, or monkey. They would certainly care, for the reason just given, that Johnny not be jumping in the rack with the hit guy, of whatever gender or species. It made it harder to take him out if circumstances required. Johnny sighed. He and E.F. had too many good times ahead. He was just going to have to produce another dead hit guy, taken out for no reason at all except to provide cover for E.F. with the club.

"Yes, sir," Johnny said as he exhaled a cloud of cigar smoke. "It always makes me feel rotten to double-cross one of our contract guys. Word gets around; it just makes it harder to recruit the next one."

"The old man's gotten too big," Mr. King said. "When he goes down, they're gonna come lookin'."

Mr. Rossell said, "I don't know, Stanley. Who's gonna be sore? Not the Commies down there. They hate him as much as we do. Not our guys, these 'Free Cuban' whatevers. They want him gone. From what I hear, the U.S. government . . . the jackass president, the CIA, all that crowd . . . want him gone. They want the Free Cubans as much as we do. So are they gonna come lookin'? I don't think so. The dumb-ass press'll make a big story out of it until the next Lewinsky comes along. . . ."

There was a general chuckle. Stanley King said, "I don't dispute what you're sayin', Mr. Rossell. I'm just talkin' insurance, is all. No clues. No fingerprints. Nobody sellin' a big story some years from now. That kinda thing."

The raspy voice said, "You gotta do it, Johnny."

Within an hour, Johnny was in his car headed out of the club and down the beach where E.F. had rented a secluded cottage under the name of Liz Scarlett. Although E.F. had begged to visit the club, Johnny insisted that there be no record of her identity there—for her own protection. So, since her return from Cuba a few days ago, she and Johnny had wrecked the bed, along with most other semiflat surfaces in the house, regularly and had left some interesting dents and curves in the beach sand. She met him on the darkened front portico and had his shirt off before he got through the door. The rest of his clothes marked a path to the bedroom where a freshly uncorked bottle of champagne waited in a bedside silver bucket. E.F.'s wraparound towel fell somewhere between Johnny's teal green slacks and his bright red Jockey shorts.

After his third workout of the day, Johnny lit a cigarette and sighed. "It looks like I gotta kill you."

Leaning on one elbow, a hand still between his legs, E.F. said, "Why? 'Cause I missed?"

"Nah," he groaned. "You're gonna go back and get it done. Tomorrow. But after you do, I gotta kill you. The guys decided. Can't have a shooter of a world-famous old guy walkin' around talkin' about it."

She rubbed his hairy stomach. "I'm not going to talk, Johnny. You know that. It's not my style."

"You know that, and I know that," he said. "But they don't know that. They don't know who you are. They don't want to know who you are. They just want me to take you out when the job's done."

"Is it the money?" she asked. "The success fee?"

"Nah," he said. "They could care less about that. They just don't want you decidin' to make yourself famous."

E.F. put her hand back between his legs and husked, "So get your gun out and kill me."

Johnny hated it when she did that. So, presently, he groaned and rolled on top of her and all she did was laugh. And almost killed him.

Shortly before dawn E.F. and Johnny made a plan. When she completed the job, she would make her way through several South American and European capitals to a small hotel on the Algarve. Johnny would pack up the success fee and, after transiting through an equal number of different cities, would meet her at the hotel named on the matchbook that she gave him. He would explain to the Leeward Island Club officers that he was carrying out his instructions to hit the hit guy and would drop off the radar screen for a while.

By midmorning she was on a commuter flight through Puerto Rico to Havana dressed in a flowery sun dress, a large straw hat, and sunglasses. Mingling with a vibrant group of Italian tourists, there was little, except a spectacular taut figure, to attract attention to her. Within twenty-four hours, she had a small room in the Hotel Deauville with the Italian tour group and had recovered her gear from the tree trunk in Havana's southern suburbs near the airport. She had pretty much decided to go for the close hit.

The day after she returned to Cuba she went shopping along La Rampa to find some clothes that a semistylish Cuban woman might wear. She had studied the styles and fashions, mentally grimacing at the garish tastes, and had a pretty good idea what it would take to make her look like an average urban thirty-five-year-old *Cubana*. Then, with her plastic shopping bags she toured the Plaza de la Revolución in the off chance that Ernesto Blanco might hold a snap rally there in the closing days of the campaign.

In his corner office in the Palacio de la Revolución overlooking the Plaza, Victor Pais would not have noticed E.F. passing by some hundred yards away. He was too deep into his argument with Vilma Espinosa to have looked out the window.

"Vic, I'm telling you for the hundredth time, we don't have a choice," she stormed. "Don't always be such a goddamn nice guy. We're in a war here. And we may be losing."

The stress of the campaign had put him back on the cigarettes and he hated himself every time, as now, he lit up. "Forget about nice guy. Just think practically. This 'asset' of yours kills the old guy and there will be a public response like we haven't seen since Che's bones came back. Can't you understand that he's at least as dangerous dead as he is alive?"

She kicked a plastic coffee cup across the floor and cursed. "I've seen the numbers that these hotshot Yanqui pollsters turn up, Victor, and it's close as it can be. With him still around, we could lose. We may not lose to the Miami gang, but we could sure lose to this 'precious republic' or whatever he calls it."

Pais shrugged helplessly. "We've got every one of the party people out on the streets. We've handed out more jobs and chickens and birthday cakes than there are people in this country. What do you want me to do?"

"Leave me alone," she shouted, "just long enough for me to get rid of this old sack of bones. I'm telling you, fifteen minutes after he's gone they won't miss him. They'll forget who he was. It'll totally destroy the morale of his crowd. They'll either vote for us or stay home. Sure as shit. I'm telling you. There is no 'movement' without him. It'll fold up like a tent in a typhoon."

Pais then looked out the window and watched the passing strollers, E.F. among them, in the Plaza below. "I don't agree with it and I don't want to know about it, Vilma. If I told you to cut it off, you wouldn't listen to me anyway. But I'm telling you. I don't like it. I don't believe in it. And I wish you would forget it. We'll win it the right way."

"There is no 'right way,' Vic," she said, "when you're talking about power. We've got it now. And, by God, I'm going to do whatever it takes to keep it." She started for the door and turned back. "Besides, there are a lot of other people besides us that want him gone. If something does happen to him, I've already got a press release that blames it on the CIA and their pals the goddamn 'Free Cubans.'"

That night Vilma had a meeting in the darkened park called the Loma de Lenin in the community of Regla across Havana harbor to the south. She arrived after ten when the small park with its small tree dedicated to Lenin was sure to be dark and vacant. Coughing and puffing from years of heavy smoking, she staggered up the metal steps to the hill providing a spectacular view of the city to the north and west. She saw a still figure wearing a hat waiting on a stone bench. She crossed the park and sat down.

"We only have five days," she said. "What do you plan to do?"

The man said, "I'll only have one chance. The minute he sees me, he'll know what I'm there for."

"You got to do it," she said.

The man grunted. "I like him, you know. This isn't easy."

"Neither is going back to prison easy," she said, lighting a cigarette. "You got a choice." Then she added, "I know what you're thinking. 'He's just an old guy. He's not hurting anyone. He's harmless.' All that bullshit. Well, I am telling you, he is a big problem. You don't need to understand all the reasons. Let's just say it's politics. Okay? A lot of stuff you don't have to understand. The one thing you do have to understand is, this thing has to be done and we don't have any time now to find some other way. We spent four or five months for you to develop the confidence and to get close to him. Then you had your chance. And you failed." She blew a stream of smoke skyward. "I'm not saying it was a bad plan. I'm just saying that it didn't work. I'd say you have about one more chance to make it work."

The man gave a sigh. "I cannot shoot him. I don't have the courage to shoot anyone . . . particularly someone I know and have traveled with. He'll look me in the eye. I know he will. So I have to do what I know about. You know . . . the bombs."

Vilma Espinosa snorted. "Do you think I care what you do? I could care less. Just . . . get . . . it . . . done! You understand?"

"The bomb means other people will get hurt too," he added.

"You don't listen very well, do you?" She sneered. "All I care about is results. Sometime in the next five days. Get rid of him. If somebody happens to be standing around—especially that crazy Yanqui TV woman—too bad. That's their problem." She stood up. "We know where you are. Our people are watching. Don't try to run. Don't try to hide. We're right on you. Do it, and do it fast."

"What about the other side," he asked, "the ones that took the shot at him? They're going to try again, for sure."

She uttered a foul curse. "You saying we should rely on that gang in Miami to eliminate our worst nightmare? You crazy? Talk about a gang that can't shoot straight—they already proved that. Of course, they're going to try again. They want him gone almost as much as we do. But those guys are fools and they'll screw it up."

He was silent. She dropped her cigarette and crushed it with a booted foot. Then she stalked off to descend the steep metal steps and enter the official government car waiting below. He knew that if he didn't kill Ernesto Blanco, he would return to prison for the rest of his life—if he were lucky. He knew that if he did kill Ernesto Blanco, Vilma Espinosa's special security forces would probably kill him on the spot and take credit for trying to save the old revolutionary.

But he also knew two things that Vilma didn't know. Reliable sources in the Cuban criminal underground had recently revealed a secret. A tight group of bad boys in the Bahamas had the contract out on Ernesto Blanco and the shooter was, of all things, a sexy *señorita*. She was the one that climbed the Sierra to try to take him out during the television broadcast. His former cellmates had even showed him a grainy picture of her in some kind of combat gear. If somebody had to kill Ernesto, he hoped this woman would relieve him of the duty. She had almost saved him from the necessity of planting the bomb in the getaway truck some days ago.

But he had an even more important secret. He had gone to the clinic that day for the third time and the doctor had confirmed, based upon tests over the previous days, that he had no more than six months to live in any case. As he stood to look out over the lights of the city where, except for his young days as a revolutionary, he had spent most of a disreputable life, the man who called himself Otra Vez smiled. The political bosses had a lot less leverage over him than they thought.

4 5

On rare occasions in human history there are unseen tides and currents that pull large numbers of people together—people who are not even aware of this tidal pull—and that carry them in ever growing numbers toward a common destination. When this occurs, the great numbers of people carried forward by this force arrive at their destination surprised to find so many others there with them. They were not aware of the breadth and depth of the force that pulled them from their comfortable place and pushed them in a direction they could not have imagined only a short time before. They had become so accustomed to their conventional lives that they thought they lived in isolation from universal currents. Such people—almost all of us—forget that we are born with very powerful instincts common to most of our brothers and sisters. So that when a great and rare historic force arises, it can be and usually is a reminder that we are all waiting to be led toward some common destiny. We are just waiting for the historic energy that accumulates the tiny rivulets, sends them toward the larger streams, distributes them into the flowing rivers of humanity and then into that ocean whose massive tides can change history.

In trying to analyze it later, some said there was a peculiar moon at that time. Others said it was a weather phenomenon like El Niño. Some older people said they felt a powerful spirit and visited the *babalao*, the Santería priest, to try to determine if it were evil or benign. More sophisticated people in the city said it was simply a case of mass hysteria, some kind of weird crowd psychology that, once let loose, could not be stopped. Observers *del norte*, including in the CIA, tried to determine—for possible future use—if some drug had, perhaps, been put in the water or the food that caused people temporarily to go a little crazy, or perhaps whether it was as simple as some sinister forces handing out a lot of beer and rum.

We probably will never know. Or if we were to know, we would probably not understand. For, whatever the cause, sometime in the three days before the election on the first of May, 2000, a trickle of people drifted out of tiny villages and off faraway cane fields and began to move toward the historic capital, Havana. This early sign of migration, driven by some instinct shared with birds and butterflies, had been facilitated unwittingly months earlier when the authorities had decreed, in the announcement of the terms of the proposed national elections, to permit voting by qualified citizens at least two days before the election day itself. There were two practical reasons for this decision. The first was that all ballots would be cast and counted by hand, not by the machines of more sophisticated venues, machines that few in Cuba would have trusted. The second reason was the difficulty many rural and elderly people would have in getting to a polling place in one twelve-hour period. Given these realities, every person of eligible voting age was permitted to cast a ballot within the three-day period ending with the close of the polls on the first of May.

The analysts did agree later that this decision to vote over a three-day period had as much to do with this mass migration phenomenon as anything else they considered. Whatever the reasons, empirical or metaphysical, a tide of Cuban humanity began to trickle toward the capital from Mantua, Ciudad Bolívar, Dimas, La Palma, Cubanacán, Candelaria, and a host of other villages in the west, from Melena de Sur, Madruga, Perico, Mordazo, Condado, and many other small towns in the central provinces, from Jucaral, Guayabal, San Andrés, Dos Caminos, Bayate, El Catao, Imías, and hundreds of other like places toward the east. Most times there would be no special signal, just a *vaquero* on an old horse, a couple of *campesinas* on the road, a few young people on bicycles, one or two extra people on the bus, a family on the train. But anyone watching would have noted a few more people than usual headed for Havana. Toward the afternoon of the twenty-ninth of April, there was a perceptible increase in traffic, both of those on the public transport and those making their own way. Those making a long transit found places along the way to stay for the night, some with relations and others simply camped out at convenient roadside parks. As the trickle, then the stream, of faraway travelers made its way through the intermediate villages and towns, those predisposed already to make the pilgrimage drew inspiration from the human tide and found the courage to join it. Trucks from farm collectives were loaded up with people and put out on the roads and onto the highways. An abnormal number of donkey- and ox-drawn carts joined the tide. All were headed for Havana and they all hoped to get there for election night. The growing crowds along the way seemed carefree and celebratory. There was a hint of possibility in the air, a sense of history, the taste of revolution. It would later be reported that one had to go back four decades, to the triumphant march of *los barbudos* from Santa Clara to Havana on New Year's Day, 1959, to find a precedent for such a mass migration across the countryside.

In every community in Cuba in those hours the workers for the True Republic were pleading and urging, cajoling and motivating every voter they could find. "May we have your vote? Give us your support, *por favor*. Stand up for Cuba. Do it for your children. Now is the hour of our freedom." And back from the people came, "Where is Ernesto? We want to see the leader. We will meet him in Habana. Ernesto to the Palacio de la Revolución." The workers gave out lists of True Republic candidates for the national offices and the legislature. They helped people find the polling places and reminded them to take their identification papers so they could vote. Free Cuba Party and Cuban Social Democratic Party representatives were visible here and there in the larger cities, but neither had the nationwide network of dedicated volunteers that the True Republic could produce.

Meanwhile the quiet missionary of the true republic movement sat on the fragile porch of a shepherd's hut high in the Sierra. He was reading a well-worn book, writing in his ever-present journal, and giving no evidence of awareness of a political tidal wave surging beneath and around his mountains. Rafael and Nick were down in the city of Santiago helping the local supporters get out the True Republic vote. Alejo had made a trip down to the nearby town of Guisa for food and supplies. Fifty yards away, Victoria sat on the ground in a sunny clearing with her back against a log. She had put down the small sketchpad and pen she had been using to try to preserve the opulent natural surroundings that so characterized her new, revolutionized life and was brushing her thick red hair, now beginning to lengthen after her self-administered bob. From the porch Ernesto now looked up and studied her, a slight smile on his wrinkled face. He went inside, poured fresh hot coffee in the cracked cup, and walked toward the sunny glade. He briefly tried to remember a happier time in his life, but simply could not.

When he handed her the cup, she looked up at him and smiled. "Are you satisfied?" she asked.

"Ah, lady," he said, "a true revolutionary is never satisfied. Not so long as there is someplace else that requires a revolution." Both knees popped as he sat down beside her, and he grimaced at the creaking sound.

"But for Cuba are you satisfied?" she persisted.

He smiled the glistening white-toothed, youthful smile and touched her cheek with his fingers. "In truth? *Sí*, for one reason only I am pleased. I have done my best. Now it is up to them. Now it becomes their revolution." He paused, still smiling. "I am also pleased because I have made one or two new friends here."

Victoria said, "I want very badly to ask you what you will do now. But I know you will not tell me."

He took the cup and sipped the bitter, cooling coffee, then studied her face illuminated by the oblique rays of the spring sun. "Even more interesting is the question of what you will now do."

"At great turning points in your life," she answered, "it is always clearer what you will not do than what you will do. I will not go back to TPN. I will not return to broadcasting. Most of all, I will not go back to the kind of life I was living. I was headed into a very dark cave when I met . . . when I came here. The only thing I know now is that I have to do something that is more worthwhile, that gives me a greater sense that I am helping someone else." Then she laughed. "Maybe I will find a country to revolutionize."

He joined her laughter. "*Bueno. Bueno.* Why not? But permit me to offer a thought. I believe that you are very good at what you do, or what you used to do. I believe you were recognized for doing good work in the television. You can recapture what integrity you feel you may have lost while still using your skills for good."

She took his hand and looked quizzically at him. "I don't understand. Television was corrupting me. My life was corrupting me. Now you are saying I should continue?"

"I do not know, dear lady," Ernesto said. "I do not know the television. But surely there must be some way for you to use its power for good. Can you not make stories about the Cuban people? Can you not make stories about hungry children in the world? Can you not make stories about the injustice of hoarded wealth and hoarded power? Can it not be used, this television, to give people important information and educate them about the world they live in? Can it truly not be done?"

"Of course it can," she said, "and on some rare occasions it is. But it has become so much about money—and the power money brings." She looked into the distance, remembering a time perhaps in her idealistic younger years. "I would love to do that. That's what I really wanted to do and for a long time thought I was doing." She shook her head. "Then I suddenly woke up one day and I was just an aging and very disposable part in a giant money machine."

Briefly seeing the face of a disappointed woman, Ernesto leaned toward her and kissed her cheek. She embraced him and held him tight. "You alone should decide," he whispered. "I should not seek to direct your life."

She whispered back, "I want you to direct my life. I want to regain some goodness and something noble I can believe in. Please help me do that." He could feel emotion shaking her.

"Your heart will do that," he said to her. "Your heart is good. It will show you the way. You must trust your heart. If it is pure, if you genuinely wish to make a difference for having lived, then you will find the right way." Now he studied the scenic panorama stretching out for miles around. "I know. It took me more than thirty years, years that most would say were wasted. Years in exile. Years when no one—except those I met and lived with—even knew I existed. But I knew I was not done. I knew I had yet another revolution—someplace—sometime. My heart told me it was my destiny." He gently placed a weathered hand between her breasts. "Your heart will too."

After moments of silence, Victoria said, "When you go away—and I know you will—when you go away, will there ever be some way that I can find you?"

"Ah, lady," Ernesto said, "from you I will never go away. You will not need to find me. Because I will always be here, where your heart is beating so strongly. When your heart beats, it will be mine. When my heart beats, it will be yours. There is no distance then, you see. Wherever I am, there you are. And wherever you are, there I am also with you."

"Ernesto," Victoria said, "you have given me so much. You have changed my life. I am one small country you have revolutionized." She now touched his lined cheek. "There is no gift I can give you in return."

His eyes twinkled merrily. "Oh, yes, dear lady. You have given me very much. You have given me something only a goddess can give. You have given me back my youth. When I met Alejo, when I was just getting started, I was just a cranky old man, angry at the authorities and at the powers. Then, one night, when I saw you down in the cantina near Santiago, it was like a sunrise. I felt like a spirited, foolish young man again. I did not want to meet a *periodista*. I did not want to perform like a monkey for the television. But . . . I did want to know you. So I devised this scheme to entice you into our camp. If you lived with us and followed us, then maybe we would do the television performance. Then I saw you transformed from a big-city, high-powered *gringa* into an *auténtica* creature of the sunlight, a warm human person with a very great heart." He put his head back and looked straight up. "It was then I think—just before they tried to shoot us—that I felt my love for you."

As Ernesto held her tightly in his arms, her head on his thin shoulder, Victoria smelled the wild orchids in the nearby trees and heard the exotic birds of the Sierra chattering and singing. She shook with laughter and with tears. She thought of Marshall and her hostile colleagues and imagined their collective shock if they were to see her. She thought of how inconsequential had become all the things that were a few weeks ago—a lifetime ago—matters of utmost consequence. She knew her days with Ernesto Blanco could be counted now in hours. Her mind was a chaos of doubts and fears for her future. But her heart held a peace that she had never known.

Finally she said, "You will be needed here to govern, to offer direction, or at least to provide inspiration." It was a statement intended as a question, and even more as a wish.

She felt him shake his head in the negative. "No, my lady, I am not needed here. I have no answers for these people. My job was simply to ask the questions that helped lead them to their own freedom. Now they have it. Now they must, without my presence, learn how to use it." He sighed deeply. "Late in my life, I have become a teacher and a poor one at that. Like Socrates, I know only how to ask questions. When the people discover the answers, for themselves, then the teacher is no longer needed." He waved a hand out across the panorama. "There are others, somewhere, who may also need a teacher."

They heard Alejo whistling "Guantanamera," the signal that he was returning, not to catch them by surprise, and that it was indeed he. Reluctantly, they rose to meet him. Behind him came Rafael and Nick, whom he had fetched up on the trail. Alejo had two string baskets of food. The two younger men were panting, wide-eyed and red cheeked. They had been running.

Rafael gestured as he entered the small clearing. "They are coming from all over, Señor Ernesto. They are filling the roads and highways. They are all going." He bent forward, hands on knees, gasping for breath.

Equally breathless, Nick added, "He's right, Señor Blanco. There were a lot of them leaving Santiago. Not everybody. Not the old party people or the slick ones from the FCP, but a lot of other people, ordinary people. It's like a march, like a crusade or something." He too gasped for air.

Alejo said, "What are you boys talking about? You sound crazy. Who is going? Where are they going?" Suddenly, he dropped the bags and rushed to Ernesto's side, looking wildly in all directions. "Are they coming here? Are they coming into the Sierra?"

They both shook their heads no. "They seem to be heading for Habana, Señor Alejo," Rafael panted. "We—the True Republic people—got all the people in Santiago city we could to vote. Many voted today. Many others will vote tomorrow and on the election day. But many of those who voted today simply decided they would go to Habana."

Nick added, "There seems to be some kind of human earthquake. They are behaving as if some revolution is taking place. No one can explain it because no one is in charge."

Ernesto listened to them but seemed deep in thought. Victoria studied him searching for a reaction. According to the role assigned to him by fate, Alejo simply looked worried. Ernesto said, "They will expect someone to meet them."

Quietly, he instructed Nick to return to Santiago the following morning and to get to Havana as quickly as he could. He was to make contact with the leadership of the True Republic movement in the capital city and begin to organize a rally for Cuban democracy and independence to be held as the polls closed exactly two days hence. If the True Republic had the good fortune to succeed, its victorious candidates should address the crowds. If the True Republic did not succeed, he would talk to the people about the need to go forward toward the goal of the republic of the people nonetheless. Rafael he asked to arrange transport for Victoria, Alejo, and himself from Santiago to Havana the morning of the first of May. Since none of them had eaten all day, Alejo immediately set to work to prepare the usual dinner of black beans and rice.

As the sun was lowering behind the tops of the Sierra trees, Ernesto said to Victoria, "I would like to ask one more favor from you."

She did not like the finality of the request. Instead of "one more," she heard "one last." But she smiled by way of acceptance.

"If Alejo takes you into Santiago or Manzanillo tomorrow, could you make arrangements with your network . . . your former network . . . to send—what do you say, 'broadcast'—a message from Habana on election day?" he asked.

She nodded affirmatively. If what was going on below was what she thought might be going on below, TPN would be wild for anything she might send them. Having no camera, she would have to give an audio feed, she thought in passing. Never mind. Live audio, with a studio backdrop picture of her or Ernesto—why not her and Ernesto, from the satellite interview—could still be dramatic, depending on what she had to say.

"Of course," she said, "if that is what you want." Then she asked, "What do you want me to say?"

"I will know when we get to Habana," he answered. "But, if you do not mind, please make the preparations. I think it may be necessary . . . to explain things . . . to explain the outcome of the election to others in the world who might be interested. And," he added as an afterthought, "maybe to explain it to the Cuban people as well."

The following morning Rafael and Nick started for Santiago and, just as Alejo started to lead her down the trail, Victoria returned to Ernesto. "Will you be safe here?" she asked, then felt foolish for doing so.

Ernesto smiled, his eyes gently glinting in the morning sun. "My dear lady, I have been safe with myself for well over three decades. It is much too late to begin to worry about safety at this stage." Then he put one hand on her shoulder and one hand on her hair. "These mountains and these trees, and the flowers and beautiful birds, they are my friends." He kissed her mouth. "Please, hurry back soon."

Hours later, down below in Manzanillo, Victoria made her collect call to Sam Rapport in New York. Once again, he was extracted from a business lunch, this time at Le Cirque. "Vic," he spluttered, shouting and spraying expensive food into the phone brought to his table, "where the hell are you? What are you—?"

"Shut up, Sam, and listen," she shouted back. "I can't talk long, but here's the deal. I want airtime—prime time—election night. After the polls have closed here and they have some kind of count to report. I need a slot—maybe five or ten minutes—around nine o'clock. Can you do it?"

"What have you got, Vic?" Sam begged. "What can you give us? What the hell is going on down there?"

She heard him say excitedly to the table, a hand only partly covering the phone, "It's Vicky Savidge . . . somewhere in Cuba. Where are you, Vic?" Then back to the table. "She's got something for tomorrow night. You know, the Cuban elections." Then back to her. "Vic, give me a lead. I'm going to have to go to Marshall for this."

Victoria shuddered at the mention of Marshall. "Do whatever you need to do, Sam. That's your concern. Just take my word, I'll make it worth your while. It will be either Señor Blanco or just me. But I don't know yet."

"Vic," he shouted. She could almost see the food spraying from his mouth out across the table. "Vic, we're hearing something is going on down there. Is something going on down there? Tell me. Tell me!"

"Something is going on down here, Sam. I will call you election night." Then she added, "Sam, get the airtime."

Alejo and Victoria made their way by car back to a different trail into the mountains. They changed their route every trip. Alejo whispered some secret code word to a nearby *campesino*, who delightedly gave them a ride in a donkey cart as far as he could. At the trail head they left the *campesino*, and, after he had turned back, entered an almost invisible path that gradually led back to their weathered cabin.

As Alejo once again cooked the same simple meal, Ernesto took Victoria for a short walk through the orchid-clad trees and, once away, embraced her. She assured him that they would be able to send a message the following evening and he seemed pleased at the chance. "I may ask you to speak for me . . . for us," he said.

"It would be an honor," she said.

Dinner awaited the returning Rafael, who reported success at arranging the necessary transportation. The *alcalde* of Santiago, an ardent true republican, offered the use of his own car to take his leader to the capital. Following dinner, Alejo had a short private conversation with Ernesto, who simply nodded. Presently, Alejo and Rafael quietly took their bedrolls and blankets through the trees a short distance away. As Victoria slipped on her light flannel nightshirt, a ritual she now performed without self-consciousness, and prepared for sleep, she saw the two hard, ancient bunks pushed together. She sat on the edge of the outer bunk until Ernesto came in, sat down, and slipped off his sandals.

"They thought we might want to be next to each other tonight," he said quietly.

■ ■ ■

Professors will tell you that the whole history of human politics is simply about power. The writers I've read divide the world between the idealists and the realists and, these days particularly, they come down strongly on the side of the realists. I suppose that's because Hitler and Stalin have reminded everybody of the dark side of human nature and made Machiavelli fashionable again. You have to be a fox to avoid the snares and a lion to overawe the wolves. And so naturally Tío Sam hires a guy like Kissinger to run his foreign policy. People like that are foxes, all right, and they use the military—and the CIA—to make themselves lions.

That kind of approach will get you by in Europe, where they think along those lines, and maybe even in Asia, where they understand wiliness and "strength." But we poor dumb Latins, we have never figured out, aside from conquest, what a big power like Tío Sam is up to down here. You take a place like this—Cuba. These people are so used to being colonized, they're conditioned to think in those terms. The Yanqui is just a colonialist with a Coca-Cola and a smiley face. What's he up to, they're asking themselves. What's he really want? Power. Power over us. If nothing else, power to sell us his stuff and get our sugar cheap for his cereal and his chocolate and his Coca-Cola.

That's about where "realism" leads you. Do I feel responsible for that little experiment we tried here forty years ago? Of course. We didn't create utopia. We didn't understand human nature. We were too much "social realists."

Because it seems to me there is something else always going on beneath the surface. I won't call it "idealism" because the twentieth century trampled that notion. I'll call it longing. Longing for something better. Now your materialist thinks that longing is about things. And, for the poor guy, there's something to that. Everybody longs for the basics for himself and his family— shelter, food, a job. But there is more. I mean the longing for peace, for healthy children, for clean air and water, for goodwill in the community, for hope for a better life for your children. Maybe also not to be totally dead when you're dead. But that's a story for another time.

It doesn't seem to me you can talk about Aristotle's "golden mean" or Rousseau's "social contract" to people like these who aren't even on the ladder yet. Aristotle was dealing with Athens, which, despite that war they had— that crazy Peloponnesian one—was a well-off place, and Rousseau was dealing with Enlightenment—though pretty corrupt—France. These Cubans aren't even there yet. Now let's look at T. Jefferson. He was dealing with a society that had roots in the Enlightenment and a yeoman culture and a stable middle class and an educated, more or less egalitarian leadership. But he also understood something basic about people, something that could be applied even to a poor society like this one. He saw that the idea of equality, if applied to a political system of republican representative government, and if truly democratic, could offer hope, could give ordinary people the chance to improve their lives.

That's what this revolution is all about. As I keep writing and saying to myself and saying to these people: This is a test of their character. We have to give them a chance. If they take the chance and they assume responsibility, that's all they can ask for. Neither I nor anybody else can guarantee the outcome. It might not work out. Not everybody can be as lucky as Tío Sam. *But at least they have to be able to try. If the True Republic wins tomorrow, that will be their chance.*

If this is an idea whose time has come, then we'll see it catch on in other parts of the Latin world and the African world and the Asian world. Who knows, maybe it might even catch on del norte.

∎ ∎ ∎

4 6

◼

Much more than Ernesto Blanco or the small band traveling with him could possibly imagine, the idea of the true republic had indelibly seized the imaginations of an amazing gamut of people in other parts of the world. At the State University of Moscow and the University of Beijing, True Republic organizations were formed to track the outcome of the Cuban election and to discuss whether the movement's manifesto could be adapted to their respective societies and cultures. This was also true of hundreds of universities throughout the world. Someone in Italy created a True Republic website that had become one of the most frequently "visited" sites on the entire Internet. The True Republic Manifesto had been downloaded hundreds of thousands of times, photocopied, and distributed to even more hundreds of thousands without computers. Publishers throughout Europe and North America reported a dramatic increase in demand for *The Republic*, for *The Portable Thomas Jefferson*, for *The Rights of Man*, for *The Anti-Federalist Papers*, and dozens of other such works. This demand came largely from students, but there were also a surprising number of homemakers, businesspeople, teachers, editorial writers, and a host of others searching for the roots of the ideas of Ernesto Blanco.

The Montana history professor running for the United States Senate under the True Republic banner had created a surprising grassroots network of volunteers throughout his state as well as around the country. The polls showed that he was running even with the incumbent Republican senator who had filed a lawsuit to prevent Professor McLemore from using the word "Republic" in his third party title on the dubious legal theory that it was confusing and misleading. Under questioning, this senator admitted that he had "never read any long-dead Greek who calls himself Pluto or Plato or any one of those fancy foreign names." An unusual number of Washington political journalists were beginning to follow the Montana Senate race to determine if some premonition of a groundswell might be detected. The professor was financing his grassroots, volunteer-based campaign with small contributions—he had established a maximum contribution limit of $20—which were beginning to pour into his storefront campaign headquarters in Helena from all over the country. His finance chairman, another professor, announced that their campaign had received 129,000 contributions, averaging $17.34 each, which had yielded more than enough to make him competitive. It was later reported that virtually every political direct mail company in America, Wager-Down among them, had been making desperate efforts to get their hands on that computerized list of contributors.

On American campuses the True Republic drama had reawakened student interest in politics and public service. Long dormant since the activist 1960s and practically dead in the high-finance era of the Reagan Revolution and the Contract with America, a new generation of Americans was being energized to take on the problems of race, of poverty, of social justice, of political empowerment. Young radical writers were challenging the "one-party" political system in America. They attacked the "Party of Washington (D.C.)." They satirized the stranglehold that special-interest money had on the political process. They assaulted the Culture of Lobbying that controlled the nation's capital, and they shook a potent fist at the lack of access ordinary people, including themselves, had to people in powerful positions. They created dramatic perform-ances that lampooned politicians and their leechlike consultant append-ages. They lampooned the press and the Culture of Scandal that had destroyed serious journalism in the name of media conglomerate profits. Some of the ubiquitous and anonymous "observers" in the press thought they felt the trembling of a cultural earthquake beneath their feet.

In the previous few days, U.S. television networks and other media outlets had begun to report regularly on the impending Cuban election. Viewers attentively followed the three-way race and besieged call-in talk shows to ask questions about the True Republic movement and Ernesto Blanco and tried to get the experts to tell them what it all meant. This caused discomfort if for no other reason than that the experts did not know. Despite the presence of a swelling international press corps in Havana, there was still considerable confusion as to who this character was, where he came from, and what his agenda was. The is-he-Che-or-isn't-he debate raged on with neither side able to pin its opponent def-initely to the mat. Aside from Victoria Savidge's interview some weeks before, no one had actually interviewed him. A small number of re-porters claimed to have raced to a Blanco sighting somewhere in the Havana vicinity but none could provide more than the most cursory description. As usual, then, myth filled in the great gaps in fact. He didn't exist. There was more than one of him. He was an obscure Amer-ican actor seeking a reprise. He was a whiskey priest. He seduced young girls. He seduced young boys. He was some kind of witch doctor who conducted elaborate blood rituals involving human sacrifice, bestiality, naked dancers, and voodoo magic.

For its part, TPN tried every maneuver to capitalize on its tenuous claim to the Blanco franchise. The dramatically interrupted Victoria Savidge interview was rerun over and over. The audio feed from Vic-toria—though a blatant political commercial—was also rebroadcast as breaking political news. No heed was given to her dramatic on-air resignation. The network persisted in identifying her as "TPN's award-winning international correspondent inside the True Republic campaign in Cuba." Now, TPN was screaming hourly that it would have an exclusive report from its "award-winning international correspondent on election night from Havana with an up-to-the-minute report on the outcome of the dramatic election in Cuba." There was not a journalistic cliché that TPN had not worked to death.

Ernesto, Victoria, Alejo, Rafael, and the *alcalde* of Santiago de Cuba drove their antique Chevy across Cuba toward Havana. As they traveled westward, they noticed a stream of people along the roads and highways, both on the thoroughfare and along the shoulders. The mood of the people was festive and celebratory. Horns on the bewildering variety of motorized vehicles honked back and forth. Many of the people were wearing FCP baseball hats and smoking CSD cigars. But virtually to a person, everyone was wearing—in a buttonhole, a shirt pocket, a skirt waistband, the band of a straw hat, or just in the hair—the white mariposa of Cuba. At first Ernesto did not notice, so absorbed was he in writing in his battered leather journal, whose pages were almost full now. But next to him Victoria studied the faces along the way and began to notice the ubiquitous flower. She did not yet know of it symbolism, until finally she said to Rafael, "All these people are wearing the same flower."

Rafael turned sideways in the crowded front seat and grinned. "*Sí,* Señora Victoria, it is the flower of Cuba. The people have taken it as the symbol of the True Republic."

Ernesto suddenly looked up. He looked out at the stream of people traveling on their bicycles, their mules, their oxcarts, their pushcarts, and every kind of means of transport. Almost all had the white mariposa. For the first time since he had appeared months before in the *plazuela* of the village up in the Sierra, Ernesto Blanco was speechless. He had known that a human tide was moving and that it was moving to Havana and that it was somehow a declaration of democracy, a celebration of the first truly free election of the modern times. What he had not understood until this very minute was that it was a march for the *revolución de la república auténtica.*

As he looked at Victoria in wonder, the people along the road began to point, then to chatter among themselves, then to shout to their friends along the road ahead. And sensing that an event of consequence was occurring around them, people studied the buses, trucks, and cars as they slowly proceeded through the thickening traffic. They saw the car with a handkerchief attached to the radio antenna on the back, a handkerchief the *alcalde* had not attached until his occupants were aboard. On it was drawn the mariposa symbol of the True Republic. Inside they saw the *alcalde* driving, a young man in the middle of the front and a thin old man on the passenger door side. In the back was a Yanqui woman with dark red hair and . . . Ernesto Blanco himself! Could it be? Look! Is it him? Is it *el viejo*? It is, María! It is, José! It is him! It is Señor Blanco! It is Ernesto himself! There he is!

Then the shouts went up, shouts that would follow them intermittently, as people off and on became aware. *"Viva Ernesto!" "Viva la república auténtica!" "Viva la causa!" "Viva la República de Cuba!" "Viva la república auténtica!"* over and over as they went.

At first Ernesto looked away, embarrassed. Then, as he became caught up in the festive mood, he began to respond. He nodded his head in recognition and, occasionally, waved a hand. To Victoria, he seemed, uncharacteristically, to be blushing at the recognition. Still astounded at the growing flood of humanity and the tide of the True Republic movement, Ernesto seemed almost bewildered at the phenomenon he had helped create. He could think only of the hundreds, possibly thousands, of village square discussions, the oceans of coffee, the shared plates of rice and beans with those who often had barely enough for themselves, the countless demonstrations of hospitality by the ordinary people who had little room to share with a stranger, the curiosity of the young, the suspicion of those with a little power, the bold new assertiveness of women like the independent Margarita, the stoic endurance of the *campesinos* and *campesinas*, the endurance of the poorly compensated teachers and nurses and doctors, the tenacity of the *vaqueros*, the expanding network of true republic believers who opened their houses and volunteered their time, the serious students, and the round-eyed wonder and smiles of hope of the children. Especially he remembered the children who had studied him through curtained windows, over the tops of broken fences, along the sides of trails and footpaths, from behind the skirts of their *madres*, and from the countless passing vehicles. He hoped and believed that the people along the road understood they were marching for their children.

When the traffic slowed and his fame caught up with him, Ernesto Blanco was threatened with the celebrity's public embrace. People left their vehicles and crowded around the overheating car, peering through the windows, pressing noses and hands against the glass, reaching in through any opening to touch their *compañero*. Then the traffic would speed up and the *alcalde* gently extracted his ancient car from the press of humanity. Then, after a few miles, the traffic would slow and the process would repeat itself. And so it went, throughout the day of the election. As the traveling party neared Havana, the roads widened and the traffic speeded up. But in the late afternoon near the town of El Colorro, on the outskirts of Havana, the traffic congested as vehicles entered the main highway from a network of side roads. As before, Ernesto was recognized, a cry went up and grew in volume, people crowded around, things ground to a halt and would not move. The white flower was everywhere.

There was a growing clamor throughout the traffic jam as word spread that the famous Ernesto Blanco was right there with them. People every-where were shouting and looking. Some climbed on hoods, trunks, and tops of their vehicles looking for their leader. Horns were honking fu-riously. Those around the car containing Ernesto pointed and yelled that they had found him. Victoria turned white, afraid that they might be crushed. Ernesto turned to her, touched her face, and grinned his young-man grin. Then he got out of the car with Alejo and Rafael piling out of the front to protect him. Instinctively, people backed away and gave him space. Just ahead of them was a large farm truck. Its driver, a burly, tough-looking man, saw Ernesto in his rearview mirror and got out of the cab of the truck and went back.

He gestured to the truck bed. "Señor Ernesto, it would do me a great honor if you would let me take you and your party into Habana with style."

Ernesto returned and brought Victoria from the car. Together, with the help of the driver, they both climbed onto the tall truck bed. Alejo and Rafael quickly joined them. Ernesto looked around him and the gathering crowd gave a great cheer. From the enhanced perspective of his high vantage point, Ernesto saw up the highway ahead that the traffic was breaking loose and beginning to gain speed as it headed to the capital. He raised both hands and shouted, "*Compañeros y compañeras,* ahead lies Habana. Let us go there together. Let the True Republic enter the Capital City. Let's go there and take back this country for all the people! *Viva la república auténtica! Viva Cuba!*"

With a great roar the crowd broke up and headed for vehicles spread all over the place. In seconds, the smoking, honking, roaring engines formed a great caravan. Someone sprinting past handed up to Rafael on the truck bed a large white flag as big as a bed sheet with the mariposa emblem painted on it. Rafael raised the flag and Ernesto thrust his right arm forward. The revolution prepared to take the capital.

4 7

■

No place more dramatically marks the departure from *Habana vieja* and the entrance to twentieth-century Havana than the Parque Central. At the top of the Prado, the wide boulevard that leads from the Castillo de San Salvador de la Punta where the Malecón arises at the mouth of Havana harbor, eight blocks to the south grandly sits the *parque*. The architecture surrounding the Parque Central is nineteenth-century European Cuba at its finest. On the west side of the two-block-long *parque* are the Gran Teatro, still called by many *Habanistas* the García Lorca, and the Hotel Inglaterra along whose front sidewalk, called the "Louvre sidewalk," young Cuban independence fighters used to debate and call for Cuban liberation from the colonialists, drawing, as in 1869, deadly fire from the troops of their Spanish rulers. The Gran Teatro, a rococo pile worthy of a European palace, was completed in 1837 and still houses, in its several concert halls and auditoriums, ballet, opera, and dramatic performances. Next to it, the Inglaterra, finished in the 1880s and among Havana's most famous hotels, still attracts foreign tour groups to its eighty-four rooms and Moorish main-floor grand dining room.

Just off the *parque* to the south is the Capitolio Nacional, stunning especially to a Yanqui in that it is an exact replica of the United States

Capitol building, stone for stone. It was meant to house the newly in-dependent Cuban government, executive and legislative branches, after its completion in the 1920s. But mid-century revolutionaries saw too much of a shadow of the oligarchical past on it and too much of the spirit of *Tío Sam* in it and converted most of it into a technical library and the run-down Museo Nacional de Ciencias Naturales. Still the old national capitol and unintended symbol of Yanqui influence can be seen lurking over the *parque*.

In late-twentieth-century revolutionary Cuba, the *parque*, with its marble fountains, leafy bordering trees, stone benches, and ubiquitous José Martí statue imperturbably reviewing the parade of generations of human folly, is a central meeting point, a rendezvous for lovers, a forum for discussion—though not too vigorous debate—an oasis for whatever purpose human contact may require, perhaps even a meeting place for spies. By default, and without authorization, it had become the venue for the election night rally for the True Republic movement.

Responding to his instructions from Ernesto, his *jefe*, Nick Ferre had made his way across Cuba the previous day, struck with wonder at the moving tide of humanity headed in his direction, and made contact with the student True Republic organizers at the Universidad de la Habana. From advance outriders, they were already aware of the internal exodus and had begun the massive undertaking of establishing camping facilities in parks. From Ernesto Blanco through Nick they received approval to gather the throngs at seven o'clock, the evening before election day. The program would be simple. Exhilarating Cuban music would wel-come the people. The candidates for national office would speak to the crowd. Then Ernesto himself would say a few words. Those who wished to stay and celebrate with dance and song would be welcome.

The request by the True Republic movement for a permit to rally in the huge Plaza de la Revolución was rejected summarily by the Ministry of Public Works. The Cuban Social Democratic Party had reserved the Plaza for its own inevitable victory rally months, possibly even years, ago, they were informed. In fact, according to the ministry officials, virtually every open space in Havana had been reserved that night, just by coincidence. Sensing wholesale manipulation, the student organizers made a plan. They would circulate word throughout the organization that people were welcome to congregate spontaneously in the Parque Central. Nothing prohibited that. And once a sufficient number had gathered peaceably, who was to say that a few speeches could not be given. As to the music, it was as much a part of Havana street life as the air and the dust.

Since they had no permit, the True Republic student leaders could not erect even a temporary speakers platform. So, using Nick's credit card, they rented a suite with a small balcony on the front corner of the Hotel Inglaterra for election eve. Then, wouldn't it be a surprise if the national candidates and the intellectual and spiritual father of the True Republic just happened to be in that suite say around eight or nine o'clock that evening? And what could anyone say if they happened at that hour to want to feel the soft breeze from the west lifting through the *parque*? And what a coincidence it would be if, catching sight of a few people down below—not to say perhaps a monstrous crowd spilling over and beyond the perimeters of the *parque*—the leaders of the movement heard the outcry of joy from the crowd and the demands for a few remarks. And could any sensible public official possibly deny that those leaders would have no real choice but to respond to the crowd's demand lest it become unruly, then a mob, then a threat to public health and safety? No, indeed, it could only be interpreted as a public service of truly historic proportions for the leaders of the movement to acknowledge the crowd's acclaim and satisfy the outcry for a few patriotic words.

So it was done. Word was quietly circulated to the arriving multitudes that something big was going to take place on the eve of the election at the Parque Central. Pass the word. Spread the news. But, be careful. Keep it quiet. Don't invite the authorities. Don't provide them enough warning that they can close the *parque* or ring it with troops or frustrate the rally plan.

Even as Ernesto and his party were making their way across the country on the day before the election, *el primero de mayo*, at the Inglaterra Nick and his student friends were busy setting up a buffet table of food for the evening, a cooler of drinks, arranging some flowers in the vases, white mariposas everywhere. An art student drew the mariposa on a sheet that they would drape around the balcony just before the speeches began. They made sure the hotel supplied extra towels for the travelers, so unaccustomed to the pleasures of hot water and thick towels, who would soon arrive. They had arranged for other students to go out to the main highway coming in from the east to intercept Ernesto and his group and bring them by back streets and circular paths to the rear entrance of the hotel where other organizers were posted to bring them up through the service elevator to the second floor and down the hallway to the corner suite. Then, after the speeches and the rally, the other political leaders and organizers would leave, Ernesto would spend the night in the suite, and in the morning he would be taken out through the same back entry they had used to get him in. Every plan and every arrangement were rehearsed and double-checked several times over.

But no one had time to think about where exactly Ernesto would be taken the following morning. Indeed, for those who had given it any thought at all, there was no consensus on what his future role would be. Everyone hoped and believed that the True Republic campaign would succeed, that miraculously it would have a governing majority in the new legislature, and that its candidate would occupy the Palacio. That would mean, surely, that Ernesto Blanco would be the éminence grise, the guiding spirit, the statesman of the nation, the one who really ran things. But, truly, the chaotic turbulence, the explosive momentum of the past few weeks had given no one time to think anything through, including the future position of the one who started this whole *revolución*. No one in the Hotel Inglaterra could think beyond the next few hours.

Others, though, were thinking beyond the next few hours, thinking of the later evening, thinking of the following morning, thinking of the next few weeks. E. F. Scarlatti for one was thinking of the Algarve and Johnny Gallagher in the bed, then on the beach, then back in the bed. She thumbed absently through the thick airline ticket tossed on the bed with her things to be packed. The ticket took her to Buenos Aires through Mexico City the following morning. Then after a day or two it took her on to Lima, then to São Paulo, then back to Mexico City, then Amsterdam, then by train to Brussels, then to Lyon, whence she would drive herself across southern France and Spain into southern Portugal—and Johnny. Johnny would have two very useful things with him. One of them would be a satchel full of cash. After she was tired of the other, Johnny would suddenly find himself alone one morning in that lovely exclusive hotel on the beach with a very large rental bill to keep him company. And she would be . . . well, that was a secret only she would know.

E.F. had returned from some surveillance and reconnaissance. Wearing a tight white dress and a mariposa in her hair, she had ascertained from a muttered conversation near the door of the True Republic store-front near the campus of the Universidad de la Habana that *el viejo*—along with a horde of several hundred thousand other people—was on his way to Havana. That would mean, she reasoned, that the horde would be gathering somewhere. If they gathered, she reasoned further, that would mean that the old guy would show up. There were not a lot of places in Havana to put that many people. The Commies wouldn't let them use the great Plaza, so the choices were narrowing. She snagged a passing young man, the cutest one she could find, as he raced out of the office door. She placed her manicured nails on his slender wrist, looked with great tenderness into his eyes from no more than a foot away, and whispered, "Oh, please, please, I have been working so hard in Trinidad for Señor Ernesto. I know he is coming. I must see him. I must just once see his wonderful face and hear his inspiring words. It will mean everything to me. It is my whole life." She placed her other hand tenderly on her moist, slightly parted lips and brought a tiny tear to her eye. The fingers on his wrist she moved gently up and down.

"*Señ . . . señora . . . señora,*" the dark-eyed, dark-haired boy stuttered. "I am only . . . you see . . . just a small worker here. I . . . I do not know . . . exactly . . . what is to be done. But . . . but . . . you seem so sincere. And I understand your feelings. My friends and I have also worked so hard. We are also like you." He looked nervously over his shoulder but saw only other young people racing busily in and out of the narrow storefront carrying hastily printed leaflets and homemade signs for the rally. "I have heard . . . I do not know for sure . . . but I have heard"—here he leaned so close his lips were almost on her ear—"that if people like us . . . those who believe in the True Republic . . . come to the Parque Central"—she was briefly thrilled to feel his warm breath in her ear—"perhaps around eight tonight, then there is a good possibility that he . . . *el viejo* . . . will appear." He makes it sound like the mystical appearance of a dead saint, she thought.

"Oh, young man," she whispered breathlessly, "I do not know how to thank you. You have truly fulfilled my lifelong dream." She leaned up a few inches and kissed him firmly on his downy cheek. He turned dark red, briefly thought of asking to escort her, and then was called away by passing friends racing down the street.

Now we know where and we know when, she thought. We must now decide how. She set off eastward toward the *parque*. She was there in fifteen minutes. Although it was still midafternoon, there was an uncommonly large number of people already gathering. Good job I got here early, she thought. Also good job there are enough people that I don't stand out. She swung her handbag like a tourist on a stroll while carefully scanning the entire terrain. Now she was at her best. She specialized in logistics in the Marine Corps. He would have to speak, even if just a few words. That meant he would have to be seen, up above the crowd, even for just a few moments. No stand was being built. The authorities wouldn't permit that. They'll have to use something already elevated. She scanned the *parque* again. There will be no speaker system, so he will have to be reasonably close to the crowd. Then she saw it. The only place near enough to the two-block *parque* where one could be seen and heard was one of the balconies on the Hotel Inglaterra.

E.F. found an unoccupied corner of one of the stone benches in the middle of the park facing the hotel. She studied the park, the surrounding trees, the fountain, the angles from a wide variety of positions around the park. She filled the park with people in her imagination and heard the noise and felt the push. She worked from the proposition that a sniper approach required the long gun. The long gun would be more easily spotted and more difficult to ditch. She shook her head. She could see no way to set up a sniper shot without being protected. Even getting to the top of, and then back down from, one of the surrounding buildings would attract too much attention and involve too many people seeing her. She got up and walked across to the hotel. Inside, she passed through the spacious, ornate lobby, past the large Moroccan-style dining room on the right, and walked toward the grand staircase straight ahead. She could have been any one of the dozens of guests or hundreds of tourists that traversed the same path every day.

She slowly ascended the staircase as it rose dramatically, landed, then turned upward and to the left to the second floor. She paused at the landing and looked back, imagining herself being announced at a state ball of some kind. Then quickly she went up. She started to turn left down the hallway running along the front of the hotel when the sound of hubbub and confusion to the right distracted her. At the end of the hallway behind her she heard the excited voices of young people. It sounded as if orders were being given; debates and discussions were being batted back and forth, and a sense of urgency emanated through the open door of the corner suite. Bingo.

Adjusting the white mariposa before a hallway mirror, E.F. started down the short hallway to the right trying to look as lost and innocent as possible. Just before she got to the end suite, a corridor opened to her right leading to the back of the hotel. As she quickly started down it, she saw an open door. She heard the excited voices starting to emerge from the corner suite when a maid already in the room accosted her. She explained in hyper-Spanish with flamboyant gestures that a very angry boyfriend was chasing her through the hotel and she had to hide for just a moment. The solicitous maid could not be more understanding. E.F. peered around the corner of the door as three young people hurried down the main front hallway toward the front staircase. The maid whispered in her ear, "Isn't it exciting? *El viejo*—Señor Ernesto— will be speaking this very evening from the room the students have just left."

Thanking the maid for her protection, E.F. left the room in a dash down the hallway toward the back. She didn't want the students to see her—to prevent future identification—and she wanted to explore the back entrance. Along the hallway running the length of the back of the hotel she found a service elevator used by maids and serving staff. She entered, descended, and found herself in the middle of the kitchen. As curious cooks and waiters stared at her, she gave a confused smile, shrugged her shoulders, and followed a waitress out into the large dining room. Passing through the kitchen, she had seen the double back door through which food and hotel supplies were delivered. That is where he will be brought in, she reasoned, then up the elevator to the second floor, then to the corner suite.

E.F. had one more job to do. After exiting the hotel through the large front doors, and studying the balcony once again from the front, she casually circled the south side of the hotel on the street that passed between it and the Gran Teatro, and walked up the narrow passageway behind the hotel into which delivery carts and hotel staff entered. It was now late afternoon and she guessed that she would have little time to wait. She found a place where she could see hotel staff departing. In less than an hour the second-floor maid who had befriended her left by herself. E.F. followed her out onto the street and caught up with her. Quickly and passionately she explained her great desire to see the great Ernesto just once, up close. Would the kind lady, she pleaded, just let her use her maid's uniform for the evening—of course for ten dollars

U.S. that she quickly flashed in her unclenched fist. The deal was quickly struck and E.F. followed the maid to her crowded flat in the nearby Vedado section. Retrieving the uniform in exchange for the ten dollars and promising to return it later in the evening, E.F. made her way back to the Deauville Hotel.

In less than two hours she would be back in the Inglaterra kitchen at a spot between the giant industrial freezer and the delivery door that she had already selected as the place where she would deliver her present to Señor Blanco. She changed into the ill-fitting maid's uniform, much too large, put the silenced pistol into a large inexpensive purse, and packed the rest of her belongings—including the thick airline ticket— for the early morning departure.

4 8

■

He's going to appear about eight or nine tonight," the burly man said. "The Inglaterra."

Vilma Espinosa crushed a cigarette with yellow-stained fingers and stared at her lover *du jour* who, along with that job, got to be a high-level official in the State Security Department. "That means he has to go in . . . and . . . he has to go out." She pulled her booted feet off her desk. "Bring him in here."

The mustachioed muscle man crossed the large office, beckoned through the door, and escorted Otra Vez into the room. The older wrinkled man, hat in hand, and grinning with his broken, irregular teeth stood before her cluttered desk. "Señora?"

Vilma stood up and leaned across the desk toward Otra Vez. "Here's the deal. We'll pick you up at eight. That's"—she checked her watch— "less than two hours from now." He started to say something and she held up her hand. "Don't worry. We know where you're staying." She came around the desk and stood directly in front of him. She was shorter and stockier and, on this occasion, had reverted to revolutionary combat fatigues. Otra Vez wondered if she had ever tried to grow a beard so that she could truly be one of *los barbudos*. "Dress up. If you need nicer pants and a shirt, we'll get them for you. Remember, you are there to patch things up . . . to join the celebration . . . to give a present."

Otra Vez had no choice but to nod in agreement.

"We'll take you—him and me—in a car to the back of the hotel," she continued, nose just below his face. "You have to walk in there—like you know what you are doing. You carry your 'present' up the service elevator to the second floor. Go up the side hallway to the front. He will be in the corner suite. You get your present inside. That shouldn't be too tough because there will be a lot of people around and nobody will know what's going on."

Otra Vez nodded.

Vilma snorted derisively. "Then"—she smacked his thin shoulder—"then you're on your own. Once we're sure you've done your job, then you're a free man."

Otra Vez gave a gap-toothed smile and nodded his head in thanks. He knew very well she had already given the orders for him to be shot as he tried to escape through the back door of the Inglaterra. That way the Cuban government could claim that, with great regret for the loss of Señor Ernesto Blanco's life, they had quickly and surely apprehended his murderer, a disaffected supporter, and prevented his escape. Otra Vez could almost see the muscle man fingering the automatic pistol in his shoulder holster. This hulk would be given a medal for his heroism. And he, his poor rotten old corpse riddled with gunfire, would be put quickly on public display as evidence of the dissension and corruption that permeated the so-called True Republic movement.

"Any questions?" Vilma asked. "Have you got what you need for the device . . . your 'present'?"

Otra Vez nodded his head again. "*Comandante*, your people gave me all I needed. Excellent supplies. I could not ask for anything more."

She turned her back on him and waved a dismissal. "Get back to your place, then, and we'll pick you up in a couple of hours. As an afterthought she said brusquely to her consort, "Get him some decent trousers and a shirt."

My burial clothes, Otra Vez thought grimly as he escaped the office's foul atmosphere.

*   *   *

While Otra Vez waited for the black government car to pick him up from his shabby room in the Cerro district, E. F. Scarlatti was walking from the Deauville Hotel south down the Avenida de Italia five blocks to San Rafael where she turned left three blocks to the rear of the Hotel Inglaterra. The baggy maid's uniform concealed her figure as well as a very simple black dress that covered it. She wore cheap soft-soled shoes and had her hair tucked up under the maid's cap. She wore no *maquillaje*. She carried only the large handbag that, in turn, carried only the silenced pistol. The farther east she proceeded toward the hotel along San Rafael, the more she could hear the loud samba music and the noise of the gathering crowd. Beside her along the sidewalks and in the streets were hundreds, behind her even thousands, of people, all laughing and eager to join the election eve rally.

Reaching the back of the hotel, E.F. entered the small passageway and positioned herself twenty yards beyond the delivery door in the back. There was a lot of excited traffic going in and out of the door. Coolly, she lit a cigarette and watched. If she saw Blanco and his party arriving to enter the hotel through the back, she would quickly and quietly position herself in the space next to the freezer just inside the door and take her shot from no more than six feet away. The fall-back plan was to wait until he left the hotel after whatever speech he was to give and carry out the same operation. She had no doubt that, in the inevitable chaos that ensued, she would have little trouble escaping into the night. She would have at least six bullets left in the clip to handle anyone who might be inclined to stop her.

To her dismay she was joined by another maid who bummed a cigarette. "He's just a regular old guy," she said, "just like *mi abuelo.*"

Lighting her coworker's cigarette, E.F. said excitedly, "You saw him? You saw one of his speeches?"

The young woman blew smoke. "No, I saw him fifteen minutes ago. He just came in. There were only about four or five people with him. I thought there would be a mob."

Shit, E.F. thought. There goes plan A. "So he is already in the hotel. How exciting. He is on my floor, you know. I must go in there. They may need something. Besides," she said conspiratorially, "maybe he will need me." She nudged her *compañera.* "I hear he likes the younger ladies." They both giggled hysterically at the idea.

"If he needs more than one," the other woman said, "I am on the

third floor." They giggled again as E.F. hurried through the confusion
at the back door.

Ernesto Blanco, Victoria, Alejo, Rafael, and Nick had been led by one
of the student leaders through the back door only a few minutes before
E.F. arrived. The students had created a distraction in the front of the
hotel minutes before that by bringing in the national True Republic
candidates, led by the youthful Universidad de la Habana philosophy
professor who was the candidate for president. That grand entrance had
created a huge uproar that drew all attention—including that of the
kitchen staff who had raced to peer through the windows into the
lobby—away from the back. The service elevator had been waiting on
the first floor and the small party was whisked unnoticed to the front
corner suite. They were shortly joined by the presidential and vice presidential candidates, who would precede Ernesto on the balcony.

"Señor Ernesto," the presidential candidate said, "only history will
prove the role you have played in leading the democratic revolution in
Cuba, in creating the ideal of the true republic that all of us can follow."

Ernesto showed his white teeth. "If all goes well tomorrow, you can
demonstrate your feelings by governing this country well and making
sure the power is held by the people themselves."

Outside a chant was going up. "*La república auténtica. La república
auténtica. La república auténtica.*" It grew in volume. Rafael was peering
through a hotel curtain. He turned, his face white. "*Señores,* outside are
all the people in Cuba . . . maybe in all the world."

Nick looked at his watch. The leader of the students gestured to the
vice presidential candidate. "*Señora,*" she said, "*por favor.*"

Two students parted the curtains to the balcony. Two other students
went out and hung the banner of the white mariposa from the balcony
railing. A huge roar went up from the crowd, a crowd now resembling
a thick animated blanket covering every foot of the *parque* and stretched
down the side streets and the broad boulevard of La Rampa to the north
as far as anyone could see.

The candidate for the vice presidency stepped out onto the balcony
and held her hands up for silence. Gradually, the cheers of "*La república
auténtica*" and "*Viva Cuba!*" began to die down and she began her remarks. Behind her in the suite Ernesto picked a glossy apple from the
fruit bowl. He studied it carefully. He had not seen an apple like this in

many years. He tentatively took a small bite. Across the room Victoria saw him and smiled. He looked like a tired, white-haired, wrinkled boy. He also, she thought, radiated a happiness and contentment known only to those who possess a dream and who dare greatly. She crossed the room, took the white mariposa from her hair, and carefully tucked it in the top pocket of his simple *guayabera* shirt. She wanted to kiss him but decided it might embarrass him in front of the students.

The vice presidential candidate concluded her remarks and, as she began her introduction of her running mate, the True Republic candidate for president, an official government car made its way carefully through the crowd that spilled down San Rafael behind the hotel, the same street E.F. had walked up less than an hour before. The car had to stop about fifty yards short of the hotel.

Vilma Espinosa sat forward in the backseat that she occupied with her body builder escort and hissed at Otra Vez, who sat in the front passenger seat, "All right. Take your 'present.' Get it in the suite. Get out of there as quickly as you can. Come out this back way. We will be on Industria street, just behind El Capitolio, waiting for you. As soon as you get to the car, we'll be out of here before the damn thing goes off." She whacked him hard on the shoulder. Otra Vez winced and nodded.

He motioned for the driver to open the car trunk. They went around to the back. Otra Vez very carefully removed a nicely wrapped package, more than twice as large as a shoe box with a large bow on top, from a large plastic shopping bag. He gingerly stepped back and motioned the driver to close the trunk. He muttered, "Make sure you wait where there are no people. I don't want anyone to see me when I come back."

With that he walked toward the back of he hotel and entered the narrow passageway. He could feel Vilma and her bully boy watching him. As he got to the door, a waiter came out for a smoke and held the door for him. "Gift for *el viejo*," he said. "Got to be from a very nice lady, I think." They both laughed. Otra Vez made his way through the crowded kitchen, out into the lobby, and then proceeded up the wide front staircase that by now was crowded with people hoping to get a glimpse of the True Republic leaders, *their* leaders. He was desperately afraid that someone from the Sierra camp—Rafael or Alejo—might see him. Yet no one did. He got to the second floor, where young people were holding whispered conversations and racing about, and started down the right hall toward the corner at the south end of the hotel, where a small group of people were clustered. A young man stopped him.

"May I help you?" he asked.

Otra Vez said, "A present for Señor Ernesto . . . from the True Republic workers in . . . Matanzas," he quickly added. "I simply want to take it to him personally."

The young man grabbed the large box and said, "*Muchas gracias, señor*, I will make sure he gets the package. I am afraid he is now about to say some words to the crowd. He will be very happy for this, I am sure."

Otra Vez continued to hold the box. "How do I know it will make its way to Señor Ernesto himself? It is very important that he opens it. He is my very good friend. I must be sure that he opens it himself."

"*Señor*," the young man said as he jerked the box away. Otra Vez flinched. "You have my word of honor. It will go to Señor Blanco himself. I will personally give it to him. He will open it."

Otra Vez saw a table of food emerging into the front hallway from the corridor running to the back of the hotel. He started to reach for the box and then he shrugged. "*Joven*, I must trust you to give this present to *el señor*. And, *por favor*, make sure he reads the note inside himself."

"I give you my most sincere promise, *señor*," the young man said as he turned, went down the hallway, and entered the room.

Otra Vez started to go back down the stairs when he noticed a maid peering around the corner of the side hallway toward the door of the corner suite. She carried a large handbag which he thought strange. And something about her gave him a chill. She somehow did not look exactly like the usual hotel maid. She had sharp, attractive features, the look of a woman of style and quality. She could rise above the serving job on her looks alone. But there she was. Perhaps she is, he thought, the kind of person drawn to dramatic events and dramatic personalities. With that, he headed down the grand staircase pushing his way through the people packed on its steps and through those filling the lobby. Instead of going out the back way, however, he exited through the front doors into the throng pressing against the front of the hotel. He squeezed his way into the front ranks so that he could look almost directly up onto the sheet-draped balcony some forty feet away. He had a perfect spot from which to view what was about to happen.

What was about to happen was the introduction by the True Republic candidate for president of the founder and leader of his movement, the inspiration, he said, that had brought them all to the very heart of the capital of Cuba here tonight and that would bring them to the gates of power when the polls closed in less than twenty-four hours. "He is," the candidate said, "a man whom we all know, admire, respect, and, yes, even revere. But a man not very many of us have seen very much." This brought a cheer and a great laugh from the crowd that knew Ernesto Blanco's reclusiveness had become itself magnetic. "He is," the candidate shouted above the noise of the crowd, "the father of democracy in Cuba. He is the architect of the ideal of the true republic. He is . . . Ernesto . . . Blanco!"

A gigantic roar, a noise equal to past receptions of *Fidel* in the Plaza de la Revolución on New Year's Day, rose from the tens of thousands in and around the Parque Central. The noise bounded off the tall facades of the buildings bordering the park. The presidential candidate stepped back. For a moment the balcony stood empty. Then suddenly onto the balcony stepped the slight, white-haired figure of Ernesto Blanco. The roar doubled. Otra Vez felt a chill. The *revolución* had returned. Inside, behind the slight figure timidly waving a hand, Rafael yelled until he embarrassed himself. Everyone in the suite was applauding. Nick thought to himself that the loss of his career was well worth it, that he would never have come this close to the epicenter of a genuine, historic democratic revolution had he remained a careerist. The excitement was so intense and the waves of noise pounding against the hotel facade so great no one noticed that Victoria had gone into the adjoining bedroom with tears streaming from her eyes.

Ernesto Blanco managed to quiet the crowd only after several minutes. Then he said, "*Compañeros y compañeras*, tomorrow marks the liberation of Cuba." Great cheer. "Tomorrow marks the beginning of a new kind of country . . . not just a new country for Cuba . . . but a new kind of country in the world." Another cheer. "Starting tomorrow, this country . . . you people . . . have a chance to show the others how it is done. To show the rest of the world that ordinary people can exercise the power to run their own lives. No big state to run your lives. No big money to run your lives. Just *you* to run your lives." Another cheer. "If you vote tomorrow, you will win your freedom and win the power. Then, *mi amigos y amigas,* then you must earn the right . . . by showing your responsibility." Huge cheer. Then he shouted, "Good-bye, my friends, I will always love you."

The roar that greeted Ernesto doubled in volume as he raised his hand and stepped back from the balcony. It echoed and bounded back and forth across and up and down the Parque Central. Even in the hotel suite itself the noise was so great no one could speak a word. Nor could they hear a sharp explosive report. Had they heard it, they would most certainly have thought that it came from a couple of blocks to the south, somewhere in the vicinity of the Capitolio Nacional.

4 9

■

The note said:

You have given me my life back, *che.* So, in my own small way, I am doing the same for you. We won't see each other again. But you brought the revolution back to life, and in a better way. Keep it alive—for all of us.

Con mucho respeto, Otra Vez

Ernesto studied the note and the old work shirt Otra Vez had always worn that had been in the box. He could only guess—but he had a good guess—as to what it meant. Clearly Otra Vez had been sent by the Cuban power structure to stop him. But something—probably we will never know, he thought—changed his mind. Of course, he had always been a little suspicious of Otra Vez. There had always been something not quite right there. But deep down, Ernesto had always thought Otra

Vez was a good man. Circumstances had given him a bad life. You could see it in his face. But that did not mean he was a bad man.

Outside the crowd noise had dampened enough that the sirens of emergency vehicles could be heard and through the south windows of the hotel suite a small glow somewhere behind the old capitol building could be seen. The connection between these phenomena and Otra Vez's note would never really be known. Because no one else was alive who could identify Otra Vez as the Cuban Social Democrats'—more precisely Vilma Espinosa's—designated hit man to eliminate Ernesto Blanco. And of course no one, save Otra Vez himself, knew there had been two boxes in the large plastic bag he had brought from his small room and deposited in the trunk of Vilma's official car. Nor could they know that he had intended the benign one for Ernesto since he left the doctor's office a week before. Even had the Cuban authorities known Otra Vez's identity, an effort to retaliate for eliminating one of their key leaders would have failed. For no one could remember seeing Otra Vez ever again after election eve.

The Parque Central was not the only dramatic forum that evening. In an upstairs office at the Free Cuba Party headquarters on the Prado some blocks away, Eddie Alonzo was on a conference call to Olivero Sanchez and Micky Mendoza in Miami. "A lot of people have already voted," he reported. "And we can't get any reliable data from the exit polls."

"Why not?" his boss Micky demanded.

He said, "Why not is because these people thought we were from State Security, so they all told us they voted for the CSD. If they are telling the truth, it's a landslide for the guys in power."

"That can't be," Sanchez insisted.

"Of course it cannot be," Eddie responded. "Every in-depth poll and focus group we've done, where the people we sampled had confidence in our confidentiality, show that it's a horse race—even three days ago. It was a third, a third, and a third."

"Yeah," Micky said, "but the problem with those polls is that they don't show an undecided. There have to be some undecideds."

Eddie said, "I agree, Micky, but these people will not admit they haven't made up their minds."

"So," Sanchez said, "we just have to wait until the votes are counted."

"I'm afraid that's where we are, Olivero," Micky said. "We're down to the last twenty-four hours."

"Eddie," Micky continued, "how long will the count take? They got several million paper ballots. It'll take forever."

"Don't think so, Micky," Eddie said. "With so many votes cast yesterday and today, they have already been counting a lot and they will count all day tomorrow. They're going to post preliminary results as soon as the polls close tomorrow night at seven and then keep updating them throughout the evening. Unless it's very close, we should have something definitive well before midnight tomorrow."

Olivero Sanchez said, "Yeah, and if it's close, we know how that call is going to go. Those guys down there are going to be discovering some mystery ballot boxes."

"Don't think so, Mr. Sanchez," Eddie answered, "Jimmy Carter and the international busybodies are all over the place down there. They have somebody looking over every counter's shoulders. I think it's going to be honest."

"Just so it's honest in our favor," Sanchez concluded. "I hope Carter and his crowd got their instructions from the White House."

And during roughly the same hour, just after ten o'clock the night of the thirtieth of April, an equally tense telephone call was placed from Miami to the Leeward Island Club in the Bahamas. Johnny Gallagher said, "We still haven't heard from our guy."

"*Your* guy, Johnny," Harry Rossell reminded him ominously. "*Your* guy. You better have some news for us soon because, as I recall, the contract runs out at midnight tonight. And right now it's . . . let's see . . . it's less than two hours."

Johnny could not keep the anxiety out of his voice. "Believe me, Mr. Rossell, this guy is the best. I will wager a lot that our guy . . . my guy . . . is about as close to the target as sh . . . as he can get." His voice shook. He almost gave it away. Nerves.

"I wouldn't wager any more if I were you, Johnny," Rossell warned. "If the job's not done successfully by midnight, my recollection is that we get the down payment back. That's a good deal of money, as I recall. Do I recall correctly, Johnny?"

"Yes, sir, Mr. Rossell," Johnny said as he tried to keep his voice steady.

"It's returnable. That's the deal." Five hundred thousand. Having made one too many trips to Vegas recently, Johnny didn't have that kind of money handy. "My guy's good for it. But, believe me, there has never been one time when . . . he's . . . he's let me down. Besides, he'll want the other half badly enough to get the job done. For sure."

"Tell you what, Johnny," Harry Rossell said, "you call me back here in . . . let's see . . . one hour and a half. Okay? And I would suggest in the meantime that you find someplace to watch the news wires. If your guy is successful, I have to believe we'll hear about it pretty quickly. Don't you think, Johnny?"

"Yes, sir," Johnny responded quickly. "The press is all over things down there. We'll hear about it right away."

Johnny's "guy" was as conscious as her employers of the sand running through the hourglass. She wanted the other half of the contract—the success fee—badly. It was key to her long-range plan—her escape. Besides, even though she had almost all the down payment, she had no intention of returning a dollar of it. Johnny would have to make it good. His club didn't know who she was. But, it did mean Johnny would be looking for her. She didn't need that. Johnny had some resources. And she didn't want to spend the next several years ducking those guys. So she had to move and she had to do it soon.

Where *was* he? she kept asking herself. He had given his speech. Now he was still in the room. Meanwhile, she had to keep moving. Due to the turmoil in the hotel, especially near the corner suite, and the outside pandemonium that had become a giant street party, she had been able to avoid a challenge from any of the regular hotel employees. She found spare towels to carry up and down the side hall. If she found an unattended serving cart, she requisitioned it and pushed it up and down the corridor. She was running out of ploys. Besides, she had to keep the handbag close by and, for a maid, that was a curiosity. But she had to stay close enough to determine when the old man left so she could get down to the rear door ahead of him. She certainly could not stand around in the kitchen or loiter near the back door. That would be even more obvious. Fifteen minutes before, when all those sirens went off somewhere nearby, the other politicians had left and a lot of the students with them. There could not be very many people left in that suite with the old man. For the third time in five minutes, she looked at her watch: 10:45. She did not have any time left. She would wait a few minutes more, then she would have to force the issue. Where *was* he?

Ernesto was talking to those who had come to Havana with him and had been with him much of the way—Alejo, Rafael, Victoria, and Nick. They were alone in the room, sitting in a circle. "Victoria and Nick, you *norteamericanos*, you have shown that the people of your country are not against Cuba. You have both sacrificed your careers for your belief in a democratic cause. You have shown us that the image of *Tío Sam* that has become such a bad thing here for so long can become *Amigo Sam*. And Alejo, *gran amigo mío*, you have cooked so many rice and beans. *Por favor*, do not cook one more plate of rice and beans." The old man smiled shyly, recognizing his *compañero*'s compliment, and looked as if he were about to cry from the pride he felt. Ernesto turned to Rafael. "*Joven*, I don't know what caused you to leave your home for this cause. But this movement is not for us. It is for you, because you are the future of Cuba."

Rafael studied the carpet in the hotel room, unaccustomed to such finery. "Señor Ernesto, I only wanted to find the mule and find out how to make him go." He looked up and smiled. "That's what you promised."

Ernesto ruffled Rafael's unkempt hair. "I did it too, didn't I?"

E.F. paced up and down like a taut, caged cat. There was a maids' room at the end of the corridor. She would go there for a smoke. She reached in the pocket of her uniform for her cigarettes. She felt something else in there and pulled it out. It was a key. It had to be a master key. There was a room near the front of the side hall that she had not seen anyone enter or exit all evening. Quickly she tried the key. It worked. She slowly opened the door and flicked on the light switch. Empty. She slipped inside, turned, and peered out. Perfect. She flicked off the light and stood in darkness. She could stand just inside the door and see anyone moving from the corner suite toward the front stairs or, more likely, coming down the side hallway past her to the back elevator. She put her handbag on the floor, took out the gun, charged the chamber, and waited. If he does not come out in half an hour, she thought, I'm going in.

Just then, a young man came past the door, only three feet away, heading toward the corner suite. Action, she thought. He went around the corner to her right and she heard him tap quietly on the door. She could hear a greeting and a quick discussion as the door opened. They are moving him, she thought. This is it.

Earlier in the evening, when it was clear the festivities outside would go on into the night, and when Ernesto had stated his unease with the comforts of the hotel and his desire to spend the night in a humbler place, the decision had been made that he would leave once his conversation with his closest friends was ended and he would be taken to spend the night in a small village along the coast outside Havana. When Nick answered the door, one of the student leaders said, "The car is ready. It's in back waiting."

Nick turned back into the room and told the others he would be back to bring them out as soon as he checked to see that all was clear. Then he followed the student leader out into the main front corridor and quickly turned left down the side hallway leading to the back. He had gone less than thirty feet when the door to a guest room opened to reveal a maid in the darkened room with her right hand behind her back. He hurried on a few feet and stopped. He knew that woman! Who was she? Whoever she was, she was not a maid. His mind raced back over the weeks and months. Someone he had met. Someone he had talked to. She wasn't a maid! Then why was she dressed as a maid? A reporter, he quickly thought. She's lurking to get a picture or grab a quick interview when Señor Blanco comes out. He grabbed the shirt of the young man with him as he turned back. As he started to go back the few feet to the door, the woman's face emerged and she looked directly at him. Ms. Scarlatti! That was it! E. something. E.J., E. something. Scarlatti. With the Free Cubans. Why is she here?

All this raced through his mind in a few quick seconds. He stepped back to the door.

"Ms. Scarlatti," Nick said. "You remember . . . Nick . . . Nick Ferre. From the Interests Section. . . ."

She looked at him grimly . . . blankly. Then her right hand came from around her uniform and she pointed a pistol with a very long barrel directly at him. He knew immediately and instinctively that she was there to assassinate Ernesto Blanco. With the same blank look—expressionless, emotionless—she waved the long gun barrel back toward the corner suite.

Nick stared at her. He was frozen. He would not move. Again she silently wagged the gun barrel twice.

Suddenly, in a desperate attempt to get help, the student started running down the back hall. So quickly Nick could hardly believe it, E.F. dipped her knees slightly, brought her left hand up to the gun, pivoted to her left, and shot the young man in the back. Nick had heard that sound up in the Sierra some weeks before. It was like a loud cough.

Very deliberately, Nick whistled the first few bars of "Guantanamera." Then he stepped directly toward her and grabbed the gun barrel. She shot him straight through the heart. He was dead before he hit the floor.

E.F. stepped over Nick Ferre, turned to the right, and started for the corner suite. As she got to the front hallway and started toward the door twenty feet away, a thin, high scream erupted from the corridor behind her. She looked over her shoulder and saw a waiter and waitress wheeling a food cart toward the corner room. They saw the gun first and then Nick's body. The waiter shouted, "You crazy bitch—*loco en la cabeza*—!"

As before, she squatted slightly, swung the gun around with both hands, and fired off two shots. Cough! Cough! Seeing her turn, the waiter and waitress, the latter screaming, ducked behind the tablecloth draped over the cart. Her bullets struck dishes and glasses and the metal warmer under the cart. There was a tremendous clatter as dishes, glasses, flower vases, food, and silver shattered, flew against the surrounding walls, and crashed to the floor. The flame from the Sterno heaters in the food warmer caught the tablecloth on fire. E.F. swore as she heard footsteps pounding up the main staircase.

She swung around just as the door to the corner suite opened and in the doorway stood Ernesto Blanco. She studied him briefly, suddenly shocked to be so near her prey of the last four months. To her great dismay, he smiled at her with a row of very strong, white teeth and said, "So there you are, *señora*."

She pointed the gun at the white-haired man, less than twenty feet away, and said, "It is not personal, *señor*, it is just politics," and fired.

For a second time, the hollow-point bullet magically passed by his ear and, given much greater proximity, this time tore out a huge section of the door frame behind him. This time E.F. had been distracted by the noise behind her as she spoke to Ernesto. The hotel security man on the top steps of the staircase forty feet behind her yelled, *"No! Para!"* as he fired a round into her spine.

■ ■ ■

Why do so many good people have to give their lives just because they are doing the right thing? It is one of those great mysteries. Nicholas Ferre should not have had to die just because he believed in democracy. He certainly should not have had to give his life protecting mine.

Nick was as fine a human being as I have met. I hope, somehow, those words I sent his parents will get through. Not that it will help them that much. But they should know what an extraordinary son they created. He gave his life for his country. He gave his life for me. Even more, he gave his life for something he believed in. One night last week he told me that the weeks he spent with us, the time he spent in the movement, meant more to him than anything else he had ever done. He wanted to help the people of Cuba. That was his main goal. And he came to realize that the best thing he could do for these people was to help them get their independence from the forces of state power and the forces of private power. He believed totally in the ability of the people to govern their own lives. And he believed in the future of Cuba.

If I am not mistaken, Nick will be one of the early heroes of the new Cuban republic.

And, I believe he can become a bridge from Cuba to the United States and from the United States to Cuba. That is what his last few weeks really were. He was a bridge from his country to this one.

If our side wins, and I believe we may, then the new government should— as I have already urged our leaders to do—create a Nicholas Ferre Memorial—an exchange program of scholars and diplomats and students. Nick will smile at that.

He did more in his life than most of us do in lives twice or even three times as long. Which is another lesson. Long life doesn't guarantee any more rewards than the effort and the contribution you've put into it. Some people, like Nick, have a richer life even though it is short than people who live longer but give back little.

I suppose the votes tomorrow—not tomorrow; it is after midnight, so today—will be a confirmation of the sacrifice of Nick and the other young

*man and all the people who have risked so much to bring real democracy to
Cuba for the first time. What a legacy they will have. Greater than any I
can imagine.*

*From what Victoria tells me, our movement is spreading far and wide.
The white mariposa is flying all over the place. They have it now in some
villages in Africa and in South America and in some Asian countries. And
they have it* del norte.

I bet T. Jefferson is smiling too.

■ ■ ■

5 0

■

Ernesto had insisted on remaining in the hotel until the bodies of
the two slain young men were properly cared for and security officials
had contacted the U.S. Interests Section to notify the ambassador of
Nick's death and arrangements had been made for his return, with appropriate diplomatic honors, to the States. This despite the fear that the
dead American woman facedown on the same hallway was part of a
greater assassination plot against Ernesto. He simply would not be
moved. All the emergency vehicles and ambulances had arrived at the
rear of the hotel, so outside in the *parque* the celebration continued well
after midnight.

Then they were transported in nondescript cars provided by the True
Republic movement to the coastal town of Cojímar just east of Havana.
Protecting propriety, Victoria was placed in the simple home of the local
organizer for the movement. And Ernesto, Alejo, and Rafael were provided a separate, equally simple house nearby. Rotating shifts of student
leaders provided round-the-clock security.

When they arrived an hour or more after midnight, Ernesto saw Victoria to her door. She was tearful and badly shaken by the tragedy that had ended the triumphant evening. The others faded discreetly away into the nearby trees. He took her shaking hand, then held her tightly in his arms. She put her head on his shoulder, a hand on the side of his white head, and silently wept. "He was so good," she sobbed. "He saved your life. He saved all of our lives."

Ernesto nodded his head, agreeing. "It will not be forgotten what he did. By the people. They will know who he was and what he did. And they will remember him for many years to come. Maybe he will go into the history books to be studied by the schoolchildren. Then he will become a legend."

Victoria softly said, "But he was so young."

"He was," Ernesto answered. "But he was also, in his soul, at least as old as me. He had within him a certain spirit, a spirit that was as old as time, a spirit that guided him toward the destiny that he wanted. His destiny was to bring to the land of his parents the democracy he believed in."

"Do you truly believe that?" she whispered.

"I do, lovely lady," Ernesto said. "I believe it also about you. You have discovered your destiny here. Before that, you were lost. Now you are a complete human."

She shook. "Tomorrow—today—my destiny ends. I have nowhere to go tomorrow."

"You have everywhere to go now," he answered. "You are a new person with a new life and a new possibility. You will be very welcome here, to stay and help these people learn how the television can be used properly, how it can be used to teach and to inform—not just to entertain."

"That I believe I can do. I now can see the difference—dramatically," she said.

Ernesto added, "But you can also do the same thing in your own country and in other countries. Something so powerful as the television must be rescued from the devil and put to better use."

Despite her grief, Victoria smiled tearfully at the thought of Marshall Stuart with the devil's horns on.

"It is too much, I fear, for just one person," she said.

Ernesto held her back and looked squarely at her. "One person, armed with a great idea, is mightier than an army."

She nodded, tears still in her eyes. "You have taught me that. You have taught many people that. I will not forget it. I do not think the young people whose lives you have touched will forget it either."

He smiled. "There. I hope I have also taught you not to be afraid."

"I am not afraid," Victoria answered. "It is just that tomorrow—to-day—after I broadcast the election results—it will be the first time in almost twenty-five years that I have not had an assignment." She touched his face softly. "You will have a big assignment. You must help form a new government."

Ernesto looked at her a long time. He leaned forward and kissed her and held her again. "I do not know how to govern, dear lady," he whispered in her ear. "That is for others, as I told you. I am only a revolutionary. And once a revolutionary, always a revolutionary. My destiny is a never-ending quest—a quest for the true republic."

"This republic can be the true republic," she protested.

"It can, and I pray that it will be," he answered. "But my true republic will always be just slightly out of reach. And I must go in search of it."

She put her forehead on his shoulder and wept. "Please, don't leave."

"I will not leave, dear lady. As I have told you in the Sierra, I will always be in your heart. And you will also always be in mine. And, who is to know, as you follow your new assignment—your destiny—and I follow mine, whether we will meet again in the true republic of our dreams."

He kissed her again and opened the door for her. Over her shoulder, she looked at him again. Then she closed the door.

5 1

■

The first light of the sun on *el primero de mayo* was striking the small harbor at Cojímar as an unremarkable fishing boat put out to sea. It had a crew of three and one passenger. Nothing set it apart from many other similar vessels plying the seas off the northwest coast of Cuba looking

for fish for the tables of the fine hotels and the simple plates of ordinary
Cubans who might have the spare pesos necessary to afford the catch it
might deliver the next evening.

Except this day the boat would not be fishing. It would fish on its
return the following day. This day it would take its lone passenger to
an equally small coastal village called Playa Norte on the Isla Mujeres
off the Yucatán peninsula of eastern Mexico.

The headquarters of the True Republic movement, just one block from
the main campus of the Universidad de la Habana, was in the kind of
turmoil any political headquarters experiences on election night. The
turmoil was particularly compressed, however, by the tiny space into
which the few desks, small printing press, few telephones, stacks of leaflets and piles of placards, and hundreds of people were jammed. The
noise was intense as messages were shouted back and forth, information
exchanged at high volume, and bodies pushed forward and backward
through the narrow first floor. The headquarters, temporarily converted
from a small bookstore, also had a second floor that was almost as
crowded but not nearly as noisy. From the lone telephone at a cluttered
desk in the front of the second floor Victoria was preparing to make her
election night report to TPN and, thus, throughout the world.

Every few minutes excited young people brought the latest election
returns scribbled on torn pieces of paper to her. At eight o'clock that
evening, an hour later than promised, the Ministry of Information released its first returns representing the tabulations of ballots cast during
the first two days of balloting. The count was current through the ballots
cast up to that afternoon. A student sitting next to her translated the
announcement. "*Señora*, he says this: It is for the Free Cuba Party—
twenty-five percent; for the Cuban Social Democratic Party—twenty-
eight percent; for the movement of the True Republic—forty-seven
percent." There was an ear-splitting roar from those jammed in the
narrow headquarters. Outside, car horns were honking, lights were flash-
ing, people were shouting and chanting in the streets.

The student held up her hand. "The Ministry of Information official
is saying that this represents perhaps more than half of the votes that
will be cast. That it represents mostly the small towns and villages that
had not so many votes to count. That the returns from the major cities—
especially Habana—are now being counted rapidly, under the supervi-

sion of the international observer group, and that these results will be announced at each hour from now on."

Victoria's interpreter waved at a student with very thick glasses and rolls of paper under his arms who was starting downstairs. She brought him over and introduced him to Victoria as the movement's best vote analyst. He had calculated the number of votes throughout each province and city that would be needed to win. "It is better than we had hoped. If we sustain anything like these numbers," he said in English, "we will win the plurality very clearly." His unlined forehead suddenly wrinkled. "But it is not enough. The real contest is for control." He leaned toward her and spoke slowly against the din from downstairs. "*Señora*, we fear that the two other parties—if together they have a majority—might form an alliance of power and shut us out of the government."

Victoria said, "I can't believe that could happen. They hate each other. One is the party of the old Communists and the other is the party of the old oligarchy. How could they get together?"

"Oh, *señora*," he said. Victoria suddenly heard the voice of Ernesto. "This is politics. At the conclusion, for the others it is about power. They will form alliances with the devil himself for the power. They both know that if we win the majority, they will have only the power of a divided minority—a fragmented opposition. Neither of the other parties will form a coalition with us. And we will not form a coalition with either of them."

At nine o'clock the numbers were holding within a percentage point or two. To control the government and implement the manifesto of the true republic, the movement had to pick up at least three percentage points in the final count. The Ministry of Information spokesman stated that the bulk of the election day ballots would be counted and announced by ten o'clock.

Victoria called TPN in New York. "Here's the deal, Sam. The true republic . . . Erne . . . Señor Blanco's movement . . . is winning by a wide margin but not yet by a majority." She went on to repeat the synopsis just provided by the young analyst. "What do you want to do?"

"Call back just before ten, Vic," he shouted down to her, "and we'll put you on live at ten. You can announce the results as they are given to you. It'll be a little dicey, but it will be real time and exciting. We'll beat everybody up here with the story. And, of course, we're carrying it worldwide on the network."

Victoria said, "Sam, I have to be honest with you. When I come on, I'm going to report the results. But I'm also going to tell you—and everybody else—what it means."

"It's a deal, Vic," Sam shouted. "Everybody knows your story—that you've gone over. We're billing it that way. We had no choice given that performance you put on from the mountain up there. Everybody in the world now sees you as the mouthpiece for that old guy." Sam lowered his voice conspiratorially. "What else are you, Vic? You can tell me."

Victoria said, "I am not his—or anybody else's—'mouthpiece.' Although I am proud to be one of his voices. And whatever else I am or may be is none of your business." She hung up.

At three minutes before ten, she called TPN in New York again. The line was connected into the ongoing news broadcast that was just wrapping up and the announcer stated that the former award-winning international correspondent of TPN, Victoria Savidge, would be on live in sixty seconds from the "Pure Republic" headquarters in Havana with the up-to-the-minute and conclusive results of the historic Cuban national elections. Stay tuned.

Seconds went by and then the same practiced resonant voice came on welcoming viewers to the ten o'clock news with a special report on the closely watched election returns from the Cuban capital. Behind him there was a dramatic still picture of Victoria Savidge and Ernesto Blanco taken off the interview tape in the Sierra just before the bullet was fired. "And here is our correspondent—sorry, our 'former' correspondent— Victoria Savidge. Vicky . . ."

"We are awaiting the latest announcement from the Ministry of Information on the tally of the ballots from today, election day, here in Cuba. As your viewers know," Victoria shouted into the phone to overcome the background noise, "voting has been taking place here over the past seventy-two hours and the polls officially closed three hours ago at seven o'clock Havana time. I am waiting to have those latest results handed to me and as soon as they are I will read them. Right now the True Republic movement is leading the Free Cuba Party, the party of the Right, and the Social Democratic Party, the party of the left, by a significant margin. Analysts here believe that if the True Republic can be prevented from winning a clear majority, the possibility exists—as implausible as it may seem—that the two other parties, representing opposite ends of the spectrum, might form a coalition to govern the country and shut out the True Republic from any participation at all."

Victoria continued, "I can tell you, from firsthand knowledge, that if this were to happen, there is simply no telling what the supporters of the True Republic might do. No one is threatening violence. But there are close to half the voters of this country that, over the past six months, have been so moved by the prospect of democracy and an honest government free of the old political and financial power structures that they have literally taken their lives into their own hands and demanded a government in which they—the people—could participate. If they are shut out—especially by the kind of cynical maneuvering that many of us . . . that many people—even in our own country—are fed up with, there is no telling what they might do. So, in that respect, this is a critical moment.

". . . Just a minute. Here is the announcement of the Ministry of Information. I will read it to you as it is given to me. As of ten P.M., Havana time, with ninety-six percent of the voting units fully reporting, representing . . . what is this?" she said to the student who had scribbled the numbers. "Ninety-eight? Ninety-eight percent of the total vote, the count is . . . Free Cuba Party, twenty-six percent; Cuban Social Democratic Party, twenty-two percent . . . and the True Republic . . . is this it?" she said to the student. "Is this the result? . . . The movement of the True Republic, fifty-two percent!"

Victoria Savidge held the phone up toward the open window in the front of the tiny, jammed storefront headquarters—her arm fully extended in a gesture of triumph—so that millions of people around the world—in African shanties, in Latin American favelas, in Asian ghettos, in Middle Eastern souks, in U.S. dormitories—could hear the din. All Havana poured into the streets. A Mardi Gras of freedom had broken out.

After a minute of the echoes of human celebration, Victoria spoke into the phone. "The people of Cuba have charted a new course, not only for themselves, but for others to follow. The people here who founded this movement and some of whom have given their lives for it believe in one simple ideal—the ability of people here and throughout the world to have the political power themselves to govern their own lives. For them," she said, tears streaming down her face, "for them it is more important than the security offered by the state or the materialism offered by the market. For them it is the hope of a better future built around a community that cares for all and in which all can participate. For them it is the dream of freedom and of a destiny for their children that is open to all and that leaves none behind. Since it is the dream we all share, let us wish the people of Cuba well as they set sail on this great voyage. And let us know that we are with them—as far as the human spirit can reach."

Then she said, "Good night and God bless, Ernesto. . . ."

Many miles to the west the fishing boat bobbed across the dark Caribbean sea making steadily for the Mexican coast.

On deck with the skipper was a frail-looking white-bearded elderly man. He was lying in a hammock slung on deck looking up at the stars as the captain steered and they were listening to the radio broadcast over an English-language station. When the broadcast finished, he smiled and said quietly to the night, "Good night and God bless, Victoria. . . ."

5 2

∎

Victoria asked to be taken immediately back to the small house near the beach below Cojímar. She entered the small bedroom somehow sensing the presence of Ernesto Blanco. On the bed was a letter in Ernesto's hand. It read:

Letter to Victoria—
There are only two things in life that are real. One is the love of another person. The other is a purpose for our life. Most of my long life,

I have not had either one. Then the first one you gave me. And the other I had just found for myself. The second one I hope I have given you. And the first one I will always give you.

For some people like us, to be in love with each other does not require a constant presence. We are still in love wherever we are, whatever we are doing. That is what it means to be inside each other's hearts.

For some people like us, to have a purpose—to serve others—almost guarantees that we will not always be together. My purpose requires me to be a gypsy of the *revolución*. To sow the seeds of the people's power. And then move on. For me, I am followed by the Hound of Heaven. I cannot stay still. I must always move on until I die.

But wherever I go upon the earth, I will always carry two pictures in my mind. One is a picture by a famous Cuban photographer of a very small poor girl. She holds in her hand a simple piece of wood. It was, perhaps, her only toy. He called the picture "La niña de la muñeca de palo"—The girl of the wooden doll. It is reported that she died soon after of leukemia for lack of access to the medicine in the United States that might have cured her.

The other picture is a happier one. It is the picture I have of you in my mind as you stood one day next to the tree covered by orchids at our camp in the Sierra. The sun was on your hair. Your lips were smiling. Your eyes were shining. You were then—as you still are—the most beautiful creature I have ever seen.

So these two pictures I will always have with me. The one of the child that represents the purpose of my life. And the one of you that represents the love of my life.

I am always with you—

The letter was signed, in his characteristic scrawl, "Ernesto."

On the bed next to the letter was a white mariposa. Victoria pinned it in her hair.

EPILOGUE

■

High in the Meseta Centrale de Chiapas in the state of Chiapas in Mexico, near the Guatemalan border, lies the tiny village of Las Margaritas. The mountain range surrounding it very much resembles the Sierra Maestra mountain range in eastern Cuba.

The hardy Chiapas Indians still farm the rocky land and drive their cattle from range to range. They usually wear the black wool *serapes* against the cool of the evening at the high elevations. On market days they go into Las Margaritas for their supplies.

There is a small square or *plazuela* in the center of the village, much like villages throughout the region. It is, except in the season of the rain, dry and dusty. But it is the meeting place of the people, the place where they share their experiences and trade their stories and discuss the issues of the day.

Toward the end of May one evening, a lone white-haired elderly man, a stranger, sat at the only outdoor table in front of the only cantina in the village. He sipped a cup of coffee.

Across the square, a young boy leaned against the cracked and faded wall of one of the low buildings. He watched the stranger who moved only to lift the cup of coffee to his lips.

Then, *el viejo* smiled a large smile, lifted his hand, and slowly beckoned to the boy.

suddenly turned to the camera, his idea clear, and the words poured forth like a torrent.

"I did not spend my life being a revolutionary to see the world now pass me by. Once a revolutionary—a true revolutionary—always a revolutionary. Look at what's going on." Now he left the confines of the desk and began to perambulate the whole studio. The outmatched camera did its best. "The whole world is trading. And we are left out. The whole world is getting computers. And we have only a few. The whole world is opening up. And we are closed." He was stumbling over television cables and pausing in front of stunned technicians and wide-eyed staff members holding cups of coffee. With wildly gyrating results, the cameraman had lifted the camera from its mount and was now producing combatlike footage as he followed the restless warrior around the studio.

"No more," shouted the scarred old veteran, his combat fatigues clashing dramatically with the technological cage that, for the moment, contained him. "No more." He suddenly reached in the breast pocket of his green jacket. He produced a signature Cohiba Esplendido, the kind his doctors made him give up a decade before. "No more," he shouted once again. With a flourish and a wink at the camera, he struck a long wooden kitchen match and, with the style of a seasoned professional, slowly rotated the tip of the cigar in the blue flame until it glowed.

Pursued by the sweating, beleaguered cameraman, he resumed his pacing, puffing as he went. "We have to make some changes here. Changes *muy grande*. Despite the Yanquis, we will open this country up. Everybody can come and damn *Tío Sam*. We're going to give every Cuban kid a computer."

The crowd in El Papagayo cantina in Manzanillo was mesmerized. Where in the hell was all this going? Had the old man finally gone over the edge from the lifelong battle with *el Norte*? Until the time that Castro got up from the desk, those in the back had been silent. But when he lit the Cohiba, a cheer went up from them and people began flocking in from the street to find out what was up. Outside, the street traffic was thinning. All across Cuba people were scrambling for the nearest television set.

"The revolution brought health care to the Cuban people . . . better than anybody in Latin America. We have fewer babies dying than in Washington, District of Columbia, capital of the U.S.A." He poked the cigar at the camera, which jumped back as if from a heat-seeking missile. "We have schools for our people. The best in the southern part of this hemisphere." He paused; then, his eyes widened dramatically, he shoved the cigar at the camera: "Now, it's not enough. Now we have to have computers if we want to be civilized and give our kids a chance. The next revolution is . . . computers." This last was delivered more softly and thoughtfully. His voice was sad and wistful, as if he were contemplating a mystery which he could not fathom.

In the back of the cantina sat a solitary elderly man dressed in the simple clothes of the mountain villages. Though crowded about by intense auditors of the performance, his dress, age, and demeanor marked him as singular. As he listened, he gazed more often out of the window into the night sky than at the fuzzy electronic screen. Seeing his occasional enigmatic smile, those around him assumed him to be slightly drunk or at least, like the leader to whom they now listened, of an age unable even to contemplate the wonders of the silicon chip and the microprocessor.

"That is why I am going to let others take over this new revolution." An impressive figure even at five inches on the television screen, *el Comandante* now stood behind the desk. He puffed on the cigar thoughtfully. "Nobody should stay in one place forever. I'm going to start traveling to countries that don't even have what we have, countries in Latin America and in Africa and in Asia. They need to know what we've done here and how we did it." He started to sit down, then changed his mind. "If I travel the world speaking about revolution, then I don't have time to run this country anymore. We have to pick some new leaders."

The cantina crowd, like thousands of cantina crowds all across Cuba, watched in stunned silence as an inch of ash fell, unnoticed by *el Jefe*, onto the desktop. He reached into an inner pocket of his green combat jacket, his eyes twinkling and a slight, provocative smile on his lips. He pulled out a folded sheet of paper and opened it up. He put on reading glasses. "Here the U.S. president says, just two days ago, 'Our policy toward Cuba will change when the Cuban people can pick their own leaders.' " Through the thick beard, large white teeth gleamed as Castro held his large hands palms up and shrugged dramatically. "I thought that's what we've been doing all these years. But, I guess *Tío Sam* still doesn't understand our system.

"Okay, Mr. President. Okay." The old revolutionary consulted a